Questioning Lips

"What other things are pleasing to men?" Alicia asked as Travis's kisses strayed to her earlobe, then to her breasts, deliciously teasing her.

Daringly, she slid her hand beneath the opening of his shirt. Her fingers caressed the bronzed expanse of his chest. The tension had not completely left her, she was still afraid. But she was willing now, her breasts burning against him as he unfastened the rest of his shirt.

The sensation of his nakedness opened a yearning within her, and Alicia could hold off no longer. Sliding her hand up to the tempting hair at his nape, she raised her gaze to meet his.

"No more questions," she whispered, as his lips closed hungrily over hers. . . .

Lord Rogue

Patricia Rice

AN ONYX BOOK

NEW AMERICAN LIBRARY

NAL BOOKS ARE AVAILABLE AT QUANTITY DISCOUNTS
WHEN USED TO PROMOTE PRODUCTS OR SERVICES.
FOR INFORMATION PLEASE WRITE TO PREMIUM MARKETING DIVISION,
NEW AMERICAN LIBRARY, 1633 BROADWAY,
NEW YORK, NEW YORK 10019.

Onyx is a trademark of New American Library.

SIGNET, SIGNET CLASSIC, MENTOR, ONYX, PLUME, MERIDIAN
and NAL BOOKS are published by NAL PENGUIN INC.,
1633 Broadway, New York, New York 10019

First Printing, January, 1989

1 2 3 4 5 6 7 8 9

PRINTED IN THE UNITED STATES OF AMERICA

Author's Note

Except for the intrepid Roosevelts, the characters of this book are entirely fictional, although I have revived the names of several of the inhabitants of early St. Louis for the sake of historical detail. We know these people existed, but detailed biographies of their characters are unavailable. I have used the writer's privilege of imagining them.

The story of the steamboat *New Orleans* and the New Madrid earthquakes comes entirely from tales of that time, including eyewitness reports and the log of the *New Orleans*. While the steamboat did not record picking up any extraneous passengers after the quakes (as a matter of fact, it avoided doing so, much to Lydia's dismay), I have again used poetic license to bring reality into touch with fiction. I have also compressed time and distance to some extent to get the boat to my hero and heroine in time, but the journey over that particular stretch of river did occur between December 16 and January 2, and the rest of the events are all too real. The marvelous Roosevelts sailed through the Louisville shoals, the New Madrid quakes, Lydia's pregnancy, fire, Indians, and all the other tribulations of travel at that time to prove the viability of steamboat travel. The trip even included the marriage of two of their passengers, but that's a story for another time.

1

THE DECEITFUL September sun burned warmly against the weathered wooden planks of the keelboat. Lower than normal, the river provided little current to rock the boat against the barren shore, but the boat's half-naked occupant knew these things instinctively and paid them little mind now. When he was ready, the current would carry him where he wished to go.

Red-bronze skin glistening with the day's warmth, he worked idly at a slender piece of cherry wood in his hands. Hunkered down on his heels, his broad, muscular back propped against the cabin wall, the keelboatman whittled away another shaving and lifted the carved figure to the light, admiring the feel of the wood as much as the product of his craftsmanship.

Hands so broad and callused they did not appear capable of holding such a delicate figurine, no less producing it, turned the wood to polish a smoother line. Above a nose naturally bent like a hawk's beak, dark eyes gleamed with satisfaction, and a thin, almost sensual mouth turned upward in a sardonic grin. Though these features taken by themselves seemed oddly disparate, they fit together well behind high, prominent cheekbones and a wide brow. The unfortunate occurrence of heavy, shoulder-length black hair tied back by a cotton bandanna and a gold ring in one ear masked any of nature's attempts at handsomeness.

The keelboatman whistled softly to himself as he continued his carving. He held the wood lovingly, as if the woman appearing beneath his talented fingers were real. Surprisingly, the delicately carved female was fully clothed and not the crude attempt at lasciviousness many another whittler laughed over. Gowned in long skirts lifted at the hem, as

7

if the figurine were about to step over a foul puddle of
water, the carving portrayed a remarkable likeness to a
regal lady, from the toes of her slipper-shod feet to the
feathers of her broad-brimmed hat. The whittler chuckled
idly at his own conceit and turned the piece carefully in
his hands, searching for flaws.

An aspect of sadness tinged his smile as he admired the
carving's wealth of upswept hair. If only a real woman could
be produced as easily as a wooden one, he would be a
happy man. But finding a lady like this one in the frontier
wilderness of the Ohio had as much likelihood as this piece
of wood coming to life. He had deliberately left all that
behind, now he must make do with what he found.

Grinning cheerfully, if somewhat cynically, at the prospects that opened for him, the boatman set aside his toy
and reached for his discarded shirt. The whores down at the
tavern wouldn't object if he arrived clad only in deerskin
breeches, but he had no intention of courting whores. If he
were to settle down, he wanted a lady, and, as the good
women of Cincinnati had made clear, they held no desire
for a half-breed keelboatman, he would be moving on.
Tonight—well, tonight the whores offered definite possibilities.

He stooped to retrieve his carving, then propped himself
back in his earlier position as he heard the sound of an
approaching boat. His fingers automatically reached for the
polishing stone as he cautiously awaited the new arrival.

Angry voices carried over the water along with the slap-
slap of current against wooden keel and the knocking of
long poles against rock as the other boat maneuvered into
shore. Playing his role, the half-Indian carver remained
motionless, seemingly intent on his occupation. Until the
distinctly feminine accents of one of the disputants caused
him to look up just in time to catch the fleeting glimpse of a
slender ankle and a long stockinged limb swing over the
boat's keel to the shore. Heavy black skirts quickly ob-
scured this alluring sight, but his attention was instantly
captivated.

Slowly, savoring every detail, his gaze traveled upward
from that revealing slippered toe, past the thick skirts of a
mourning gown, to the hint of slender hips and a long,
elegantly curved waist. He hesitated, afraid this dream would
become a nightmare should he look farther, but not un-
courageous, he continued his exploratory travels. He swal-

lowed hard as his gaze encountered the full curve of a
generous bosom disguised beneath that revolting black gown,
then lifted his eyes—to stare directly at the image in his
hands come to life.

True, she wore a practical bonnet instead of the feathered
creation of his imagination, but he could tell from the long
curls escaping about her face and throat that she hid a mass
of thick chestnut hair that would glow like polished mahogany in the sun. And her features—by the grace of the Great
Spirit!—were finely carved and delicately boned and proud
as any queen's. At the moment they seemed to be striving
to contain some emotional outburst, whether of fury or
despair he could not ascertain. But the desire to see her
eyes had him on his feet before he realized the topic of the
argument.

"But you said you could take me to St. Louis! What am I
to do in this godforsaken spot? How am I to find another
boat? Where am I to stay?" Anger fought with tears as the
woman confronted the sneering boatman leaning on his
long pole.

"You can go this side of Hades for all I care, Miss
Uppity. The river's too damned low to travel farther without promise of more reward than you're ready to give. I'll
take my chances on the whores and a cargo of lead before
I'll take the likes of you any farther."

"If I had been a gentleman with a purse full of gold, you
would have taken me where I want, I warrant! Why must a
woman who travels alone submit to this treatment? My gold
is as good as any man's!"

The Indian had to smother a grin at this taunt. Tucking
the back of his shirt into his pants, he sauntered closer to
the fray, eyeing the crew of the other boat. They all seemed
to be enjoying the argument hugely. Did the fool woman
really think she could travel alone all the way to St. Louis
with a boatload of women-starved men? Especially men of
this ilk, accustomed to doing as they pleased, when they
pleased. He wondered how many knifings the captain had
had to put down before they reached this point.

"All the gold in hell won't pay me to risk my neck to take
you to St. Louis on a river like this. I don't relish finding a
knife in my back hauling this rig over the falls while you
dabble your toes in the water. Go find a man to protect you
so I can do my duty."

"Protect me! I can protect myself, as you well know! Give me my bags. I'll get to St. Louis without you." Anger had obviously won out over tears as she stamped her elegant foot and set her hands on her hips, glaring defiantly at the taunting boatman.

The Indian came up silently behind her, eyeing the other man's reaction to this demand. Knowing full well the reputation of these men for mischief, he could imagine the possibilities a lady's trunk of fripperies would provide. It seemed an appropriate time to intervene.

"Give me the trunk, boys." The deep, calm voice of authority brought instant attention.

The woman turned and gasped at the physical nearness of this lean giant who had materialized beside her. Then she bit her tongue against the terror inspired by his appearance. The glittering black eyes beneath the faded red bandanna augured ill will to any defiance, and the muscular strength rippling casually beneath the half-fastened blouse bespoke the ability to carry out any threat. She could see the scars of other battles on his cheek and upper torso, and she hastily stepped back as his long fingers rolled into fists.

The other man eyed him without trepidation, however, merely giving him a nod of acquaintance as he dismissed his troublesome passenger. "Aye, Lonetree, she's all yours." Turning his head to his grinning crew, he barked orders: "Haul out the lady's trunks, boys. Be gentle about it. Lonetree's taking up the assignment."

Hoots and catcalls followed this admonition, but the trunks were delivered in order, stacked upon the rocky shore beneath the lady's disdainful glare.

Silently the man called Lonetree heaved the heavy trunks aboard a mule-drawn wagon near the river's edge. Without so much as a glance to the black-clad lady, he untethered the mule and hitched it to the traces. When everything was prepared, he waited patiently beside the wagon.

Alicia Stanford gripped her reticule tightly beneath gloved fingers and, raising her chin, approached the dilapidated wagon as if it were the comfortable carriage to which she was accustomed. The journey from Philadelphia had been long and hard, and she had grown immune to the shocking inconveniences that must be endured to accomplish her goal. If she must ride beside a savage into this timbered fortification that presumed to be called a town, she would do it with dignity and without a trace of the despair and fear that ate at her insides.

Lonetree watched this performance with the hidden admiration of a professional. Tear-drop blue eyes behind a thick fringe of black lashes displayed no trace of emotion as she accepted his assist into the wooden seat. A faint whiff of perfume drifted from the voluminous folds of her skirts as she settled them modestly about the lovely ankles she kept carefully concealed from view this time. He might as well not exist for all she noticed him.

Alicia held herself as stiff and distant from this odd stranger as the wagon seat would allow. She had expected him to stink, as did so many of the ruffians she had encountered lately, but other than a faintly masculine aroma she could not quite define, he seemed surprisingly clean. Even the odious shoulder-length hair appeared as clean as her own, a definite asset after the vermin-laden heads of the boatmen. Shuddering, she stared blindly out over the streets they passed.

Shanty-built log and frame houses gave way to an occasional brick edifice or two-story dwelling, but this burgeoning frontier town on the Ohio held no promise for her hopes. For the thousandth time since she had left Philadelphia, Alicia wondered if what she went toward was not worse than what she had left behind. But the memory of the shame and humiliation kept her from turning back, and pure obstinacy erased any trace of self-pity. She would reach St. Louis if she had to die in the process.

The silent Indian halted the wagon outside one of the larger structures Alicia had seen, but the tavern sign swinging overhead did not increase her hopes. With trepidation she took his callused hand and leapt from the wagon, staring blankly at the wooden walls while her driver went to retrieve the trunks. Hotels apparently did not exist this side of the mountains. But a tavern?

Without a word of explanation Lonetree shouldered open the tavern door, and heaved the first of the trunks upon the polished plank floor inside. Then politely holding the door for his passenger, he waited for her to enter.

Before she could set foot inside, a screech of outrage carried through the opening. "Don't you set your filthy foot inside my portals, you heathen savage! Begone with you before I take a hatchet to your head!"

Startled, Alicia glanced up to the stoic face of the man who had so politely come to her rescue. To her surprise, one twinkling black eye appeared to close in an outrageous wink before he turned and staggered into the tavern.

"Brought paying guest, Red-Haired Dog. Give me two bits." The self-assured giant who had come upon Alicia so silently now staggered across the uncarpeted floor like a herd of buffaloes, crashing into a wooden hatrack and knocking over a brass spittoon before collapsing against a brilliantly polished mahogany bar. The red-haired, elfin man behind the counter turned purple with outrage, and reached for the afore-mentioned hatchet mounted prominently on the wall, until his glance happened to catch upon the lady standing, horrified, in the entrance.

"Oh, my word, my apologies, madam." He hastily dried his hands upon a linen towel and sent the long-haired Indian a scathing glance. "Carry in the lady's bags, heathen. Then you'll get your money."

Alicia could swear there was a self-satisfied smirk upon the Indian's face as he turned his back on the bar and swaggered out the door, but she did not dare look him directly in the eyes again. Too confused and too tired to examine the intent of this absurd charade, she turned pointedly to the innkeeper.

"I seem to be stranded in this city for a few days, sir. Would you have a decent room that might accommodate me until I can find further transportation?" This haughty tone had served her well upon many an occasion, and it did not fail her now, as she had suspected. The subservient bartender bowed meekly and hastily produced a ledger.

"I have a fine front room vacant that you should find entirely to your satisfaction." He produced a quill pen and scowled again as the Indian entered carrying the last of the bags. "Be careful where you put them, you lazy lout. You'll mar the floor!"

Beginning to understand something of the innkeeper's nature, Alicia turned her back in disgust and rummaged in her purse for a dollar piece. The Indian had neatly stacked her bags at her feet and stood now staring down at her, a singularly odd expression in his eyes. He was younger than she had first imagined when he had spoken with such authority, and despite the flagrant insult of his unkempt hair and gold earring, he had a striking visage. She could not complain of his deliberate antagonizing of the horrible little man behind her. Under other circumstances she would have found it amusing. Still, he had no right to stare at her in such a disconcerting manner.

With as much graciousness as she could muster, she offered the coin. "Thank you very much for your assistance, sir. I hope you will accept a token of my appreciation."

The dark face broke into a white-toothed grin as he palmed the coin and insolently made a rude gesture to the clerk behind her. With another audacious wink he walked out.

"That was a mistake, miss, if you don't mind my saying so. He'll just drink it up. All Indians are like that. Worthless drunks, the lot of them. You took a terrible chance in traveling with that one. Mean, he is. Just as soon scalp you as look at you."

Since she had the spine-chilling feeling that the Indian had enjoyed looking at her, Alicia hastily turned back to the business at hand.

Signing the guest book, she inquired, "Could you recommend any guides familiar with the western part of the river? Or a boat that might be leaving downriver soon? I am trying to reach my father in St. Louis as soon as is practicable."

The little man snorted and swung the book around to read her name. "Well, Miss—or is it Mrs?" he glanced at her heavy mourning.

"Miss," she responded automatically, then regretted it instantly. "Mrs." she corrected. "We were married only a short while."

The innkeeper took a bent pair of wire-rimmed glasses from his pocket, and polished them carefully before putting them on to better observe his attractive guest. "Well, Mrs. Stanford, were it me, I'd not step a foot farther into the interior. The Indians are on the warpath downriver, and the only settlements beyond here are stinking holes of filth and low-life riffraff. And St. Louis is overrun with those heathen Frenchies and Spaniards. You'd do well to stay right here, Mrs. Stanford. Cincinnati will be as grand as its name one of these days. Biggest little town on both rivers."

"I'd rather assume New Orleans claimed that title," Alicia commented dryly. "But I shall consider your advice. Thank you."

As she climbed the stairs to her new room, she considered

the prospect for all of one minute and discarded it promptly. She had not suffered the agonies of travel to come this far and give up. She had no purpose in staying here. She had no purpose at all anymore. The only thing that kept her chin up and her mind from the brink of despair was the possibility of finding out what had happened to her father. She needed that goal to keep going. Even Indians on the warpath presented no obstacle for one in her state of mind.

2

By THE TIME the next day had spent itself, Alicia had almost despaired of her foolish obstinacy. No one would recommend a boat ride downriver, particularly for an unaccompanied woman. Perhaps in the spring when the flatboats carrying settlers and their families arrived she might find safe transportation. But spring would be much too late. She would not be able to travel in the spring.

Fighting the tears pricking behind her tired eyes, she stopped at a small general mercantile store close to the river. The proprietor watched her with friendly interest as she stared in perplexity at the bewildering array of rifles and shotguns upon the wall.

"Might I help you, miss?" he inquired genially.

Alicia shook her head. "I'll not ever be able to hold one of those. Don't they make small ones?"

"Small ones ain't much use for nothin' but close to. Ain't any animal fool enough to get that close—exceptin' man, of course," he added wisely.

"Of course." Alicia turned from the wall, wondering which wild animal she feared more, man or the ones in the woods.

Shoving that conjecture aside, she trotted out her well-worn question. "Do you know of any guide who might take me downriver? I wish to reach St. Louis while the weather holds."

The genial storekeeper studied her with concern. Tired circles ringed long-lashed eyes of a disconcerting blue, and it was apparent from the way she dressed and spoke that she was a lady from back East. Though she was of above average height, there was a frailness about her that made it entirely possible that she might shatter upon contact. He shook his head with doubt.

"Ain't no one going to take a lady out on that river this time of year. Water's lower than I've ever seen it. You'd have to portage around the falls and more. A good keelboatman might do it if it were worth his while, but you don't look to have a cargo you want hauled."

Alicia smiled at the expected response. "If you know a good keelboatman, I'm prepared to make it worth his while. Surely there's somebody in this town willing to take a risk."

He frowned. "Only one crazy enough to try is Lonetree. Makes the best damn keelboat on the river. Doubt if he's got a crew ready this time of year, though. If you were a man, he could pirogue you downstream, but that ain't no trip for a woman."

Remembering the frail little shells she had seen bouncing on the river's waters, Alicia had to agree with that insight. Drowning might be favorable to scalping, but the name Lonetree provided another objection. Surely there could not be two of such a name.

"Lonetree?" she inquired lightly, hoping to gain information without revealing interest.

"Half-breed lives down by the river. Can't hardly miss him. Big fellow with a gold earring. Best guide on the river, but a savage brute. Bit a fellow's ear off once. Nearly got hanged another time when he carved a white man's face like it was one of those pieces he's always whittling. His friends got him out in time, but most of the places in town are closed to him now. Take my word for it, you don't want to mess with that one."

"No, of course not," she murmured, strolling toward the door. "I thank you for your time, sir."

She swept out, her long skirts swishing along the dusty road as she walked swiftly toward the river. Savage brute he might be, but no less savage than this entire town she found herself in. The Indian at least had acted instead of talking.

Stripped to just his tight buckskin breeches as he labored in the late afternoon heat to finish the cabin roof, Lonetree looked up in surprise at the sound of light footsteps on the rocks below. His surprise intensified as he recognized the widow lady of the day before. Even in this sun she wore that damned awful bonnet, but she appeared amazingly cool as she held her hand to shield her eyes and called to him.

"Mr. Lonetree, might I speak with you a minute?"

With a wicked grin of delight, the half-naked boatman

slid from the low roof and landed lightly on his feet in front of her. Dancing black eyes judged her consternation as she stepped backward when suddenly confronted with his rather awesome state of undress, but she retreated no farther than that. He gave her credit for that small hint of courage and for her daring in meeting his eye. A man learned to judge by such small actions out here.

If he had known the horrifying swell of near terror at his masculine nakedness Alicia had to swallow before she spoke, he would have given her credit for a good deal more courage than he supposed. The boatmen on the way down here had occasionally stripped to the waist, but she had been able to discreetly look another way and avoid the sight for all practical purposes. She had never really seen a man's torso naked before, and this particular man lent an even more frightening air to the experience. Though he possessed not an ounce of fat and his tall frame was more wiry than broad, the muscles of his shoulders bulged with the labors of his occupation, and she could trace the scars of his battles across the rounded planes of his chest. A tattooed band of blue about his arm accented the ferocity of his appearance. After hearing of his reputation, the proof of the rumors did not dispel the distress of Alicia's stomach.

She had to keep her eyes on his to keep her mind off the rest of him.

"Mr. Lonetree, I've been told you build the best boats on the river. How long would it take for you to build one for me?"

The insistence on calling him "mister" made him smile, and he was nearly distracted by a burnished curl dangling beneath her bonnet and blowing in the wind off the river. He liked tall women. They were a hell of a lot easier to kiss.

Finally bringing his thoughts back to the subject, the Indian's smile disappeared. "What do you want with a boat?"

Heavenly blue eyes glared at him with less-than-angelic venom. "What does one normally do with a boat? I intend to make St. Louis before winter, and a boat would seem much faster than walking."

Amusement flickered across his sharp features. "You planning on rowing it yourself?"

"Of course not." Unable to bear his masculine proximity any longer, Alicia walked toward the shore. "I'll hire a crew to take me. How many men would it take to handle a boat like that one you're working on?"

"More than you can handle at one time. What you need is a flatboat and some nice family to travel with."

Alicia spun on her heel and glared at him. "If I hear that one more time, I'll scream. I want to go to St. Louis. I want to go now. What do I have to do to get there?"

She spoke in insultingly simple terms, as if to a particularly dense child, but the man in front of her had the sense not to take it personally. Indeed, he admired the ferocious light in her eyes as her irritation grew, and he had all he could do to keep the grin from his face while she spoke. "I can think of any number of pleasant answers to that question, but as I am in no humor to be slapped by a lady, I'll answer you honestly. You can buy my keelboat and hire me and my crew for a princely sum, or you can hope old Daniels will come off his drunk to pirogue you downriver, or you can see if you can pry LaRouche from his wife and family long enough to maneuver a flatboat to the Mississippi. You'd have to take horses upland from there."

Alicia stared in astonishment at this breathtakingly honest speech. She had spent the day listening to platitudes and worthless opinions, but this renegade with the look of an uneducated river rat spelled out her options in concise terms even she could understand.

But when she opened her mouth to reply, the words that came out were not what she had intended. "How is it that you speak like an English professor to me, but grunt like an animal to that toad of an innkeeper?"

The Indian's grin grew cynical as he leaned over and swept up his discarded shirt from the boat's deck. Shrugging it on without bothering to fasten it, he tucked the tails in his breeches, still leaving a disconcerting expanse of bronzed chest exposed.

"How is it that a Mrs. Stanford travels without so much as a maid or a ring on her finger?" he asked with disinterest. "We're not all what we seem out here, and you'd do best not to question."

"But you are an Indian," she asserted, refusing to be led astray by his perceptiveness.

"I am a Delaware," he agreed. "A half-breed, I believe is the term most frequently used. Now, if you will excuse me,

Mrs. Stanford. . ." he pointedly began walking toward the boat.

"Wait!" Alicia ran after him. "This LaRouche, with the wife and family. Where can I find him?"

He turned a skeptical eye on her. "He'll not come cheap, either. It will take a fair sum to pry him from the comforts of home. Or are you thinking a family man is a safer bet?"

As that was exactly what she was thinking, Alicia stopped some distance from him and met his stare stubbornly. "Just tell me where I can find him."

He hesitated, then nodded acceptance. In a few terse lines he described the Frenchman's location, then impolitely he turned his back on her and returned to work.

Alicia found the house without difficulty, a neat cottage with a row of straggling late summer flowers along the planked wall. At her knock a short, plump woman of middle age appeared, her pleasant smile addressing the world and including the intruder.

"Mrs. LaRouche?" Alicia had already decided she had come to the right place if the husband were anything like the wife. The Indian might be the best boat builder on the river, but she wouldn't trust him past the front door. This woman she trusted instantly. At the woman's nod she inquired, "I'm Alicia Stanford. I've been told your husband sometimes guides boats downriver. Is he home?"

The woman's smile never wavered, though clear, perceptive eyes took in every inch of her visitor's appearance. She stepped aside and waved Alicia in. "I doubt that he can help you, but please do come in, Mrs. Stanford."

A sunny sitting room with braided rag rugs, spinning wheel, and a well-worn rocking chair welcomed her. At a trestle table in the far corner, a small man rose to his feet but made no effort to come forward. His hair was thick though peppered with gray, and his weathered face wrinkled into a smile at the sight of the lovely young woman on his doorstep.

"Jacques, Mrs. Stanford is inquiring after a guide. Do sit down, Mrs. Stanford. And you, too, Jacques," the housewife chided. "You'll hurt that foot again if you keep your weight on it like that."

Now that her eyes had adapted to the room's light, Alicia could see that the man's foot was heavily bandaged, and he

leaned on a cane for support. Hope that had risen just
moments before quickly dashed itself to pieces.

"Mr. Lonetree said you were one of the best guides
around, and I had hoped . . ." she began in explanation,
but a wave of disappointment prevented her from repeating
her foolishness.

The wiry man beamed and pulled his chair closer before
sitting. "Lonetree said that? *Merde*, but I never thought him
a fool. You can't find no better guide than that no-count
half-breed, you can't." He used the terms with affection,
laughingly. "Me, I'm laid up with this leg, see, and I promised Martha, no more the wanderin' for me. I do a bit of
trappin', a bit of tradin', but it's good to sleep in one's own
bed at night." He winked roguishly at his pleased wife.
"You got cargo you want hauled? Lonetree the one you see.
He take care of it fine."

Alicia perched at the edge of the wooden chair she'd been
offered, twisting the strings of her reticule as she tried to
fight back tears. She never used to cry, but it seemed a
constant state of affairs now. She hated it. She hated being
helpless and she hated asking for help. But she just couldn't
do it all on her own anymore.

"Is there no one else?" she finally whispered. "I have no
cargo. I need to reach my father in St. Louis. Lonetree
mentioned a Daniels. Perhaps a pirogue. . ."

Sensing her visitor's emotional distress, Mrs. LaRouche
came to the rescue with a cup of herbal tea, while shaking
her head vigorously behind Alicia's back. Her opinion of
the other guide was well known to her husband, however,
and he ignored her warning.

"St. Louis? That is a long way. It is dangerous. Daniels is
an old man, a good one, a very good one, but old, you
unnerstan'? You go talk to that rogue Travis. He take you
fine enough." The Frenchman grinned happily, as if he'd
solved all her problems.

Alicia looked up with a glimmer of hope. "Travis? Where
might I find him?"

LaRouche waved away this misunderstanding. "Lonetree.
He make like an Indian, but he called Travis. Damned fine
guide. You go tell him I said take you."

If she had not held the cup, Alicia would have thrown up
her hands in despair. She was going around in circles and

getting nowhere. "Please, I would rather speak with this Mr. Daniels. Is he in town? Could you direct me to him?"

The first hint of a frown dimmed the Frenchman's merry expression, but a meaningful gesture from his wife brightened it again with some sudden understanding. A flashing white grin broke across his dark face. "Me find him for you. He traps and he wanders. Me find him. You come back here, say, day after tomorrow?"

The mixture of relief and worry on the young woman's face was too much for her kindly hostess, and tentatively Martha LaRouche offered, "Would you come to dinner that night? We have a daughter—she'd enjoy meeting you. Unless, of course—I mean, we can't offer anything fancy. . ."

Alicia grasped the reason for the woman's hesitancy. The house was neat and comfortable, but a far cry from the homes she had visited back East. Even her servants had lived better than this, and she didn't know how to respond to this unexpected invitation. But it was time she accustomed herself to her new environment, and the warmth of this couple eased some of the aching loneliness she had known since leaving home.

Alicia's smile of gratitude was genuine as she rose to depart. "Please, I would love to come, if I won't be a nuisance. Just tell me the time—"

"I come get you. Lady like you don't walk these streets at night. Babette, she love to see you. Maybe we ask some others, have a fete to welcome you." Jacques leaped from his seat again in the excitement of planning.

Somewhat overwhelmed by his sudden enthusiasm, Alicia quickly shook hands and returned to the street. She may not have found a guide, but she felt as if she had gained friends.

In her room that night, Alicia listened to the revelry in the tavern below, and wondered once again if she had made the right choice. Perhaps she should turn back now, throw herself on Teddy's mercy, and become the fashionable young matron she had been raised to be. But the idea of even being in the same room with Edward Beauchamp III again sent an icy chill down her spine and a feeling of revulsion to the pit of her stomach. The stress of these past days and weeks caught up with her now, and violent shivers rocked her shoulders as she threw herself upon the bed, fighting the emotions rising to overwhelm her. God in heaven, if she could only kill him. . . Her fists curled in tight balls of rage

as she beat upon the bed and tears of frustration rolled
down her cheeks. She had thought this stage past, that she
had learned control, but she wanted to scream and cry and
raise an uproar that would be heard all the way to St. Louis.
She wanted a knife and a gun and the strength to wield
them.

Furious with herself, Alicia flung herself from the bed and
stalked to the window. Never, never would she allow herself
to fall to the level of these knife-wielding, gun-toting, violent strangers around her, not even if her present state
condemned her as being as ill-bred and uncivilized as they.
She was a Stanford, and she was a lady. No matter what the
circumstances, she would behave as one, even if her soul
screamed in outrage and her heart cried acid tears that
corroded everything she saw or touched. She would not let
him destroy her. She would not.

Raising her chin and covering the churning pain in her
insides with her palm, Alicia vowed silently never to contemplate returning again. She would swim the river before
she would turn back.

In another, less respectable tavern by the river, the half-
breed called Travis lounged against one wall, his arm draped
over his propped knee as he contemplated his raucous surroundings. Taking a swig of ale from the mug he held, he
bent a cynical smile at his thoughts.

In another ten, fifteen years, that could be him over at
the bar chugging a jug of cider on a dare from one of his
boatmen. Or brandishing a knife over a game of bones like
those two at the table. Or more likely, the keelboat captain
over there, tickling one of the barmaids and running a hand
up under her skirts while she bounced on his knee. That was
the future in store for him if he did not carve out a niche
where he could belong. He could wander the river until the
Indians or the outlaws or syphilis or his own pure meanness
did for him. And wouldn't that be a fitting end to a fine old
family tradition.

Grimacing as if he had bitten something sour, Travis rose
to his feet and dropped his mug on the nearest table. Before
he could elbow his way to the door, the strong aroma of
sweat and cheap perfume encompassed him, and he found
his path blocked by the full figure and garish undress of his
favorite lady of the evening.

Wrapping her arms around his waist and pressing her bounteous beauty against his chest, she leered laughingly up at him. "So early, lover? You weren't going to leave without kissing me good-bye, were you?" she taunted.

Travis grinned down at her painted face and red-dyed hair, and pinched a plump buttock beneath the thin material of her cheap gown. Molly was about as honest a woman as he'd ever hope to find, but she wasn't what he had in mind right now. He had his sights set on a lady, and he knew where he could fine one.

"Molly, my little chickadee, you can kiss me good-bye and weep little crocodile tears when I'm gone, for it's off to distant shores I'm bound."

She appeared on the verge of protest, but the kiss he planted on her rouged lips took her breath away, and not until he was gone did she realize how the hard sinews of his embrace had left her aching for more.

3

ALICIA DEBATED her choice of gowns for her first invitation to dinner since leaving Philadelphia. The stagecoach and keelboat down here had not given occasion for formal dress, and she longed to don something feminine and flattering, but she hesitated. She had worn only black since her mother's death, and her choices were necessarily limited, but the decision to dress formally at all caused the greatest dilemma. Did these people dress for dinner? Or would the other guests be wearing deerskin and calico?

Setting her lips defiantly, she drew out the slender black silk with interwoven metallic threads of silver. She had ordered it shortly before her journey and knew it to be of a daring fashion even for Philadelphia. The Empire waist and low neckline emphasized her high breasts and slender hips, and it fit so snugly, chances were good that she might never be able to wear it again. She would wear it this once, just for herself.

Alicia had grown accustomed to doing without the services of a maid these last weeks, but she wished desperately for the nicety of a large mirror for just this one evening. Fastening the gown, she tried to judge its effect by the tiny washstand mirror, to no avail. She ran her hands over the straight fall of the skirt, praying her figure had not changed too much since the last fitting. The ruffle of black lace at the neck provided respectable coverage, if also presenting a tempting invitation. She was unaware of the latter effect, however, and merely wondered if she ought to wear pearls or silver to accent the black.

Finally deciding on a simple silver locket, she carefully checked the myriad pins holding her heavy hair in its old-fashioned upsweep. Small curls dangled at her ears, but all else remained securely under guard. Alicia smiled in satisfaction as the knock came at the door notifying her of the arrival of her escort.

Jacques LaRouche grinned in masculine delight as his guest appeared on the stairs with only an ornately crocheted silk shawl to cover the effect of the delicate gown. Behind him the tavern's occupants hooted their appreciation, but the Frenchman ignored them all, gallantly bowing and offering Alicia his arm.

She stood half a head taller than he, but Alicia was grateful for his protection under the circumstances. Never had anyone hooted at her when she made her entrance before. Averting her pinkening cheeks from the men at the bar, she hurried outside after her escort. Next time she would take out her opera cape.

"You honor us, Mrs. Stanford," Jacques intoned solemnly as he helped her into his wagon. "Martha, she love to cook and to have the fetes, but she think we too poor, nobody come. For her, I thank you."

Embarrassed by this gratitude for her own selfishness, Alicia shook her head. "If you knew how much I appreciate this chance to be with friendly faces, you would realize I should be the one thanking you. I never knew how much it was possible to miss friends and family."

He nodded sagely. "I too once was alone. For a man it is not always good. For a woman. . ." He shrugged with eloquence. "A beautiful lady like you will not lonesome be for long. You see."

Alicia had to smile at his Gallic assurance, and she arrived at the LaRouche cottage with more confidence than she had expected. These were good people, and she was determined to enjoy herself.

When she caught a glimpse of Martha LaRouche and her daughter, Babette, she was glad she had made the decision in favor of formality. Although their gowns were the fashion of a decade ago, they had garbed themselves with an eager desire to take advantage of this rare social event. The room rustled with heavy petticoats and taffeta as they hurried forward to greet their guest.

In no time Alicia found herself describing the world she had left behind to a captivated Babette while Martha and Jacques greeted their few remaining guests. At seventeen, the French girl was still somewhat awkward and self-conscious, but her dusky beauty would soon attract many a suitor. Her laughter chimed enchantingly at Alicia's description of the meeting of the French and English ambassadors in her aunt's drawing room. The war between their countries might rage with saber and cannon, but the tongues on the two politicians had cut a wide swath through that evening. Alicia's wit portrayed the occasion with verve.

Even though the raw new capital at Washington was to be the seat of government, Philadelphia continued to be the meeting place of the influential. Alicia was well accustomed to formal social occasions with aristocrats from all over the world, and she quickly adapted to this new country she found herself in.

Just as she began to feel relatively secure in her new surroundings, the cabin door opened one more time, and Babette let out a screech of delight.

"Travis! You came! Mama said you would!"

The young girl threw herself into the arms of a frock-coated gentleman who hugged her with as much enthusiasm as she greeted him.

"Babette, you dangerous little peacock, you grow more beautiful every time I see you. When are you going to marry me?"

Babette laughed gaily at this facetiousness and led the newcomer into the room. Recognizing the deep baritone somewhat resembling mellow whiskey, Alicia stared in disbelief at the newcomer. How could the elegantly attired gentleman with his shining black hair pulled back in a neat queue be the half-naked savage from the river? The velvet coat of a deep chocolate brown molded perfectly to broad shoulders not requiring padding, and the sophisticated striped waistcoat of gold and ivory satin accented his lean waist as well as good taste. Alicia shied away from gazing more closely at the buckskin breeches buttoned tightly to muscled calves and thighs. If they were as exquisitely tailored as the coat, she would not be able to hide her embarrassment.

Instead she gazed upward to the high cheekbones and black eyes of his bronzed countenance, and met a faint trace of sardonic humor.

"Mrs. Stanford, I believe," he drawled lazily. "How good it is to make your acquaintance again."

Speechless, Alicia could scarcely conceive a fitting reply, but fortunately Jacques LaRouche intervened.

Slapping Travis on the back, he laughed. "We had to ask this no-count renegade. He the only one hereabouts who have the fancy coat to wear!"

A curl of amusement turned up one corner of Alicia's mouth as she held out her hand to the Indian. "I suspect I was invited for the same reason. I am pleased to meet you again, Mr. Travis."

"Oh, no, not Mister! I'm Jacques, he, Travis. We no need titles here," the Frenchman protested in vain, for neither of his companions was listening.

Travis allowed his gaze to saunter slowly over the inviting presence before him. Waves of rich chestnut hair crowned an elegantly high forehead from which stared brilliant eyes of sapphire blue, trimmed with a thick fringe of dark lashes and accented by eyebrows that seemed to peak in perpetual curiosity. The straight, narrow nose bespoke aristocracy, and the soft curves of her nearly oval face provided the ideal setting for a wide, inviting mouth of natural rose. He had no need to see the expensively delicate gown she wore to know he stood in the presence of a true lady. The truth was revealed in every pampered, unlined inch of her lovely cream complexion. He grinned.

"I suspect you are right, Mrs. Stanford. Martha and Babette here have a penchant for civilization that the remainder of the community sadly lacks." He casually hugged the shoulders of the giggling young girl at his side. "I dare say they have met their match tonight." This time, his gaze swept approvingly over the slender black gown that left a shocking expanse of ivory shoulders and arms bared to the cool evening air.

Alicia froze under his appreciative gaze and immediately turned to her host, coldly ignoring the flirtatious respect of the tall man at his side. "I don't believe I have met all your guests. If you would introduce me. . ."

Acknowledging her request, Jacques led her away, giving his puzzled friend only a slight shrug as he passed him by.

Undeterred, Travis insinuated himself into a seat across the table from Alicia when she sat down to eat. Well-known by Jacques' guests, he kept the conversation flowing around him and made certain it included the guest of honor. Since she was so obviously embarrassed by his frank stare, Travis made his presence unobtrusive by surrounding himself with others, but he held her attention just the same.

Once she became a part of the familiar flow of conversation, Alicia relaxed and began to enjoy the evening. The meal was a simple one, consisting mainly of recently harvested vegetables: beans and corn and early squash cooked with chunks of fat and bits of bacon, plus a haunch of venison for the hungry. Since the trestle table scarcely contained room for all the guests, people roamed about, carrying their tin plates wherever they might. Some of the men disappeared outside to smoke their pipes and pass a jug, while their womenfolk eagerly gossiped by the fireside. Martha and Babette bobbed back and forth from the kitchen, keeping the dishes filled from steaming pots and received their appreciation from the swiftness with which the food disappeared. Alicia held back a smile at the manner in which a tasty loaf of bread was ripped to crumbs before it reached the end of the table.

The man across the table from her caught that smile and frowned. Was the elegant lady from back East laughing at the country manners of his friends, or was she truly enjoying the evening in a milieu she had never found herself in before? Travis didn't really want to know the answer to that. He'd found fault with every woman he had ever known, except one perhaps, and even she had failed him. If he were to set his plans in motion, he must seize the opportunity offered and overlook the drawbacks. She was definitely the best thing he had seen in a long time.

Unaware of her place in the schemes of the man across the table, Alicia began to warm to the easy ambiance of the French trapper and his friends. A fiddle appeared from nowhere and began to sway out a merry tune that was soon joined by the lilting sounds of a mouth harp. Well warmed by the juice of a jug, a few men dragged out their reluctant wives into a small space cleared on the cabin floor, and the walls began to rattle with their foot-stomping appreciation of the serenade. Laughing, clapping, caught up in the music, others quickly joined them until only Alicia and Jacques remained at the table.

Unaware of her wistful expression as she watched Babette swing around the circle in the arms of her tall Indian partner, Alicia almost jumped at the sound of the deep voice behind her.

"Out here a woman cannot live alone. If she not have family, she must find a man." A wide, white grin broke across the Frenchman's dark face as his guest turned to face him. "And there are many, many men out here to choose from. A widow marries quickly. There is no time for mourning when the logs need chopping and the pot needs meat for cooking. Why don't you dance and make merry like the others?"

Since she had refused every offer she'd been made, the question was an honest one, but Alicia was incapable of answering it. Even she was uncertain of the truth. She only knew she was an outsider and would remain an outsider. She could force herself to do many things, but there was no purpose in forcing herself to join the dancers. She would never marry, so she need not submit to the touches of total strangers. She shook her head politely.

"My father is in St. Louis. I am not without family," she offered in explanation, though she knew she bent the truth sharply. Her father had been in St. Louis five years ago. Whether he still walked this earth at all was a matter of pure speculation.

The evening ended before midnight, and as the guests slowly drifted out into the night, and Babette and Martha began the process of cleaning the ruins, Travis appeared before his host to say his farewells.

"I thank you for the evening, Jacques. It will give me something to remember on those long nights down the river."

Helping Babette fold up a rug so the remnants of someone's tobacco could be shaken out, Alicia tried to ignore the polished accents coming so strangely from this man she knew to be an uncouth boatman if not half savage. But her efforts were unsuccessful. The knowledge that he intended to travel downriver compelled her to listen.

"You goin', then?" the Frenchman asked with interest. "They say Tecumseh and his warriors are refusin' to treat with Harrison. Them filthy redcoats be promisin' the heavens to the heathens. Can't be healthy for travelin'."

Travis's thin lips quirked in a wry smile. "That should be no problem for a redcoat renegade like me. You worry too much, Jacques. You're getting old. I've got a hankering for new places. I'll write you when I find them."

Jacques snorted. "A river rat never stays one place for long. It will kill you, my friend."

Before the conversation could get more personal, Alicia

stubbornly intruded. "Did you say you were traveling downriver, Mr. Travis?"

Dark eyes swept inquiringly to the intruder. "The boat is nearly done, Mrs. Stanford. I did not build it for amusement."

Taking a deep breath and avoiding his quizzical stare, she turned to her host. "Have you found Mr. Daniels yet?"

Jacques shrugged. "He no return. I keep looking, but he is a man prefers wilderness to town." He shook his head slightly to silence his friend. It would not do to tell the lady the man she sought lay in a drunken stupor under the back stairs of a local tavern.

Gathering her courage, sensing somehow that the elusive Mr. Daniels might never return, Alicia swung back to the cynical gentleman. "Would there be room for a passenger on this boat of yours, Mr. Travis? I would pay well."

Since he had built the boat purely on speculation and scarcely had half the cargo necessary to fill it, he would normally have agreed immediately. But Travis was taking no chances on any misunderstanding with this one.

"Madam, I will be traveling with a crew of nine men on a river that is so low we may have to pole our way down it. Without rain, we will have to portage around the falls and any sandbars. The discomfort of traveling in such a manner is difficult enough for strong men, but with the added danger of Indians on the warpath and river pirates on the banks, I would not recommend the voyage to anyone, especially not a woman traveling alone."

Stung by his scorn, Alicia drew herself up to her full height, her proud chin tilting at a stubborn angle, though the gazes of her admirers were more attracted to another asset to which her stance drew attention. Unaware that her shawl had fallen from her shoulders to reveal the lovely curves exposed by her low-cut bodice, Alicia answered his challenge with tenacity.

"You need only promise to curtain off one corner of the cabin for my privacy. I can walk the same as any man if we must. The Indians and the outlaws are a risk I must take no matter when or how I travel. I fear the actuality of my traveling companions more than the possibility of other dangers." She eyed Travis with doubt. "If I may take Jacques' word that you are capable of behaving with a better degree of courtesy than the cutthroat who left me here, I am willing to take the risk if you are."

Travis laughed softly and a hint of admiration gleamed in his eyes as he surveyed his delightfully intrepid passenger. "I am not so certain I trust myself so much as Jacques does. But if you are foolish enough to accept the risks, I will accept your offer of a generous fee. My cargo may not sell as well in St. Louis as New Orleans, and the going is a mite more difficult."

Beginning to shake with a combination of joy and fear, Alicia simply nodded in reply. She would pay any price to be as far gone from Philadelphia as she could, and the possibility of finding her father again filled her with elation, but the prospect of the journey ahead marred any foolish notion of immediate happiness. That, and her predicament, kept her feet firmly on the ground. She was a survivor, but some days the struggle made her wonder if it were worth the effort of surviving.

With arrogant self-assurance Travis turned to his host. "I'll take the little lady home, Jacques. You rest that foot and take Martha off to bed before she works herself to death. Give both your women a kiss from me."

Torn between outrage at his presumptuousness and the guess that the young girl behind her would prefer to be kissed by this stylish renegade than her father, Alicia lost her chance to control the situation. Somehow repeating her farewells and appreciation, she found herself led out into the starlit night in the company of a man she instinctively knew to be dangerous.

"Where is your earring tonight, Mr. Travis?" she asked acidly as he took her elbow and steered her toward the street.

"You like my earring?" he returned cheerfully. "I'll wear it in the morning when you come down to quarrel over the terms of our arrangement."

"I see no reason why I should speak with you again until it is time to leave. Simply name your price and date of departure."

Travis gazed down at the stack of lovely hair that came just past his chin. Other women wore their hair down about their shoulders or in long ringlets that danced around their throats or in other enticing arrangements. He'd love to loose the pins in those thick tresses, but this one was so starchy she probably did not even wear it down in bed.

"You open yourself to some interesting propositions with

that offer, Mrs. Stanford. No wonder Captain Danforth was
so irate at your lack of interest. But I will not insult Jacques'
wisdom by naming the terms that first come to mind. Come
down to the boat in the morning and we will talk money and
preparations. The nighttime should be reserved for more
pleasant things."

Alicia bridled at the lewd implications of his words, but
she would not lower herself to arguing with a creature that
probably referred to himself as "half horse, half alligator"
like the other keelboatmen. One didn't argue with less than
human mentalities, it would be akin to whipping a dog.

"I cannot fathom what further preparations might be
needed, but if you will not discuss terms tonight, then there
is no point in your accompanying me any longer. Thank you
for your company, but I can see myself back."

The frostiness of her tone served to amuse Travis even
more. She had not condescended to take his arm when he
offered it, but he wasn't about to be dismissed like an
unruly child, either. Keeping his voice as neutral as was
possible under the circumstances, he informed her, "I promised Jacques to see you home, and I will, if I must hog-tie
you and carry you screaming through the streets. If you are
to travel with me, Mrs. Stanford, you must learn to obey
orders, or I will put you off on the first island we come to.
A boat cannot be run down this river unless all hands are
prepared to jump when ordered. Perhaps you had better
think twice about signing on with me."

Shocked at being spoken to in such a manner, Alicia
fought back any hasty reply. She needed this arrogant,
presumptuous half-breed to take her away from here. It was
most vexing to be placed at such a disadvantage, but she
would have her own back one of these days. St. Louis was a
civilized city. They would listen to a lady's complaints. Then
let this black-eyed monster look at her the way he was doing
now. She longed to slap him, but that would be lowering
herself to his level. She would wait for her revenge.

"I shall do that, Mr. Travis," she replied coolly as they
reached the tavern door. "If I am not down at the river in
the morning, you may find yourself another passenger. Good
night."

Stunned by the possibility that she might choose to stay
behind rather than travel with him, Travis hesitated long
enough to allow her to get through the door before he had

the presence of mind to kiss her, as he had planned. Grimacing wryly at the realization of his own arrogance in assuming she would rather travel with him than stay here, he hastily shoved open the tavern door and followed her in.

She was scurrying toward the stairs when his voice boomed over the murmur of voices at the bar. "It was a pleasant evening, Mrs. Stanford. I look forward to seeing you in the morning!"

Alicia turned on the stair and stared at him in dismay, until the reaction of the other men in the room caused her to choke and flee for her chambers. The Irishman at the bar was fighting apoplexy at the sight of the richly frock-coated Indian standing head and shoulders above the crowd. And the others were pulling themselves up out of half-drunken stupors to stare in disbelief at the cultured tones coming from a half-breed they had arm wrestled and drunk with for untold nights past. The sight of Alicia's frail silk disappearing up the stairway topped it all off, and within minutes the saloon was in an uproar.

Travis merely smiled, bowed politely, and departed.

Upstairs in her locked room, Alicia stared out the moonlit window to the street below. The midnight terror had her in its grip, and her hand clutched convulsively at the tiny rounding of the place between her hipbones. Never, ever would she let another man touch her again. Just the thought of it made her tremble violently until the sickness returned. But this was a man's world she was entering now. Why had she not thought of that when she fled the horror she left behind?

She had been given fair warning of the violence she faced that first night in Pittsburgh. The stagecoach had left her at what had been promised as a respectable hostelry, but the ruffians inhabiting it had been little better than the ones below, including the women.

Closing her eyes against the memory of the knife flashing in the hands of the woman at the bar, Alicia tried to calm herself. She had never seen a knife fight before. The blood. . . ! It sickened her to remember it, sickened her to remember a woman had been the one to wield it. But most of all, it sickened her to remember the wild surge of vengeful delight she had felt as the man fell to the floor. Filled with loathing for herself, she had run from the room, but the memory haunted her still. She now knew the fiend she could become, the kind of person he would make of her if she let him.

Slowly dropping her shawl to the dresser, Alicia stared blindly at the tiny mirror. She could not let the madness inside of her be released. She must fight it with every ounce of pride she had left, though he had left her little. To give in would be to lower herself to the same level as that knife-wielding harlot, and that way lay destruction. She had been raised a lady. Even among savages she must remain a lady, at whatever cost.

Torn between helpless fury at the violence that had been done to her and the need to preserve what remained of her shattered pride, Alicia rocked slowly back and forth in front of the mirror. She could not let another man do that to her again. Never again. She would buy the means to prevent that in the morning. Before she went to the river.

4

TUCKING THE SMALL pearl-handled pistol she had just purchased into her bag, Alicia turned to leave the general
mercantile store. A well-endowed, somewhat eccentrically
garbed woman with flamboyant red hair stopped in the
doorway before Alicia could leave, and the two women
gazed at each other with curiosity.

Alicia had heard of women like this before, but protected
as she had been, there had never been any possibility of
meeting one. The revulsion she felt for what this woman
must do for a living provoked an irrational curiosity to know
more, but she would have passed silently by had not the
other woman spoken first.

"Well, I declare, if it isn't the little lady what has the
whole river talkin'! How do you do, honey? I'm Molly
Malone, or so's they call me, leastways. Meeting Lonetree
this morning, ain't you? Mind if I walk a ways with you?"

Unable to refuse politely as the larger woman followed
her out, Alicia covered her confusion with silence. The
woman's nearly lashless eyes looked her over with open
curiosity, but there appeared to be no animosity in them.
Her garrulousness prevented conversation from lagging.

"Mite on the quiet side, ain't you, honey? Lonetree's an
odd one. Might be he prefers 'em like that, but I can't see
how a proper lady like you would get mixed up with the
likes of him. I'm not meanin' to be nosy, honey, but I take
an interest in my friends."

Alicia's footsteps slowed to a halt with the impact of these
words, and she turned her head slowly to stare into the
brash, honest features of this overdressed, overweight woman.
The woman's complexion showed the effects of an excess of
liquor and paint, but despite the artificiality of her appear-

ance, there seemed something genuine in her concern for
the elusive half-breed.

"Mrs. Malone, I appreciate your interest, but I fail to
understand your meaning. Mr. Lonetree or Travis or whatever he is called has offered to transport me to St. Louis and
my father. It is strictly a business arrangement. If there is
something else I should know, please feel free to confide in
me."

The woman broke into a grin and looked Alicia up and
down admiringly as if she were some strange creature in a
zoo. "Well, honey, you got a mite more gumption than that
prissy gown gives you credit for, I'll say that. Maybe Lonetree
knows what he's doin'. Usually does, that's for certain.
Never saw such a man for getting what he wants, providin'
he knows what he wants. But when a man starts putting on
fancy duds and goin' to town instead of taking up a lady's
invitation to her bed, it sure sounds like he knows what he
wants. He's a mite on the wild side, that injun blood in him,
I reckon, but he's a good man. You ain't going to find none
better out here. Always wondered what that boy had in
him, but now I see what he's been after. You don't want
him, just send him back to me. I'll look after him."

Incredulous, unwilling to grasp the outrageous implications of these words, Alicia simply shook her head in disbelief. "I'll keep your recommendation in mind, Mrs. Malone.
I thank you for sharing your thoughts with me."

"Honey, that's what we're put on God's good earth for. I
do like your style. Some of these so-called ladies around
here cross the street when they see me comin', and there
ain't no way I can be of help to them. But I thought if
Lonetree picked you, there's got to be a reason, and I was
right. You got class, but you're a woman just like me. Men
are hard on a woman, but we can't live without them. You
take care now, honey. I reckon we won't be seeing each
other again soon."

Molly Malone rolled off, her wide hips swinging generously beneath outdated petticoats and stiff skirts. She reminded Alicia of a battleship she had once seen plowing
through the waves of the harbor, her mighty keel reducing
the roar of the ocean to mighty splashes. God help any who
floundered in her path.

Somewhat shaken by the encounter, Alicia turned her
feet reluctantly toward the river. Just what had Molly meant

when she said they were both women? She seemed to hint that the other ladies of town were somehow excluded from that class. Surely she did not take her to be of the same sort as. . . Alicia shook her head in bewilderment. She felt as if she had fallen through a hole in the ground and come up in another world.

Travis looked up to follow her progress as Alicia picked her way daintily over the rutted clay and rocks of the path down to the river. She had abandoned black for a deep navy blue, but she still wore one of her infernal bonnets with the brim pulled around her face so only someone standing directly in front of her could see more than shadow. The sensible muslin gown showed no hint of the frills or lace of last night, but was shrouded in a cloud of light blue gauze, concealing any hint of the creamy skin beneath. Despite all that, he smiled in pleasure at the sight of the slim figure silhouetted beneath the thin gown as she swayed gently down the hill. If she had any idea how much those fashionable little gowns revealed, he suspected she would dust off her mother's old full skirts, but who was he to deny the world the pleasure of what he viewed right now?

Alicia glanced suspiciously at the smirk on his lean face as Travis climbed down from the cabin roof to greet her. At least he had the presence of mind to wear his shirt this day, though he had refrained from tying it closed at the throat. True to his word, he had returned to his savage costume, his long hair tied back in a bandanna instead of neatly in a queue, and the gold earring glittering infamously in one earlobe. But the image of the proper gentleman he had appeared the night before somewhat blurred his uncivilized image of the day. She no longer looked on him with stark terror, but an immense amount of curiosity.

"Beautiful day, Mrs. Stanford." White teeth gleamed in a bronzed countenance, and the crook in his nose did nothing to detract from his striking appearance.

"But you would prefer rain, I take it?" Alicia asked acerbically, refusing to be taken in by his charm.

His eyebrows went up in surprise at her grasp of the situation, but he nodded agreement. "This trip would be a good deal safer in the rain, admittedly, but to wait for it might place us too close to winter and other hazards. It might take longer than usual, but I can get us downriver without the rain."

"Good. I've been told you are a competent man and assured that you get what you set out for, so I'll not doubt your ability to achieve this goal."

At the ironic tone of this pretty speech Travis glanced at her from beneath black brows. "And who have you been talking to that is so generous in my praise?"

"A Mrs. Malone, I believe. She left me with a most singular impression, but I don't suppose you would care to clarify her implications?" Clear blue eyes peered out from beneath the bonnet's brim with piercing intensity as she gauged the keelboatman's reaction.

Travis opened his mouth to speak, closed it again, and stared at her with incredulity and disbelief before he broke out in laughter. "Molly! My God! What were you doing talking to Molly?"

Tapping her toe, Alicia frostily waited for him to control himself before she replied. "I believe it was more a case of Molly doing the talking. I would prefer it if my name did not become a household word. Just what is everyone saying about me that she would confront me in such a manner?"

Sobering, Travis leaned back against the boat's keel and picked up the latest stick he had been carving. Pulling out his knife, he looked up at her obliquely. "I don't know who you're hiding from, Mrs. Stanford, or why, but any woman traveling this river alone will start tongues wagging. You should have changed your name if you wished to conceal your identity, though I doubt any man in his right mind would fail to recognize your description."

Uneasily aware that he had come closer to the truth than she cared to admit, Alicia averted the topic. "I am just not accustomed to being gossiped about in such a manner. Now, shall we discuss the terms of our agreement?"

Travis continued to whittle at his stick, studiously watching the shape forming beneath his fingers. He had promised himself not to look too closely at the flaws of this woman who had stepped so miraculously from the water practically into his arms, but he could not avoid certain niggling doubts. She was some years younger than he, but no longer a child. If it were not for her mourning and her insistence on the title "Mrs." he would have thought her a maiden, though. Her modesty went to an extreme for a woman who should have known the physical aspects of men and matrimony. Now this fear of being known added to the mystery. Had she murdered her husband? Or just run away from him? Judging by the innate good breeding she displayed, Travis rather suspected the latter, which certainly complicated matters seriously.

However, he was in no position to ask questions, and since he could think of no better plan than the one he had conceived, he shrugged laconically.

"The price of the boat is forty-five dollars. If I make less money on my cargo in St. Louis than I expected in New Orleans, I will expect you to make up half the difference. If I make more, I will split the profits. In either case, the boat is yours to do with as you wish when we get there. But over and beyond that, I expect you to obey my orders. Can you shoot a rifle, Mrs. Stanford?"

Alicia swallowed her relief at the price. To pay for the entire boat was outrageous, but she was in no position to haggle. She had feared he would somehow know the limited funds she carried on her and demand all her remaining cash. Under the circumstances, forty-five dollars was reasonable, but the other conditions might not be. She glared at him dubiously.

"A rifle, Mr. Travis? I have never even held one."

He snorted and shoved himself to an upright position again. "I figured that. We'll have to give you some lessons, Mrs. Stanford. At times, every hand is needed, and yours will be no exception. Hampered by those fool skirts of yours, you will more likely be a nuisance than anything, but putting breeches on you certainly won't solve the problem. 'Tis a pity you're not a squaw. They at least know how to dress sensibly."

Seething over his insults, Alicia fought back the urge to retaliate in kind. Her upbringing did not permit vulgar quarrels, but never before had she been so induced to indulge in one. Perhaps her condition rendered her emotionally unstable. If so, she had all the more reason to resist telling this insufferable man what she thought of him. She would not lower herself to his level, regardless of the provocation.

"Mr. Travis," she replied icily, then catching herself, she forced herself to inquire, "Is it Travis Lonetree or Lonetree Travis? It is most difficult addressing you without a proper introduction."

He watched with admiration as she visibly choked back her fury. The women he knew would have taken a knife to

him by now. She was a lady, no doubt, but one obviously in
the last stages of losing control. It would be interesting to
see how a lady reacted to the travails in store for her.

"Neither. Just call me one or the other, preferably without the 'Mister.' I'll answer to just about anything. You had
something else you wished to say?"

Alicia's chin jutted dangerously. "I only wished to say,
Mr. Travis, that I am quite capable of wearing breeches or
deerskin or blankets, if necessary, should it get us to St.
Louis any more quickly. Just inform me of the approved
garb and I will acquire it."

That he had not been expecting, and it took Travis a
minute to formulate a reply. It would be severely tempting
to recommend breechclouts and turkey feathers as his mother
had worn, but he would not test his luck too far. Smiling his
approval at her practicality, he recommended, "I trust your
judgment in not wearing anything to inflame my men any
more than necessary. Other than that, I recommend anything that allows you to walk with comfort without entangling
itself on every briar. Normally, it would not matter, but we
may see a lot of walking this trip. Moccasins would be more
comfortable for your feet than those dainty slippers." He
indicated the pieces of material laced elegantly about her
ankles.

Alicia blushed at the realization that his sharp eyes had
not missed any detail of her garments. She was unused to
such scrutiny, but she refused to allow him to throw her off
balance.

"Can you recommend a place where I might purchase
some moccasins, then? And tell me what date we will be
leaving so I can have my luggage delivered in time?"

Travis could not help but grin to himself at the meekness
with which she complied to his commands. That would not
last long, but he would enjoy it while he could.

"I'll take care of the moccasins for you. One of my men
will have the wagon at the tavern at daybreak. I'm ready to
go as soon as you are, Mrs. Stanford."

Startled, but relieved at the knowledge that this unendurable
voyage would begin so soon, Alicia merely nodded her
acceptance. She did not know how she would survive countless days in the company of this unnerving savage, but she
would endure anything to escape what she had left behind.
She would run barefoot through the woods if required.

"I will be ready at dawn, Mr. Travis. Thank you." Averting her eyes from that penetrating black stare of his, she turned back to the path toward town.

Dawn arrived more quickly than she was prepared for, but since she had scarcely slept all night, Alicia was up and ready when the ancient wagon pulled to a halt outside the tavern. Hastily she checked the black kerchief wrapped snugly about the dove-gray muslin bodice, and straightened her gray bonnet to effectively hide all sight of her hair. She knew from experience that heavy tendrils would escape before day's end, but she would start this journey with proper decorum. She looked the part of a Quaker lady, she surmised, and wished she had the white apron to confirm it.

The knock on the door startled her, though she had been expecting it, and with one last nervous knotting of her bonnet strings, Alicia unfastened the door.

To her surprise Travis stood there, his shirt properly tied and topped by a buckskin jacket with fringes along the arms and yoke, his hair cropped to an almost respectable length about his sun-browned throat. She must have been staring, for he gestured silently at her trunks, distracting her gaze.

She nodded and hurried to gather together her pelisse and purse and the smaller carpet bag. Travis effortlessly lifted the largest trunk and carried it into the hall, gesturing with his head to another man outside to go after the last. They marched through the silent tavern without exchanging a word. Not until they reached the street did they even encounter another human being.

A lone couple strolled arm in arm through the dusty, half-lit street, dawn's rosy hue providing little more than shadow in the early morning coolness. They appeared to be respectable people, perhaps walking to work at one of the local groceries. At the sight of the small procession loading baggage into the wagon, the woman whispered urgently into the man's ear. The man in turn stared at the tall, broad-shouldered figure helping the lady into the seat.

Without a word of provocation he spat in the dust at Travis's feet, muttered, "Damned, no-good injuns," and steered his companion across the street.

Alicia stared after the couple, too stunned to react in any other way, until the tension of these last minutes broke with an hysterical giggle. Travis had merely shouldered the last of the trunks into the wagon and climbed into the seat beside her. At her outburst he raised a quizzical brow.

"That's what Molly said they did when she came to town. Are you a whore, Mr. Travis?" As she had never said such an improper thing in her life, she hastily covered her mouth with her fingers and looked surprised, but the dignified man beside her did not seem in the least disturbed.

"No, Mrs. Stanford. Are you?"

The casualness of his question shocked Alicia into further giggles, until she could not control the hysterical gulps of laughter rocking her body. Until now she had kept torturously tight rein on her emotions, but today she felt free. The burden of a thousand travesties lifted from her shoulders, and fell by the wayside as the wagon rumbled down silent streets to the river below. Home and family lay far behind and the great, wide West loomed before her. She wanted to shout "Hallelujah!" and dance a jig, but she did not know how. Instead she laughed until the music of it filled the streets and the men in the wagon with her began to grin.

"Mrs. Stanford, if you can laugh that way at every insult you are given, you are destined to lead a long and merry life," Travis predicted.

"That sounds as if you expect me to be insulted frequently, Mr. Travis," she giggled as the wagon came to a halt by the river.

Travis swung down from the seat and with a lazy, muscular grace grasped her by the waist and lifted her to the ground. Black eyes twinkled wickedly as he held her a trifle longer than necessary.

"If it keeps you laughing like that, I'll make it a habit to insult you daily."

Growing uncomfortably aware of the crew of keelboatmen leaning over the side and lounging against the cabin watching this scene with great interest and no small amount of grins and jests, Alicia hastily disentangled herself from Travis's presumptuous hold.

"You grow too bold, Mr. Travis. I thank you to keep your hands to yourself."

Hands on hips, he laughed at the twin spots of outraged red coloring her cheeks. "Didn't anyone ever teach you, Mrs. Stanford? We Indians respect no one but the moon and sun. Children of nature, some poor poet called us. Creatures of impulse is the usual epithet. Beware, Mrs.

Stanford, or I'll scalp that dreadful bonnet right off your pretty locks."

With a roar of laughter at her expression, he shouldered the first of her trunks and headed for the boat, leaving Alicia to follow in his path.

It was pure madness even to contemplate this trip, but as she gazed at the wooden partition in the back of the cabin obviously installed just for her convenience, she smiled with pleasure. This Travis/Lonetree might be a rude, arrogant, presumptuous Indian, but he was the closest thing to a gentleman she had encountered west of the Alleghenies. And with satisfaction she set her bags down at the foot of the crude bed constructed just for her.

For the first time since leaving Philadelphia, she felt confidence in her plans. She just wished she could have seen Teddy's face when he pulled up to the Stanford mansion and found the windows boarded and a "FOR SALE" placard on the door. He wanted the house so badly, let him buy it. Only this way, she wouldn't come with it.

5

By NIGHTFALL some of the pleasure had dissipated, and weariness masked whatever remained.

The reverberations of shotgun blasts still echoed in Alicia's ears, and her hands and gown still stank of sulfur from the day's lessons in loading and priming. The lesson would have been simple enough if Travis had not insisted on holding her hands to guide each step. His proximity had made her so nervous she became all thumbs and the lessons took twice as long, much to the appreciation of the grinning crew.

Grimly she contemplated the warm bucket of water some thoughtful person had provided for her to wash in. What she wanted was an enormous bath to rid herself of the stench of sulfur and the memories that still made her ache with pain and her skin crawl with disgust. The presence of so many overtly masculine, half-dressed men around her did nothing to alleviate her distress. If allowed, her imagination would go beyond control.

Remembering the small pistol neatly tucked beneath her pillow, Alicia gave herself permission to relax a little. She would not be caught unawares the next time. Now that she knew what could be expected of men, she could prepare herself. For that reason she had endured this day's lesson. Now she knew how the weapon operated. Weariness momentarily stripped away her mantle of respectability. She would not become a victim of violence—or man, again.

Unbuttoning the high-necked gown she had chosen and lowering the bodice and chemise, Alicia washed in the luxury of hot water. After the first part of her trip, this journey with Travis seemed to be a decided improvement in quality. He was obviously worth the money spent if the remainder of the journey met today's standards.

The lavender soap erased all traces of gunpowder, and, feeling considerably refreshed, Alicia fastened her clothing again and prepared to join the others over the evening meal. Travis had declared this part of the river safe enough to land and hunt fresh meat, and she could smell the results of the hunt cooking over a fire now.

She debated leaving off the cotton kerchief so she could enjoy the cool evening air against her skin, but, remembering the Indian's warning, she pinned the additional covering over her shoulders. She would not be accused of offering anyone enticement. On her way out, she grabbed a shawl as extra precaution.

Travis hid his grimace as his passenger stepped from the boat wrapped to the neck in dreary gray and black, and huddled beneath bonnet and shawl like some ancient spinster. He meant to have no trouble with his men over this woman, but she had taken his words too far. He had already made his claim on her, and there wasn't a man aboard who wouldn't honor it. They knew he would skin them alive if they attempted to steal his property. But he wasn't about to explain that pertinent piece of information to the lady.

He ignored her as she found a secluded spot on a log just out of reach of the fire light. He had never seen a woman shy so from his attentions, but he attributed it to her fear of his race. This all must seem strange to her, so he would not push too hard, too fast. She seemed to be learning quickly, and without the prejudices of those who had lived this life too long. She might learn to respect his intentions, given a little time. If not, there were other ways of bringing her around.

Travis sat back on his haunches and sipped at the bitter brew in his cup while covertly studying the woman across the glade. It was a good thing she had been married before. Untried maidens could be a bit hysterical at first. From what he had learned of this one thus far, she would be furious, but her upbringing would prevent her from becoming violent. No, if he had to resort to desperate measures, she would submit soon enough.

The restlessness this thought stirred in his loins made Travis smile. Once she grew accustomed to the idea, he would teach her the pleasures her first husband obviously had not. It had been a long time since he had bedded a real lady, one who smelled of soap and perfume instead of horse

lather and sweat. He remembered the smooth softness of
skin untouched by sun, the feel of satin sheets, the taste of
sweet wine upon his lips. Where in hell would he find wine
and satin sheets out here?

Standing up, irritated by the path of his thoughts, Travis
slipped into the shadows of the trees to work his way around
the clearing to the lone figure at the clearing's edge. To his
surprise, when he arrived at the log, she was gone.

Alicia cautiously followed the faint trail she had found
into the woods. The need to relieve herself so frequently
could become a nuisance under these circumstances. She
detested being forced to go out in the open like some
creature of nature, but she feared returning to the boat
alone even more. When Travis was there, she felt relatively
protected. But she did not know or trust those barbarians he
called a crew. She preferred the security of the woods.

Accomplishing her objective, she adjusted her skirts and
petticoats and glanced about her. She could see an occasional star through the canopy of leaves above, and knew
this night would not bring rain. The various murmurings and
stirrings in the underbrush around her made her uneasy,
and she lingered no longer. Perhaps the others were ready
to return to the boat by now.

As she stepped out onto the path again, a wild screech
tore through the air just behind her, and a hideous noise of
beating drums and slapping leaves erupted all around. With
a scream of terror Alicia ran for the safety of the fire.

And collided directly with the tall, unyielding frame of
the half-breed. Lonetree's arms instantly circled her, cradling Alicia against his linen-covered chest as she babbled
incoherently of savages and wild beasts. His lack of fear
calmed her. The muscular strength holding her shielded her
from the unknown. And the soothing stroke of his capable
hand down her spine brought her to her senses.

Instantly alert, Alicia pushed his chest, trying to distance
herself from the very masculine body pressing into her.
Travis yielded a short distance, but did not free her completely as he stared like a cat through the darkness at her
upturned face.

"What is it, Alicia? Did you see something?"

She sensed the tension in his voice, but her fears of this
man overwhelmed the fears of a moment ago. She squirmed

to be free of his hold, not even noticing the familiarity of his address.

"No. I heard a noise. . ." She wriggled from the loose hold of his hands on her waist and breathed easier. "A horrible noise. Like I'd imagine a banshee."

She could almost feel his grin in the dark.

"That screech owl a moment ago? If that's all, you're safer with him than with me."

With that inane remark he held his hands to his mouth, and emitted a screech that could have deafened a devil had one been around. Alicia covered her ears and stared at him with incredulity.

"Whatever on earth possessed you to do that? One in a night is quite sufficient."

Travis caught her shoulder with one arm and turned her to face back the way she had come. "I'm going to teach you the stupidity of wandering off by yourself."

A shadowy figure emerged from behind a copse of trees and shrubs. Even in the darkness Alicia could discern the near-nakedness of the red man not three yards from where they stood. If it had not been for Travis's arm holding her firmly in place, she would have turned and fled.

"There is your screech owl," he muttered before breaking into a soft murmur in an unknown tongue.

The Indian approached cautiously, and Alicia could trace the fierce scars of tattoos across his chest and upper arms. She averted her eyes from the loose breechclout that provided his only covering, and welcomed the protection of the strong arm around her. She huddled closer to Travis's side, but he didn't seem to be aware of it.

The men exchanged a few brief words in a foreign language before the Indian turned his gaze to Alicia. At the same time Travis jerked the concealing bonnet from her head, revealing the thick mass of chestnut hair curled above a frightened oval face and brilliant blue eyes. The stranger smiled.

"Pale face," he scoffed in clear English. "You grow soft, Lonetree."

Suddenly realizing they were discussing her, Alicia jerked from his grasp and snatched her bonnet back. With a glare to her irritating guide, she turned on her heel and beat a hasty retreat to the fire.

Their laughter followed her all the way back.

She could hear the sound of a mouth organ and singing as she approached the clearing, but her fury and chagrin prevented lingering. Skirts sweeping the long, dry grass, she kept on toward the river. She understood now that Lonetree would never be far behind. She need not fear his men, but she had better learn to steer a wide course from their captain.

Slamming her cabin door and throwing the latch, Alicia curled her arms around her middle and stared at the thin partition as if it might turn to smoke. It didn't, but it wasn't long until she heard the sound of footsteps on the roof overhead and along the narrow deck outside. The men were settling in for the night.

She waited, huddled in the center of her narrow bed, listening to the sounds of talking and laughter outside. Her heart had slowed its pace, but she still did not divest herself of a single garment. The touch of the Indian's arms about her held her petrified. She feared he would come looking for more.

Then she heard the soft sound of footsteps in the long cabin outside her door. The other men walked with heavy tread, stomping their hard boots against the wooden deck. She recognized this softer tread. Travis might tower half a head above every man on the crew, but he walked as quietly as any cat in the woods. Alicia held her breath as he approached, then emitted a sigh of relief as she heard the sound of barrels shifting a short distance from her door. She should have known he would make his bed there.

Relaxing, at last, she removed her outer garments and retired to bed in her chemise. The small port hole of a window allowed little circulation and the night was warm. Exhausted, she slept instantly.

The gentle rocking of the river current woke her in the early hours of dawn. A light rain beat against the cabin planks, and a cool wind discovered the port hole and swirled about the tiny room. Alicia's stomach churned violently, and she automatically reached for the chamber pot to heave up last night's supper.

Groaning softly, she wrapped herself in a quilt and lay upon her narrow pallet, waiting for the waves of nausea to settle. She had thought this part over and done, but the river's motion had unsettled it again. If she were to be sick all the way to St. Louis, she would never survive the trip.

A gust of wind made the boat rock more, and she bent to spew the last burning remnants of bile into the pot, trying desperately not to think of the trap her body had become. To think was to experience an anguish well beyond her capacity to control. That way lay madness. She must act, force herself to go through the motions of controlling her life, though she knew she had lost all ability to steer her own course months ago.

A knock sounded at the door, but she could do no more than groan and roll back into the comfort of the quilt. The voice on the other side expressed instant concern.

"Alicia! Are you all right?"

She pressed her eyes closed at the sound of Travis's deep baritone. That was all she needed. "Go away," she muttered, hopefully loud enough for him to hear.

"We're casting off in a few minutes. If you want your breakfast, you'd better be quick." The voice was curt; he had heard her, but there was still a note of questioning in it.

Alicia didn't answer. Travis frowned at the silence, then turned on his heel, and left her there. He had heard the sound of retching often enough to recognize it, though usually it accompanied a nightlong bout of drinking. He didn't think Miss Nose-in-the-Air indulged in nightlong bouts of anything.

He yelled orders at his men in a voice that warned of the dangers of disobedience. The crew jumped into action, giving the half-breed looks askance. His surly temper was known to all, and they had no intention of crossing it. Wearing his fringed coat in deference to the wind and rain, Travis still managed to look more Indian than white man with his straight black hair held back in the red bandanna and a gold earring glittering against his swarthy skin. The fact that half the men on the boat dressed in a similar manner made no impression on their fear and respect for the man who had made this trip more times without incident than any other they knew.

When Alicia finally appeared, her face pale and drawn against the crow's black of her cloak and bonnet, Travis set his mouth in a manner that left grim lines on either side. What did he know of this woman, after all? Remembering his earlier suspicion that she ran from her husband, he swore at himself. All he needed was an irate husband coming after him with a gun.

He watched as she helped herself to the pot of hot coffee, but touched nothing of the fried meat and potatoes left warming over the brazier for her. His gaze traveled over her tall, slender figure, but he could detect nothing beneath her billowing cloaks. Cursing himself for three sorts of a fool, he leapt from the roof and approached her.

"Are you OK?" he inquired gruffly.

Alicia jumped backward as if she had been hit, then recovering herself, met his black gaze coolly. "OK?"

"All right. Feeling well." Irritated at having to explain himself when he felt certain she knew the connotation of his slang, Travis made no attempt to be polite.

"Not that it's any of your business, but I am fine." Alicia clasped her hands around the warm mug, striving frantically to keep all the frayed pieces of her nerves together while she confronted this half savage man towering over her. She was unaccustomed to having to look up to meet a man's eyes, and the experience did nothing to calm her. For some reason he looked particularly fierce this morning, and she hid her shudder at the grim lines of his chiseled face.

"Pardon my existence," he replied sardonically. Without another word he turned his back on her, and strode off to shout furious commands to one of the pole wielders.

Shaken and on the verge of tears, Alicia returned to the safety and comfort of her cabin. She did not possess the strength to fight the world today.

When the sun came out later that day, she reappeared on deck, hoping to find an inconspicuous corner to huddle in. The smooth lines of the hull and narrow deck made that an impossibility, but craving fresh air and sunshine, Alicia settled on a crate at the bow near the cabin door.

Whereas Travis deliberately ignored the delicate figure wrapped in shawls, his crew went out of their way to perform for her attentions. Like mischievous boys, they sang lusty songs, performed daring—and totally unnecessary—feats with their poles, and insulted each other's performances loudly. Alicia attempted to ignore them, but her need for laughter was so great, she could not always hide her smile at some particularly apt remark. When they turned their gifted tongues upon their captain, her obvious delight encouraged them to soaring new heights.

Until Travis dropped lightly from his lookout perch upon the cabin to land in their midst with a wicked grin that did

not bode well for his brash comrades. He had shed his
jacket, and the loose linen of his shirt sleeves billowed in
the cool September breeze as he stood, hands on hips, and
grinned at his suddenly nervous pole men.

"All right, you ring-tailed polecats, you're feeling mighty
feisty today. Which of you wants to put your money where
your mouth is and try to take me down tonight?"

Alicia noticed a certain hesitancy before they all clamored
to join the battle, and she gave the Indian a darting look.
Though taller, he was leaner and less heavy than the majority of his crew, and she wondered at his confidence in taking
on such a challenge. Keelboatmen were notorious brawlers,
and only the strong survived in this habitat. It appeared to
her that he had a less than even chance of winning any
brawl with his men.

The idea of fighting just for the pure meanness of it left a
sour taste in Alicia's mouth, but she had no right to interfere. Any comment she made would be turned against her,
but the challenge took some of the sunshine from the day.
As they eagerly clasped their fists around a long pole to see
who would come out on top, she lifted her skirts and quietly
disappeared inside the cabin. She had not meant to cause
this scene, and she certainly had no intention of encouraging
it.

They landed the keelboat early that evening at a sliver of
an island some miles upstream from the town of Louisville.
Alicia coldly ignored Travis's offer of a helping hand, and
stepped to the muddy shore without his aid.

Travis expertly caught her elbow as her slipper heel slid in
the river clay. "Tomorrow we will portage around the falls.
Wear your moccasins. Taking the boat down the falls is a
tricky operation, and I want my men in top shape. That's
why I didn't take them into town tonight. I trust you will be
well and ready to travel first thing in the morning, also?"

She didn't like the tone of his voice as he asked that
question, and she shook her arm free from his steady grip.
"After brawling half the night, you might well ask yourself
that, Mr. Travis."

She turned to follow a narrow path up the bank, but he
kept in easy stride with her. "I don't do anything without a
purpose, Mrs. Stanford." He emphasized the "Mrs." wryly.
"Just follow my orders, and we'll get on swimmingly."

Alicia glanced up in surprise at this odd expression, but

Travis was already cutting across the clearing in the direction of a small grove of trees. She stared at his broad-shouldered back for a few seconds before shaking off her reverie and walking on. He was a strange mixture of Indian and frontier white man, but every once in a while . . . She shook her head at the incongruity of her thoughts. The British still held outposts in the vast interiors of this uninhabited land. Who knows? Maybe the savage had lived among the British in their forts for a while. It certainly would be in keeping with the reports she'd heard of British and Indian warfare in these parts.

Not in the least reassured by these conjectures, Alicia held herself aloof from the company at the campfire. As the men groused and teased and made bets over the upcoming fight, she began to understand Travis's purpose in this at least. With the temptations of the taverns and women of Louisville only a few miles away, he offered a different entertainment to keep his rowdy crew occupied. With the opportunity to see their leader out-matched, they scarcely cared about missing the city's delights.

She meant to return to the boat before the brawl started, but while they ate, two burly boatmen blocked the path, and a circle had formed around the fire before she finished her meal. She sensed some of the men leaning against the trees at her back, and though all politely ignored her, Alicia realized she had no chance of escape. They wanted an audience, and she was to provide it.

Someone offered her more coffee, and she sipped it nervously. She had paid no attention to Travis's whereabouts, but she knew by now that he would not be far away. She was both grateful and irked by his constant watchful protection. If she felt it were only her safety that interested him, she could be more gracious about his proximity, but she had learned to suspect the motives of all men. Seldom did they act out of the pure generosity of their hearts.

That was something else which she had no wish to think long upon. So, when the two combatants finally appeared in the ring, she almost felt grateful for the distraction. Wearing only their tight buckskin breeches, bronzed, muscled shoulders gleaming in the firelight, they threw giant shadows across the clearing as they moved cautiously toward one another. As Alicia had predicted, Travis was lighter than his opponent, but the older man's weight tended to fat more than muscle. She shivered as the heavier man dived at Travis with every intention of smashing him into the ground. This would be a no-holds-barred contest, and she clenched her eyes shut at the first grunt of pain.

There was no heavy thud or shaking of the ground as she had expected, and the men's cheers forced Alicia to peek quickly to see what had happened. With a grin Travis now stood on the opposite side of the fire, while his opponent shook his head free of cobwebs and gasped for air after the blow to his midsection. Not only was the keelboatman heavier, but less fleet of foot than the wily Indian. Alicia began to realize there never had been a chance at a match. Even as she watched, Travis sidestepped another charge, as if he knew every thought in the other man's head. This time a blow to the jaw made his opponent stumble and nearly fall into the fire.

With the advantage of quick wits and athletic grace to add to his muscular strength, Travis had every man in the crowd bested, and they knew it. They fought only with the hope of a surprise blow bringing him to the ground, where their heavier weight might take the lead. Alicia shook her head in dismay as time after time the crewman struggled for a hold on his captain, only to find himself stumbling just to stay on his feet. The men roared and cheered or cursed mightily as their wagers led them. This was a performance, pure and simple, and she grudgingly admired his finesse.

In no time at all Travis had his opponent on the ground with his arm twisted behind his back, conceding defeat. White teeth bared in a grin, Travis rose to acknowledge the cheers of victory, and with a brief expostulation on the folly of insulting a giant among men, half alligator and half horse—and here he winked broadly in Alicia's direction—Travis accepted a cup of whiskey from the jug offered. Then, with a gleam in his eye, he made his way straight toward their captive audience.

Alicia rose, posed to flee, but thinking her eager to acknowledge the victor, the men pushed her forward. Still holding his cup and to roars of approval all around, Travis trapped her with his free arm.

Before she knew what was happening, Alicia found herself bent in the embrace of this sweaty, half-naked savage as he lowered his whiskey-flavored mouth against hers. She tried to scream, but he was too quick, catching her lips with a fierce kiss that left her breathless.

Then, as if he had done nothing untoward, Travis set her back on her feet again, grinned that self-satisfied smirk of his, and strode back to the fire for another pull from the jug.

Thoroughly shaken, unable to put one foot in front of another, Alicia collapsed back on to the seat she had made of a pile of rocks. She pressed the back of her hand to her mouth and tasted the salty flavor of his kiss. He had not bruised her. He had not even disturbed the carefully pinned lace of her bodice or shawl, although she could feel several tendrils of hair falling from their pins from the swiftness of his move. He had not done any of those things she had learned to fear in a man, but every fiber of her body shook with terror.

Travis appeared not to notice when she finally gathered her strength and slipped from the clearing to the safety of the boat. Yet within minutes of latching the door, Alicia heard the catlike tread of his footsteps upon the planks outside. She gave a cry of fear as the sound came closer, and with desperation she dove for the small pistol beneath her pillow.

Travis heard the cry and scowled. The fight had set his blood racing, the whiskey had brought a roaring to his ears, but the light of admiration in her eyes had been his inspiration. He had the taste of her sweetness upon his lips, the feel of her supple body in his arms, and he wanted more. But that whispered cry of fear brought him to an instant halt. He wanted her, and he would have her—he had no doubt about that—but the pleasure would be doubled when the lady wanted him. He would wait.

6

THE SICKNESS and the rain returned the next morning, both increasing in equal intensity. Alicia buried her groans in a pillow and refused to come out upon command. The boat lurched and jerked onward as the crew propelled it into the river, and the wind and the rain lashed it forward.

By the time they reached Louisville, Alicia had managed to don the first gown she encountered in the trunk, but she left her hair in the heavy braids she had plaited the night before. Merely winding them around her head took all the energy she could summon.

The churning in her stomach had subsided to a dull ache in her lower abdomen by the time the boat landed at the first stage of the portage. Alicia felt the jar of the landing and came out of her cabin of her own accord, making her way with difficulty down the aisle through the cargo of heavy crates and barrels.

On his way to fetch his recalcitrant passenger, Travis met her at the door, and his eyes narrowed grimly at the sight she presented. The pale oval of her face was white and drawn, her lips pinched and colorless as she grabbed at the door frame to steady herself. For once she wore something besides black or gray, but the brown gingham hung loosely on shoulders too frail for even that light burden. The wind whipped the velvet bonnet from her hair, and the childish braids stopped his tongue. When she lifted smudged eyes to meet his, he cursed the fates.

"We'll be hauling the cargo out to wagons most of the morning. Why don't I take you up to the tavern and call for a physician? You don't look well enough to travel."

Alicia straightened her shoulders and pulled her cloak more closely about her body. She met his concern with stubbornness. "'I do not need a physician. I'm perfectly capable of traveling. How might I help?"

Travis drew a deep, ragged breath and prayed for strength. He ought to heave her over his shoulder and forcibly carry her to the care of someone more knowledgeable than he, but she had not appointed him her bodyguard. He knew little enough about female disabilities. Maybe she was right. Maybe she was fine. But she damned well wasn't in any state for traveling.

"Go back to bed. Keep out of our way. That will help more than anything." The gruffness of his tone hid his concern.

Alicia glared at him, but his implacable gaze brooked no argument. Something in the stern cut of his lean jaw and the way his black eyes watched her from beneath those arched brows spoke of an ability to command and to enforce his commands. Without another word she swung around and retraced her steps. A lady did not argue with strangers.

She dozed on and off, listening to the scraping of crates and barrels and the patter of rain upon the roof. The river should be rising. That should make the journey swifter. She calculated the number of days it might take. With luck they could be in St. Louis by early October. That would be time enough to see a physician.

She wondered if her father would understand, but the possibility of finding her father in this wilderness seemed so remote, she could not concern herself overmuch about his thoughts. There were too many other things on her mind. She went over her plans again, rehearsing what she would say, what she must do. She had a new life to carve out, and she drew up the strategy with the accuracy of a general on the field of battle. It would work. She knew it would. She would make it work. But the knot in her stomach drew tighter.

The quiet knock on the door startled her from an uneasy sleep. The nausea had departed, but her body ached, and she could scarcely summon the will to move.

When Alicia came to the door without bonnet or cloak, her brilliant eyes heavier and duller than before, she resolved Travis's dilemma. The thin gingham she wore did nothing to disguise her full breasts and reed thin waist, but the full skirts hid all else. Travis relied on his senses for what his eyes could not see, and his senses told him she wouldn't travel half a mile on those ancient, unsprung wagons waiting outside.

"The river is rising. Without the cargo we should navigate the falls without too much difficulty. The ride will be rough but swift. Prop yourself somewhere that you will not fall, and you need not come out in the weather."

As she swayed in the doorway, Travis had the sudden urge to catch her in his arms and wrap her in that old quilt and carry her to a doctor, but Alicia's haughty aloofness made him wary of acting on impulse. He reminded himself again that he knew little or nothing of female illnesses, and even less about ladies. What she needed was a husband to look after her. If she had one, he would like to box the fellow's nose to let her run away in this condition.

"I do not want to be an inconvenience," Alicia protested. "I am perfectly capable of riding in the wagons, or walking if necessary."

"I am certain, madam, that you are quite capable of flying, if you so desire, but in this case it is not necessary. I said I would get you to St. Louis, and I mean to do it with you still in one piece. Lie down, wrap yourself in quilts, and hold on. We're taking the falls."

Travis slammed the door and stalked away. Alicia felt an enormous sense of relief at not having to expend any further effort. With a sigh she removed her pillow and blankets from the cot, and rolled up in them on the floor. The idea of traversing a waterfall might be horrifying, but nothing could be as bad as what she had already suffered. If Travis thought it safe, she would not worry.

Not realizing the implications of this weary thought, Alicia prepared herself for the commencement of their hazardous journey.

With the aid of his right-hand man, Travis poled the keelboat into the river's current, relying on his instincts and his experience to gauge the narrow channel that would take them past the treacherous rocks to the lower river. The falls were actually no more than a gradual downgrading of the river over stepping stones of wide rocks that created rapids of rushing water as the river tumbled over them. When the river was high, they created little problem. After a dry summer they made a dangerous trip. Travis gambled on the rain and his own knowledge to avoid collision with jagged ledges in shallow waters.

Normally the thrill of the wild ride and conquering nature's obstacles gave Travis a sense of exhilaration as he flew over the white water and navigated to safety. This day he felt only a nagging sense of worry every time the boat shot into the air and landed with a jolt. He kept seeing Alicia's pale face growing paler with every tumble, and her wide eyes growing larger and more luminous with each frightening lurch. When the boat finally reached the more placid waters above the landing, he locked his pole in place and literally ran back to the cabin.

The weak cry of pain beyond the door was sufficient to propel Travis into the cabin without the niceties of knocking. He nearly fell over the bundle of blankets and quilts on the floor before realizing the moan came from there and not the bed. Cursing violently, he dropped to his knees and tried to unwrap the tangle, searching for Alicia's pale face and chestnut hair.

When he encountered the sticky wetness of blood, the truth hit him with the force of a hammer blow, and Travis gave a cry of anguish and rage. Wasting no time, he fled to the bow. With the city behind them, he knew only one place to go.

Under his curt commands, the keelboat shot past the landing filling with wagons of cargo. The startled faces of his men stared as their boat sailed on past, downriver, without them.

Alicia tossed restlessly in the oppressing heat, and the empty pain in her middle made her cry out. The tall figure propped in a chair beside the crude fireplace jerked awake and came to stand at the bedside, but she still slept. The wide, wet paths of tears down her cheeks told the tale of her dreams.

He wandered to the window, pushing aside the coated paper to stare out into the moonlight at the two tiny white crosses outlined on the hillside. He shouldn't have brought her here. He should have tried to pole her back upstream toward town. He should never have brought her downstream at all.

The cold emptiness of his friend's cabin laid a chill upon his heart. Out of all the men he knew, LaRouche and Robert were the happiest. Both had deserted the wandering life for homes and families. He had left LaRouche safe and content in Cincinnati, and he had expected to find the friendly aid of Robert and his wife here. The sight of those carefully carved and whitewashed crosses outside spoke tales he didn't wish to hear.

Remembering other deaths, other families destroyed, victims of war and disease, Travis felt the pall of loneliness enshroud him. Returning to the chair, he leaned back and willed sleep. Maybe settling down wasn't such a good idea. Maybe he was better off dying with his boots on, his knife in hand, instead of in small, agonizing pieces, as each tormenting loss ripped out a part of his heart.

He wished Robert were here. He should have brought Auguste up from the boat. He closed his eyes. Anything would be better than sitting here listening to her helpless cries, hearing her fevered breathing, knowing she was beyond his help.

Alicia shivered and instinctively sought for covers. They lay in heavy stacks all about her, weighing her down, pushing her back against the cushions . . . stealing what was hers alone.

She screamed, shoving against the imprisoning weight, kicking frantically at the beast holding her, entrapping her in the tangle of clothes. A man's voice spoke above her, and she screamed again, screamed as she had not dared to before, screamed as if her life depended on it. She would not let him do it again! She would not!

The weight lifted and the drowsiness came over her again. He left her alone. Good. Maybe he would stay away. She would have the maids call the sheriff if he came again. Just because she was alone now did not mean she was unprotected.

Alone. Tears crept down her cheeks, squeezing out from beneath her lashes despite every attempt to hide them. All alone. They all had left her, one by one, all had gone away. She was all alone. Even the hated thing growing inside her had gone. She sensed the emptiness like a hollow place where life had once been. She hadn't wanted to admit it, had refused to acknowledge life, fearing another loss. She was glad it was gone, so now she could be all alone again. She didn't deserve better than that. She was a wicked whore, a wanton woman. He was right. She deserved what he had done. She deserved to lose the only thing she had left.

Her sobs tore at his heart, but Travis had learned better than to approach her. She screamed at the sound of his voice, fought the touch of his hand. He could only watch her waste away with fever and wish he knew a woman to bring to her.

If he ever met the man who had done this to her, he would kill the bastard with his bare hands.

A jay cackled somewhere in a bush outside. No sunlight had reached the room, but Alicia sensed it was not far away. Her body ached. When she moved, the soreness tore open the unhealed walls of grief, and she choked back sobs of anguish.

In the darkness someone moved, and she forced her eyes open. The embers of a fire glowed in the dirt hearth across the room. Her eyes widened, not recognizing her surroundings. She glanced around, finding the rough-paneled door in a frame of logs, the papered window, the tilting shelf above her head. She had never seen this place before. Where was she?

As if she had spoken the question out loud, a tall figure rose out of the corner beside the stone chimney, where he had been whittling a loose piece of kindling. She scarcely recognized the shadowed face with several days' growth of beard, but the gold ring in his ear caught some small flicker from the fire, and Alicia relaxed. Travis was here. Lonetree. What a terrible name. Lonetree Travis. Travis Lonetree. Lone Travis Tree. Lone Travesty. She giggled and slept again.

Travis stared at her sleeping face surrounded by the heavy tumble of chestnut curls, and wondered if he were imagining things. The giggle had caused an inexplicable surge of hope. Now he stared at her pale face, drained of the artificial color of fever, and wondered if that were not a smile upon her dry lips.

The next time Alicia woke, it was day, and she was in full command of her senses. Her sense of smell told her someone was cooking something delicious, and her insides told her she was starving. Anything above and beyond that had no importance.

Spying the tall man poking absently at the kindling in the fireplace, she persuaded her dry tongue to speak. "Travis?"

He swung around as if confronted by the devil, then relaxed as he read the unfevered intelligence in her eyes. "The doctor said you would be needing some meat broth. Will you try some?"

"Please." She watched eagerly as he spooned the broth into a bowl and carried it carefully across the room.

She struggled to sit up, but her muscles refused to obey. With dismay she watched as he set the bowl on a table beside the bed. She would spoon it all over herself from this position. Her tongue stuck to the roof of her mouth, and her dry, cracked lips barely produced a sound.

"Water?"

Travis nodded and went outside to the well. When he returned, she was struggling desperately with the covers, her fingers plucking the awkward quilt while she tried to raise herself up on one elbow. At his entrance she nervously tucked the loose hair about her face behind her ears, and he almost laughed out loud at her expression. The lady was back.

Setting the pitcher of water down, Travis leaned over and lifted her shoulders from the bed, tucking her pillow and some old blankets behind her until she could rest comfortably sitting up. Every muscle in Alicia's body knotted at his touch, but she was in no position to refuse.

Travis sat on the bed and helped her drink from the ladle of water. So great was her thirst, she did not notice his proximity. Hunger replaced her embarrassment when he began to feed her from the bowl by the bedside. She did not dare think about what had gone before, when she had no consciousness of his presence.

And after she had eaten, she slept. Sleep was so much easier than facing the appalling facts. She had lost a baby, and this man—not even a physician—had tended to her. She could not deal with that reality, not yet.

In the days that followed, however, Alicia discovered how much she had to rely on Travis, and the struggle with her pride collapsed beneath the burden. He had the decency to leave the cabin often enough that she could use the chamber pot without fear of interruption, but she had not yet the strength to empty it. This task he performed without comment, as he provided her with clean linens and rags that he must have washed himself. The embarrassing intimacy of these chores made it easier to accept his help in managing the smaller tasks of eating and washing.

He brought her trunk up from the boat, and she watched with some amusement as Travis sifted gingerly through the feminine garments inside to find the clean nightgown she requested. At the hint of laughter in her voice, he turned and held up a pretty garter of blue satin and lace.

"Is this what you wear beneath those grim gowns of yours?" he inquired boldly, hoping to encourage this first small hint of spirit in his patient.

"That's for ballrooms, Mr. Travis," Alicia informed him politely, hiding a titter of laughter as one dark eyebrow arched sardonically at this piece of information. When he produced a pair of lacy pantalets, an extravagant new fashion she had indulged in, she could no longer hide her grin. She never thought there would come a time when she could watch a man handling her most intimate garments and laugh, but somehow he had managed to go beyond the barrier of his sex to become a friend.

"Now, I'm not entirely ignorant of a woman's underthings, madam, but I've never seen the like." Travis held up the long pantalets admiringly. "If it weren't for all the furbelows, they might even be practical."

"That's what I thought, but my maid almost died when I threatened to wear them. Now do give me my gown, Mr. Travis, before you embarrass me further."

He scooped up a long blue cambric and lace concoction that lay hidden at the bottom of the trunk, and throwing it over his arm, carried it to the bed.

Alicia read the determined glint in his eye and hurriedly scooted herself to a sitting position so she did not feel quite so intimidated by his greater height. He had been gentle beyond belief these past days, but that small grain of distrust had planted itself deeply. Men were too unpredictable.

"I can't wear that one," she protested as the frothy fabric drifted into a tiny pile on the quilt.

"Are you going to tell me you wear black even in bed, Mrs. Stanford?" Travis asked mockingly. He noted the spot of color in her cheeks and the indignant shine of those lovely eyes, and mentally patted himself on the back. She was a fighter, and who better than he knew what a fighter needed?

"Of course not," Alicia replied indignantly, then sensing his self-satisfied smirk, she capitulated grudgingly. "You will have to keep the fire well stocked if I'm not to freeze in this thing. It's meant for summer nights, and it must nearly be October."

With any other woman, at any other time, he would have

made a risqué remark about not needing fires to keep her warm when he was around, but not with this one. Any reminder that he was man and she was woman would send her skittering back over the brink of that cliff from which he had just pulled her. He walked uncertain ground every time he approached her.

"A good, hard freeze and the trees will put on a spectacular show for the remainder of your journey, Mrs. Stanford. Maybe a few chilly nights will help you to rise from that bed a little sooner."

He grinned and walked out, leaving Alicia to the task of struggling out of her old gown and into the new. Just pulling off the gown made her blush, remembering how it got there. Travis had burned the bloodstained gingham she had worn the last day on the river. He had undressed her and dressed her again in this old lawn shift he had found in the cabin. He had seen all of her there was to see and never said a word. His tact endeared him to her more than anything else he could do.

By the time Travis returned to the cabin bearing the ingredients for that night's meal, Alicia had washed, changed, brushed her hair into an orderly chignon, and fallen asleep again. He stared down at her pale face outlined by the heavy curve of her hair and wished she would let it flow free. The thin blue nightgown left most of her arms and shoulders bare except for a small puff of sleeve, and he could watch the rise and fall of her high, full breasts beneath the delicate material, but these temptations did not satisfy him. Realizing the foolishness of these thoughts, Travis swung back to the fire.

Travis seemed somewhat pensive when he served her the stew he had prepared, and Alicia watched furtively as he moved with lithe grace about the cabin. He wore his usual garb of open-necked linen shirt and buckskin breeches and boots, but he had apparently abandoned the bandanna and the earring. His black hair was pulled back from his sharp cheekbones with a rawhide thong, and he looked more than ever the Indian in the firelight. Only the slight hook in his nose marred the perfect evenness of his strong features.

"Has the boat gone on without us?" she inquired softly as he stared into the fire, his back turned to her.

Travis helped himself to a bowl of stew and came to sit down in a chair beside the bed, leaning it against the wall near her head and propping his boots upon the pallet. "They can't go anywhere without us. They're terrorizing Louisville until you get better." He fished a piece of meat from the stew with his finger and savored it thoughtfully.

Alicia stared at the dregs of her own bowl. "What have you told them?"

"I've simply told them you are ill. They think Robert and his wife are still here, but I daresay they will allow their romantic fantasies to stray a little. I have acquired something of a reputation, I fear."

"As have I by now, I suppose." Alicia pressed her eyes closed against the heat of her tears. The night was the worst, when she had nothing to do but think of the utter failure she had made of her life, and of the child's. She could not think too much of the child yet. It had not been real before. It was even less real now. Only the horror and the pain remained.

The smallness of her voice scraped at his heart, and Travis lost all interest in the food before him. He watched her bent head with sympathy, wanting to touch the vulnerable nape just visible beneath the stack of chestnut curls.

"Are you going to tell me about it?" he inquired gently, striving to hide the depth of his curiosity.

"What is there to tell?" she asked bitterly. "I'm not a widow, I've never been married, and I cannot even successfully carry a child. I don't seem to be capable of doing anything right. I had hoped to save my reputation by coming out here, but even that is to be denied to me, it seems."

Relief at learning no avenging husband followed her was quickly replaced by his earlier rage at the man who had done this. Travis found it hard to imagine this haughty creature succumbing to the ways of passion without the proper ceremonies. Her fear of him led him to believe an even greater crime had been committed, and a knife of anger twisted in his gut. Never would he have suspected the extent of her fragility that first day he had seen her—tall and proud and courageous, combating the evils of the world with her ladylike tongue. But he knew it now, and a strange urge to protect her from further harm overtook him.

"I will see that you arrive in St. Louis with your reputation untouched, if we have to hire a maid and a duenna in the process. Your only task is to get better so I can take you there."

Alicia threw her loyal guide a quick, grateful look. He had not condemned her, nor inquired into the sordid details. Half Indian he might be, but in her eyes at this moment he was all gentleman.

"You spoke of a Robert and his wife. Is this their cabin? Where are they?"

The change in subject did not relieve the heaviness of his thoughts. Travis set aside his bowl and shoved his hands in his pockets, staring at the toes of his boots. "Dead, most likely. At least Eleanor is, I imagine, and probably the child she carried. Robert's probably drinking himself into an early grave. I never saw two people more in love than they, the last time I was through here."

As if the subject had preyed on his mind these past days, Travis rose abruptly and stared out the window at the two tiny crosses, speaking his thoughts aloud. "He brought Eleanor from back East. She was his childhood sweetheart or some such. When he got tired of the roving life, he staked out this place and went back to marry her. She had actually waited for him and followed him out here willingly. I used to be so jealous of his luck that I could scarcely stand to see them together. She was a delicate little thing, like a woods violet. He should never have brought her out here. Anyone could tell she wasn't strong enough."

Alicia stared at his broad back in amazement. She had thought him self-centered, overbearing, and arrogant, but he spoke with a wistfulness and anger that gave evidence of another Travis/Lonetree than she knew. What man ever considered the inconveniences a woman suffered to follow her husband through life? It was a theme she had heard often and knew well. That this half-savage keelboatman contemplated the perplexities of such a life opened her eyes.

"I think, perhaps, she wouldn't have been happy without him," Alicia responded shyly, wanting to ease his pain but fearing to speak her thoughts. "Don't you think it better to live briefly and die happy than to live long in misery?"

Travis turned and eyed her with curiosity. "Do you believe that?"

Sitting up in bed with one burnished curl escaping her chignon and falling on a nearly bare shoulder, Alicia appeared more a Grecian princess than a philosopher. But knowing what he did of her, Travis listened carefully for her answer.

She contemplated her reply, not responding immediately. Dark-lashed eyes became wells of pain as she tackled her thoughts. "I am a coward, I fear, but I would rather act than suffer in silence. I'm not certain happiness can be obtained in this world, but if I thought it were, I would pursue it. Life is too brief as it is to endure it instead of living it."

A rare smile of genuine warmth cracked Travis's hard visage. "I believe you're right. To suffer in pursuit of happiness would be much more gratifying than suffering for nothing. I don't suppose you'd consider marrying me and ending both our miseries?"

Alicia laughed and slid down among the covers. "I greatly suspect that would only give us a new assortment of miseries to suffer. You're not the marrying kind, and heaven only knows, I don't intend to try it. Good night, Travis."

She closed her eyes and turned her back on him, but Travis continued to stare at the slender outline of her form beneath the covers for a long while afterward. He had every intention of marrying her, but there was a very good chance she spoke the truth. She might kill him before it was done with, but at least he'd die happy.

Grinning, he began to stoke the fire.

7

ALICIA MET HIM at the door wearing a light woolen gown the shade of spring violets, her hair loosely pinned upon the crown of her head and already spilling from its confines. Travis knew she brushed it in the darkness before dawn, before he rose to light the fire. It was the one piece of privacy she had managed to preserve, and he granted it without comment, though he often lay in the darkness wondering what she looked like with her hair down, curling about her shoulders and breasts.

He had the same thought now as she stood in the doorway, the setting sun sending glittering beams across polished mahogany, accenting the brilliant blue of long-lashed eyes. She was still too pale, too thin, but that did not stop his thoughts from straying to the loveliness he had glimpsed beneath the layers of clothing she contrived to wear. It would be a long time before she was ready for a man, though. He would have to find a woman soon or scare her off for certain.

She smiled with delight as he produced the pie hidden behind his back. "Wherever in the world did you steal that?" she exclaimed, moving aside so he could carry in the delicacy.

"The doctor's wife sent it. Said you should be needing a little pampering now." Travis slid it onto the crude table and began moving about the room, depositing the packages he had carried back from Louisville, stirring up the fire beneath the soup she had been simmering.

Alicia blushed and moved farther into the shadows. "She doesn't even know me," she protested.

Travis shrugged and continued with his tasks, keeping his gaze averted. Now that she was up and about, he had great

difficulty keeping away from her. "This isn't a very popu-
lated area and the women stick together. You'll find it
different from back East."

"I wish I could thank her for the thought." Wistfully
Alicia drifted from the shadows, catching a drop of syrup
oozing from the crust with her finger. "Will the boat be
ready in the morning?" She licked the syrup from her finger
unthinkingly.

Smiling at this childish gesture, Travis broke off a piece of
the crust and sampled it. "I thanked the lady prodigiously
and assured her I would take excellent care of you. And
yes, the boat will be here in the morning."

Uncomfortably aware of the way his black eyes followed
her, Alicia moved to the fire and stirred the broth. While
she had been ill, the barrier between them had disappeared,
but now she felt the tension returning. She missed the easy
camaraderie of earlier, but did not know how to return to it.

"The soup is ready if you like. It is not much, I know, but
with the pie. . ." She gesture helplessly.

"Actually, I wasn't expecting anything at all. I didn't
know ladies could cook."

Alicia swung around, angry words on the tip of her tongue,
but the smile in his eyes tore them away. After all he had
done, she could not yell at him. She didn't know what she
wanted from him, but she wished he wouldn't look at her
like that.

"Your friend's wife must have had a lovely garden. There
are herbs out there that couldn't have grown wild." She
turned back to spoon soup into a battered bowl.

She was so very vulnerable, and the longing in him was so
unbearably strong, that Travis could think of no good reply.
Life was going to be pure hell these next weeks.

"Let me bring in some more kindling before dark, then
we'll see what Eleanor's herbs and a lady's cooking can do."
He strode out whistling, fully expecting a pot to be thrown
at the back of his head. He would enjoy a good, rousing
fight if he were to be denied the pleasure of lovemaking.

She disappointed him, but that didn't matter. He fully
intended to find out if she were as cold as she tried to
appear; it would just take longer than he had planned.
Besides, if he wanted to marry her, it would take different
tactics than just wooing her to his bed. If he had done
nothing else in this world, he had learned patience. He

would take all the time necessary to make this a successful engagement.

The prior night's frost had burned away in the warmth of the day's sun, but the first nip of chill had returned to the air when Travis reached the woodpile by the creek. He kicked at the weathered logs, warning any hidden vermin of his intentions, but his mind was wholly on the woman waiting in the cabin. He tried to picture her warm and willing in his arms instead of cold and aloof and jumping nervously every time he approached. He smiled at the image his mind created and bent to pick up the nearest log.

A sharp sting of pain rocketed through his hand, and with incredulity Travis stared into the beady eyes of the copper scaled serpent with its fangs sunk firmly into the broad base of his thumb. A second later his knife flashed and the snake slithered to the ground, but already the venom burned trails of fire through his veins.

Alicia heard his shout and flew to the door, visions of rampaging Indians and man-eating bears racing through her mind. What she saw nearly terrified her as much, for she had come to think of Travis as an indestructible giant, invulnerable to the hazardous world around them. To see him with his face pale beneath the bronzed tan, fingers rigidly clasping a swollen, bleeding hand, sent her into momentary shock.

But only momentary. The cold, clear, calculating mind that had brought her this far served her well now. Her mind raced over the possibilities as she met him on the path. The anger in his eyes startled her, but she ignored it in the presence of his obvious pain.

"Snake?" she asked quickly before he could offer explanations.

Travis nodded. "I've cut it open and tried to suck the venom out, but it's not enough. You'd better go fetch Auguste down at the river."

But she was already running back to the cabin, grabbing rags and a wooden spoon and a bucket. As Travis staggered in the doorway, she commanded, "Keep that arm down! Sit there." She pointed at the cabin's only chair.

When he fell into it, she wrapped the rag around his arm, knotted the long-handled spoon into it, and began to twist until Travis nearly screamed with the pain.

"What in hell are you doing!"

"Cutting off the circulation. Hold it there while I get some water from the well. I had to break the ice on it this morning, so it can't be too warm." Alicia picked up the bucket and hurried out the door, leaving Travis to stare after her with anguish.

It was a hell of a time to die. There was too much he had to do. Just when he had decided what direction his life should take and found someone to share it with, it seemed a cruel blow to be cut down without setting one foot down the path. It did not help to see the concern in her eyes and know he had reached through her hard shell but would never know what he had gained. Cursing, Travis leaned his head back against the wall and felt the poison throbbing through his arm.

Alicia returned, and rolling up his shirt-sleeve, dashed his hand into the icy water, numbing it to the elbow.

"I didn't know freezing a man to death cured snakebite," Travis muttered through clenched teeth.

"I don't know, either, but it sounds sensible. One of my suitors in Philadelphia was a doctor and he preached this theory about blood to anyone who would listen. He said it goes around and around in the body and we can't stop it, but things like cold will slow it, and he showed me how to tie a tourniquet in case I was ever in danger of bleeding to death. Now, hold still while I put these on."

Travis opened one eye and peered dubiously at her slender figure kneeling beside him, until she produced two particularly nasty specimens of creek leeches from the bucket. "You're out of your mind," he protested weakly. "Why didn't you marry this brilliant fellow?"

"He died," she replied matter-of-factly. "Besides, he was married to his work. The cholera epidemic claimed him."

Alicia began placing the slimy creatures down the inside of his arm where she could see the veins sculpted beneath the tanned, hard skin. The muscles tightened beneath her fingers until every sinew and tendon stood out, but she had no fear of his greater strength now. She knew only she could not let this man die, for her life depended on him.

"My God, Alicia, I won't have a drop of blood left in me." Travis uttered the protest without conviction. Whatever she was doing now could not stop the poison that had already entered his bloodstream, and he could feel himself weakening by the minute. It took all his remaining strength to sit upright, and he continued to mentally curse his ill luck and poor timing. He didn't want to die now, but he had to prepare her for the possibility.

He tried to open his eyes to watch her as she worked over his throbbing arm, but the pain made his head swim, and he rested it weakly against the wall as he spoke. "Go to Auguste. He can be trusted. He will get you to St. Louis. Don't delay. Shawnees are getting restless."

Tears rolled down Alicia's cheeks as she loosened the tourniquet slightly so his hand wouldn't turn blue, then tightened it again. She sensed the pain in his abrupt phrases, and the needlessness of this occurrence made her rage inwardly. Perhaps Travis was not the best of men. She suspected he drank too much, fought too much, and frequented the wrong sort of women, but he was not a bad man. Remembering the gentleness of those broad palms as they lifted her from the bed, helping her to sit, to dress, to eat, she touched his callused hand with tenderness. The leeches were beginning to swell with his poisoned blood, but it might already be too late. She knew so little of this cruel life, and her helplessness sent tears streaming down her cheeks.

When Travis began to slide from the chair, Alicia helped him to the bed, carefully keeping the injured hand hanging down and still. The soup over the fire bubbled and steamed, but she paid it no heed. The fire under it would die soon enough. Her only concern lay in the man tossing restlessly on the covers of the bed. She had to keep him still until as much of the poison was drawn from his body as was possible.

She tried kneeling beside the bed and holding his hand down in the icy bucket of water, but even in pain he was stronger than she. Travis drifted in and out of consciousness, and he fought her for possession of the hand, tearing it from her grasp and rubbing it, cursing incoherently.

Finally furious and on the verge of frustrated tears as he knocked off newly placed leeches, Alicia rose and sat on the edge of the bed so he couldn't reach the arm hanging over the side. His big body left little room for her on the narrow pallet, but she succeeded in calming him to some extent.

In one of his lucid moments Travis opened his eyes to find her nearly perched on top of him, and he managed a half grin. "Lie down, Alicia. Don't hover over me like an anxious vulture."

"You say those things on purpose to make me angry, don't you?" she inquired with curiosity, bending to inspect her handiwork and loosen the tourniquet some more.

"You keep everything inside. It's not natural." Travis closed his eyes again, breathing in the scent of her. Even out here in the wilderness, she contrived to smell good. "Lie down. I can't hurt you, and if I'm to die, I'd like to die with a woman in my arms."

His soft insistence tugged at a chord in Alicia's heart, and she glanced down at his angular face, finding nothing to fear in the pain-racked features.

"And your boots on," she finished for him, not without a touch of irony.

"Lie down." Travis tugged her arm with his good hand, pulling her down toward him. When she capitulated, curling in the narrow space he left at the edge of the bed, he smiled in satisfaction. A spasm of pain rocked through him, making him grit his teeth, but he fought the reminder of his mortality by concentrating on the intriguing woman next to him.

"You've never shared a bed with a man, have you?" It was more statement than question, and Travis heard the sharp intake of her breath, but to keep his senses, he had to focus on something. She held his interest more than any other topic.

"No," Alicia responded curtly, trying to find a position that did not leave her lying practically on top of him. Her only satisfaction lay in keeping his shoulder pinned to the bed so he could not move the injured hand.

"I thought ladies didn't go out unchaperoned with gentlemen." His voice began to fade, but Travis struggled to keep conscious.

"It was just a Sunday afternoon ride," Alicia whispered into his shoulder, knowing to what he referred without being told. The subject lingered, ever present, between them, neither willing to speak it out loud. Until now. The pain and humiliation had eaten her insides to a black pit of nothingness, and all that had happened since had left her numb. She could not think, she could not feel, but the words came without effort. "We'd known each other forever."

"You were engaged?" His tongue felt thick and dry, but Travis led her on, determined to have the story.

"No." Alicia's voice was so low she almost spoke to herself. "He'd asked me, but I was in mourning for my mother, and I told him I couldn't make any decisions like that. But he kept asking, insisting. I almost gave in. I had other suitors, and everyone said I should decide. With my mother gone, I was alone in the house. Except for the servants."

She was avoiding the subject, but telling Travis more than she knew. She was as alone as he in this world and disliking it just as much. He said nothing, but let her talk without interruption.

The words poured faster, encouraged by his silence. Perhaps he slept. It did not matter. She needed some outlet, some way of puzzling it out.

"Teddy took me out, made me forget. My mother always told me the only men interested in me were the ones who wanted money, but Teddy's family was wealthy." Alicia felt more than heard Travis's grunt of protest, but she ignored it. He did not know the society she moved in, had never seen the petite, dainty women with winning smiles and infectious laughs that the men preferred. She scared men away, she knew. They called her a bluestocking behind her back, and perhaps she was. But it was better than being a fool. She had been a fool once; she wouldn't try it again.

"Teddy made me nervous, but I thought he was my friend. I didn't see any harm in driving out with him. That's all I did wrong. Why did that give him the right to do what he did? Call me those names?"

Her voice broke, and Travis roused himself from his pain to stroke her hair and hug her closer. Anger began to boil in his veins again, and it felt good. He wanted to rip this Teddy's head off and parade it on a pike. My God, she couldn't be much more than twenty now. She had been just a child, one who had just lost her mother and was desperately looking for a way to turn, and that bastard had ripped the rug right out from under her.

"He was a polecat, Alicia. Forget him. You did nothing wrong." He croaked the words, hoping she understood. He could feel her tears dampening his shirt.

"But I must have!" Alicia choked back a sob as she relived the horror of those moments. "He told me I'd teased him long enough and he would settle the matter once and for all. I screamed, but we were miles from anywhere. I must have hit my head when he pushed me down in the seat, because I don't remember how he—" She gulped, unable to relate the swiftness of events, remembering only finding her skirts thrown up to her waist, and his nakedness pushing against her. She barely had time to scream and try to push away when he had torn at her innocence with a viciousness that still made her cry with anguish. The pain stayed with her, and the humiliation as the hairy beast pushed and shoved and groped at her most private parts. By the time he reached his final convulsions, she had been rigid with disgust as much as pain.

Travis didn't need to hear that part of it. He had seen men rape before. It was not so uncommon. But now he understood the depth of the injury, and that he could never, ever touch her in such a way.

"He sounds like a desperate, weak man, Alicia. I know men, believe me. It wasn't your fault."

His voice seemed somehow stronger, and Alicia raised herself on one elbow to gaze down at his face. His eyes were closed, and his mouth was set in a grim, bitter line, but his skin burned beneath her touch.

"He thought I would have to marry him." She lay down again, secure in her position beneath his arm. "But I wouldn't. I wouldn't even see him again. I went to stay with Aunt Clara and told the servants to say I was not at home. And when I knew. . . when I knew there would be a child, I put the house up for sale, packed my bags, and left. Aunt Clara thought I'd taken leave of my senses, but she took care of everything for me. When everything is sold, she'll send the money where I direct her. Don't overcharge me, Travis, I'm living on a slim budget until then."

A hint of his usual grin played about the corners of Travis's mouth. "Don't lie to me, paleface squaw. Petticoats don't weigh as much as yours. I could have robbed you blind and thrown you in the river."

He sounded so much better, Alicia grew suspicious, but his skin still burned with unnatural heat, and his hand and arm had swollen to twice their natural size. She leaned over the side of the bed and loosened the tourniquet again. It would have to come off soon, but not all at once.

When she settled back down beside him, he seemed to sleep, and she made no reply. He could have done just what he said, and she probably wouldn't have cared. She had wanted to die, but not any longer. She would make him

live, too, and then they would be even. Then she could feel
free to smack that self-satisfied smirk off his face.

She dozed off and on throughout the night, waking to
release the tourniquet and replace the leeches. Travis lay
still beside her, only his shallow, uneven breathing telling
her he clung to life. She prayed as she had never prayed
before. Somehow, out here among nature's best and worst,
God seemed closer, more real. She needed the hand of God
now and not another death to haunt her dreams.

The violence and self-loathing that had haunted her nights
these past months had retreated to some dark corner of her
soul, perhaps banished forever. If she could just survive
this, return this man's life, she would be healed. The madness would be gone. She made a bargain with God, promising this and more as the night wore on.

The last of the leeches fell off before daybreak, whether
poisoned or satiated, Alicia could not discern. She had
removed the tourniquet entirely, and his arm seemed less
swollen than before, but it could be her imagination. She
repressed any suggestion of relief. Whatever the day held,
he did not need her to hold him any longer. Gathering her
skirts, she prepared to rise.

Travis's hand caught her by the arm, holding her in place.
"Stay." The word whispered through the darkness, barely
disturbing the pre-dawn silence.

"You must be uncomfortable." Alicia turned to touch his
forehead, finding it slightly cooler.

"Never. Now I can say I've spent the night in your bed."
The words were whispered, but still carried a hint of a grin.

"You wouldn't!"

"Won't have to. Just smile knowingly when accused."

"Travis! You promised!" Angry, worried, she lifted herself up to glare at his closed face. The darkness prevented
her from seeing much beyond his bent nose and dark hair.

"Don't you ever get lonely?" he asked unexpectedly,
opening his eyes and staring up into the white blur of her
face.

Realizing he was only taunting her again, she lay down
and curled next to his warmth. The fire had finally died out.
"Yes, of course, especially now," she whispered in reply,
thinking of the emptiness within where once there had been
life. Even a life bred by violence was better than no life at
all.

"So do I." Travis made this admission without calculation or forethought, only speaking what he felt with her woman's body pressed close against his side. He would not likely find it there again for a long, long time.

"Have you ever loved anyone?" The darkness seemed to encourage honesty, and she would know more of this stranger who knew more of her than any other human being.

"I thought so, but she married another. She was young, very quiet and shy. I was ready to become part of the tribe, part of my mother's people, but even Indians can be snobs. Her parents didn't think I was good enough. I left after that. There didn't seem much point in staying."

Alicia lay against his shoulder and contemplated his words. She had not given much thought to Travis as a person, as a human being capable of emotion. He was just the indispensable guide who would lead her to a new life. But remembering all she had seen of him, the drunken Indian, the imposing gentleman, the keelboat captain, and the gentle man who had nursed her to health, she realized she had been selfishly blind. How must it feel to be half Indian, half white, and rejected by both races? Is that why there was such a ring of irony in his laughter, why even his jests hid secret hurts? He was nothing like the men she knew back home. She could fit him in no category that came to mind.

"So you've never stayed anywhere long, since," she guessed.

"Not until now. After I sell off the cargo, I mean to look around for a place. I want land around me, but not wilderness. Some of my people have settled in Missouri. St. Louis is a good place to start looking. Marry me and I promise to become a respectable businessman."

Amused, Alicia touched his forehead again, testing for fever. "You think you will live so long?"

In answer, Travis wrapped his injured arm around her waist and held her in place while his good hand brought her head down to his. His lips were warm and caressing, seeking and not demanding, and Alicia did not fear them. Gently she returned the kiss, liking the sensation, but not daring more.

At the first sign of resistance Travis released her, but he had his answer. There was no coldness in her, only fear. He would teach her not to fear.

"I aim to live, Blue Eyes." He felt her rise from the bed

and the coldness where she had been seeped through him.
"And I have every intention of making myself a wealthy and
respectable citizen of St. Louis. So you may as well agree to
marry me now and save ourselves a lot of trouble."

Alicia bent over the fire, hiding the burning in her cheeks.
He had made the same outrageous proposal to Babette; he
meant nothing by it, but it gave her food for thought. She
had thought to live in St. Louis as a respectable widow, but
now she had no need to do that. She could teach as she had
always wanted to do. But if she could not find her father,
she was as much at the mercies of her surroundings as she
had been in Philadelphia. More so. Then she had been a
respectable virgin with the opportunity to choose among
many suitors. Now she could marry no man for fear he
would despise her for what had happened. And she could
not endure the degradation of the marriage bed in any case.

But Travis knew her past and did not care. He offered
more protection than any other solution that came to mind.
Other men would leave her alone if they thought she belonged to him. Only the belonging part needed defining.
Perhaps he would be satisfied with the respectability of her
company. Perhaps—sometime far in the future—if he wanted
children, she could suffer through that act just once more.
She knew very little about children, but men seemed to
want them. There were always possibilities.

Alicia returned to the bed with a slice of last night's
forgotten pie. "It is not much of a breakfast," she murmured, not quite daring to face him yet. The small cot
seemed even smaller beneath his broad-shouldered frame,
and she could not believe she had spent the night lying
beside him.

Black eyes glittered as they discovered the hint of pink in
her cheeks. She had not laughed at him this time. He would
take that as a good sign.

8

THEY MADE a dramatic appearance on the riverbank at dawn; Travis with his arm draped over Alicia's shoulder and Alicia clinging to his waist for support, both too weak to manage the uncertain ground alone. The keelboatmen below, however, put an entirely different interpretation on the tableau, and a ragged cheer split the frosty morning air as the pair came into sight.

"You'll have to bear with it for a while, I fear," Travis chuckled into her ear. "They'll never believe the truth."

The loose sleeve of his shirt hid his swollen, blackened arm, but he favored it as he helped Alicia into the boat. Auguste leapt to take her hand, and sent two of the crew scurrying up the hill to fetch her trunk. He cast his captain a look askance, but Travis merely shrugged and watched as Alicia quickly disappeared into the privacy of the cabin. They had come closer these last days, but she still shied away from men. It would take a long time to undo the work of that animal who called himself a gentleman.

By the time the boat got under way, word of Travis's recovery from snakebite had swept through the crew. The first hint Alicia had of it was the sound of her name being called aloud. Startled, she opened the door of her room to listen and caught the sound again. From here she could hear the men chanting in time to their poling as usual, but this time her name seemed to be a part of the chant.

Curious, she tiptoed to the door of the long cabin to listen, and discovered Travis grinning like a possum as he watched the crew at work. She would have darted back to safety, but he caught her movement and dragged her out to sit on a bale in the sunshine.

"You've been immortalized in song, Mrs. Stanford." He

lounged against the wall beside her, seemingly at ease, but his sharp eyes carefully scanned the river ahead for obstructions.

"So it seems. I'm not certain I'm following the lyrics." The name "Lonetree" seemed to come frequently into play, but Alicia had heard them sing about their captain before. Now that she could hear the chant better, a slight flush colored her cheeks.

"Well, it's safe to say you figure as a cure for copperhead bites, but let's not go into the details of how you do it." Travis gazed down at her with amusement as she reddened more. "Were you always such a prude, Mrs. Stanford?"

"My mother raised me to be a lady, Mr. Travis. I had no hint of what the rest of the world was like."

Some of his smile slipped away, and his bronzed countenance grew thoughtful as Travis gazed upon her bent head. "Perhaps we ought to drop this 'Mr.' and 'Mrs.' bit. It is rather inappropriate. You can go back to being Miss Stanford when we reach St. Louis."

To his earlier delight, she had chosen a sky-blue woolen gown to wear this day instead of her usual crow's black. She looked very young with her pale cheeks colored by wind and embarrassment, and very beautiful. She had made this much progress, Travis determined he would see it further.

"With this chant traveling up and down the river, I had better find a new name entirely," Alicia answered wryly. "Else, if I should find my father, he will have us both horsewhipped."

Travis looked mildly alarmed. "Is he normally a violent man?" He wasn't concerned for himself, but he'd be damned if he'd turn her over to a man who would lay a hand on her.

Alicia laughed. "No. Perhaps if he had been, he would have stayed in Philadelphia and Mama would have run away. But Papa is very mild-mannered, very gentle, at least, with me. Only, he would be very disappointed if he thought I'd behaved less than a lady."

Travis attempted to work out this new piece of information. "If he is a kind man, why did he desert his wife and daughter?"

Alicia leaned against the cabin wall and turned her face to absorb the sun's rays. She would be as weathered as Travis if she kept this up, but the sun and air felt good. She felt the blood stir in her veins for the first time in months.

"My father and mother did not get along. I was too young to understand, but knowing what I do now, I suspect my mother did not return his affections, if you understand me."

Travis couldn't prevent a grin. "And just how much do you know about affection, Blue Eyes?"

Alicia threw him a glaring look, then glanced away. In this light, in command of a crew and boat, his hair tied neatly and without the bandanna, Travis became strikingly handsome. Well, perhaps not exactly handsome, but extremely capable and almost unbearably masculine. Still, she held her ground, avoiding his implications.

"I know enough to expect very little of it. I suppose my mother loved me, but she made my life hell with her lectures on the evils of men, meaning my father. And I know my father loved me, but he left me, and then forgot about me. I have not heard from him in five years or more. And certainly whatever made my parents marry does not show a good example of sensibility, whether affection can be blamed for that or not."

"I begin to understand you," Travis replied with care. "Love is rather a fragile thing, it seems. My parents must have loved each other very much to do what they did, but it obviously wasn't enough to overcome the obstacles. Perhaps just a good, healthy respect for each other would be wiser."

Alicia's mouth bent into a wide smile. "That would destroy the writers of ballads and romances. How can you write about the devastating effects of respect?"

Travis grinned his appreciation of this riposte, but he made no further comment. The high-minded lady would not approve of his view of love and marriage, and he avoided the subject by leaping to the cabin roof to shout orders at a lackadaisical crewman in the rear. Should he tell her a woman was meant to bear a man's children and keep his house, she would most likely strike him dead. All this nonsense about love was for the writer of ballads and romances she spoke of and not for the world they lived in. A good healthy respect for each other would suffice, as she soon would discover. That, and the mysterious chemistry that made one woman better than another in bed would cement a marriage more securely than sweet words and sighs.

Warmed by the sun and lulled by the boat's gentle rocking, Alicia remained blissfully unaware of Travis's growing confidence. She only knew her own confidence was slowly returning, the cracks in her brittle facade gradually mending with each passing hour. That Travis was partially responsible for this she vaguely recognized, but not with any conscious thought. If she thought about it, he would be too alien to her world for his attitudes to affect her. But on some deeper, less conscious level, she felt a kinship for this half-savage keelboat captain, and his approval of her actions bolstered her self-assurance.

In the days that followed, Travis did not press his suit or apply any other pressure, but Alicia was constantly aware of his presence. He would appear to share a biscuit with her at breakfast, stop to comment on her reading material when she sought a sunny spot on deck, and ate his dinner at her side, regaling her with tales of the river. She came to accept, and then enjoy, his company once she learned he presented no threat to her well-being.

Although he often strode about the deck in bare feet and shirt sleeves, Travis had discarded his earring and bandanna and appeared less the river pirate than before. The fact that he seemed all muscle and sinew even when he crouched beside her, idly whittling some stick, made Alicia uneasy, but she attempted to disregard this distrust of his masculinity. He made no attempt to extend the familiarity that had sprung up between them, and their only physical contact was the occasional brush of their hands. Someone else apparently tended to his arm, and Alicia gradually relaxed her guard.

The river had risen with the earlier rains, and there was no further need to portage. Alicia's strength began to return with these days of enforced idleness until she almost wished for the opportunity to stop along the banks and walk awhile. Travis's cautiousness wouldn't allow it, however. He docked on islands whenever he could, or at the base of cliffs where they could not be reached from shore. His explanations of the unsatisfactory treaty talks with Tecumseh and his Shawnees did not satisfy Alicia's restlessness, but she bowed to his greater wisdom in this. The incident with the Indian and the owl had been sufficient to convince her there could be a brave behind every tree and two squaws behind each rock.

They passed by the settlement at Red Banks without stopping. Alicia stared in curiosity at the crudely built cabins and wondered in despair if St. Louis would resemble this collection of hovels. The isolation frightened her, striking too close to the loneliness that haunted her dreams. She had left behind everything and everyone she knew and loved, and the future loomed impossibly bleak before her. The slate was clean, and she had only her hand to write on it. Could she do it?

That evening, when they made camp on an island rather larger than the others before, Travis allowed the crew to go ashore. Noting his passenger's reluctance to join them, he frowned slightly. He had thought her recovering from the melancholy that had embraced her, but he should have known it was too soon.

Carrying a half empty bottle of wine, Travis came up behind Alicia and caught her elbow, helping her from the boat to the ground. Without the need to call herself a widow any longer, she had begun wearing some of the lighter hues from her trunk. For the cool October air she had chosen a coppery velvet that clung without any discernible reason to her too-slender body, but she had covered the low neckline with a heavy shawl of shimmering bronzes, successfully concealing what the gown had been meant to reveal. The slender skirt made climbing from the boat difficult, however, and Travis was rewarded for his efforts with the glimpse of a stockinged ankle.

"I trust you're wearing those long, frilly things under that skirt, Blue Eyes. There's a nip in the air tonight," Travis whispered in her ear.

Alicia blushed crimson and attempted to brush off his helping hand, but Travis cheerfully kept his hold as he guided her toward the fire. He knew how to be patient, but he also knew what to do when his prey sensed danger and was about to flee. It was time to move upwind.

The campfire had been kindled within a circle of trees, out of sight of the river. They had stopped early this evening, before the sun set, and there had been time to catch a few squirrels and rabbits to add to their simmering stew. Alicia's stomach growled appreciatively at the aromas arising from the pot, but Travis's possessive hold prevented any outward show of emotion. She held herself straight and silent as she walked along at his side.

Travis couldn't refrain from darting her a look of curiosity. "Are you not feeling well?"

"I am fine." Diverting his attention from herself, Alicia questioned, "Why did we stop so early?"

Travis kicked an old log closer to the fire and helped her to sit on it. "I don't want to pass Cave-in-Rock at twilight. I prefer dawn, when the occupants are deep in drunken stupor. The sheriff was said to have run off the last lot, but there's always some lowlife looking for a hidey-hole. I'll not take any chances." Travis lowered himself to sit beside her.

Politely, Alicia did not edge away, but she was very aware of the muscular thigh stretched out beside her and the broadness of the shoulders rubbing hers. Travis seemed sublimely unaware of their proximity as he commanded a cup and partially filled it with wine. She was grateful he wore his fringed jacket. The thick deerskin seemed to provide a barrier of decency between them.

She accepted the wine and tried to imagine herself in a polite drawing room making conversation. "You are saying there may be outlaws somewhere ahead?" she translated.

"River's full of them, but Cave-in-Rock has the worst reputation. It's wilderness. There's no real law to hold them. And they can spot a boat for miles before it arrives. We won't look real appealing to them. Too many men and too little cargo. They prefer easy pickings, greenhorns with no guns and all their worldly possessions." And women, but Travis had sense enough not to mention that. He meant to keep her well out of sight until they passed those dangerous straits.

Alicia accepted his confidence and tried not to worry. Travis had steered them safely thus far; she would not doubt his abilities now.

The wine provided a small glow of heat in her empty stomach, and Alicia began to unbend slightly. She took the bowl of stew someone offered her and concentrated on it instead of the half-Indian keelboatmen beside her.

"You said you were thinking of settling in St. Louis. What will you do there?"

Darkness had descended and all Alicia could see of Travis's face was the dancing reflections of the fire on the bronzed skin over sharp cheekbones and high forehead. Still, she knew he laughed at her question.

"A place like St. Louis offers plenty of opportunities. I'll just nose around a little until I find something comfortable. But I'm not much of a city man. Sooner or later I'd like to look into land around there. They say Kentucky is the best place for raising horses, but just across the river can't be too bad. And it's open territory. A man could put roots down there and grow with the place."

Alicia could see nothing funny in that. It sounded quite sensible in a roundabout way. She was unprepared for the proprietary hand that touched her chin and tilted her head up until dark eyes burned into hers.

"I'd not take a wife unless I could afford to keep her. It won't be Philadelphia, but it will be a place for a lady. Don't fret about the future."

His callused hand grazed her cheek gently, and Alicia jerked her head away, inexplicable tears welling in her eyes. "You presume too much," she said huskily.

"I presume nothing at all. I work for what I want." Travis bit into his bread, leaving her to think what she would.

Had she dared to return to the boat alone in the dark, Alicia would have walked off and left him. Instead she continued to sit silently, listening to the raucous tales of the crewmen and sipping on the wine. The wine crept slowly into her veins, giving her strength. She had a will as great as this arrogant man's. He could not force her to do anything she did not want to do, except physically, of course. But she was beginning to realize Travis would not use physical force on her, and part of her fears slipped away. Since that day Teddy had attacked her, she had lived in terror of so many things. It was nice to discard one and meet this man on equal terms.

As she accepted a second cup of wine, she heard Travis chuckle. Instantly suspicious, Alicia swung her head to glare at him. He clinked his tin cup against hers.

"Never let it be said that I did not warn you. That wine is a mite stronger than you're accustomed to, I suspect." With those words of caution he took another drink from his cup.

Alicia grimaced. "I noticed. I was just trying to be polite."

Travis grinned at this glimmer of honesty. "Would you have poured it on the ground while I wasn't looking or politely drunk the whole thing?"

Holding the cup up before her, Alicia stared at it in bemusement. Then with a rare grin she admitted, "Probably drunk the whole thing. By now, I'm beyond tasting it."

That grin struck Travis with unexpected force. The shock of it exploded somewhere inside of him, sending reverberations of excitement through his veins. It took all his self control not to wrap her in his arms and kiss her until the grin became a permanent fixture on both their faces. Only knowing that she did not share his excitement prevented him from acting on impulse.

Travis took the cup from her hand and handed it to one of the crew. "I will remove temptation from both of us." He stood and offered his hand. "Walk with me?"

With the fire at his back, his face fell into shadow, and Alicia could read nothing of his expression. With the wine still giving her strength, she accepted the offer and rose to stand beside him.

Her head came up past his chin and the sweet scent of her hair sent another surge of excitement through Travis. He had thought to have seduced her by now. This prolonged abstinence had come as an unexpected blow, but he could endure it. He would not cause her pain if it could be avoided. He took her fingers and placed them around his arm, leading her into the deeper darkness outside the clearing.

"How can you always be polite?" he inquired once they were out of sight of his men.

In the darkness, when she did not have to see his broad shoulders and masculine frame, Alicia lost all fear. She considered his question with interest. "Habit, I suppose. Is that bad?"

"No, I suppose not. It makes things go more smoothly, avoids confrontations, something I'm notoriously bad at doing," Travis thought out loud. "Out here it is probably less important than in the city where you have to deal with so many people all the time, but it is a nice habit to have. It is one of those things that make it more pleasant to escort a lady."

A wry smile turned the corners of Alicia's mouth. "You prefer ladies who politely drink your wine into drunken stupors?"

He chuckled. "That too. And a lady is less likely to scream and slap and kick. A cold shoulder offers a certain amount of challenge."

A soft laugh escaped Alicia's lips, a sound so fragile the song of a tree frog nearly drowned it, but Travis had been listening for it. He relaxed as the pressure of her fingers on his arm tightened.

"If you behaved as a gentleman, it would not be necessary for women to kick, slap, and scream."

"The habit of being a gentleman is not so well ingrained

in me," Travis admitted cheerfully. "I am a man first and a gentleman as an afterthought. If you live out here long enough, you will learn to be a woman first. The instinct for survival is greater than the need for civilization."

Pensively Alicia released his arm, using both hands to lift her skirts and avoid his touch. "There are times when I'm not certain I am a woman at all."

She had been told often enough that she was a bluestocking, cold and uncaring, and she had certainly been trained for the part. While other girls learned the etiquette of coquetry, she had been encouraged to stay home with her mother and her books. She had never learned to attract a man's attentions and had never felt any desire to do so. That there might be something wrong with her was just one of her many fears.

Travis did not find her admission particularly shocking. Catching Alicia's elbow, he swung her around to face him. Her pale cheeks were just a blur in the moonlight, but he could see the sapphire blue of her eyes in his sleep.

"Oh, I don't think there is any reason to doubt you are a woman," he replied casually before sliding his arm around her slender waist and drawing her against him. "Shall I prove it?"

He gave her no time to reply or protest. Warm lips closed invitingly over hers, silencing her words. Alicia tasted the wine on his breath, and the aroma of smoke from the campfire circled around them. She pressed her palms against his chest, but his heat through the thin linen alarmed her as much as the pressure of his hands at the small of her back. Only the gentleness of his kiss kept her from succumbing to panic. His mouth moved tenderly along hers, inviting response, not demanding. Alicia felt her heart pounding frantically beneath her rib cage, but some of his warmth seemed to seep into her veins. Her fingers curled helplessly against his shirt as her lips slowly began to respond to his.

The taste of wine is sweet and tempting, but Travis dared not sample too deeply of this forbidden liquor. Even as he felt the heady victory of her kiss, he sensed the tension forming along her spine. Before she could flee his grasp, he released her lips and pressed a kiss to her forehead. His hands continued to stroke the supple length of her back.

"I warned you I was no gentleman." He spoke first, taking the offensive. With this one he had to be quick.

Alicia stepped from his hold, pulling her shawl more tightly about her. She could not look him in the face. That she had allowed herself to be kissed by any man was shocking enough. That the man was a ne'er-do-well half-breed who had no place in the world as she knew it was totally incomprehensible. She could still feel the strength of his callused hands where he'd held her, and she shuddered. Better had she stayed with the gentlemen in Philadelphia than succumb to this savage who held no respect for the conventions. His greater strength left her feeling vulnerable, and the absence of it made her feel very alone.

Her words, when they came, surprised even herself.

"You are more of a gentleman than some I know." The bitterness was clear, and she could not take it back. Instead she covered it by taking a step toward the boat. "I can find my own way back."

Travis did not allow it, of course, but escorted her properly to the silent keelboat. As he helped her aboard, moonlight illuminated the sharp angles of his cheeks and the high planes of his forehead, accenting the blue-black smoothness of his thick hair, and Alicia had to check a gasp of pleasure. In this light, against the primitive backdrop of trees, he was one with the beauty of the night. Shakily, she had to remember he was a man and not a painting, and she vowed never to sample his wine again.

9

ALICIA LISTENED to the lapping of the river against the boat's hull and shivered in the eerie early morning silence. The keelboat moved swiftly with the current under the guidance of an unusually quiet crew. Travis had ordered her to stay below and the men to hold their tongues until they passed the notorious outlaw hideout. Alicia fretted at this confinement, but in truth, she was not certain she was ready to meet Travis face-to-face this morning.

Memories of the prior night made her blush, and if there had been room to pace the floor, she would have worked off her nervous restlessness that way. She had torn the incident apart from every angle imaginable and could only conclude the fault lay in the time spent in Louisville. Their familiarity then in that lonely cabin had encouraged this extraordinary familiarity now. She could think of no other reason why she had allowed herself to be kissed by this man who was so genuinely her inferior.

She should be furious with his presumption, but she knew she was as much at fault as he. She had never openly rejected his advances, nor been firm about the familiarities he took. She had been too ill and too frightened to discourage him at first, but she had no excuse for last night. What would he think of her now? True, he had not tried to invite himself in last night, but how long would that last? Her mother had warned her that one thing led to another, and Alicia now had some glimmer of understanding of what that meant. Holding hands led to kissing, and kissing led to more kissing, and beyond that she chose not to imagine. She would have to put an end to this nonsense immediately, or she might wind up an Indian squaw in the backwoods of the Louisiana Purchase.

*   *   *

From the opening in the sheer rock cliff above the river, a red-flanneled arm scratched at an odorous armpit while its owner sighted along the slowly rolling current. A grin broke out on the man's bearded face as he sighted the approaching keelboat, a grin that revealed the blackened stumps of his teeth.

"Up and at 'em, laddies," he cried in exuberant delight. "Mattie told you he'd find you a woman. Here she comes now."

With varying degrees of enthusiasm, curiosity, and drunken disinterest, the motley inhabitants of the cave straggled into the dawn's light. Since Mattie had arrived last evening bringing word of a female on a keelboat, they had stayed awake drinking and scheming. Women were rare in these parts, even more so as the river travel slowed with the coming of winter. But a woman on a keelboat full of men was a rarity indeed, and deserved serious consideration. Any woman who could service a keelboat crew would provide several nights' entertainment for the bored outlaws of the cave.

As the others spied the boat rapidly approaching, they began to scramble down the narrow path between rocks and shrubby sassafras and pine to the river's edge. Judging from identical crops of thick, bushy black hair and beards, three of the malodorous group were related. The others merely possessed the mean, hungry look of the chronically unstable, men who could not live in peace with their neighbors, but took what they wanted without fear of consequences. None stayed for long in this isolated outpost, but the present gathering had come together just long enough to reach the camaraderie that made this raid possible. Brave in numbers, they clambered into the waiting skiffs at the river side and shoved off into the current.

Alicia heard the first shout of warning without registering its significance. She had flung herself on her small bunk and opened a book in an attempt to avoid her thoughts and the light tread of moccasins overhead. She did not know how Travis balanced on that angled roof, but he moved along it with astonishing agility. It was the sound of those footsteps racing urgently to the bow that returned her to sensibility.

She jerked upright, discovering the dawn silence had changed its tune. So accustomed had she grown to the continuous curses of the crew that she had not noticed when they had returned to the refrain. But instead of the usual jovial bantering, they practiced threats this day, a growing rumble that sent chills down her spine.

The answering cries had naught to do with the bragging challenges of keelboatmen. While Travis's men bellowed their intentions of ripping the competition from stem to stern, chewing them up, and spitting them out for breakfast, the shouts from the other boat or boats made little or no sense. Raucous cries and roars came closer, and Alicia wished desperately for some means of looking outside.

The explosion of a gun and the crash of one wooden keel against another sent Alicia stumbling backward into the bunk. She had not even realized she had stood to open the door, but she knew better than to make that attempt again. Though Travis would not thank her for being underfoot at a time like this the awful helplessness of sitting here and taking no hand in their fate brought tears of frustration and anger to her eyes. Fate had been too cruel before; she could not trust in it again.

More gunshots roared, and a man's scream made Alicia's blood run cold. The seriousness of the situation finally sank in. Her Indian guide had seemed invincible, but he was just a man and could die like any other man, like the man groaning just outside the cabin now. She had no idea how many attackers there were, but their bold shouts rang in her ears as another boat collided against the keel. Sheer terror swept her soul as the battle outside erupted in another place.

She could hear Travis's voice as he shouted orders, but he never seemed to stay in one place. The stench of gunpowder drifted through the planking, making Alicia choke, but she muffled the coughs in her pillows. The gunfire had diminished as the opportunity to reload was lost, but the grunts and curses of men rolling about the decks in violent battle echoed on both sides. She had seen the wicked knives the men used for everything from shaving to gutting fish, and she had no desire to visualize the manner in which they were employed now.

To her horror, she could hear someone crashing through the cabin door where the freight was kept. The partition that separated her bunk from the freight was a thin one, meant for privacy and not protection. Instinctively her hand reached for the reticule where she had stored the small pistol and forgotten about it. She did not even know if it were loaded, but her trembling fingers wrapped around the cold ivory handle and pulled it from its hiding place.

Somewhere outside her door a scream of fear stopped short and died a gurgle that made Alicia want to retch. She had heard no other footsteps in the cabin, but knew instantly that Travis had followed the man in, that he was out there now, standing over the body of a dead man. No one else could move that silently.

A loud thunk in the roof over her head caused her to swing from this horror to the next. A scream leapt to her lips, but Alicia muffled it, refusing to reveal her presence to whatever vile creatures attacked them. Hand over mouth, she backed against the far wall as the sound crashed against the roof again, this time with an ominous splinter.

Shouts from his crew warned Travis not to tarry. He threw a quick glance to the closed door at the end of the cabin, then raced back to the deck. The silence from the end of that long corridor haunted him, but he could not stop to investigate. Lives hung in the balance.

When he reached the deck and discovered the reason for the shouts, Travis felt a rush of cold rage down his spine. A filthy black bear of a man swung a glittering ax at the roof above Alicia's quarters, tearing through the split wood shingles with ease. The man not only ripped at Travis's carefully honed handiwork, but he threatened his woman. That was beyond the acceptable boundaries of battle. Rage rolled up in Travis's throat and roared out in the ear-piercing battle cry of his youth.

Stunned by the sound of an Indian war cry in the midst of the river, several of the combatants made the mistake of looking up, only to find themselves quickly in trouble. Lonetree's crew knew the violent sound well enough and took advantage of the surprise, but the brute on the roof continued mindlessly hacking a hole to his prey.

The opening was large enough for Alicia to see through by the time Travis traversed the length of the roof to challenge the intruder. She had been given a full view of the outlaw's uncovered, furred chest and massive hands, and could read the lust in narrow eyes as he caught sight of her. She felt trapped like an animal in a cage. The horror of an earlier day when a man had looked at her like that came back vividly. She could feel his heavy weight pushing her down, his groping hands pawing, the violation that had destroyed her life. Her mind went blank as her trembling hands lifted the pistol. She aimed upward, striving for the power to pull the trigger.

Although she heard no sound of gunfire, the outlaw suddenly staggered backward, roaring in anger. Blood splattered in bright red droplets on the bare floor. Alicia closed her eyes, but she could not shut out the sight emblazoned across her eyelids. Through the gaping hole Travis stood half naked and, knife in hand, carving the outlaw as if he were a piece of wood. The raw savagery on his bronzed face as he drove the knife home curdled Alicia's blood, and the revulsion she felt kept her frozen in place.

With his enemy properly dispatched to a hell of his own choosing, Travis glanced downward through the splintered wood. Furious despair swept through him as his quick glance noted the pistol pointed in his direction and the pale face of the stricken woman behind it. He had no time for a woman's recriminations. Without another look downward, he leapt to the deck to rid his vessel of the intruders.

As the last of the outlaws scrambled back into their boat and paddled away, Travis gave orders to clean up and move on. The look on Alicia's face stayed with him as he worked furiously to get the boat back on course and out of danger of running aground. He had not known she possessed a gun. From the look on her face, he knew what it was meant for. He did not doubt that if he had gone a step closer, she would have used it on him.

But he could not let her terror stand in his way. He had plans for that lady. He had not yet met a challenge he could not conquer, and he had no intention of being defeated by a woman. Today was just a temporary setback. He would bring her around again.

Travis had no knowledge of the stubbornness of the Stanford pride or the precariousness of Alicia's sanity. He discovered both when—with his duties done and his boat on course—he knocked upon the door of his passenger's cabin. Receiving no reply, he attempted to open the door, only to find it blocked by her heavy trunks.

"Alicia!" Angry and suddenly afraid that she might have been hurt, Travis pounded furiously on the thin partition. "Open the door!"

"No, thank you," came the polite but distant reply.

"How in hell am I supposed to talk to you through a damned door?" he cried indignantly. He could not remember ever being openly defied like this, and the newness of the experience astonished him.

"Don't," was the pert reply.

Travis's eyebrows nearly rose to his hairline, and the thunderous expression on his features would have warned Alicia of her danger had she seen it, but she could not. Terrified but hiding it behind the icy politeness that was her only protection, she sat curled in a corner of her bed clutching the book she had tried to read earlier. The surge of violence that had risen in her today had terrified her as much as the man who had caused it. She had thought herself healed and her presence of mind returning, but the rawness of the wound had opened wide again with the sight of Travis wielding that knife. She could not believe she had actually aimed that gun at him. She was no better than he, and he was an uncivilized savage. Self-loathing made it easy to ignore the pounding at the door; terror at his violence prevented any action at all. She protected herself in the only way left to her. Escape.

At the black fury on their captain's face as he erupted from the cabin, the crew dug in and kept silent. Most of them had seen that look before and knew its results. They had no desire to lose their ears or a piece of their hides.

Alicia let out a scream and pressed against the wall as Travis's lithe frame dropped through the hole in the roof. The tiny chamber scarcely held room for one. His broad shoulders nearly filled the space of the narrow wall.

Travis glared at her pale, frightened face and cursed himself. It was too late now. At least he should be consoled she still did not point a gun at him. Without a word he lifted the trunk blocking the door and flung it back in the corner. Then he opened the door and placed himself in the doorway.

"I have told you I will not tolerate disobedience. The next time I call, you will answer." Travis strode out, slamming the door behind him.

This time her scream was one of outrage, and Travis smiled grimly at the sound of the book hurtling against the hollow partition. At least he had succeeded in destroying that ladylike aloofness.

For the moment perhaps, but not for long, he discovered with some regret later when the next meal was served. Alicia promptly appeared when called, her head held high, her hair pulled severely into a knot, and her high-necked gown enveloped in disguising shawls. She accepted the cold offering handed to her, and just as promptly returned to her cabin without speaking a word.

The crew glanced surreptitiously from one to the other, and hid their snickers at the expression on their captain's face. Never had they seen him thwarted by any man, no less a woman upon whom he had turned his attentions. This promised to be one hell of a fight, and they sat back to relax and enjoy it.

To their surprise Travis only scowled and returned to his meal. The lady ate alone.

The tense silence lasted until they arrived at the swampy land spit that marked the end of the Ohio and the beginning of the Mississippi. A cluster of shanties marked this meeting place of two grand rivers, but other than a horde of mosquitoes, none of the inhabitants came forward to greet their landing. The sound of the boat scraping the rocky shore brought Alicia from her cabin, and Travis threw her a look of annoyance when she appeared on deck.

"Go back inside. This is no place for a lady." His words were curt to the point of rudeness as he leapt to the soggy bank to help drag the low-lying keel on to dry land. No dock existed, though a number of the craft along the bank indicated the need for one.

The day was overcast and a wind off the river picked up the fringes of Alicia's shawl and whipped it around her. She stared at the collection of shanties and wondered about their occupants. They couldn't be pirates if Travis felt free to land here. She was tired of her own company and the same four walls. It was time she learned to fend for herself.

"Then pretend I'm not a lady," she replied dryly, following the rest of the crew and stepping from the boat to dry land.

"Suit yourself." Exasperated, Travis turned on his heel and stalked toward the largest of the log buildings. He could just imagine the reaction of the men inside when she appeared, her cheeks pink from the wind, chestnut curls peeking from that abominable bonnet, blue eyes wide and innocent, and wearing one of those damned skimpy gowns that revealed every curve. When the stampede began, he'd have to rely on his crew to get her out of there. Then maybe she would learn to take orders.

He had not taken into account the effect Alicia's tall grace had on men who had seen nothing but prostitutes and little of them in countless months. They stared, they looked away, and they edged out in embarrassment. Travis's lip curled as he watched one man after another sidle from the tavern as Alicia settled herself at a table in the corner, her large eyes sweeping the room with curiosity. These men may have stayed too long in the company of other men, but they remembered well the standards of cleanliness preferred by their wives and mothers. Travis reckoned the tavern's lone bathtub would receive a good workout this night.

Understanding none of this, Alicia studied the cabin's crude interior with interest. Mud filled the chinks between the logs, and no window broke the large expanse of walls. In summer it must be stifling, but the large fireplace at the far end kept the place pleasantly comfortable on a day like this. She wasn't certain what kind of place it was, but the large number of plank tables and assorted crates and stools used for chairs indicated it was a gathering place of sorts. She was disappointed that no other women appeared to be present. Travis's promise to provide a maid and the other accoutrements of respectability had taken on new meaning now that they had reached this crossroads. St. Louis lay at the end of this leg of their journey.

Alicia watched as Travis casually questioned the men remaining. His black hair brushed the collar of his deerskin coat, but he had long since abandoned the scarf and the earring. There was almost an aristocratic elegance in the proud line of his angular profile, in just the way he moved his shoulders and carried his weight. She knew men born to the society of drawing rooms who could not hold themselves so erect and with such grace as this savage. She hated him for appearing one thing and being another, like all the rest. She felt revulsion at her admiration of this violent savage. If she were ever to have peace of mind again, she must free herself from this domination by violent men, rise above their world where they could not touch her.

Vowing not to be trapped into complacency again, she swiveled her attention to a slight movement at the curtain dividing this room from some room in the back. The light from the fire did not provide more than shadows, but gradually Alicia discerned a slight figure and a pair of eyes staring back at her. Curiosity and not fear made her continue to stare, although she knew it was not polite to do so.

Finally, giving a furtive glance to the man serving drinks at the back of the room, the small creature moved forward. Before she made it even halfway to the fireplace, the tavern keeper cursed, strode across the room, and cuffed her back toward the curtain.

Alicia instantly came to her feet, and her movement alerted Travis and his crew. The sudden threatening protectiveness surrounding the lady as she approached the object of the tavern keeper's wrath prevented any reaction from the other men in the room. When Alicia knelt to help the fallen child to her feet, Travis moved lithely and quietly between the man and the two females, his hand on the hilt of his bone-handled knife.

The child scrambled to her feet, and Alicia could see that though she was small in stature, she had the figure of a woman, and the expression of her dark eyes and thin lips spoke of bitter experience. She might be young in years, but older than Alicia in knowledge of the world. Standing, she cast Alicia a quick glance, as if to be certain of her protection, then she faced her attacker defiantly.

"I heard the man. You promised to put me on the next boat to St. Louis."

"He's looking for crew, not passengers. Now get back in there where you belong." The tavern keeper's heavyset bulk moved threateningly toward the rebellious waif.

"I am looking for a maid." Alicia spoke crisply and firmly, startling the onlookers. "Come back to the table with me and we will talk about it." Cool blue eyes turned to the burly tavern keeper. "Bring us something suitable to drink, please."

Trailing a whiff of lavender cologne, Alicia strolled regally to the table she had occupied earlier. She might know little about frontier life, but she understood the servant mentality. Had the tavern keeper been a man at all, he would never have treated the child in such a manner. Those who treated others brutally were extremely susceptible to similar treatment. She couldn't apply physical violence, but she had other methods. He would respond simply to the force of her commands.

The girl scurried after her, astonished that no meaty hand

reached out to jerk her back. Sitting in the chair indicated, she craned her neck to watch in amazement as her tormentor drew mugs of ale from kegs and handed them to the tall Indian in buckskin. The Indian's face was expressionless as he carried the mugs back to the table, but the girl sensed an undercurrent of tension between the lady at her side and the approaching man. This one had no fear of the lady's high-handed ways.

Her curiosity grew as the keelboat captain set the mugs on the table, ignoring her but staring intently at the elegant lady.

"We'd better have a talk before you make any rash decisions." Travis kept the tone of his voice neutral.

"Very well," Alicia agreed politely. "You are the captain and I would not wish to interfere with your journey."

The girl could see the muscles in the Indian's jaw bunch and his hands knot into fists, but she did not understand this reaction to the lady's icily correct words, or his reticence in refraining from striking her if that was his wish. She had never seen a man restrain himself before, and she had certainly not expected it of this one. She could tell by the way he held himself tautly, his fingers near his knife, that he was ready to spring at any false move. And she knew what he intended to tell the lady.

Travis turned his dark stare upon the bedraggled child hunched fearfully beside Alicia. The flat, round face spoke of some Indian ancestry, but not of the eastern tribes with which he was familiar. The white complexion and flashing green eyes reflected more dominant genes, Irish, most likely. He could guess her origins and knew of a certainty the problems she would create, but she couldn't be more than sixteen, if that. He couldn't leave her here.

"If you have any possessions, pack them," he ordered, jerking his head to indicate she leave.

The girl understood and scrabbled quickly from her seat, leaving Travis to face the cold stare of the lady.

"If you mean to take her, then there is no need for this discussion, is there?" Alicia kept her voice deliberately without inflection, although her heart pounded a little faster beneath his glare.

"I just want you to realize that I nearly had to kill a man over a two-bit whore. I hope your need for a maid justifies the cost."

To Alicia's knowledge, no one had ever used that term in her presence before, and she blanched with anger and a sinking feeling of despair. She didn't know whether to believe him or not, and she allowed anger to rule her reply.

"You have no right to speak to me in that way. If you object to my helping a child in distress, you might phrase it more politely and give rational reasons for doing so. Otherwise, we have nothing further to say to each other."

Travis controlled his rage with an effort that should have cost him a blood vessel. He had known women of all stations in life before, but never had he met one so deliberately irritating as this one. She sat there so coolly, waiting for him to do something violent, to confirm her opinions of him and men in general, and damned if he didn't want to. Instead he forced himself to calmness and, taking a step backward from the table, made an icily formal bow.

"Forgive me for intruding. I only meant to warn you the child has been sleeping with Hans in exchange for room and board since she arrived here, and will most likely feel obligated to do the same in return for her fare to St. Louis. I trust her reputation will serve to protect yours."

He strode away then, leaving Alicia to stare at his broad-shouldered back with incredulity and growing despair. Damn the man! Did he always have to be right?

10

SITTING BENEATH the tarp Travis had nailed over the gaping hole in the roof, Alicia listened to Rebecca Whitefield's sorry tale with detachment. The girl was reluctant to speak and even more reluctant to tell the truth. The only words over which she grew animated were her insistences that she would learn to be a proper maid and live a proper life now. Alicia had her doubts, but like Travis, she could not abandon the child to the brutality of the tavern keeper.

Before they could travel anywhere, Alicia insisted Rebecca would have to bathe. For that she needed Travis's aid. As soon as she heard his footsteps on the deck outside, Alicia swept from the cabin to confront him.

To her surprise Travis agreed readily and sent one of the crew scouring the town for a barrel while others gathered wood for a fire to heat water. This late in October, the river would be too chilly for bathing, particularly for an undernourished child.

He extracted his due, however, detaining Alicia while the fire was built.

"What has she told you?" Dark eyes noted Alicia's withdrawal from his proximity, but Travis counted on her upbringing preventing her from ignoring a direct question.

He was right. Even in the rapidly gathering twilight Alicia could feel the intensity of his gaze, but she could not turn her back on him and walk away. "Nothing that I can believe with any surety. She claims her mother is a beautiful actress who died and went to heaven, and her father is waiting for her in St. Louis, that somehow they were separated. That is the part that makes sense to a certain degree."

The wry grin on Travis's lips was hidden in the darkness. She had chosen the story most like her own to believe, but

did not recognize the similarities. An inveterate liar always
knew when they were believed and stuck with the best
story. Whatever her past truly was, Rebecca Whitehead had
just rewritten it to suit her new employer.

He added his own discoveries to Alicia's. "According to
one of the men I talked to, she came here with a man who
claimed to be her father. They were looking for transportation up the river and ran up a sizable bill at the tavern while
waiting. Apparently her father either made a deal with Hans
or just decided to slip off without paying his bills. One
morning he was gone and she was still there. The girl has
kept pretty much to herself since then. With any luck, she
won't present too much difficulty."

Alicia could not help but be grateful for this small reassurance, but she shuddered at the horror of this story. Hers
was a small misfortune compared to the tragedy of this girl's
life, and she vowed to see it righted.

"I don't think she enjoyed what she was doing. It should
not be difficult to keep her from your men." Her concern
for the girl held her thoughts, temporarily erasing the image
of savagery that had haunted her nightmares since the pirate
attack. With the twilight disguising Travis's masculine physique, Alicia could respond to his educated speech rather
than his appearance. Her fears faded when they talked.

Travis looked at her with curiosity. Alicia's innocence was
almost frightening, but charming too. He had forgotten how
protected an unmarried lady could be, and he saw no need
to enlighten her now. He just added a few words of caution.

"I won't worry about my men, but I've hired new ones to
help pole us up the river. They'll know her story. It won't
be easy to silence them."

The stories of a boat crew would never reach the ears of
Alicia's world, and she shrugged the warning aside. "There
is little I can do about that. We cannot leave her here. How
long will it be before we reach St. Louis?"

The breeze ruffled a curl escaping from Alicia's bonnet,
and Travis had the urge to grab the intrusive cloth and fling
it in the river so he might see the chestnut tresses beneath.
Instead he steadied his hand by leaning it against the cabin.

"The current is low and slow this time of year, but it will
not be an easy ride. It will be November, I suspect, if all
goes well."

Alicia hid her despair by turning to watch the progress of

the fire builders. November seemed eternity, but it was closer than before. "Thank you for taking on Rebecca," she murmured before turning to head back to the cabin.

Travis caught her elbow, preventing her escape. "Don't shut me out, Alicia." The timbre of his voice was low and deep and meant to be reassuring.

She turned and gave him a cool stare. "The door was never open. Please release me."

She hurried away to the tune of Travis's curse. She didn't know what made her say things like that. They had weeks of each other's company to endure. She should not deliberately antagonize him, not when he tried to be reasonable.

But as Alicia stood guard over Rebecca's washing later that evening, she realized her reactions were instinctive, designed to keep Travis at a distance. It was better that way, she decided. He was much too bold, and she had too little experience to hold him off. She had seen him unmasked and knew him for a savage, and she must not let herself forget. Rebecca would give her someone to talk to and remove the temptation Travis's conversation offered.

Rebecca had willingly submitted to bathing and, because her clothes were no cleaner than herself, she spent that first night wrapped in a blanket while her newly washed wardrobe dried. She made no complaints of sleeping on the hastily constructed pallet on the floor of Alicia's room, and even offered to brush Alicia's hair before she went to bed. The fact that the boat would not leave land until morning might have had much to do with her good behavior.

Still, even when the crew poled the keelboat out into the Mississippi and out of sight of the tavern and its occupants, Rebecca kept quietly to her employer's side. Alicia could not exactly describe the girl's behavior as meek, for her eyes were everywhere, watching everything—which included a large number of half-dressed men—but she behaved respectably. It might be possible to believe she wished to change her ways.

However, it was not possible to carry on intelligent conversations with her. Her uneducated speech became lessons in English more often than not, but the lessons at least gave them some common ground to converse on. Rebecca's mind had a distressing habit of sticking to one path, and that was a path in which Alicia had little knowledge.

Becky watched boldly as Travis's broad-shouldered, slim-

hipped figure walked away from them after he had stopped
to politely inquire after Alicia's comfort. The wind had
grown considerably cooler these last days, but Alicia had
been unable to bear the confines of the cabin for long.
Becky had observed the way Travis's dark gaze lingered on
Alicia's pink cheeks before he duly noted that she had
wrapped warmly in a fur-lined spencer. Now she turned her
speculative gaze back to Alicia's nervously clasping and
unclasping fingers.

"If you like him, why ain't you let him know? He's more
than willin'," Becky commented dryly.

Alicia was glad for the cold wind against her hot face.
Becky's one-track mind kept catching her by surprise and at
the worst possible moments. Travis had taken up a pole
behind them and could see every move they made. Luckily,
he could not hear.

"I hired Travis to take me to St. Louis. There is nothing
else he needs to know. I'm not certain what you mean by
willing, but it does not sound like a proper subject for
discussion."

Becky made an exasperated noise. "Every time I speaks
of what everybody's thinkin', you tell me 'taint fittin'. What
do proper folk talk about iffen you can't say what's on your
mind?"

Alicia couldn't help but smile at this interpretation of
propriety. Certainly other people must have more on their
minds than Becky, but she was beginning to question if her
maid were not closer to the truth than she wished to imagine. On this trip, even her own mind had begun to play
tricks on her. Surely, when they reached civilization, she
would find other topics of more interest.

"What's on my mind is that it is very chilly and I would
like a hot bowl of soup and a good book. I'm going in."

Becky shrugged at this reply and cast another look backward. "It ain't cause he's got injun blood, is it? He's too
fine-talking to be a real injun. He talks better than any man
I ever knowed. Looks better too," she added as an afterthought.

"How many men have you known?" Alicia asked wryly,
gathering her skirts around her and preparing to depart.

"Lots of 'em," Becky responded grimly. "But I reckon I
know a good one when I see him. He don't even look twicet
at me when every other man on this boat done tried their

mightiest to get me alone. Any woman alive could see he's got his eye on you. Don't you like his looks?"

Growing annoyed, Alicia ignored this inquiry and stalked back to the protection of the cabin. Her cheeks flamed with the implications of the child's words, though Becky could scarcely be considered a child. After being so cruelly used by men, why did she continue to look at them with such avid interest?

Instead of following Alicia into the boring interior as usual, Becky idled her way to the rear, where Travis had taken up the position of rudder. At this sluggish pace, brawn was needed more than brain, and he had no need to tell his men what to do. His piercing black gaze found Becky instantly, and a frown formed over his hawklike nose.

Her childish stature and open stare were somewhat disconcerting, and Travis leaned on his pole to stare back. She grinned at this ploy and boldly stepped closer.

"Are you an injun?" she demanded.

"Are you?" Travis replied politely. He didn't know what the little demon was up to, but he was well prepared to find out. He hadn't been able to get close to Alicia since they'd left the Ohio, and this one was a major reason.

Becky looked mildly confused by this turnabout, but she was game for any sport. She tried again. "I might be, but that don't seem to bother Miz Stanford none. Reckon she likes injuns just as well as other people."

Travis choked on this ingenuousness, but managed to keep a straight face. "I reckon Miss Stanford just likes some people more than others. Don't you?"

The ambiguity of his question never struck his listener. She shook her head. "No, I reckon she likes me well enough, she must like everybody. I ain't ever heard her say nothin' agin nobody. She's just"—she scrambled for the proper word for the educated lady—"backward." She chose the only fitting word in her vocabulary.

This time Travis could not control his shout of laughter, but the pint-sized midget didn't seem to mind. She calmly waited until he recovered himself before interrogating him again.

"But you ain't backward. Iffen I'm in the way, why don't you say so? I owe you one. I'll sleep somewheres else if you want to be alone with the lady."

A broad grin crept across Travis's face. "Midget, if the lady heard you say that, she'd have your scalp. If you want to keep your job, you will have to be a little more discreet than that. You stick with Miss Stanford and look out for her. She's not much used to these parts." Hands on hips, Travis glared down at her warningly. "But when you see me moving in, you clear out. Got it?"

Becky grinned delightedly. "Yes, sir, Cap'n, sir. I got it."

Happily she wandered back to the cabin. Travis stared after her, the odd conversation replaying in his mind. Backward! He wondered what Alicia would think of that description. He wondered what Alicia would think about a number of things, but he was not likely to find out unless he pressed his suit quickly. St. Louis wasn't that far away.

He found his opportunity two nights out of St. Louis. The day had been a brilliant autumn spectacular of reds and golds, the lingering warmth of the sun scenting the leaves and stirring the blood. The brown current filled with the floating remains of summer and excitement rode high at the expectation of reaching their goal shortly. Even Alicia had come out of her shell long enough to bask in the sun and laugh merrily at the crew's high spirits. Now was the time.

Travis watched as she slipped away from the campfire. Becky usually followed, but she had sense enough to wait and see what he would do. Without a glance in the maid's direction, Travis strode after his prey. Becky smiled and stayed behind.

The brisk air and clear skies did strange things to his insides, stirring primitive longings that could so easily be assuaged. Travis could imagine lying on a blanket beneath the stars with a willing woman in his arms as the peak of happiness right now. He had not been with another woman since first laying eyes on this one, and his needs were strong. He knew better than to expect much, but just a small melting of Alicia's cold reserve would suffice. To just lie with her by his side would free his mind for plans for the future. The rest would come with time, he felt confident.

Alicia too felt the spell of the night. She rummaged in her trunk until she found the deep emerald redingote that she had worn last winter, wrapping it about her to keep out the autumn chill. Then she propped herself on the edge of the cabin roof to drink in the river's silence, and salve her injured soul with the peace of the stars and the water's gentle rocking. She had learned to love these moments, and almost regretted the journey's end. St. Louis could very easily be the end of her hopes, and she was not prepared for still another disappointment.

She had thought about her arrival for so long, she feared any flaw in her plan would destroy her. She wanted to teach. She knew she certainly had the education to do it, and even her doctor beau had told her she would be good at it. He had expressed his regret that she was wasted on the role of perennial debutante. Now she had shed that role and could be anything she wanted to be, could make her life anything she wanted of it.

Unless she found her father immediately. That question loomed in Alicia's mind larger than any other. Surely St. Louis had schools and needed teachers of some sort; she had heard the frontier towns were desperate for education. But her father—would he have forgotten her after all these years? Was he alive? Would he still be living in St. Louis? And if he were, could he accept a daughter who had no interest in marrying, but simply wanted to teach?

Her thoughts had carried her so far away, Alicia didn't hear the noiseless tread of Travis's moccasins upon the deck, and had no awareness of his presence until he swung up to sit beside her. Startled, Alicia nearly fell from her precarious perch, but Travis caught her and held her firmly until she recovered her balance. His hand remained disconcertingly close behind her.

"I didn't mean to frighten you." It was not an apology, simply a statement of fact.

"I know you didn't mean to," Alicia acknowledged, reluctant to have her peace disturbed, but somehow not sorry he had intruded upon her troublesome thoughts. There was so much space out here, and she knew no one in it. She had known loneliness before, but not a loneliness so thorough and all encompassing as this. Even this disturbance became a welcome one.

Travis smiled wryly at the phrasing of her words. His gaze traced the soft silhouette of her fashionable bonnet and caped coat, and knew she had donned a protection more complete than a suit of armor. Somehow he had to find some way to divest her of it.

"Do you know where you will go when we reach St. Louis?" he inquired carefully.

"I have the address of my father's last letter. If he stayed there, surely it must be suitable. And if there is no room there, I will ask for recommendations. It cannot be so very difficult."

Travis noted the wistfulness in her voice and wished he could reassure her, but words would never accomplish that. "He has written you?"

"Five years ago." Her voice was so soft, the night nearly carried them away. "He wrote my aunt and gave her the address and told her if I should ever want him, I could reach him there. I wrote and I wrote, and I never had an answer."

The cry in her words was so distinct that it was all Travis could do to keep from taking her in his arms and kissing away the tears. After all these years the pain of desertion must still be raw. He took her hand and she did not resist.

"Perhaps he never received the letters. It takes six weeks or more for a letter to get out here. Maybe he had moved and the people at the address simply threw the letters away. Things like that happen."

"He could have written to tell me," Alicia whispered. For years her father's desertion had torn at her heart. She had thought he loved her. He had taken her with him everywhere, treated her as an adult, showed her off to his friends and then one day, he was gone. He had tried to explain, but she had not understood. She had not known he meant to go away forever. The mind of a twelve-year-old does not comprehend forever. Those first few years he had written lovely letters, and she had replied eagerly, but gradually the number of letters grew fewer until there were none at all. Just that last one to her aunt. He was gone now, no longer part of her life. But Alicia could not make her heart believe it.

"Don't blame him too harshly, Alicia. Life out here changes a man. You will change, too, if you stay here long enough."

Tears ran down her cheeks, but Travis could not see them in the darkness. She turned to look up at his angular profile, the high cheekbones and slightly hooked nose. She had the strongest urge to stroke his face, but never would she have the nerve to do such a thing. She wanted desperately to be held, but not the way this man would hold her. Just the sensation of his hardened fingers wrapped around hers upset her equilibrium. The power in his hand was terrifying.

"Did you know your father at all?" The question came

out unbidden, and Alicia could feel his penetrating dark gaze focus on her.

Travis shrugged. "I lived with him for a good many years. That does not mean I knew him."

"But you love him?" Alicia did not understand the pattern of her questioning, but she had a need to know.

Travis considered this a minute. "Yes, I suppose I do. I have to respect him. Marrying my mother defied every social and moral tenet he must have known."

"But it didn't work out." Sadly Alicia heard what went unspoken.

"How could it? He had responsibilities elsewhere and her life was here. Perhaps—" Travis shook his head, preferring to change the subject. The past was no longer a part of him. The future was what he sought now. "It does not matter now. Our lives are what we make them."

It seemed a strange philosophy for a man who seemingly had spent his life idly wandering up and down the river, and Alicia doubted its truth. So far she had not made much of her life. It had all been done by others.

"I wish I could believe that," she murmured, mostly to herself.

Travis tightened his hand around hers, willing her to understand. "You can, Alicia. Good or bad, you made the decision to come out here. Now open your eyes and see it realistically. It's not Philadelphia. It's something completely new and different. There is a place for everybody out here, if you just take advantage of what God has given you."

Alicia laughed dryly. "God gave me a wealthy father who deserted me and brains that don't seem to be worth very much in this world. I'm not lacking in blessings; I guess I just haven't learned to use them yet."

"He also made you one of the most beautiful women I have ever seen," Travis reminded her. "Or haven't you noticed?"

She had never learned to deal well with polite flattery, and had certainly never expected to hear it from this man. She stared at him with a mixture of embarrassment and confusion.

"You have been too long in the wilderness, sir. I am tall and thin and too plain, as I have been told often enough. I certainly never intended to trade on my looks. Do you tell me my education will be unwanted out here, also?"

In exasperation Travis ripped the bonnet from her head

and threw it where the wind could catch it and blow it out to sea or hell or wherever. He never wanted to see the damned thing again. His long fingers ran deep into the thick upsweep of her hair, and his other hand caught her shoulder to keep her from jerking free.

"You have hair like warm mahogany and eyes the color of flashing sapphires, and if you let me dwell on the topic of the rest of you, you would have good cause to slap my face," Travis informed her with intensity. "Men will always want you, and you had better become accustomed to that fact quickly. Men out here aren't shy and aren't in the habit of sending posies and candy. It will be up to you to make the rules and abide by them. I know you are not ready yet, but my offer still stands, Alicia."

Before Alicia knew it, Travis's arms circled her waist, and his mouth came down hard and possessively across hers. The fear and excitement he had generated in her with his words now deteriorated into pure physical panic. She fought him, fought the strength of those warm arms holding her, the liquid hunger of his kiss, the yearning urge that had allowed him to go this far. She beat his chest, trying to drive away the demons that brought his body so close to hers.

She scratched and kicked and bit until he finally released her. Then she dropped to the deck and hands on hips, attacked him scornfully. "Don't ever, *ever* do that again, Travis Lonetree. I will never marry, but I am certainly not likely to consider changing my mind for a violent savage."

She stormed off and Travis could hear the trunk being shoved in front of the cabin door once more. The hole in the roof had never been mended beyond the tarp, but she knew he wouldn't use that route again. Not after what she had said.

Cursing, Travis stalked off to find a spot for a cold bath. Ladies weren't worth the trouble. The first warm and willing woman he found would do.

11

TRAVIS HADN'T CHANGED his opinion by the time they docked in St. Louis, and neither had Alicia. They had spent two days coldly ignoring each other, much to the distress of every other occupant of the boat. The winds of winter couldn't have chilled the craft any more thoroughly.

While Travis busied himself with the process of docking, Alicia sent Becky to find someone to haul her trunks up the bank and look out for some form of transportation. By the time she had seen all her trunks carefully packed and tied, Becky was back.

Polite to the very last drop of her blood, Alicia forced herself to locate Travis. With the exertion of poling the boat into position and hauling freight into place, he had cast off his coat and stood now in only shirt-sleeves and breeches, muscles straining at the seams of both as he heaved a crate aft. When he sensed her presence, he stood with hands on hips, glaring down at her, a scowl on his bronzed visage.

"I have come to say farewell. I recognize that you have gone beyond your duty in looking after me, and I wish that we could have been friends—" That was not what she had meant to say, and Alicia hastily changed her direction and finished formally. "When I find a place, I will send you my address so that we might settle the final costs of the journey. Should you find a buyer for the boat, please let them know I am willing to sell."

This businesslike little speech cost her much effort, particularly as Travis made no attempt to relieve her of it. He merely continued to look at her as if she were a stranger intruding upon his day, and nodded acknowledgment when she finished. When it became obvious he had nothing fur-

ther to say to her, Alicia swung smartly on her heel and
stalked away.

Becky gave her a look of curiosity as she marched up the
hill without another look back, but her maid's opinion held
no weight with Alicia. If the girl had stayed with her as she
should have, she might at least be taking leave of the
keelboatman with some degree of amiability. The sour taste
of dissension marred her arrival in this new life.

At the top of the hill a gentleman in a horse-drawn buggy
lifted his cap in greeting and smiled approvingly at the new
arrival in her fashionable Eastern traveling gear. "Good day
to you, miss. Your maid tells me you are in need of transportation. It is not often I can be of service to a lovely lady.
I am Dr. Bernard Farrar. Where might I take you?"

Alicia smiled up in delight at this civilized greeting, and
her smile widened at the sight of the young doctor. Perhaps
St. Louis society would not be so heathenish as she feared,
and she looked around her with renewed humor.

"I wished to go to the address of a Mrs. Bessie Clayton.
Do you know of her?"

"Of course. Let me give you a hand." He extended his
gloved fingers to help Alicia into the carriage. With quick
dispatch her trunks were loaded in the rear with Becky
bouncing on top, and he switched the horses into motion.

Excitedly Alicia gazed around at the streets as they drove
through town. Relief swept over her as she realized this was
no frontier outpost with timbered cabins and makeshift for-
tifications. The fort on the hill spoke of an earlier need for
protection, but the graceful establishments glimpsed through
rows of fruit trees and orderly hardwoods gave her an impression of the civilization she had yearned for since leaving
Philadelphia. Verandas with delicate wrought-iron traceries
lent an exotic air to elegant stone residences, their towering
walls giving a permanency to a town not yet half a century
old. She could see signs for milliners and boot makers, a
dancing academy, and even an assembly room. It exceeded
the bounds of her hopes, and Alicia sighed happily as she
leaned back in the seat to enjoy the ride.

The physician smiled at this reaction. Obviously St. Louis
had just passed inspection. He dared intrude again. "How
do you come to know Bessie? Is she a relative of yours?"
Even as he asked it, he doubted the connection between this

elegant Easterner and the down-to-earth Bessie, but it was a means of breaching the gap with the lovely lady.

"Oh, no. I have never met her." Rather than go into details, Alicia explained simply, "A relative recommended her. I am looking for a place to stay."

The doctor gave a snort of laughter. "You and half the town. Since Jefferson bought the territory, people have been moving in faster than they can build houses. Even private homes are taking in boarders. I myself am staying at Mr. Robidoux's home. The only other doctor is French, and Robidoux was eager to see an American, which explains my good fortune."

At Alicia's crestfallen expression, the doctor hastily added, "But I'm certain Bessie will make room for you. She's taken in boarders since her husband died. She's exceedingly respectable and keeps a good table. You were well informed."

The doctor's assurances came through as promised. Bessie Clayton took one look at the proper young lady on her front porch, nodded a welcome to the young doctor, and ushered Alicia and Becky into her comfortable home.

"So you're Chester's daughter!" Bessie bustled about her spacious kitchen, preparing coffee for her guest, slicing a cake just from the oven. A small, plump woman, she was as warm and comfortable as her kitchen. It never occurred to her to entertain the new arrival in the unused parlor.

Alicia responded with overwhelming relief to this friendly reception. "You know my father?" she inquired eagerly, foolishly. Of course she did, if he had lived here.

Bessie laughed cheerfully, settling her plump frame into the chair across from Alicia and making certain the poor, half-starved maid had an extra large slice of cake.

"Chester stayed right here with me for nigh on to two years while he was building his business. A gentleman through and through. He had that upper back bedroom overlooking the garden. It's occupied now, I'm sorry to say. It's my best room, but don't you worry. We'll find a place to put Chester's daughter until he returns."

Alicia's heart skipped two beats and did a back flip. She could scarcely breathe long enough to get the words out. "My father . . . He still lives in St. Louis, then?"

Bessie looked mildly startled. "Why, of course, child. He travels a good deal and is out of town much of the time, but he's just built himself a place up by the hill. Not certain it's even finished yet, what with him not being around and no woman to look after it, but it's a lovely place. I thought certain he'd asked you to come out to make it into a home. Always set a mighty store by you, he did. Used to sit right here in this chair and tell me all about you. Like to broke his heart to leave you behind. But a girl's place is with her mother. He was right about that."

Tears of happiness and disbelief rimmed Alicia's eyes, and she fought to keep them down. The last few months had been long and exhausting, physically and emotionally. These friendly words nearly brought on a hysteria of relief. Her hand trembled as she set the cup back in its saucer. Her father was not only alive, but he loved her! It seemed too incredible to be true. She wished for the whole story, but just this small portion of it had nearly destroyed all her defenses.

"Mrs. Clayton, you don't have any idea how much those words mean to me. I just . . . I'm so tired . . ." Blinking back tears, Alicia tried to explain, but all she wanted to do was lie her head on a pillow and cry. She had not slept well at all these last nights.

The landlady looked at the girl's suddenly very pale face and overly-large eyes and exclaimed, "My heavens! Whatever am I thinking of? You've come all this way in a filthy boat with no proper meals or bedding. Of course, you're exhausted! Let me take you to my room for now and while you're sleeping, I'll have something done with that little room behind the parlor. We'll fix it up all nice and neat and cheery. Come on with you now, off to bed!"

Bessie and her boardinghouse provided the healing balm Alicia needed to piece together all the torn and wounded fragments of her spirit. Bessie wrapped her in warmth and comfort and security, and her house became a haven to retreat to at the end of each day in this strange and curious new home.

With Rebecca at her side, Alicia set out each day to explore the sprawling river town and acquaint herself with the inhabitants. Her first stop was at the imposing residence of Auguste Chouteau, where her father resided when in town. She made no attempt to call on the family, but merely left a message to be given to her father when he returned. The black servant impassively accepted the message, and

Alicia made no attempt to discover when her father would return. She dared not get her hopes up.

The sight of a city where trees and gardens were as much part of the streets as buildings excited her. Her mother had never left the house so she had done little traveling, but St. Louis was much like Alicia would have imagined a European city to be. In fact, St. Louis was more cosmopolitan than Philadelphia in some respects. Everywhere she went she heard the chatter of foreign tongues and saw the influence of the years of Spanish and French occupation. But even European cities couldn't boast the exotic flavor of red-skinned Indians roaming through town with their packs of furs and blankets to trade, or the boisterous and occasionally obnoxious presence of the half-wild trappers who came in for their supplies. Each moment was an education unto itself, and Alicia returned to the boardinghouse bursting with questions at the end of each day.

Unfortunately, freedom had its price, and Alicia was exceedingly aware of the cost, particularly in monetary terms. The gold she had paid Travis for the boat had severely depleted her cash reserves. She had written Philadelphia to give her aunt her new address and request that the bank transfer her funds, but if Travis were right, it would be three months before the letters could go back and forth. With winter arriving, it might be even longer than that. In the meantime she had rent to pay and a maid who had no suitable clothes.

Becky protested vigorously when Alicia marched her down to the dressmaker's shop for a fitting, but she succumbed to the delights of the lovely wools and heavy cottons Alicia chose for her. She would have preferred the red satins and yellow silks that caught her eye in the shopkeeper's window, but she grudgingly agreed they would not be very sensible against winter winds. When Alicia promised her the gift of a lovely paisley shawl of many colors to wrap over the drab blues and browns, Becky brightened considerably.

As a personal maid, Becky was worse than useless, but as a protector of Alicia's reputation, she was a veritable bulldog. She knew no fear when they were accosted on the streets by drunken trappers or curious Indians or even well-dressed gentlemen. She promptly dispatched them all with very little variation in finesse. Alicia had to reprimand her sharply when Becky almost took her booted toe to one poor young man who merely bowed and doffed his hat in their direction.

Alicia hid her laughter at the gentleman's startled expression until they were around the corner, and then she could no longer cover her chortles. Still smarting from the scolding, Becky sent her a suspicious glare.

"What you laughing for now?" she demanded. "I thought you didn't want no more men bothering you. And then you let that one get away just 'cause he dresses toffy."

"He only bowed, Becky. He was being polite. I can't stop people from looking. It's better just to ignore them," Alicia tried to explain. In truth, these walks had taught her that Travis was right once more. The men of St. Louis did notice her, for whatever reasons, and she rather enjoyed the attention.

"Hmph," Becky snorted. "I bet if Travis fixed himself all up proper like that, you'd not turn your nose up at him like you did."

The mention of Travis was like a slap in the face, and Alicia grew sober instantly. "Mr. Travis is not a gentleman and has never pretended to be one. Instead of spending your time thinking about men, you'd best turn your observant little ears to finding a suitable position for us if you wish to eat these next months."

That sobered Becky. She had been without food before, and had no intention of ever returning to such a dismal state of affairs again. She had thought Alicia wealthy beyond her dreams, and was prepared to do anything to please her so she could continue living as comfortably as she had these past weeks. The possibility of the money running out had never occurred to her. The thought of working hadn't, either. Becky's quick little mind turned to Travis. Alicia's turned to the ever knowledgeable Bessie Clayton.

When confronted with the problem, Bessie smiled unconcernedly. "Your father will be back before your money runs out, child, don't you worry. Whatever would he think if he returned to find his daughter working for her room and board? 'Why, Bessie Clayton,' he'd say, 'You know better than to let my little girl work.' Oh, he'd give me a proper dressing-down, he would."

With much argument Alicia convinced her she wanted to work, that she had come to St. Louis so she could work, and Bessie had to accept the inevitable. If Chester's daughter left before he returned because she couldn't get a job, he would never forgive her.

She nodded her head reluctantly. "I suppose things are different than in my day. Bless Mr. Clayton's soul, I always had to work, but then I was never a proper raised lady like yourself. I'll see what I can find out. A teacher, you say? Seems like there's always room for a teacher. But a young and pretty one . . ." She shook her graying curls thoughtfully. "We'll see."

Bessie was as good as her word. Within the week Alicia had an invitation to an interview at a small academy for ladies that had just lost one of their teachers to marriage. Married teachers were taboo, Alicia quickly learned, but her assurances that she had no fiancé and no immediate prospects of one pleased the academy's spinster owner. The fact that she was Chester Stanford's daughter and a lady by birth pleased the owner even more. A dozen little nine- and ten-year-olds running unsupervised made the position a certainty. Alicia was hired on the spot.

Alicia had no experience whatsoever with the eager minds and active bodies of a younger generation. She had been tutored at that age and never had the experience of playing with other children. By the end of that first Monday, she began to wonder if she had ever been a child. By Tuesday evening she wondered if she would even survive. Friday, when all the spelling tests came in nearly perfect, she began to think she might possibly have some grasp of the situation.

Sunday evening Travis knocked at the door.

Bessie hurried down the hall to the small chamber that had been made over into a bedroom for Alicia. When her boarder opened the door, Bessie whispered in distress, "It is a gentleman. At least I think he is a gentleman. For you. I've showed him into the front parlor."

Puzzled, Alicia searched her brain for a reason for a gentleman to call on her. She had met no one but the doctor, and Bessie was acquainted with him. For that matter, Bessie was acquainted with everyone.

"Did he not give a card?" Perhaps gentlemen didn't carry cards out here. Very likely they didn't.

Bessie shook her head, gray-blonde curls flying. "I was terrified to ask. He's so tall." She emphasized the last word as if it answered everything. "And fierce. Like an Indian, but not like an Indian. If you know what I mean."

Alicia knew what she meant. Travis. She breathed a little easier and patted her hair to be certain all the pins were straight. She still wore the wine-colored velvet she had worn to church with its high frill of white lace about her throat, and she felt appropriately garbed if he had come as gentleman. She nodded approvingly to her landlady.

"He is captain of the boat that brought me here. I left him with some business to transact for me. Don't fret." Her lips turned up at Bessie's concerned expression, and the older woman broke into a wreath of smiles.

"I must say, he's a handsome devil, but I could not imagine what your father would say if you started stepping out with someone as ferocious-looking as that!"

Alicia was laughing when she entered the parlor, her eyes twinkling and her cheek dimpled with amusement at Bessie's caricature of her caller. Travis turned at the sound of her entrance, and the sight nearly knocked the breath from his lungs. He held his hand out to the mantel to steady himself, and his gaze swept with fascination from polished mahogany curls over rich wine-covered curves, to tiny slippers peeking from beneath lacy frills. And back again to laughing sapphire eyes.

"I see you are faring well," he commented dryly, remembering his manners and sweeping a gallant bow.

"And you," Alicia replied without antagonism. He did look well with his hair cut fashionably to fall over his forehead and trimmed in back so it did not touch his immaculately white cravat. The forest green of his coat suited him well, the beautifully tailored cut emphasizing the breadth of his shoulders and coming short at his waist to disclose the discreetly gold and green waistcoat and fawn trousers over his trim abdomen. He looked considerably less ferocious than before, and the thought of Mrs. Clayton meeting him when he wore bandanna and earring made her smile again.

"Might I inquire as to what you consider so amusing?" Travis asked with a degree of irritation. He had not meant to finish this business in person. Only Becky's impassioned pleas had caused him to swallow his anger and make certain the spoiled lady had not come to grief. And now she laughed at him.

Alicia was instantly apologetic, indicating a chair by the fireside that he might sit. "Not you, I am sorry. Or maybe, yes, just a little. Please, sit down." She took the chair opposite him, unable to contain her inexplicable happiness at seeing him again. "You terrified my landlady. Whatever on earth did you say to her?"

A flicker of something akin to understanding flashed in dark eyes, and Travis relaxed in the seat offered, admiring the picture she made with the fire light dancing across her lovely cheeks and throat.

"Perhaps I did sound a trifle surly. I shall try to make it up to her on the way out. I trust you won't mind conducting a little business on a Sunday?"

"Of course not. I had not expected you to sell the shipment so quickly. Did you take much of a loss?" Alicia prayed quickly. A substantial loss would empty her coffers even faster than anticipated. She was unaccustomed to cutting corners.

"On the contrary, we did quite well. They are desperate for everything that can be hauled up the river. St. Louis is not quite so conveniently situated as New Orleans."

Travis removed a small purse from his jacket and set it on the table beside her. The coins clinked nicely. "I also have an offer for the boat. You will take into consideration that it is in need of repairs."

Alicia sat forward expectantly. From the sound of the coins he had put beside her, she would be able to provide a merry Christmas for Becky and Mrs. Clayton, and even buy small trinkets for her students. The sale of the boat would see her comfortably until the money arrived from Philadelphia.

"Your offer?" she demanded eagerly.

She was enjoying this, Travis realized admiringly. The Philadelphia heiress had adapted readily to this life of living by her wits and talent. Another woman in her place would be despairing of the comedown from mansion to boarding house, a dozen servants to one, overflowing purse to single coins. This one seemed to be thriving on the challenge.

"I've been given license to offer twenty-four dollars," he mentioned casually, watching her reactions as if this were a poker game.

Alicia considered the offer. That much would tide her over nicely, but it was scarcely half what she had paid. If St. Louis were really desperate for whatever came up the river, it seemed as if she could get a little more. She tilted her head consideringly.

"I think that's a trifle low, don't you agree? Surely the boat isn't much worse off than when we started, except for the little hole, of course." She refused to allow herself to think of the cause of that hole. She could not picture the gentleman across from her carving at another human being the way Travis had that outlaw. It was unthinkable.

Travis grinned and crossed a booted leg over his knee. "Best damn boat on the river, pardon my language. I build them to last. What are you asking?"

That disconcerted her slightly. She had hoped he would give her an idea of what the boat was worth in this market, but he just sat there grinning at her. So be it.

"Let's say thirty-five dollars," she replied firmly.

"With what I just gave you there, that means your journey not only didn't cost you a cent, but you made a profit on it," he reminded her.

"It cost me more than money, Mr. Travis," she answered in a low voice, all laughter gone now. "I would be quit of it as soon as possible. Of course, you must take a fair commission for arranging the sale."

The haunted look was back in her eyes, the veiled anguish that Travis had so desperately wished to remove. He had been a fool to think she could forget so easily. It would take time and patience to see those wounds healed. And he, who had prided himself on his patience, had nearly opened them up again. Perhaps ladies weren't worth the effort, but in that moment Travis decided this particular woman was. He would not accept defeat.

"I did not mean to remind you, Alicia," he said quietly, before diverting the topic to safer ground. "I will sell the boat for enough to cover my costs and get you the thirty-five dollars. Have you heard anything about your father yet?"

The change of topic worked. Alicia's face glowed like a thousand candles. "He is alive! He is out of town on business, but Bessie says he can be expected back before the snow comes. And she says he used to talk of me all the time, and write. She doesn't understand what happened to the letters. She says he seldom received mine, either."

Travis felt a moment's trepidation at this news, but he didn't allow it to deter him from his goal. He smiled with her pleasure.

"I am happy for you, Blue Eyes. Now I had better go before your landlady believes I am holding you hostage."

He rose and held out his hand to the captivating woman at the fireside. Her fingers curled trustingly in his, and again he felt his breath catch. He would have to find a woman soon, or this one would drive him out of his mind.

Alicia looked at Travis with curiosity. In this light the angular planes of his face were shadowed, and she could read nothing of his expression. He had obviously arrived in anger, but now he seemed to be looking at her in a way that made her heart beat too quickly. She could not help but remember all he had done for her, been to her, and embarrassment lightly flushed her cheeks. Still, she dared not offer him the friendship she craved. He presumed too much.

Instead she shook his hand briefly and led him to the door. Mrs. Clayton had left the parlor door partially ajar, apparently to better hear Alicia's screams, she thought wryly. Her gaze met Travis's at this thought, and he grinned wickedly.

"Perhaps you should introduce me to your guard dog," Travis suggested.

"Of course." Alicia lowered her eyes demurely so he couldn't see the leap of laughter there. Sometimes he understood her too well.

Bessie bobbed a slight curtsy as Alicia introduced her guest as Captain Travis, for want of a better name for him. He commented warmly on her lovely home and what good hands Miss Stanford found herself in until Bessie was blushing with delight. Then he made his farewells.

Outside, he encountered a slight figure hovering in the bushes, and his frown returned.

"Rebecca Whitefield, come out of there!" he commanded.

She darted forward, gazing at his stern profile with anxiety. "Is it OK, then? Did she take the money?"

"I didn't see any evidence that she was starving, and she just cost me a pretty packet with her haggling. What made you paint me such a bleak picture?"

"She said we'd both be starving if we didn't find jobs soon!" she protested. "And you told me to look after her and so I did." She stood up to him pugnaciously.

"Seems to me Miss Stanford is the only one working, Miss Whitefield. I don't suppose you considered taking on employment before you came to me?"

Becky straightened her shoulders indignantly. "And who would look after her if I did? You don't want all them fancy dudes hanging around her, do you? And besides, I been helpin' out Miz Clayton, too."

Travis laughed. "I'm sure you have. Well, then, Rebecca, I suppose I must reward you for your loyalty." He flipped her a coin, but his expression became stern. "Just you remember to stay with Miss Stanford and keep her from harm, or I'll come after you with a stick. Do you understand?"

Becky grabbed the coin and nodded eagerly. She had no intention of losing this easy job. Besides, she was beginning to take an interest in how the Indian would woo the lady.

12

To Becky's disappointment, Travis made no overt attempts to call on Alicia after the one visit. The money from the sale of the boat was delivered by messenger, and that seemed to be an end to it.

Alicia didn't have time to consider her thoughts on the subject. She devoted all her time to conquering the challenge of her first position, an exhilarating experience for one who had been confined to the same stultifying activities for the better part of her life. If she missed the occasional rewards of her previous existence—the music, the witty conversation, the access to influential and interesting people—she gave no evidence of it as the month of November ran into December. Lesson plans became more concise as Christmas drew near.

Alicia had never been away from home for Christmas before, but neither had she ever planned her own Christmas. At home, tradition had dictated the decorating and gift giving and parties to be held. Here, everything was new, and she had to adjust to different traditions, different people, even different weather. Although natives swore the winter was the coldest they had ever seen, no snow turned the dry grass to a wintery white, and sleigh bells were mostly a tale told by those who remembered them from their past homes.

Homesickness struck in mid-December with the sight of a carriage full of young people gaily dressed in holiday garb and bearing colorful gifts laughing and chattering merrily on their way to a party in one of the large mansions on the outskirts of town. Alicia stared wistfully after the departing carriage, and wondered if she would ever meet those of her own kind hidden behind the stone walls and gardens of

town. She had scarcely even had the opportunity to meet
the wealthy parents of her students.

Loneliness crept beneath her skin and lodged there. She
had never been allowed close friends at home, and now it
seemed she would not have the opportunity to make any.
Christmas would have to be shared with Becky and Mrs.
Clayton.

It could have been much worse, she reminded herself
strongly as she walked on in the darkening twilight. The day
had become heavily overcast, and she had stayed late after
school working on costumes for the Christmas play. The
first flakes of snow began to fall as she hurried down the
block to the welcoming two-story home of Mrs. Clayton.
The thought of what Christmas could have been had she
stayed in Philadelphia with Teddy made her feet hurry faster.

The smell of cookies baking enveloped Alicia as she entered the door, and the sound of Becky chattering happily in
the kitchen brought a smile to her face. The wizened, owlish-
child she had first met had slowly transformed into an almost normal sixteen-year-old these past weeks. She was still
crafty and wise-mouthed when given the opportunity, but
lately her chatter had all been of Christmas. The plans for
Mrs. Clayton's Christmas dinner had awed her into silence,
and the greenery now decorating the chandeliers and banis-
ter and mantels had been lovingly laid by the child's hands.
Alicia doubted if her little maid had ever celebrated Christmas before.

At the sound of the front door closing, Bessie Clayton
bustled from the kitchen in the rear of the house, wiping her
floury hands on the starched apron she wore.

"You're home, at last! We didn't think you would ever
arrive. I just heard from a friend of mine . . ." Bessie stopped
in the hallway to smile happily at her lovely young boarder,
and her eyes danced with excitement as she savored Alicia's
anticipation. "Your father was seen riding into town not two
hours ago."

The impact of this message staggered Alicia abruptly into
the nearest chair, and her hand went to her mouth as she
contemplated all the implications. Her father was home for
Christmas. He was alive and in St. Louis and she could see
him again. Her head swam with the delirium of happiness
produced by these few words. Tears danced in her eyes, and
she made no attempt to remove bonnet or pelisse.

What if he didn't know she was here? That thought struck wildly and could not be banished. She had left her messages weeks ago. Perhaps he would not even return to the Chouteau house, but had made arrangements to stay in that empty house he had built. Perhaps the servants would forget to deliver her message altogether. The possibilities seemed endless.

"I must go to him," she murmured distractedly, securing her bonnet strings and straightening her pelisse.

Bessie frowned slightly. "That is foolish. It is getting dark and you have to go all the way across town. Wait until morning and then you can send Becky."

Alicia shook her head stubbornly, standing and pulling on her gloves again. "He may leave town again by morning. The streets are safe this time of day. Becky has a cough and shouldn't be out in this cold. It will take me no time at all."

Bessie's protests went unheard. The miracle of finding her father after all these years overrode all else. Alicia found herself walking briskly along nearly empty streets as the last rays of daylight faded into obscurity. Lanterns appeared in windows, oil lamps flickered in the interiors of the houses she passed. Stores and businesses closed for the day, leaving patterns of shadows across the street. The snowflakes increased but threatened no danger. They blew and danced in the streets, and Alicia reveled in their freedom.

The Chouteau house loomed formidably large and set apart from the others, but Alicia scarcely noticed its imposing facade. Her thoughts centered wholly on the man who might even now be sitting in that lighted study or conversing with the occupants. How much would he have changed over all these years? Would he remember her? Would he be pleased to see her? Alicia refused to allow doubt to enter her mind. She marched boldly up the front steps and let the brass knocker fall loudly.

Eventually the tall black servant she had encountered before came to the door. He stared impassively at the unknown lady elegantly clad in deep green velvet bonnet and pelisse.

"Is Mr. Stanford in?" she requested politely, not betraying the pounding of her heart against her rib cage.

The servant blinked once or twice and considered the question before replying. "No, ma'am. He only stopped for a moment and left in a hurry. Don't know where he's bound this time."

The awfulness of this announcement shattered Alicia's euphoria. Gone again. She stepped back as if struck, managed a stammered "thank you," turned around, and fled.

She should have known it was too easy. Had he been in too much of a hurry to see the message she had left? Or had her message produced the hurry? Perhaps he had fled at the discovery that his daughter had arrived in town. What else could have sent him so precipitously from his home so soon after his arrival?

Blindly Alicia rushed through the darkened streets, fighting the torrent of tears burning behind her eyelids. Until now she had fully believed her father hadn't wanted to leave her, that he loved her still, that he would welcome her with open arms. And now this. A door slammed in her face. A cold shoulder she could not ignore. Fool. Fool that she should believe any man cared for anything other than his own selfish pursuits. Her mother had been right all along.

Loud music and a splash of light crossed her path, but Alicia paid it no heed. The sounds of drunken revelry from the tavern had no part in the empty pit of loneliness gaping before her. Somehow she would have to leap that terrible pit and go her own way. The world around her scarcely existed.

She stumbled to a halt as two men staggered from the saloon directly into her path. A frozen puddle made her abrupt back step a slippery maneuver, and the two men hit the ice with equal indelicacy. One grabbed her shoulders and the other fell to the ground with a stream of curses nearly drowned by his companion's roar of laughter.

Alicia attempted to jerk away from the crude hand molesting her shoulder, but her movement only served to return the drunkard's attention to her presence. Garbed in filthy buckskin and unwashed linen, he smelled of more odors than Alicia cared to define, but the stench of whiskey was overpowering.

"Look what I found, Earl!" he exclaimed proudly, twisting his captive more securely until he held both shoulders. "We don't need those fancy women in there when we got this out here!"

His equally grubby companion staggered upright and beamed blearily at this evidence of manna from heaven. He whistled lewdly and pawed her bonnet.

"What have we here? Reckon she's new?"

Panic finally took its hold as Alicia realized she had no protection whatsoever against their drunken advances. She did not even wear boots that might scar their shins. She struggled futilely against the larger one's hold, but he was not so drunk as to lose his powerful grip. He pulled her closer until his stinking breath scorched her face.

"Let go of me or I'll scream!" she hissed between clenched teeth, trying to kick but hampered by heavy skirts and pelisse. Terror gave her more strength than she possessed, and she jerked one arm loose, swinging violently at her attacker. She reacted with pure instinct, all ladylike manners lost as she opened her mouth to scream while her fist beat awkwardly at the hand holding her.

The trapper attempted to silence her protests with his broken-toothed, foul-smelling mouth, but Alicia kept eluding him, jerking this way and that. Her hysterical screams produced little effect against the raucous revelry from within the tavern.

And then a tall shadow blocked the yellow light, and a hand casually grasped the collar of the trapper's jacket, flinging him backward into his companion. A familiar voice warmed Alicia's ear as a strong arm caught her reassuringly by the waist, pressing her closely to his side.

"It's all right, Alicia. In the name of all that is holy, don't cry." Travis held her tightly, feeling the hysterical tremors quaking through her slender body. He turned and scowled at the burly men staggering back to their feet, the fierceness of his planed visage emphasizing the threat of his words. "If you ever lay hands on this lady again, you'll account to me."

His casual drawl contained a menace that caused Alicia to glance quickly to his sunburned profile, but not a flicker of emotion marred Travis's hard features. The two men stared at the elegantly dressed gentleman with a mixture of anger and respect, but they made no attempt to question Travis's authority.

"Didn't know she was yours, Lonetree," one stammered, backing away from the light. "It's a cold night and when you wouldn't let us—"

Travis cut him off sharply. "Go sleep it off somewhere. Don't annoy the lady further."

The men melted into the night, leaving Alicia stricken and shivering in the hold of the man she knew to be more of a danger than any other she had met. Too ashamed of her departure from the civilized course she had set herself, she could not meet his eyes.

"What in hell are you doing out here alone?" Angrily Travis kept his grip on her, even though he sensed she shrunk from him, or perhaps because of it.

"I wasn't thinking." Hurriedly Alicia tried to explain and escape. "I was upset and wasn't watching. I've got to get back. Mrs. Clayton will be worried." She pulled away, backing toward the safety of darkness.

Travis stepped forward, catching her elbow and steering her from the noisy confusion of the tavern. Only now did she realize he was garbed formally in tailored velvet frock coat and elaborate cravat, the gold buttons of his satin waistcoat winking in the occasional flicker of light. He had whipped his tall beaver hat back on his head when he took her arm, and in the shadows she could not have distinguished him from any Philadelphia gentleman attired for a formal evening.

"Will you tell me what upset you, Alicia?" Travis's voice murmured low and husky against her ear as he walked her toward the safety of her home.

The story poured out without bidding. Too tired and shaken to hold anything back, Alicia soon felt tears scalding her cheeks, but she kept her face averted from his penetrating gaze.

"Perhaps your father received your message and hurried out to find you," Travis calmly suggested at the end of her tale. She was as cold and stiff as any board in his hands, but he sensed it had little to do with himself this time. She was a wounded creature who feared all offers of help. He prayed fervently that his words were not far wrong. She could not bear another such rejection.

Alicia considered his reassurances doubtfully, but her steps became a trifle quicker. "We shall see," she replied evasively before changing the topic. "You seem to have done well since we arrived. Have you found what you were looking for?"

Travis grinned in the darkness. "I'm just doing what comes naturally. There's money to be had for the taking out here. I'm just taking a little of it while I look around."

His cheerful tone steadied Alicia's nerves to a degree, and the warm touch of his arm beneath her hand became less of a threat. He matched his long stride to hers as they strode toward the boardinghouse.

"By that comment and your whereabouts this evening, I take it that you are not exactly making an honest living?" She strove desperately to keep her voice normal. He had seen her too near the verge of emotional disaster too many times.

"More honest than many I can name," Travis protested. "I'll admit I don't frequent the best houses as yet, but I mean to. How is your employment coming along?"

She did not feel any surprise that he knew of her job. She suspected he knew a lot of things about a lot of people, but kept his mouth shut. There were many things she liked about this man.

Alicia gave a brief description of her duties as teacher, but her heart had already begun to pound again at the sight ahead of Mrs. Clayton's parlor spilling over with light. Her fingers tightened convulsively against his arm.

Travis too noted the unusual display, and his jaw locked determinedly. There had not been time enough to establish his position as a person in society, but he fully intended to meet Alicia's father on his own terms. He didn't know what kind of man Stanford might be, but Travis realized he would be the biggest hurdle to cross in his pursuit of Alicia. He wanted to know his opponent's strengths.

"It appears Mrs. Clayton has company. Shall we go in?" Dark eyes searched the pale oval of her face. He expected to be turned away and was already planning his argument, but she merely stared at him with wide, frightened eyes and nodded. That brief glimpse of fear cut Travis to the bone, and made him more determined than ever. Someone had to protect her, and it might as well be he.

They entered the welcoming warmth of the Clayton front hall together, the tall, slender young lady on the arm of a bronzed stranger. The happy chatter of voices in the parlor ceased, and the two occupants swung to stare at the newcomers.

Bessie stood beside a graying, distinguished man of middle height. His conservatively cut coat and trousers spoke quietly of wealth. His self-assurance as he stepped forward, his gaze fixed on the young woman in dark curls, spoke strongly of good breeding and lifelong security. He had no doubt of his position in this world. He scarcely cast Travis a second glance.

"Alicia?" he spoke softly in a voice of joy and wonder.

Sapphire eyes lit from within, transforming Alicia's cold features to radiant beauty. With a sob she cried "Papa!" and flew into his waiting arms.

Over their heads Bessie and Travis exchanged glances. Bessie wiped a tear from her eye with a corner of her apron, and Travis looked away. Even the most cynical of men would be moved by this reunion. He had to be happy that Alicia had found her father at last, but he could only pray it did not mean an end to his own dreams.

Gradually, as exclamations and bewildered questions slowed, Alicia remembered her manners and stepped back so that Travis could be introduced. Thrilled with the discovery of his daughter, Chester Stanford only had eyes for her and scarcely gave her tall young man a second thought.

"Papa, this is Captain Travis. But for him, I would never have made it to St. Louis."

Travis gave a wry smile at this introduction and cast her a quick glance, but she seemed totally sincere. He took Chester Stanford's hand and shook it firmly. "Most pleased to meet you, sir."

"Good to meet you, Captain Travis. I owe you more than I can repay for returning my daughter to me. If there is ever anything I can do . . ."

Travis bowed his head politely and with a nod toward Alicia and Bessie moved toward the door. "I don't mean to intrude upon your reunion. It's been a pleasure." Returning his hat to his head, Travis strode out, leaving the singular impression that a well-bred gentleman had just departed.

Alicia appeared mildly confused by this behavior in a man whom a moment before had practically admitted to being a gambler or worse, but the presence of her father quickly obliterated all else. She turned and threw her arms ecstatically around his neck again.

Chester chuckled and drew her into the parlor, leaving Bessie to tactfully disappear into the kitchen in search of refreshments.

"Your young man is very imposing. Why ever did he have you out on a night like this?"

Alicia looked startled at this turn of conversation, but she quickly dismissed her father's assumptions. "He is not my

young man, Papa. Captain Travis merely escorted me home
when he found me wandering in the dark. I heard you were
home and rashly went looking for you."

Chester looked affectionately at his beautiful young daughter. The cold had brought a rush of color to her cheeks, and
her eyes sparkled like her mother's never had. He did not
imagine for a minute that any man could look on her without desiring her. He was relieved that she had not allowed a
mere boat captain to worm his way into her affections.

"Never mind, dear, I will soon introduce you to some of
the best and brightest young men this country can offer. It
will be my pleasure to introduce you to society."

An alarm should have sounded in Alicia's head at these
words, but her pleasure was too great to read any serious
disturbances into her father's predictions. She desired only
his company and his approval, and she had both. At long
last she was content.

13

CHESTER STANFORD opened his newly built house with a dinner and dance on New Year's Eve. The best of St. Louis society turned out for this celebration within a celebration. The arrival of Chester's beautiful daughter and the expected announcement of his engagement to the widow of one of St. Louis's oldest residents made this the social event of the year.

The polished floors were as yet uncarpeted. The piano and much of the furniture had not yet arrived from New Orleans, and the servants were all new and poorly trained, but none of these factors diminished the gaiety. Chandeliers gleamed with a thousand flames, and every professional musician within the limits of the city had been called upon to provide entertainment. The chance to shine before the wealthy and the powerful inspired both guests and entertainers.

Standing on the curved mahogany stairway overlooking the glittering crowd, Alicia found her father proudly introducing Letitia Labbadie to the new governor. Letitia wore a narrow gown of blue velvet over her short, rather full figure, but the simple cut of the gown served only as a backdrop for her elaborate parure of diamonds. Alicia had not had the opportunity to get to know her stepmother-to-be very well, but her father's announcement that he meant to marry again now that he was a free man had left her vaguely shaken. Watching the couple, she realized she had no right to deny them the happiness they sought, but she felt excluded from the loving warmth that surrounded them.

True, her father had insisted that she must come to live with him, and Letitia had warmly repeated the invitation, but Alicia could not bring herself to surrender her brief independence for a home that wasn't hers. She knew she had hurt her father's feelings by delaying her departure from the boardinghouse, so she had attempted to make it up to him in other ways. She wasn't certain how long that would satisfy him.

Her gaze wandered over the crowd, most of whom she had met these last few weeks. They were an odd lot, scarcely the statesmen and aristocratic families that she had known in Philadelphia, but they had their own levels of aristocracy here. The wealthy French and Spanish families that had formed this settlement still dominated society, but the American politicians now governing the territory had become an important part of the local scene. The American businessmen and professionals who had begun to arrive with the Louisiana purchase found their expertise and their ready cash equally welcome. The talk this evening was of the act being introduced in Congress to carve out the land west of St. Louis as the Missouri Territory, to be governed separately from the rest of the purchase. Politics seldom changed.

Alicia discovered a towheaded young man determinedly striding toward the staircase, and she sighed, wondering if she dared escape to the room that was to be hers for the evening. The eligible men she had met these last weeks were not so very different from those she had known back East, though several were considerably more hotheaded. They spoke of duels and gambling and racing as if they were still in New Orleans, where many of them came from. She had learned to take much of their charming, soft-spoken flattery with a grain of salt, but she found the flattery more pleasant to listen to than the arrogant boasting of some of her suitors.

Catching her father watching expectantly, Alicia accepted the young man's offer to dance and allowed herself to be led out into the company. At least these fast-moving country dances alleviated the necessity of conversation. She enjoyed intelligent conversation, but the young men thought suitable to court her seldom indulged in that pleasant activity. She supposed they must talk among themselves of things other than the weather and her beauty, but those seemed to be the only topics appropriate between men and women.

True to form, as they left the dance floor and approached the buffet, the young man complimented her on the loveliness of her gown. Defying her father's wishes on this point,

Alicia had chosen the black silk, high-waisted Parisian gown she had worn for the first time in Cincinnati. Her mother had been dead less than a year, and she did not find the color inappropriate. Among all the vivid colors of the holiday season, it produced a more sophisticated than somber effect. She had listened to Letitia's advice, however, and not covered the low neckline with anything other than an intricate silver necklace that picked up the silver thread shot through the brocade. She felt conspicuous whenever her escorts' straying gazes fell lower than her eyes, but she endured their attentions with grace. Looking did not have the power to harm her.

Her father rescued her from a witless exchange over the beauty of the imported crystal chandelier. She accepted his hand gladly and smiled in delight as she noticed the musicians struck up a waltz. Even in Philadelphia the waltz was shockingly daring, but she loved the music and the movement.

"It is New Year's Eve, and I am scandalously happy. Shall we see that the rest of our guests are equally scandalized?" Chester Stanford suggested wickedly as he led his daughter out onto the dance floor.

"Nothing would please me more," Alicia agreed, swinging effortlessly into the rhythm under her father's expert guidance. "However did you learn to waltz while living out here among the savages?"

"I travel widely and allowing ladies to teach me the intricacies of the dance made an excellent opportunity to get to know them better. One is seldom a stranger in the city for long if one knows how to waltz."

Alicia had to laugh at the gleam in her father's eyes. He had always been able to make her laugh. She could not understand how her mother had failed to love his charming, witty company. She supposed he had always been something of a ladies' man, but she felt certain he would have been a faithful husband had her mother allowed it. Was it possible that she had inherited her mother's coldness that she could not enjoy the company of any one man for long?

Not wishing to linger on such thoughts, Alicia fell in with his nonsense. "And has Letitia taught you so well that you have chosen her over all the others?"

Chester laughed. "Letitia will not even watch if she can avoid it. You are too young to hear her comments upon the sinful thoughts of men's minds while waltzing."

Alicia looked mildly alarmed. "If she is so religious as that, how can you—I mean—" She stumbled over the words, not knowing how to phrase them delicately. The sins of men had been one of her mother's preoccupations, and it had destroyed their marriage. Why would her father seek out another such woman?

Her father smiled gently at her confusion. "You do not need to say it. Letitia is no more religious than I, nor is she as cold as my comment made it seem. I fear it is just the opposite. She knows well what is in my mind and enjoys it, but I do not expect you to understand that until you marry. Have any of the local fellows caught your eye?"

The change of topic brought a flush to Alicia's cheeks, and she looked out over the crowd. "They are all very pleasant," she replied stiltedly.

Chester shrugged. "If there are none here, we will take you to Natchez and New Orleans and anywhere else you would like to go. You should have your choice of men. I want you to be happy."

Alicia remained silent. She knew her father still felt guilty for leaving her; he had said as much. He only meant to compensate for the missing years with these sweeping promises of eligible men and happy marriages. She could not tell him it was too late. Just a hint that she was no longer a virgin would horrify these droves of well-bred gentlemen her father promised to present. She did not even have to worry about getting past that stage to discussions of marriage. She could not marry. But how was she to explain that simple fact to a man as persistent as her father?

If he had only carried that persistence into inquiring why her letters had never arrived, he might have discovered her unhappiness and saved her from the disaster her life had become. When they had discussed it, it had become quickly obvious that her mother must have intercepted the letters and destroyed them in an attempt to force Alicia to turn against her father. Alicia had been too young to understand that then, but surely her father would have known what kind of woman he had married and guessed what happened. Only the letters she had mailed to her aunt or that she had personally mailed had arrived at their destinations. Why hadn't he found some way to reach her?

Gazing at the crowded ballroom with its glittering array of guests, Alicia could surmise the answer to that question.

Her father was an energetic man who enjoyed people and business and pleasure. He had found all three in his new life. Perhaps there were times when he missed his daughter, but those times were not frequent enough to justify returning to the family he had left behind. Once her father made a decision, he didn't look back. Little by little she was learning he was as human as the rest of mankind. She still loved him, but not with the idolatry of her younger years.

That knowledge made it easier to recognize the widening chasm between them. Her father would insist on seeing her as the eligible young daughter to be married off to one of the best men money could buy. And she could barely look those same men in the face. It put her in an unconscionable position, and one that would have to be resolved soon.

The dance ended and her father gallantly left her in the company of a bevy of young people. Alicia felt ancient beyond her years as they flirted and teased and talked of nothing more serious than the next party they would attend. She had never learned to talk like that, and she saw no point in trying now. Making her excuses, she slipped from the ballroom into the wide hall.

She heard men discussing business in the smoke-filled study, and hurried past that door to the back of the house. The main parlors and dining room had been opened up to make the ballroom, but the family sitting room overlooking the gardens and the hill beyond would be quiet and private.

She had only just entered the room when she realized she was not alone. Swinging to make a hasty retreat, Alicia halted at the sound of a familiar, husky murmur.

"Don't go, Alicia."

Her heart gave a nervous thud and all her senses told her to flee, but that would not only be rude but cruel. Slowly she turned to search the darkness, finding his tall, lean frame silhouetted against the French doors. The gleam of his cheroot arced downward as he smashed it against some hidden tray. Growing accustomed to the dim light, Alicia could discern the immaculate white of his cravat and shirt against the darker hues of his tailored coat.

"Why are you here?" The question did not come out as she liked, revealing an ambiguity she had not anticipated.

Travis took his time answering, as if debating which answer she wanted to hear. "I had some business with your father," he finally replied. He remained where he was, observing the occasional glint of silver around her throat, knowing well the full curves where the necklace rested.

The sound of his voice sent shivers down Alicia's spine. Travis exuded some virile magnetism that she instinctively feared, but could not seem to fight. She remembered being held in those powerful arms that had guided a boat load of people down mighty rivers. She remembered the tenderness in his touch when he had to feed her, clothe her, care for her as a parent would a child. And she remembered his vicious knife slashing in and out and throwing a man's life away. He terrified her. And fascinated her.

Bravely she came closer, the silk of her gown rustling sensuously in the darkness. "You are a businessman now?" she inquired lightly, wanting to know this, wanting to know everything, and not wanting him to know.

"Of sorts." The room held little furniture. Travis made room for her in front of the French doors so she might look out, and he might see her face in the reflections of lamplight from the other windows. "Why are you not in there with the others, dancing the new year in?"

He asked the question more politely than she had, and Alicia smiled at having it turned against her. "Why am I here?" she rephrased it for him. He didn't laugh, and she shrugged nonchalantly. "I don't belong in there," she answered evasively.

Travis leaned against the wall and studied her pale face in the lamplight. Ridiculously long lashes splashed dark shadows across her cheeks as she averted her eyes. Although every woman in that crowded room across the hall wore her hair in tangles of loose, feminine curls about her throat and shoulders, this one still wore hers tightly pulled in a smooth chignon. It made the frail curve at the nape of her neck even more vulnerable when she turned away, and he longed to caress it.

"I don't believe that," he answered flatly. "You are the most beautiful woman in that room tonight. The others may as well have come from other planets. Every eye is on you."

Alicia laughed softly. "I should think if there were creatures from other planets in there, it would be wisest to keep an eye on them. Why aren't you in there with the rest of them, then?"

"I wasn't invited." It was a statement of fact, without inflection.

Alicia glanced curiously at his bronzed, angular face. "Then why are you here?"

This time Travis did chuckle. "Full circle. Shall I clarify my first answer? I made it my business to be here. Your father is not averse to making money, and I can help him. But he prefers to keep business and pleasure separate."

"Not always." The strains of a second waltz struck up, and Alicia glanced back toward the hall. Her father would be looking for her. She should return.

"Would you care to dance?"

The question seemed absurd and Alicia glanced back at him quickly to see if he mocked her, but Travis only watched quietly.

"It's a waltz," she replied inanely. He seemed to have robbed her of her wits.

Travis did not attempt to answer. He circled her waist with one arm and captured her hand with the other. The unfurnished, uncarpeted room made an ideal dance floor. He led her slowly into the rhythms of the music until they circled and swept the perimeter of the room as if they were surrounded by a magnificent ballroom in a glittering palace full of courtly people.

It was unlike anything Alicia had ever experienced. The music and the man carried her away into a different world, one in which she had no care beyond the sound of music and the next step. That she could feel the heat of his hand through the thin silk at her waist, that his head bent close to hers and his breath rippled through her hair, made no difference in this world of music. She relaxed and floated in his arms without fear.

The spell held for magic moments after the music ended. Travis continued holding her hand, her waist, and looking down into her upturned face. Alicia caught her breath at the burning look in black eyes, but she did not back away.

"Let me teach you not to fear." The words were quiet, undemanding.

Alicia did not pretend to misunderstand. She continued to stare into his hard-edged face, frozen and beyond the ability to act at will. "That's not possible," she murmured.

"Let me try." More command than plea. Travis lowered his hand to caress her cheek, cup her smooth jaw in his palm. "No one else knows you as I do. You cannot live with the fear for the rest of your life. It will destroy you. You must trust someone, Alicia. Let it be me."

And she yearned to do so. For those brief magic moments in his arms she had been free, and she wanted to taste that freedom again. The tension was already returning to her back and neck, and the terrified hollow in her center made her back away. He wanted her as a man wants a woman, but she could not be that woman.

Still, she had already seen the alternatives. Her father wanted her to marry, but she could not. How could she explain to those proper young men that she had been horribly raped, had carried another man's baby, and was terrified of just their touch? Travis knew, and did not care. She could turn her back on her father and all men and go her own way, but the unbearably lonely life that stretched before her terrified her as much as the other. Travis knew that too, because he had felt the same empty winds as she.

That thought made Alicia turn her gaze back to him. He was an outcast in both the worlds he belonged in. He knew what it was like to be different, to be unwanted. She did not know his past, but she understood his yearning. Raised as an Indian but rejected as a white man. Taught to be a gentleman but scorned as a red man. His problems were more than hers, but together . . .

Before her fear could act to turn away this one glimmer of hope, Alicia replied, "I want to be normal again. If I must learn to trust, I will have to start with you."

Travis's exhalation of breath was almost audible. "You'll not regret it."

The pact was sealed without any further explanations. As Travis gazed into terrified sapphire eyes, a corner of his lips turned up mischievously. "Perhaps, occasionally, you might regret it."

A bubble of laughter rose in her throat at this honesty, but there was no time for it to escape. Alicia found herself clasped in Travis's strong embrace, and his faintly whiskey-scented lips covered hers with the branding heat of possession.

She had sold her soul to the devil.

14

BY THE NEXT day Alicia had come to her senses. She didn't know of a certainty what Travis intended, but she knew it was the height of idiocy to even be in the same room with him. Last night had certainly proved that had she any further doubts.

Looking in the mirror and touching her lips where he had kissed her, she wondered why no sign of his brand appeared for all to see. Never had she been kissed like that. His mouth had been warm and slow and sensuous as it had moved possessively from one corner of her lips to the other, plying them with honeyed gentleness until she had fallen for his promises.

That had been even a worse mistake. Alicia blushed just remembering it. How could she have been so irresponsible as to let that half-breed keelboatman take such liberties? She had been kissed before, but not like that, not with the rough rasp of his tongue stealing her breath away and leaving her powerless in his arms. She could not imagine how one simple dance could have reduced her to such spineless idiocy, but she would be certain not to let it happen again.

How she would go about telling Travis that she had no desire to see him again preyed on her mind through the remainder of the holidays until school started again. She had managed to persuade her father to allow her to stay with Bessie awhile longer, while the workmen finished up and the last of the furniture arrived. But the walk from her father's to Bessie's was a long one with all too much opportunity to think. It was easier to get caught up in activities at her father's house and stay rather than make the long walk home and think.

But once back in the familiar bustle of the schoolroom, Alicia returned to the routine, and the problem of Travis dissipated. Keeping up with half a dozen active little girls at once kept the mind well occupied. Her mind was already on the next day's lesson plan as she pulled on her gloves to leave that afternoon.

The sight of Travis in buckskin and fringe filling the school's feminine parlor with his virile, six-foot frame brought Alicia to an alarmed halt. The next sight of the school's elderly spinster owner chattering excitedly to this rampant specimen of the opposite sex robbed her of speech.

As Travis spied her in the doorway, he rose politely to his feet, dwarfing the tiny woman at the fire, who turned expectantly.

"Alicia! Bless you, child, you'll never guess! Mr. Travis says he can construct that stage we need without any trouble at all! He said he would be happy to do it. You must thank your father for bringing such a talented and generous man to our community."

That little speech brought a wry twist to Alicia's lips as she met Travis's eyes and looked quickly away again. It was a wonder Miss Lalende did not see the laughter in his eyes. She would be fired on the spot.

Resolutely she nodded agreement. "Mr. Travis is a man of many talents. A stage would be most beneficial for recitations and even graduation ceremonies."

"Exactly!" Miss Lalende held out her hand warmly. "Mr. Travis, you are to make yourself at home here. Come and go as you need. I realize you are a busy man, and we will do our best to accommodate you."

"I shall be back on the morrow, mademoiselle." Travis picked up his hat and prepared to leave. "I must see Miss Stanford home now. Thank you for your lovely company."

By the time they reached the street, Alicia was ready to burst, but whether with anger or laughter, she could not quite tell. She threw him a sidelong look. "That surpassed the drunken Indian act."

Travis nodded solemnly. "I surprise even myself sometimes."

She couldn't resist any longer. Laughter bubbled to the surface, floating clear and free in the crystalline winter air. There were times when he was so much like a small boy, she could not be angry with him.

Quite pleased with himself, Travis grinned and caught her

hand, tucking it securely within the crook of his arm. "That's much better. For a moment there, I thought you might shoot me. I only meant to make my presence acceptable to your formidable employer. She graciously supplied the extraneous details."

"I can imagine. She knows how to get things done and currying favor with the well-to-do makes her happy. How did you know to address her as mademoiselle? No one else does."

Travis shrugged. "Her first impression of me was less than the best, and she began to curse me roundly in French. I answered her."

Alicia could imagine how that would have startled the old lady. It silenced her. A half-breed boatman who spoke French. Was there anything he could not do?

At her continued silence Travis glanced down at her speculatively. "Alicia?"

She raised her eyes questioningly.

"I mean to court you properly, but if my company will cause problems, I am quite capable of using subterfuge."

They were walking down Main Street, surrounded by perfectly respectable shops, in the company of any number of respectable people. Why did he make her feel like they were all alone in a room together, contemplating the unspeakable? Something about his voice and the way he looked at her made her feel half naked and vulnerable.

"I have no doubt of that," Alicia answered dryly. "But I don't think either is necessary. I spoke hastily the other night."

Travis firmly propelled them onward. "I expected you to say that, but it's too late to change your mind. I choose to believe your words of the other night, not the rationalizations of today."

"Travis, I am not rationalizing." Alicia tried to jerk her arm away, but he held it too firmly and she did not want to make a scene. "I just want to be left alone."

Travis bent a skeptical gaze to her. "Shall we step down this alleyway and repeat the experiment? You didn't seem to find my attentions unbearable the other night."

Alicia clenched her teeth and lifted her chin in an attempt to fight off the color rising in her cheeks. "That was an exception. Everyone has moments of weakness."

As they turned the corner from Main Street onto the empty side street leading to the boardinghouse, Travis halted beneath the slender overhanging branches of a willow. A hint of amusement danced in his eyes as he gazed down at Alicia's prim bonnet and proudly tilted chin.

"I am happy to know that, Blue Eyes. You will excuse me if such a moment overtakes me now."

Before she could guess his audacious action, Travis bent to steal her lips, electrifying them with the heat of his kiss. His hand merely rested on her shoulder, applying no pressure, but she could not escape. The hunger she felt in the caress of his mouth totally disarmed her.

As if he had never molested her on a public street, Travis pulled her hand back through his arm again and proceeded toward the low gate marking the boardinghouse entrance.

"There is a church social Saturday night. I will be by at seven to take you. Will you still be at Mrs. Clayton's or will you have removed to your father's house?"

Still breathless and feeling decidedly weak in the knees, Alicia could only shake her head in reply. She didn't know where she would be. She didn't know where she wanted to be. And she certainly didn't know what she was going to do with this man who did not take no for an answer.

Travis cast her a curious glance. "It would be easier if you remain with Mrs. Clayton, but I am quite willing to appear on your father's doorstep should the need arise."

She could just imagine her father's reaction should Travis appear on his doorstep instead of one of the eligible suitors he had chosen. Travis could be as charming and polite as any gentleman, but the element of danger in his character could not be disguised. The self-assured manner in which he handled every situation gave her a false sense of security. He would protect her against all else, but who would protect her against him? No, her father was no fool. It would be best to keep the two apart.

"I am staying here for the time being," Alicia replied coolly, opening the gate. "You may appear anywhere you wish."

"I fully intend to." With a deep bow Travis left her there. He strolled away, whistling happily.

What was she going to do now?

There seemed to be little choice. With Becky peeking

through the curtains all agog and questioning persistently each time Travis walked her home, Alicia could be firm and decisive. But when her father brought up the subject of a small dinner party on Saturday night that would include several of the young men she had already met, Alicia found herself declaring she had other plans. If given the choice of two evils, she chose the familiar one.

She did her best to justify this madness. Teddy had seemed as harmless as those bland young men of her father's acquaintance, but he had attacked her horribly. Travis gave every appearance of being dangerous, but he had treated her with the most patient kindness. She would never understand men, but she must learn to live with them somehow.

Alicia's appearance at the church social on the arm of the rather foreign-looking newcomer caused a minor sensation, but it appeared only as a ripple of murmurs through the room. By the next day polite inquiries were being made, and Travis's name was tentatively added to several guest lists.

Alicia enjoyed the outing as she had not expected to do. Travis seemed to be on friendly terms with many of the men, and he quickly charmed the women. In his company the conversation never lagged, and Alicia found herself relaxing and laughing more than she had in months.

Travis took her home in a wagon she had not known he possessed. This time when he kissed her beneath the overhanging protection of the trees in Bessie's yard, Alicia did not protest. She had anticipated the moment and was more than ready for it. Still, the power he exerted over her caught her by surprise.

The bulk of their heavy overcoats prevented further contact than the pressure of mouth and hands, but Travis even made that sensation a sensual experience. Alicia could taste the hard lines of his lips as he moved them in feather-light caresses across her mouth, and she longed for them to cling hungrily as they had before. When he deepened the kiss, demanding response, she gave in willingly and still craved more. Even when he persuaded her to part her lips and his tongue invaded to take possession, she felt a hunger in her belly that had not been there before. She couldn't seem to get enough, even though this intimate mingling of their breaths and the lingering caress of his tongue left her breathless and warm all over.

As his kiss traveled upward, brushing her cheek, her eyes, and covering her hair, Alicia trembled against Travis's hard chest, not understanding what he had done to her. Was doing to her. His arms were strong and protective as they held her in place.

It seemed wisest if she put an end to this. Words were her only defense against the excitement inundating her senses.

"I don't even know who you are, Travis," she protested weakly, still taking advantage of the security his arms offered.

"Does it matter? Can't I be what you see now?" Travis cupped the back of her head in his hand, pressing it against his shoulder. He wished mightily to be relieved of the cumbersome clothes keeping him from feeling any part of her soft body but her breath, but this would have to suffice for now.

"Even that changes from day to day. How can I know what you are when you are never the same? Why do you play the part of drunken Indian one place and gentleman the next?"

"Can you not guess, Alicia? I did not think I made my intentions a secret. The river life is a lonely one and I am tired of it. I want to settle down, have a home, a wife to welcome me with open arms at day's end, and someday, perhaps, little ones to buy ponies for. Is there something wrong in my asking for what every man wants? And doing what is necessary to get it?"

Alicia tried to push him gently away, but Travis would not have it. His arms remained around her, his dark gaze searching the shadows for her face.

"You do not want me, then," she answered sadly. "Why not Babette? Why not all the other women who look at you with smiles in their eyes, as I cannot?"

A trace of a grin lifted a corner of his mouth. "Babette is much too young and foolish. I want a lady, Alicia Stanford, and I have found one. The land out here is wild and uncultured, but that is no reason that I must succumb to its forces. I will have a lady for wife, one who will raise my children properly. I do not require more than that."

Alicia began to grow angry with his arrogance. "You once told me you loved an Indian girl, but her family would not have you. Was she a lady? Was she not part of this wilderness?"

Travis dropped his arms and stared down at her. "My mother's people are called the grandfathers of all the Algonquin tribes. We are a proud race, and the woman I chose was of the family of one of our sachems. Under your standards she may not have been considered a lady, but under those of my mother's, she was royalty. Our children would have been raised to be leaders. Do not scorn that of which you have no understanding."

"I am sorry, Travis." Alicia turned away, gazing toward the welcoming light in Bessie's front window. "I did not mean to scorn. I simply do not understand. I had better go in now."

Travis caught her arm, forcing her to look back up to him. "There is nothing to understand, Alicia. I have told you before, our pasts are behind us. Only the future counts. Together I think we can make something of our lives. I am willing to try if you are."

And he was most certainly trying. Alicia offered a small smile. "I think we may both be hardened cases, but I'll not keep you from trying. Miss Lalende will benefit at least."

Travis laughed and released her. She had spunk. He gave her credit for that. Not many ladies would have been able to face him after what she had seen of him. He did not have to pretend with her. Sooner or later the fact that he was half Indian would come out and doors would start closing in his face, but not Alicia's, not for that reason. Hers would remain permanently barred because he was a man. At least that put him on an equal footing with his competition.

Alicia came to expect the noise of Travis's saw and hammer when she came out of her classroom at the end of each day. The habit of stopping to admire the platform emerging from the shavings of wood and sawdust developed without thought. Travis invariably had several of the children scrambling around the room, "helping" him, but whatever he was doing he would put aside as soon as she entered. He would dust himself off, send the children back to Miss Lalende, don his coat and hat, and escort her back to the boarding-house.

Where Bessie plied him with coffee and pie, and Becky hung on his every word. Travis accepted the attentions as if they were his due, and Alicia listened in open-mouthed astonishment as he and Bessie discussed the best way of persuading her to let down her hair a little. Alicia smacked away Becky's hand as she loosed one of her pins and tried to show what a curl around Alicia's face would look like, and she threw Travis an incensed look.

"I did not tell you how to wear your hair or your clothes when you looked like a savage. Just because you fancy yourself a gentleman now does not give you cause to criticize my fashionability or lack of it."

Mrs. Clayton appeared vaguely startled at this declaration, but Travis grinned and gave her a wink. "She's afraid some Indian will come along and try to scalp her if she looks too fetching."

Becky's whoops of laughter left Bessie even more confused. Alicia would have liked to kick him, but not only was that not ladylike, but he wore boots and wouldn't feel a thing. She doubted if Travis would feel a thing should she bring the sugar bowl down upon his head. He grew much too sure of himself.

Still, when Alicia came out of the classroom the next day to the sounds of silence, she felt a dismaying disappointment. She had no right to expect Travis to hang around waiting for her every day. He must have business of some sort to attend to, although she could not imagine what it was. No promises had been exchanged, no plans made. He was as free as she to do as he pleased.

Alicia halted in the door of the dance room to see if anything else had been done on the stage since yesterday. To her shock she found Travis sitting on the platform with his back against the wall, a small girl in his lap, and two hanging on his shoulders as he carefully carved away at a piece of wood.

The fact that the children hung around Travis did not surprise Alicia so much as recognition of which child graced the place of honor in his lap. The tiny six-year-old had been sent to Miss Lalende in desperation by doting grandparents who hoped the presence of other children would chase away some of the girl's fears and overwhelming shyness. Since her parents had died in an Indian raid on their home in Kentucky a year ago, the girl had scarcely said two words together.

The quartet caught sight of Alicia at the same time, and Alicia flushed slightly at the appraising gaze in Travis's eyes as he noted the two new curls peeking out of her bonnet in

front of her ears. But her curiosity was too great to let the
moment's embarrassment divert her. She stepped into the
room to examine the piece that Travis carved.

He handed the tiny wooden rabbit to the child in his lap,
who regarded it with awe. Alicia noted the other two children had similar talismans and surmised the youngest had
demanded the same. What she wasn't prepared for was the
child turning a frank and trusting gaze to her and asking a
complete question.

"Lonetree says there are good and bad Indians, but he's
lying, isn't he?" Wide blue eyes stared up at her for
affirmation.

Startled, Alicia met Travis's eyes, only to be met with
that unfathomable dark gaze with which he looked upon the
world. She turned back to the child cuddled securely against
his broad, linen-covered shirt.

"No, Penny, he is not lying. There are good and bad
Indians just as there are good and bad little girls. Why don't
you run along and show that lovely baby rabbit to Miss
Lalende?"

Penny digested this new piece of information solemnly.
She was well aware there were bad little girls, because one
of her cousins had pinched her and made her fall down just
that morning. She turned her solemn gaze back to Lonetree's
bronzed, angular face with wide-eyed surprise.

"Do Indians have little girls?"

Laughter leapt to his dark eyes as Travis placed the pre-
cocious child firmly on her feet. "They most certainly do.
And they love bunny rabbits just as much as you. Now, do
what Miss Alicia tells you."

The children scampered away as Travis rose to his full
height. The laughter had not quite left his eyes as he waited
for Alicia to approach.

"And what is your opinion, Blue Eyes? Am I a good or
bad Indian?"

She glanced to the broad, callused hands that could produce such delicate works of perfection and cradle a terrified
child, then back to the sharp planes of his high cheekbones.
She had once found those harsh features frightening but no
longer. In an odd way he was quite handsome; striking was
the word that came first to mind.

"I suspect that when you are bad, you are horrid," she

paraphrased the nursery rhyme calmly. "But for Penny's sake, thank you."

Travis wiped off his hands and reached for his coat, but his gaze didn't leave Alicia's primly proper figure. "I suppose most of us can say that. Will you go with me Saturday night anyway?"

The moment had come and she took a deep breath before replying. "No. My father is entertaining and would like me to be there. I have agreed."

Travis shrugged on his coat and regarded her carefully. "Fine. I will see you there."

15

ALICIA GLANCED nervously at the large paneled oak doors every time they opened, but the caller each time was one of the expected guests. As the room began to fill with men in somber frock coats and white cravats and women dazzling in diamonds and silks, she began to breathe easier. Her relationship with her father was a precarious one at the moment, and she had no desire to explain Travis to him.

She listened politely as one of her father's cronies detailed the growing tension in the northern territories of Indiana and Ohio, where the British still manned forts and outposts in strategic areas. The rash of Indian war parties and massacres in those territories he blamed solely on British instigation, and he could see no alternative but war with their former foes.

The argument wasn't a new one, nor had Alicia disdained it before. Only now, with Travis on her mind more than anything or anyone else, the words began to take on new meaning. The various tribes confused her, but Travis had said he was a Delaware. Delawares were among the tribes flocking to British forts for protection against the encroaching Americans. True, they had been the first tribe to sign a peace treaty with the newly formed American government some years ago, but that treaty had been hatcheted to death as swarms of settlers spilled over the mountains into the Ohio territories. The Delawares had been driven back until desperation made them turn on their former allies. Now many aided the British.

What made her think of Travis in connection with these incidents? He was half white. He had a father somewhere whom he had lived with, who had taught him the rudiments of being a gentleman. For all she knew, his father could live in Philadelphia and be a butcher or a tailor or a candlestick maker. What made her think of Travis and the British in the same breath? And why did it worry her? She gnawed at the problem even after the towheaded young man replaced her warmongering older companion. Sam chatted amiably of the dances at the assembly room, and Alicia only half listened. Could Travis be half British? Could he be a spy? Other than traveling up and down the troubled rivers unmolested, what would he gain from such a life?

Her thoughts had become so entangled she did not hear the front doors open one last time. Not until her father appeared in the doorway and began introducing the latest arrival did she look up. The shock of seeing that bronzed visage among this glittering company stopped her breath, and her thoughts tumbled into a chaotic frenzy.

Travis seemed to have no awareness of Alicia as Chester introduced him to Letitia and then to various other acquaintances near the doorway. Trapped in this corner with Sam, Alicia made no attempt to come forward and greet him. She did not think she had the courage to do so.

She couldn't believe her father had invited him. She had thought she would be safe here, but there seemed no escape. Alicia had not had time to learn the narrow confinement of a small community, but she was beginning to understand its dangers now. Avoiding Travis was the only means she had discovered to avoid her own disturbing responses, and now she learned she could not avoid him.

With relief she acknowledged the opening of the doors to the dining room. There would not be time for Travis to find her. She entered on Sam's arm and took her place near the head of the table with her father. Travis had been given a seat midway down the table.

Remembering those times when Travis had sat picking meat out of his bowl with his fingers, Alicia sent an occasional surreptitious glance in his direction. Other than the fact that his face was darker and more weathered, his appearance was little different from the other men. He used his napkin properly, knew the use of the finger bowls, and showed a thorough knowledge of the array of cutlery laid out beside his plate. How a keelboatman or Indian would possess any of this knowledge was beyond Alicia's comprehension, but she expelled a small sigh of relief. She had not wanted him to be any less than perfect in front of her father.

This insight into her own behavior brought a slight flush to her cheeks, and Alicia returned her attention to her table companions. The occasional laugh and the animated conversation at Travis's end of the table annoyed her because she could not hear what was said, but she was certain Travis was the source of it.

Even Letitia seemed to be smiling approvingly at the newcomer, and Alicia sensed her father's curiosity as the meal continued. The undercurrents of tension were more than Alicia could bear, and she scarcely noticed the contents of the plates set before her. She had the uneasiest feeling Travis had wrangled this invitation by dubious means, and her father would soon put an end to it.

If he did not, if Chester continued to sponsor Travis in St. Louis society, Travis was well along the road to respectability. Alicia knew this was his intent, but she began to doubt his motives. Ostensibly, he acted the part of gentleman to pursue her. That was what he would have her believe. But the Stanford home was the gathering place for not only the influential in society but in government. If there ever came a war, news would arrive here faster than anywhere else in the territory.

She had no reason to think such thoughts. They had never discussed politics. Travis had never given any indication that he was other than he seemed. That what he seemed was an impossible combination of savage and gentleman was difficult enough to absorb. Trying to piece together the man behind it would be a lifetime task.

When the ladies retired to the parlor after dinner, Alicia contemplated pleading a headache and going to the room that was hers. But curiosity kept her politely entertaining her father's guests at Letitia's side.

Her father's fiancée was an accomplished society matron, a descendant of an aristocratic French family. She made certain all her guests were comfortable before cornering Alicia briefly when she was alone.

"This Captain Travis your father brought in tonight, he is known to you?"

Alicia always felt awkwardly tall in Letitia's petite presence, and she maneuvered herself into a chair before replying. "I traveled here with him," she replied cautiously.

Letitia clapped her hands happily and perched on the edge of a delicate needlepoint chair. "Then you know all about him. Who is he? Where does he come from? What does he do?"

Lifting her coffee cup, Alicia smiled wryly. "You will have to ask Mr. Travis that. Let me know when you conjure an answer from him."

Letitia grimaced with dissatisfaction. "But he is such a gentleman, and he speaks so highly of you. Surely you must know something? He looks almost Spanish, but his speech . . . Every so often, there is this British ring to it."

Perhaps that was the connection that had been bothering her. Alicia had met men from England in the drawing rooms of her family and was familiar with the accent. Travis's American slang and occasional backwoods drawl had little relation to the pompous tones of the men she had met, but every so often—Letitia was right. Occasionally a British word or a clipped accent escaped.

"He only tells me that the past is over, and the future is what we make of it. He has never treated me with anything less than respect, and I have known him to be kind and generous. He has a talent for carving wood into any shape, and he has generously offered to contribute a stage to the school. I suspect he is like most men in matters that are not mentioned before ladies, but . . ." Alicia shrugged her shoulders, knowing her father's worldly fiancée would understand. She had learned that much about Letitia in these past weeks.

Letitia's eyes narrowed slightly in thought, and she threw Chester's daughter a look of curiosity. "He is very handsome. Now, if he is only wealthy—"

"If he is not, he will be," Alicia answered curtly as the door opened and the men began to join them. She should have told Letitia of Travis's ancestry, but that didn't seem to be her place. If Travis wished it to be known, he could do it himself. It was doubtful that it could be kept a secret with every keelboatman on the river knowing of it, and his own infrequent references, such as the use of his Indian name to Penny. But she would not make it her place to spread the word that would surely close doors to him.

Letitia drifted off to cling to Chester's arm, and Alicia again debated making her escape. Before she could, Sam hurried forward to capture her attention.

"Your father's wedding has been the talk of the town for weeks," he exclaimed happily. "Is there any chance that I might escort you? He says there will be dancing at the reception, and I have been practicing the waltz just for you."

Alicia hid her impatience and allowed Sam's chatter to tumble on. Though certainly half a dozen years older than she, Sam seemed more child than adult. The only offspring of a wealthy elderly couple, he had been pampered all his life and stood to inherit a sizable fortune, if he did not gamble it all away. He certainly seemed harmless enough, and Alicia did nothing to discourage his persistence. That seemed to please her father, she could tell by the contented glance he sent her.

Finishing his cheroot and brandy, Travis entered the parlor a short time later. Instantly he sought Alicia, and a small frown developed between his eyes. She had been with that young puppy when he arrived and had kept him entertained throughout dinner. Knowing Alicia's deep-rooted fear of men, he had never given serious consideration to competition, but he could see now that he had underestimated the situation. He should have known she would seek her father's approval, and she had certainly chosen the right mollycoddle for it. Samuel Howard had as much spine as a wet noodle. Alicia could twist him into circles and use him for another pretty bauble around her little finger.

Alicia jerked nervously as she caught Travis's approach from the corner of her eye. He seemed to be making a single-minded beeline directly for this corner, and she discerned a gleam of determination in his eye. She should have known better than to think he would leave her alone when he had evidently spent the meal impressing Letitia with his admiration for her stepdaughter-to-be.

Sam jumped as Travis clapped him genially on the back. With a polite bow and murmured greeting to Alicia, Travis turned to the younger man. "Surprised to see you here, Howard. I thought I remembered someone mentioning another party where you were expected tonight."

Judging from the deep color rising in Sam's face, the party was of a less than respectable nature, Alicia surmised. She wondered about Travis's source of information, which turned her mind back to the question of Travis's occupation. He had hinted that he was a gambler, but her father had called him a businessman. That seemed to be the way of

things with this man, as if being half of one race and half of
another made him two people, with access to twice as much
information as any other.

Within a few uncomfortable minutes Sam departed, and
Travis pulled a chair forward, making himself comfortable
while cutting off all access to the rest of the room.

"Do I have cause to be jealous?" he asked casually,
completely throwing her off balance as he had intended.

Alicia reacted angrily. "Cause has nothing to do with it.
You have no right to be. I don't know whose arm you
twisted to get in here, but I'll thank you to leave me alone."

Travis leaned back in the uncomfortably small chair, his
lanky frame looking out of place in the delicate drawing
room. "When another of the guests conveniently failed to
show and I happened to appear at the right moment, your
father invited me. I didn't twist your father's arm, though I
did surrender a rather substantial IOU to another party in
exchange for the vacancy. And you may save your thanks,
for I fully intend to monopolize your company for the brief
time allowed me. I had to plead another engagement as
excuse for appearing at the door wearing these duds."

His frankness twisted a smile from Alicia despite her
anger. She could almost feel the warmth of his dark gaze as
Travis searched her face for some reaction, and she could
not maintain the proper degree of haughtiness to put him in
his place. He knew her too well.

"You have managed to pass Letitia's inspection, though
she has cross-examined me on your background. If you are
to wrest any further invitations from my father, you had
best come up with a respectable occupation and a good
story to explain your past."

Travis admired the dangle of tiny ringlets on Alicia's
cheek as she glanced away from his penetrating gaze. To his
eyes she still seemed to possess a certain fragility that her
returning health belied. Lamplight flickered along the flawless, creamy skin of her throat above the décolletage of her
simple gown, and the locket dangling in that shadowy valley
held him fascinated. He meant to remove that trinket and
the velvet gown one of these days, replace them with sapphires to match her eyes and nothing else but the soft curl of
her hair. A surge of desire threatened his composure, and
Travis abruptly jerked his thoughts back to the subtle spar-
ring of their conversation.

"I see no need to explain myself to anyone. I have made several investments since arriving in St. Louis, and your father is aware that I am looking for others. Cash is a scarce commodity in these parts. The citizens of St. Louis are more than happy to accept mine."

"For as long as you have it. Gamblers tend to lose as much as they win and then more."

Travis chuckled at this scornful but eminently skillful manner of questioning. "You might ask your friend Samuel about that. Experience tells me that the house is the only winner in games of chance."

Frustrated by this line of questioning, Alicia was seeking another tactic when a servant appearing in the doorway distracted her attention. Instead of calmly gliding into the room bearing the caller's card, the man seemed agitated and uncertain. Catching Alicia's eye, he sidled along the edge of the crowd, avoiding his employer.

"What is it, Jasper?" Alicia asked impatiently. Such behavior would not have been tolerated in Philadelphia, but trained servants were few and far between out here.

"A man at the door, miss. Asking for you or someone called Lonetree. He's not a gentleman, miss. Should I have your father speak with him?"

Alicia and Travis exchanged bewildered glances. When Travis rose, she hurried to go with him. He gave her a questioning look but did not stand in her way.

Alicia recognized the formidable bulk of one of Travis's keelboatmen waiting in the front entrance. He had removed his dilapidated felt hat, but a dark bandanna still covered his long, rank hair. He shifted his heavy weight uneasily as an unfamiliar Travis in frock coat and linen approached with a dazzling lady garbed in velvet and lace on his arm. Though he knew this was the young widow who had laughed at their jokes and watched their brawls and eaten from the same pot with the crew, he could not quite look her in the eye under these circumstances.

"What is it, Ryder?" Travis asked impatiently. He knew they were drawing attention from a few idlers in the hallway, but his main concern was with the man's message. It had to be urgent to send him this far uptown.

"Auguste sent me. There's been a fracas down at the saloon, and the little girl's been hurt. She's crying for Miz

Stanford, but Auguste says we can't move her till the doc comes."

The entire message left Alicia thoroughly confused, but Travis seemed to grasp the meaning quickly enough. "Becky? What in hell was Becky doing at the saloon?" he whispered fiercely, catching Alicia's arm before she could charge off in one direction or another. He felt her give a jerk of astonishment, but she remained at his side.

"We were just funnin'. One of the fellows ran into her down to the docks, and he was for giving her a good time and then we remembered it was Auguste's birthday and well . . ."

Travis gave a pithy curse and turned to Alicia. "Go back to your guests. I'll see to this. Will you want her back after this, or shall I find a place for her to stay?"

The shock of his meaning knocked the breath from her, and Alicia's eyes widened as she stared up at him. She had given Becky permission to step out for the evening. She had never dreamed it would be with one of the rough crewmen. But who else would the child know in this city? In an instant she recovered her wits and gestured to the astonished servant.

"Jasper, fetch a wrap for me. Tell my father there's been an emergency and I've been called away."

The servant hurried to do as told without questioning, but Travis was not so agreeable. He shook her as if that would put sense into her head.

"She's down at the saloon, Alicia. You can't go in there. By now they're likely to be tearing the place from stem to stern. I'll take Becky to Mrs. Clayton's if you want. Get someone to escort you there."

"Take your hands off me, Travis," Alicia demanded coldly. "I don't understand what has happened, but I'll not leave Becky surrounded by great, cloddy hulks of mindless buffoons. She might deserve a beating, but she doesn't deserve that."

Jasper hurried back with a fur-lined, hooded pelisse and helped her into it. Travis frowned but knew short of tying her up he could not force her to stay behind. If anyone needed a beating, it was this stubborn female, but far be it from him to offer such advice.

Chester Stanford came hurrying out into the hall just as the front door opened, sending in a swirl of dry snow.

"What is going on here? Where are you going, Alicia?" He sent an amazed glare to the barbarian giant standing in his foyer.

"My maid has been injured, Papa. Travis has offered to see me home. Don't worry, I'm in good hands." She pressed a brief kiss to her father's cheek and plunged out into the night without a look back.

Travis could do no less than follow.

16

LIGHT SNOW blew around them as they hurried down darkened streets. Travis had not needed a wagon for himself and had not expected company in leaving. The crewman would not have gone near a horse if his life depended on it. Fortunately, the saloon was a fairly new one and not too far into town.

Travis made no attempt to prevent Alicia from entering once they reached the brightly lighted windows of the same tavern where they had run into each other just weeks before. He held the door and Alicia hurried in, her gaze anxiously scanning the interior for some sign of Becky. It did not even occur to her to wonder how Travis knew which tavern she would be in.

She held her tongue at the sight of overturned tables and chairs and a couple of men still lying about the floors nursing wounds or lost in drunken slumber. Regular patrons apparently had forgotten the row and had returned to the bar, but they turned to stare in disbelief as Travis entered with a lady on his arm. Alicia scarcely noted their stares as her own focused on the group in the far corner.

She recognized Auguste and Dr. Farrar and several of the other men from the boat huddled around the forlorn figure on the bench. The gaudily dressed women crowding in between them, however, offering advice and soothing words, brought a gasp of surprise to Alicia's lips.

She should have known Travis associated with such creatures. The encounter with Molly had taught her that. She had just never seen him in any world but her own, and this knowledge of his world shocked her. And it was obviously his world. The men at the bar greeted him familiarly, and the crowd in the corner looked up in relief at his approach.

She had wanted to know more about this renegade keelboatman. Well, now she knew. Boon companion to gamblers
and whores.

Travis read the tight look of disapproval on Alicia's face
without surprise, but to his relief she held her tongue. She
hurried forward to sit beside Becky as the doctor completed
his examination of her contorted arm, and the plain maid in
her torn finery burst into tears and fell into Alicia's arms.

"I'm sorry, Miss Alicia, I truly am. It was just a bit of
fun. I didn't think it would hurt none."

Alicia held the girl and looked questioningly over her
head to Dr. Farrar.

"The arm's broken." The young doctor showed no disapproval as he opened his bag. "She's still in a state of shock,
but she'll be feeling it shortly. We'll have to set it." He
glanced up to Travis, who had shouldered his way next to
Alicia. "It might be better if you took the lady to another
room. It won't be pleasant."

"No! Don't leave me, Miss Alicia!" Becky cried frantically, grasping her cloak. The pain and shock had decimated her usual tough defenses, reducing her to the child
she should have been.

"Auguste, you'd better hold her. Becky, stop that cater-
wauling. Miss Alicia can't hold you while the doctor fixes
that arm. Behave yourself or I'll tell her to send you back
where you belong." Travis barked orders while clearing a
space for the doctor to work in. He knew better than to
expect a response to his commands from Alicia. He merely
nodded to Auguste to lift Becky up while he grabbed Alicia
by the arm and prevented her from following.

"Take her in the back room. There's been enough free
entertainment here for the evening."

Becky's wail of protest died quickly as she found herself
encompassed in the arms of the powerful keelboatman.
Alicia tried to follow, but Travis planted both feet on the
ground and firmly held her back. There was no question of
breaking his iron grip, and she turned to glare at him.

"I can't desert her. I'm all she has. Let go, Travis."

"She'll not know who is with her in a minute, but if you
insist on fighting me, we'll provide further entertainment for
our audience." Travis placidly retained his grip on her arm.

Alicia glanced quickly at the interested faces of the various females watching them, then back to the men at the bar.

Every eye in the room seemed to be waiting to see what they would do next, and a flush of heat began to flood her cheeks.

"For pity's sake, let me go to the back room with Becky," she whispered, though she no longer struggled against his grasp.

"In a minute." Travis nodded peremptorily to one of the women. "Gladys, bring the lady some wine."

Becky's scream pierced the air before the woman could do as told. Alicia turned white and clung to Travis's arm as the scream quivered and died. Gently he pushed her into a seat and took the wine from the tray when the woman returned.

"Drink this. It will be over in a minute, and we'll take her home. You shouldn't have come. I warned you."

Alicia glanced nervously at the room's occupants. With Travis fairly well blocking her from view, most had returned to their prior pursuits, but the curiosity of the garishly dressed women had obviously been aroused. They kept glancing in Alicia's direction and whispering among themselves.

"How do you know these people?" Alicia murmured.

"I own half interest in the place. It pays to know them." Travis watched her expression carefully.

She didn't blink an eye, but she didn't look him in the face, either. "How fitting." The comment came without inflection.

His eyebrows turned down in a frown. "From the amount of wine consumed at your father's table tonight, I wouldn't think you a temperance advocate."

"There were women at the table tonight, but you wouldn't have me believe they were of the same sort as these?"

A white-toothed grin flashed across his bronzed features as Travis followed the trail of her thoughts. "Lonely men are victims of many sins. Would you deny us all pleasures?"

"That's disgusting." Alicia could not meet his eyes, imagining him in the arms of one of those frowsy, painted females. How could he kiss them and then turn to her? She wanted to go home and scrub her face.

"No, it's not," Travis informed her mildly. "They chose their profession. It is unfortunate that we cannot all have money and lawfully wedded spouses, but it is not disgusting."

Alicia glanced back to his impassive expression, her curiosity unsated. "If men cannot control their"—she scrambled for a word—"desires and so must frequent such creatures, why is it that women must remain virtuous? Because they don't have the same desires?"

Travis caught her hand and played with the long graceful fingers. "Women have the same needs as men, but society forces them to pretend otherwise. If it did not, we would be overrun with children who had no fathers."

There was logic in that, but her own experience did not support it completely. She had felt nothing but disgust for the act that a man had forced upon her. And here were women who obviously enjoyed the act, but seemed not to bear the results of it. It was all too confusing, and she was too distraught to consider it rationally.

"With a harem like that, what man needs a wife? I want to see Becky." Alicia rose grandly, her chin tilted upward.

Travis stood, but did not release her hand. "Some men are a trifle choosier than others. You will remember admitting that we all have our weaker moments." Her hand trembled in his and he brought it up to cover his arm before escorting her toward the back room. He would not lie and pretend he was an angel, but he would not declare his obsession with her, either. It had been four months since he had first laid eyes on this lady, and he had not been able to look at another woman since. She would drive him to madness if he did not break down her reserve soon.

Alicia heard, but chose to ignore Travis's meaning. If she could force herself to look at these things logically, she would have to admit prostitutes had their uses. If she must acquire a husband, it would be infinitely preferable if he were to unleash his lusts on someone else. But she wasn't certain she was prepared to be logical.

Becky moaned softly as Alicia touched her forehead with a cool hand, but she did not waken. Her arm had been splinted and strapped and a sling provided for comfort. Alicia glanced skeptically to the doctor. "She will be all right?"

"Bit of a hangover in the morning and the arm will ache, but she'll recover. She won't be of much use for anything for a few weeks, though."

Alicia managed a dry smile. "Becky's only use is flapping her mouth. I don't think that was harmed. I'm grateful for your help, sir. Can she be moved?"

Dr. Farrar threw an anxious glance to the gentleman at the lady's side. "It might be preferable if she stayed here. The incident is certain to cause talk, and the girl is obviously not a proper lady's maid . . ."

Standing in the shadows, the taciturn Auguste appeared ruffled at these implications, but Alicia's reactions calmed his anger.

"People may talk as they like. Becky is my friend and if it is safe to move her, she will go home with me. I'll not leave her in a place like this."

Travis shrugged laconically and offered his hand to the physician. "The lady is right. The girl has suffered enough and should not be vilified for one slip. We'll find a way to keep Miss Stanford out of it."

Auguste gently lifted the helpless patient and strode for the door, leaving no other choice but for the others to follow.

Bessie clicked her tongue and hovered like a mother hen while the sleeping maid was carried to her trundle bed and tucked away. Leaving Becky to the attentions of Auguste and the landlady, Alicia brought Travis to the kitchen and offered him coffee.

She had shed the heavy pelisse, and the clinging velvet evening gown looked out of place in this homey kitchen. Yet she moved about as if at home there, and Travis relaxed and followed her slender form with his gaze. In the half-light the white of her bare throat and shoulders held his rapt attention. When she bent to pour the coffee in his cup, he nearly lost control, and his hand grasped her wrist convulsively.

Alicia looked faintly surprised as Travis removed the pot from her hand to pour his own, but the tension in his grasp sent messages even she could understand. She sat down abruptly across from him, but Travis did not forfeit his hold.

His black gaze held hers before traveling downward over the feathery shadow of her lashes against pale cheeks, the small spot of color accenting the delicate bones beneath, and full lips that promised much but quivered now. His hand left the cup to trace the frail line of her jaw and slide upward to the thick waves of hair above her temples.

Mesmerized by the gentle longing of his touch, Alicia could not move away. Travis did things to her insides that

she did not understand, did not want to contemplate. But
when she looked up into the angular shadows of his face,
she had the urge to return the touch, to brush the lock of
dark hair back from his forehead and feel the heat of his lips
upon her palm. She shuddered, incapable of comprehending
how this had come about.

"This hasn't been the way I planned the evening. What
do I have to do to persuade you to come out of your ivory
tower?"

His touch sent delicious shivers down her spine, and Alicia had to turn her gaze to her cup to keep her feelings
hidden. She kept reminding herself she knew nothing of this
man, but in his presence it never seemed to matter.

"If the world I live in is an ivory tower, then I cannot
come out of it, Travis. Perhaps you are pursuing the wrong
woman."

"I'm not some young fool who falls for a pair of pretty
eyes, Alicia. I know what I want. I haven't made a secret of
it."

"But how do I know what I want?" Alicia's anguished
gaze defied answering. "I am enjoying teaching. I did not
enjoy what little I know of men. And I know nothing of you
beyond the fact that you are arrogant, presumptuous, and
persistent!"

This outraged declaration of his flaws brought a chuckle
from Travis. He sat back in his chair and gazed contentedly
at her as he sipped from his cup.

"You can teach anywhere; that's not a problem. The only
man you've known is a spineless bastard. You are as innocent of men as any virgin. So it seems the only stumbling
point is me. You know I'm not a proper Philadelphian
gentleman, but I don't think you're well suited for that
brand of dandy, and I think you know it. I think you're
constructing imaginary barriers to keep me out, but I'll
make a deal with you. There's an assembly dance next
Saturday night. Go with me, and you can spend the evening
asking me any question that pops into that fascinating mind
of yours. Then we can proceed from there."

Alicia read the devilment in his eyes easily enough. He
didn't have dancing on his mind. The assembly room wouldn't
have waltzes, and they couldn't talk while doing an alle-
mande. That was just an excuse to get her out of the house
alone. Well, she had a serious crimp for that plan.

"My father is getting married next Saturday. The reception will last well into the evening. I am expected to be there."

"I don't suppose you would consider just walking out with me on Friday?" Travis shook his head before she even answered. "No, I can see you would not. You are driving me mad, Alicia. Do I have to kidnap you?"

There was something so wistful in the way he said those words, so totally uncharacteristic of the self-assured man she knew, that it struck a sympathetic chord in Alicia's heart. He was trying so hard to reach her, and she kept backing away. What would she gain by hiding from the one man who knew her past and still wanted her? She did not think anything could come of it, but she valued his friendship. Nothing she did seemed to shock him, as it had the good doctor earlier this evening. She needed this friend whose support she could count on. And perhaps, just a little bit, he needed her.

Her gaze softening, Alicia gave in. "I can get you an invitation to the reception. My father promises lots of waltzes."

Travis set his cup down and leaned forward until the scent of her perfume filled his nostrils and he could see the crystalline facets of sapphire eyes. With the tip of his finger he lifted her chin, and his mouth came down warmly over hers.

The gentle invasion of his tongue sent a sweet languor spreading through her body, and Alicia lost all concentration, wanting only for this moment to last forever. It couldn't, however, and the sound of voices coming down the hall put a lingering end to this trance.

"We'll dance, then we'll talk, and then I will begin showing you what you have been missing."

His words were whispered so softly, Alicia could have imagined them, but knew she had not. Her heart set up a hammering that would not still even when Bessie and Auguste entered the room. She felt the heat rise to her cheeks, and Travis's proprietary hand at her back did not relieve it. She didn't know what she had done, but this time she would not back down from it.

Becky played the part of subdued and chastised patient for several days, until Auguste knocked on the kitchen door to inquire after her health and leave a small box of candy.

After that her cockiness returned, and she made a shambles
of all attempts to teach her the wrongfulness of her ways.

"Auguste is just a river rat like all the rest, Rebecca!"
Alicia admonished as she heard for the thousandth time the
man's praises on Becky's tongue. "Come spring, he will be
gone, and then where will you be if you let him sweet-talk
you into his bed?"

"No better off than you with that Indian of yours, I
suppose!" Becky retorted. "Don't think people haven't noticed how he always turns up when you're around. And I
sure don't see you discouragin' him none!"

Alicia bit back a sharp answer. The wise little brat was
right. Letitia had already warned her gently, and her father
had not been placated easily, but Alicia didn't intend to
heed flapping tongues. Perhaps Travis was using her, but
she in turn was using him. She wanted to know if she could
ever be a complete woman, and Travis would be the one to
teach her. Perhaps he would be gone by spring, but by then
it would not matter.

Perhaps there was little difference in herself and Becky
after all. With virtue gone, it did not seem to matter so
much if they fell victim to temptation. And they both preferred the not-so-tame boatmen to the proper, sedate fellows that could offer respectability. Travis had been right
about that. None of the gentlemen her father had introduced to her had induced her to consider giving up what
remained of her virtue. Only Travis with his arrogant masculinity had tempted her to reconsider her vows of celibacy.

Even knowing what he was did not dissuade her from the
folly of welcoming Travis when he appeared on her doorstep or from obtaining the invitation to the reception for
him. He built keelboats and owned a saloon and was half-
Indian and possibly a British spy, but he also made her
laugh, talked to her of subjects beyond the weather, re-
spected her decisions, and made her feel as if she were the
most beautiful woman on earth. Why should she resist him?
She had spent her life adhering to her mother's strictures
and had ended up miserable. It was time she enjoyed herself
a little and worried about the consequences later.

Travis noted this new confidence in her with wonder and
delight. The woman on his arm when he walked her home
met his gaze boldly, laughed out loud at his sallies, and
greeted the curious with polite warmth and assurance. He

began to see the confident woman she must once have been, the one who had dealt with senators and ambassadors and polite society in general. This woman could deal with the slights and barbs that would accompany her attachment to a half-breed river boatman. He had meant to have her at all costs, but this new Alicia made the future even more promising.

If ever his past should catch up with him, she would be able to handle that too.

17

ALICIA MET HIM at the door and ushered him in, the tension in her greeting and the suppressed excitement in her eyes telling Travis she had seen through all his euphemisms and participated in her own seduction. The knowledge sent blood boiling through his veins and his long-denied loins responded with an urgency that could have been embarrassing had he not still worn his heavy greatcoat.

"The wedding was marvelous. They looked so happy together." Beneath Travis's heated gaze, Alicia's voice sounded husky and artificial even to herself. She hastened to help him with his coat while the butler dealt with another of the arriving guests.

"Good. They will be so engrossed in each other, they will never miss us. When can we leave?" Travis murmured wickedly in her ear as he arranged to entangle her in his coat before the butler could come to the rescue.

Alicia sent him a shocked look, but smiled at the eagerness that matched her own. She waited until they entered the safety of the crowded ballroom before replying. "The dancing is just beginning. I cannot possibly leave until everyone has arrived and is made comfortable."

Travis threw a glance to the massive bowl of punch on the buffet and the stock of champagne beside it and grinned. "By the looks of that supply, everyone should be very happy within the hour. Dance with me every dance, and I may endure the wait."

"That's impossible and you know it," she scolded. "Make yourself at home and I will be with you as soon as I can."

He would not let her escape that easily. "Give me all the waltzes, then." Travis held her hand behind her skirts where no one could see. She looked ravishing tonight with chest-

nut curls piled in soft swirls that looked as if they might
tumble down upon her bare throat and shoulders at any
moment. She wore one of those daringly simple gowns
again, this one of some frail material that glimmered in soft
bronzes and golds depending on her movement and the
lamp light. A ruffle of delicate lace at her neckline protected her modesty, but catching his breath at the discovery,
Travis noted she wore shockingly little underneath. The
satin belt beneath her breasts emphasized an asset that
needed no further support. A moment of blind jealousy
shook him as he realized every man in the room could see
what he preferred displayed only to him.

Oblivious of this reaction, Alicia shook her head smilingly
and disengaged her hand. "Two is the maximum, sir. You
would not sully my reputation, would you?"

The look she gave him was so impudent, Travis could
scarcely keep from laughing. The wait would be worth
every painful minute. He just might occupy himself flatten-
ing any man who dared look twice at her.

He allowed her to slip away then, vowing silently that
after the second waltz they would leave. He might never
take her home again.

Alicia felt Travis's gaze following her as she circled the
room, greeting guests, making certain everyone had refreshments and that the punch bowl was kept filled. Each time
she glanced up from a conversation, she located his tall,
broad-shouldered figure easily by the magnetic pull of his
dark gaze. No matter what Travis was doing or to whom he
was speaking, he would catch her glance, and the look on
his bronzed visage would send a physical shock rippling
through her. If the thought had occurred to her that he was
using her position to further his own, she discarded it now.
He scarcely paid heed to the governor himself for scowling
while she danced with Sam Howard.

At the end of that set Travis silently appeared at her side,
his lips set in a grim line as he gazed upon Alicia's heated
cheeks. Before he could speak, Chester Stanford hurried
through the crowd to catch his daughter's attention.

"Alicia, for heaven's sake, find someone who knows how
to waltz. Letitia has agreed to dance it just this once, but
she will refuse if we are the only ones on the floor."

Alicia gazed tenderly upon her father's flushed and nervous features. He was not an overtly handsome man, but his

graying hair gave him an air of distinction. It was patently
obvious that he adored his charming new wife and wished
desperately to please her.

Ignoring the slow grin on the lips of the man at her side,
Alicia promised she would join them on the dance floor.
Only then did Chester give Travis a polite nod of recogni-
tion before hurrying off.

"The fates are with me, it seems," Travis drawled. "He
can't object to my escorting you on the floor now."

She ignored his acknowledgment that her father might
raise objections. Travis might not fit the classic mold of
society gentleman, but he conducted himself with all the
necessary aplomb, giving no one reason to complain of his
manners. They might object to his occupation or his race,
but that was an awkward nicety. Half the people here were
descendants of trappers and traders, and their races and
nationalities were blurred at best. If she did not care about
Travis's background, she'd be damned if she would let anyone else look down upon it.

When the waltz began, Chester and Letitia floated out
onto the floor. Letitia held the graceful train of her gown in
a loop upon her wrist, and her tiny feet expertly followed
the practiced ease of her new husband's steps. The look of
rapture on their faces tore at Alicia's heart strings, and her
eyes were so blurred with tears she almost missed Travis's
formal bow.

Once she was in his arms, however, pure exhilaration
replaced tears. Travis held her firmly, moving with all the
grace of which he was capable, and when she looked up to
him with the breathless pleasure of the music, the look in
his eyes burned paths of fire to her heart. The last time they
had done this in darkness. Now, beneath the glittering crystal chandelier, she could not tear her fascinated gaze from
his face. She scarcely heard the music or felt the floor as his
look and his touch conveyed his desires as no words ever
could.

Luckily, the dance floor filled and few noted the passion
with which they traversed the room, their bodies moving as
one in a ritual as old as mankind. Those who preferred to
stand and watch focused their attention on the resplendent
bride and groom.

When the dance ended, Travis refused to release his hold

on Alicia's waist. Hand firmly on the small of her back, he conducted her through the crowded ballroom to the partial freedom of the wide entrance hall.

"Where are we going?" Alicia asked breathlessly, not in the least sorry to leave the crush of dancers behind if it meant continuing this pleasant intimacy.

"Somewhere private," Travis muttered thickly, unable to tolerate the torture of waiting any longer.

"But we can't leave—" Alicia glanced over her shoulder to the merrymakers behind them. No one seemed to notice their parting.

"Just watch," Travis responded grimly. With a quick glance up and down the hallway, he steered her toward the small family parlor at the rear. It was early yet and no one had taken advantage of this haven. "Wait here. I'll get our coats."

Alarm swept through Alicia's veins as he abruptly left her in this darkened room. She had time to escape, to run back to the company and bright lights, to put a halt to this madness. No matter how much she trusted him, she could not go alone with this stranger who had so rapidly dominated her life. She could not.

But she did not leave the place where he left her. Travis was back in moments, bearing the fur-lined pelisse he recognized as hers, wearing his own hastily donned coat.

"My carriage is at the back gate. No one will see us leave." Swiftly Travis bundled her into her outer garments and half pushed, half carried her out the French doors to the garden. The winter sun had set hours before, and the darkness was unbroken by anything but the lights from the ballroom. They skirted these easily.

Once in the darkness of the carriage, Travis took the time to slide his hands beneath Alicia's pelisse and pull her to him. The heat of his hard body after the coldness of the night frightened her, but the tingling familiarity of his mouth upon hers dissipated those ghosts. Hard and warm, his lips sought the full curve of hers, playing along the corners, drifting across her cheek, coming back to incite greater longings.

"Travis, please." Alicia pushed ineffectually against his chest, panic climbing at the swiftness with which he conquered all her defenses. "You promised we would talk."

"And we will, my love. I just wanted to make certain you stayed warm." Travis caressed the length of her side in the sheath of silk and pressed a kiss upon her forehead.

"You succeeded quite nicely," Alicia admitted as his right arm pulled her closer while his left picked up the reins. Even through the layers of clothing, his palm scorched her skin. She had to be crazed, but she snuggled closer to his side until their hips touched. "Where did you get the carriage?"

"You are not the only one with influential friends. I borrowed it." He grinned, the anticipation racing through his veins producing a euphoria more effective than champagne. "I did not think it wise to parade you through town just yet."

"Wise man," Alicia commented dryly. "Where are we going?"

"To a place where we can talk undisturbed and where I can make love to you with no one being the wiser. Such places are few and far between in this town."

A small frisson of fear chilled her insides, but Alicia refused to let it conquer her. She had known this was his intention from the very first, and she felt confident she could stop him if the experiment failed.

She had not counted on being carried down the path to the river, away from all signs of civilization. She gasped in dismay as Travis lifted her into the keelboat tied firmly to the bank. The cold wind off the water blew straight through the thin silk of her fragile gown, and the lapping of the current against wood provided the only night sounds.

"Travis, this is insane. We will freeze to death," she whispered, terrified.

His shoulders made even broader by the shape of his great coat, Travis's large frame blocked out the few glowing lights of the city above. "I am not likely to let that happen," he replied gruffly. "Come see what I have done."

For some reason, it did not surprise her that Travis had been the one to buy the boat back from her. What did surprise her was the use he had made of it. The cargo cabin had been converted to living quarters and office space. A high-backed desk with pigeon holes spilled over with papers and invoices in one corner. A low-slung bed with no head or footboards other than the slats holding the corner posts together graced the far end of the room. A brightly colored

Indian blanket covered the linens, and the same design appeared again on the rug on the floor. Along one wall he had built a banquette that served as seating, its hard platform covered with cushions and piled high with pillows.

"It's lovely, Travis." Guessing he had done most of the carpentering himself, Alicia was astounded by his talents.

"Solved the housing and the privacy problem anyway." With uncharacteristic modesty Travis shrugged and helped her with her pelisse.

Escorting Alicia to the cushion-covered banquette, he lit a second lamp and adjusted the heat of the brazier. As Alicia admired his handiwork, Travis raided the small stock of wine he had built since arriving in St. Louis. Glasses miraculously appeared from one of the cabinets beneath the banquette, and he placed them on the shelf behind the cushions before filling them.

"I think you might find this more to your taste than the last batch I offered you." Travis sat down beside her and held the glass for Alicia to take.

Hesitantly Alicia accepted the goblet, throwing Travis an uncertain look. She had no head for alcohol, and she had already drunk several glasses of champagne. Just his masculine proximity made her giddy enough. More wine did not seem particularly prudent.

Noticing her hesitancy, Travis set the glass back on the shelf. "I want you to be comfortable, Alicia, not asleep. Are you warm enough?"

Without a shawl, the thin gown with its puffed sleeves provided little covering. Travis admired the firm lines of the lovely arms thus exposed, and his fingers drifted over one to test her comfort for himself.

Alicia shivered beneath his touch, but she felt no cold. "I am fine. It is quite warm in here." Nervousness made witty conversation impossible.

Travis stood and strode around the room, adjusting the brazier again, trimming the lamp wick. He removed his fitted frock coat and threw it over the desk chair, discarding his short waistcoat at the same time. In white linen and tight trousers, with his black hair tumbling over tanned skin and the unfathomable pits of his black eyes, he appeared more pirate than Indian or gentleman. Alicia could not avoid noting the muscular grace of his movements. The trousers disguised nothing of his powerful thighs and narrow hips, and his shoulders seemed to strain at every seam of the shirt as he turned to face her.

Alicia's heart pounded as he approached and sat beside her once again, but Travis did no more than bend over to remove his formal shoes.

"I don't know why people can't wear moccasins all the time," he grumbled half to himself. "If we were born to wear shoes, we wouldn't have toes."

Alicia laughed softly, wishing she had the daring to touch the thick locks of his hair curled about his collar. With sudden courage she sipped the wine he had given her. He was so close, she could draw her hand down the rippling musculature of his back, but she didn't possess that much courage.

Travis straightened again, his gaze falling approvingly on her pinkened cheeks as she sipped the wine. When she set the goblet aside, he bent to taste wine-sweetened lips.

Alicia gasped at the suddenness of his action, and her hand came up between them, but her first touch of his wide chest decimated her defenses as quickly as his kiss. She could feel the pounding of his heart beneath her fingertips, and the pressure of his heated mouth against hers melted her guard. She responded hesitantly at first, and then with eagerness as his mouth twisted across hers and probed for entrance.

As she yielded, her fingers curled weakly against his shirt, and Travis circled her waist with one powerful arm, pulling her closer. She took him into her mouth, arching against him, nearly swooning as he probed and explored and claimed this first of her treasures. Only when he felt the tension begin to stiffen her shoulders did he forego this delightful exploration. Lightly he kissed the curve of her lips and the tip of her nose.

"I know, we are supposed to talk," he responded ruefully to the accusation in sapphire eyes. "I just hope one of these days you'll understand how damned difficult it is for me to look and not touch."

Alicia relaxed as he settled her against his shoulder. She kept her hand on the ruffle of his shirt, enjoying the sensation of his heat against her palm. "I like the touching. It is the rest that frightens me," she murmured.

Travis bent a kiss to the softness of her hair. "There is no need to fear. Is Mrs. Clayton expecting you home?"

"No. She thinks I am staying at my father's." Alicia looked up to him questioningly.

"And your father is not likely to be checking your room on his wedding night, is he?" Travis gave a wicked tilt to his dark brow.

Understanding where this led, Alicia widened her eyes. "No, but the maids—"

"Will think you returned to Mrs. Clayton," Travis finished with satisfaction. "We have all night. Now, what is it that you want from me? My pedigree? My philosophy? Tell me what you want to know."

Held close to him like this, the hand about her waist playing sensuous games along her abdomen, his free hand drifting up and down her arm, Alicia could barely think, no less remember the questions. She fought for some control, and her earlier worries of his origins returned.

"Your parents?" she questioned incoherently. "How did they meet? Do you know? Such a marriage, isn't it unusual?"

Travis chuckled at this string of questions. "You needn't ask everything at once. I will give you time to ask them all." He settled his shoulders more comfortably against the cushions and while collecting his thoughts, moved his hand back and forth from her waist to the satin belt below her breasts. "I have heard the story from all sides, so I suppose I have a modicum of the truth. My mother and her family lived in a village along the Ohio that was attacked by a band of settlers seeking revenge for an Indian attack on their settlement. My mother's tribe was peaceful, the village contained only women and children, but the settlers burned it to the ground. Those who escaped eventually sought shelter at one of the British forts. My father was a soldier there."

So she had been right. Alicia moved uneasily in his hold, but Travis ignored her squirming. The story was one he had heard often, but never repeated to another. He limited himself to the barest of facts.

"The soldiers here do not marry their Indian women," Alicia protested feebly.

Travis shrugged. "In my tribe, to marry means to set up housekeeping together. If the marriage doesn't work, one of them moves out. Formality is not necessary. Fortunately or unfortunately, depending on who tells it, my mother's family had been converted to Christianity by the Moravians. She would not marry my father in the traditional Indian way."

Alicia lay against his chest contemplating this long ago conflict: the proud British soldier in an outpost in the middle of wilderness, surrounded by hostility on all sides, cut off from his family and his home, and the homeless Indian maiden, bewildered by an alien world and clinging to her beliefs. If Travis was any guide to judge by, they must have both been proud, self-willed people. The maiden had won the short term battle but lost the war. Marriage to a man who could not take her home with him would be the ultimate defeat.

"He must have known he could not take her home. Why would he do such a thing?"

That cut too close to the curses he had cast in his youth. Travis knew all the answers, but they were not ones he was prepared to give in full. Instead he ran his hand up into the sweet-smelling thickness of her hair and tilted her head up so he might kiss her long, fringed lashes and creamy cheeks.

"A soldier must be prepared to die. It is a very short-sighted life he lives. A fort does not attract the better class of women. In comparison, my mother was soft-spoken, English speaking, of noble heritage, and all those other things that are pleasing to men. Just as you are to me, my love."

His kisses fluttered across her skin, enticing and diverting. Tentatively Alicia touched the smooth-shaven skin of his angular jaw, hoping to persuade his lips back to hers. She doubted if Travis's loyalties lay anywhere but with himself, and her need for him exceeded any other problems. As he had told her before, he was a man, and as he was teaching her now, she was a woman. Their parentage had little to do with that.

"What other things are pleasing to men?" she murmured against his cheek as Travis's kisses strayed to her earlobe.

"Is that one of those things you wish to know about me, or an underhanded way of looking for a compliment?"

Alicia gasped as the front of her bodice suddenly gaped forward, undone by the exploring fingers at her back. A draft of cool air blew across her uncovered skin, but Travis gave her no time to feel the cold. Unfastening the final barrier of her chemise ribbon, he brought his lips to cover the puckering crests thus uncovered.

Shocked to the very depths of her soul by the sudden surge of desire rampaging through her center, Alicia tried to break free of his grasp, his name coming protestingly to her tongue. But as his mouth caressed first one sensitive peak, then the other, his tongue swirling around them until they grew hard and aching, his name was whispered from her tongue with different meaning.

Travis's lips came back to caress her. Bent backward in his embrace, her thigh pressed against the unyielding strength of his, Alicia slowly succumbed to the languor that stole over her.

His hands and fingers sculpted her as gently and expertly as they did his magical carvings. Travis filled his palms with the heavy weight of her breasts. He teased the aching crests to agonies of longing. He eased her gown from her shoulders, and shuddered with the strength of his need as his hands ran up and down the slender nakedness of her spine.

With grim determination Travis forced himself into control, clutching Alicia against his side, where he could feel the rapid rise and fall of her breasts against the linen of his shirt. He pressed his kiss along the fragile peak at her hairline. "Alicia, my love, have you any other questions? I do not think I can answer many more with any degree of rationality."

Daringly Alicia unwrapped his cravat and slid her hand beneath the opening of his shirt. Her fingers caressed the light covering of hair and molded against the bulge of powerful muscles. The strength kept leashed beneath her hands fascinated and frightened her. He could lock her in his arms and there would be no escape, but he chose to give her freedom. For that she was infinitely grateful.

Travis held his breath while her white hand traveled across the bronzed expanse of his chest, and black eyes watched her searchingly. The tension had not completely left her, she was still afraid, but she was still willing. High and firm, her breasts burned against his side until he unfastened the rest of his shirt and pulled it from his trousers.

The sensation of his nakedness against her opened a gaping hollow of yearning somewhere in her belly, and Alicia could hold him off no longer. Sliding her hand up to the tempting strand of hair at his nape, she turned her gaze up to meet his.

"No more questions," she whispered huskily.

His mouth closed hungrily over hers, and the pounding of their hearts in unison seemed to rock the boat.

Not until the shouts and curses and yells outside grew bolder did they realize the boat's rocking had other help. Booted feet jumped to the deck to a chorus of drunken railing.

They were no longer alone.

18

"HEY, LONETREE! Where you at?" The shout sounded from somewhere just outside the door. Equally raucous cries echoed from the riverbank and up the path to town. Drunken laughter and incoherent curses intermingled with the shouted demands.

Cursing vigorously, Travis leapt to his feet and strode to the cabin door before anyone could enter. Alicia shivered and grabbed frantically for her clothes as he slipped noiselessly from the room.

"Hey, Lonetree! Where's my money?" The man who had succeeded in clambering over the side yelled happily as he reeled only slightly on the slippery deck.

"The jackpot! He hit the jackpot three times runnin'!" came the cries from the hillside.

Lanterns flickered and swung and occasionally tumbled with their inebriated owners as the boatmen variously slid and staggered down the path.

"Lacrosse said you'd pay the pot. Fifty dollars, Lonetree!" A variety of whoops and cheers soared into the air at mention of this wealth.

Arms crossed, blocking the cabin door, Travis grinned and looked his newly acquired creditors up and down with amusement. Many were the times he had been in a party such as this, and he knew how quickly the high spirits could turn ugly. Lacrosse was lucky they hadn't tried to push the saloon into the river when they demanded payment. He'd seen it happen.

He dug into the pocket of his trousers and produced a small sack of coins. Pitching it to the winner, he informed them, "There's a down payment on the debt, gents. Take that back up and lose it in a game and I'll be up shortly to

pay you the rest. I don't carry that kind of cash on me.
Lacrosse knows better than that."

More cheers resounded off the river walls. Finally noting
Travis's state of undress, some one hollered, "Whooee!
Lonetree's got himself a woman in there. Don't expect him
back none too soon!"

More drunken laughter and inquiries into the identity of
the lucky female were met with Travis's careless shrug and
good-humored grin. "Go away, fellows, or I just might
forget I owe you anything at all. By morning you'll never
remember whether I paid or not."

A general laugh of agreement followed this riposte, and
with the winner swinging his wealth high above his head and
leading the way, the men gradually began the stumbling
journey back up the hill. Travis watched them go, then with
heart in throat, he hurried back to Alicia.

She stood in the center of the cabin, her gown primly
back in place and covered by her pelisse, the hood pulled up
to cover her chestnut curls. Travis groaned and approached
her cautiously.

"Alicia, they are gone. We don't have to go yet." He
tried to reach for her hood, but she stepped backward.

"You told them you would be with them shortly. I would
not want to hinder your enjoyment of the evening."

Her voice was cold and calm, but Travis could read the
pain in her eyes. Cursing silently, he made no further attempt to touch her.

"They would quite likely have turned the boat over if I
had not told them that," Travis informed her curtly. "I'll
not let you play this game with me, Alicia. I have done
everything within my power to ensure your privacy, but I
could not have foreseen this."

"When you play with drunks and ruffians, you should not
expect any less." Alicia pulled the wrap more tightly around
her, as if the night had grown suddenly colder.

"Damn it, Alicia! I've sold the saloon because you did not
approve of it, but I cannot turn my back on the men I have
worked with for years. You're going to have to come down
off that high horse and mingle with the common folk if
you're going to make it out here."

Travis tucked his shirt carelessly into his trousers and
reached for his coat, not giving her a second glance.

Uncertainly Alicia clung to the one word of hope he had offered her. "You have sold the saloon?"

Travis threw her a quick glance. "The papers will be signed this week. It was a good investment, but I can find others."

That he had made this sacrifice for her took some of the wind out of her sails, and Alicia's shoulders slumped slightly. She had reacted hastily, but the damage could not be undone so easily. The magic had gone out of the night and she felt only weariness.

"I am sorry, Travis," she whispered.

Instantly he was at her side, encompassing her waist with a strong arm and brushing her forehead with his kiss. "It will be all right, Alicia. You're overwrought and those damned fools didn't help. Don't think I'm giving up."

She succumbed to the reassuring strength of his embrace, resting her head against his shoulder. She had disappointed him, caused him untold frustration, but still he wanted her and protected her. Travis had more right than Teddy ever had to call her a tease; instead he tried to understand.

Cautiously she turned her head back up to meet his gaze. "You're not angry?"

Travis kissed her beautiful full lips gently before leading her toward the door. "I'm angry, no doubt," he responded ruefully, "but not at you. I'm not certain where I'll find a safer place than this, but reserve next Saturday for me. If that doesn't work, I'll just kidnap you and carry you off to parts unknown and have my way with you."

His wry tone made her laugh, and Alicia followed him up the hill with lighter heart. Travis was quite capable of doing exactly as he said, and as of this moment she would most likely not object. The evening had left her with an unsatisfied ache and a restless yearning for more of what he could teach her. Saturday could not come soon enough.

On Wednesday, to Alicia's surprise, Letitia met her after classes. Nervously listening for the pounding of Travis's hammer in the dance room, Alicia did not take in the first part of her stepmother's greeting, but she nodded politely after realizing she had been offered a ride.

"That was thoughtful of you, Letitia, but really not necessary. I am accustomed to Philadelphia winters, and though everyone complains of how cold this winter is, it is no worse."

"No matter. Your father and I don't want you feeling that we neglect you, and I hoped we could have a little talk."

Alicia mentally rolled her eyes heavenward. She could guess every topic to be covered, but shouldering the burden stoically, she gestured toward the dance room.

"Would you care to see what Mr. Travis has done for the school? It is nearly finished and Miss Lalende is quite proud of it."

Wanting to let Travis know where she went if he were here, Alicia didn't wait for a response to her question. Her skirts modestly brushing the wooden floors, she led the way to the dance room.

The platform was nearly complete, down to the last polished and waxed floorboard. As they entered the room, Penny pirouetted madly in the middle of the stage, and two other little girls slid across the shining wood as if they were on skates. Travis looked up from where he carved at an embellishment to adorn the proscenium. With a grin at their entrance, he unfolded himself with lanky grace and bowed politely.

Before he could speak a greeting, Penny flung herself from the stage into Alicia's arms.

"Lonetree says I can be a ballerina. What's a ballerina, Miss Alicia?"

How an Indian knew about ballerinas was anybody's guess, but Alicia hugged the child and after reminding her to mind her manners and producing a quick curtsy from the child, she answered, "A ballerina is a dancer, Penny. You were dancing beautifully."

When the child danced away, Alicia spoke in her most formal tones. "The platform is quite elegantly done, Mr. Travis. The girls are already eager for their first recitations."

The quirk at the corner of his mouth smoothly disappeared as Travis acknowledged her polite praise with a nod and turned to Letitia. "It is an honor to have you view my humble efforts, Mrs. Stanford. Shall I show you the benefits the young ladies will derive from having a formal setting for their talents?"

Alicia had to smother a giggle at being outdone at her own game, but she obligingly followed them around as Travis pointed out all the refinements he had made to produce a truly professional stage. Even Letitia had to admit to being impressed.

Travis surreptitiously squeezed Alicia's hand before she followed her stepmother out to the carriage. His touch served as a reminder of what they had already done and what they would do, and her cheeks flamed briefly. She didn't think her formidable stepmother would understand at all.

"Why did that little girl call Mr. Travis 'Lonetree'?" Letitia leapt right into her subject as she settled herself beneath the carriage furs.

"That is what his men call him," Alicia replied comfortably. "I don't know where Penny learned it."

"He's an Indian, isn't he?" Letitia demanded without warning.

Alicia smiled at the abruptness of this attack. "Among other things, I suspect. Why the sudden interest, Letitia?"

The French woman peered suspiciously at her stepdaughter's complacent expression. "Your father has heard that he is courting you. I told him I would talk to you first before he gets things all confused."

"I cannot imagine what he has heard. As you see, Mr. Travis is working on a project for the school. We have met several times at my father's house. He occasionally comes to call on Mrs. Clayton and to see how Becky is faring. After all, he is the oldest friend we have here in St. Louis. I can see nothing improper in his behavior." Alicia kept her answer as casual as possible. To cause a breach between her father and herself was the last thing she wished to do.

Letitia relaxed. "I am happy to see you are being sensible. Mr. Travis is an extremely attractive gentleman, but not at all what your father wants for you. What about this Mr. Howard? He seems quite taken with you."

"Mr. Howard pays attention to me only when he sees me. I have seen a peacock pursue his mate more ardently than he. Letitia, do not concern yourself over my unwedded state. I am quite content the way I am."

"Nonsense! You cannot bury yourself in a schoolroom and a boardinghouse forever. It is time you moved in with your father and me, and met a better class of people. It would do you no end of good."

Alicia bit back a sigh of exasperation. "Letitia, you do not need me moving in on you now, of all times. I am quite

accustomed to taking care of myself. I have practically run
my mother's house since I was twelve years old. When my
mother died, I took over complete control of not only the
household but the finances. I am accustomed to doing things
my way, and you would find it a sincere nuisance if I began
scolding your servants and telling them what to do. I am
quite happy with Mrs. Clayton and see no reason to change."

Letitia gave her a sharp look. "You have grown too
independent, young lady, but it does not obscure the fact
that you are young and unmarried and should be under your
father's protection. Rumors like the one about Mr. Travis
start too easily, otherwise."

As the carriage drew up in front of the Clayton house,
Letitia finished comfortably, "We will not worry about it
immediately. In March, when things are warmer, we will
take you on a tour of Natchez and New Orleans. You'll be
certain to find someone to your taste in those cities. St.
Louis is not quite cosmopolitan enough for your tastes, I
see."

Alicia controlled the urge to rage aloud and kept her
voice to a neutral murmur. "School will not be out until
June. That will be quite impossible, but I thank you for the
thought. Shall you come in?"

Letitia ignored the question and stared at Alicia in dismay. "After June is the worst possible time to visit New
Orleans. Your father has his heart set on this tour and
finding you a proper husband. Will you travel with us if we
wait until September?"

Alicia had climbed from the carriage and now turned to
meet Letitia's gaze. "School starts again in September. My
father must accustom himself to the idea that I do not
intend to marry. Thank you for the ride, Letitia."

Without giving time for argument, Alicia marched down
the path to the house. Letitia's look of horror haunted her,
but she would not back down. She might experiment with
Travis as a lover, but marriage was a commitment she was
not prepared to make for anyone's convenience. She was
beginning to enjoy her life just as it was. The inner rage that
had once terrified her had subsided gradually, finding better
outlet in this unexpected freedom. She would do nothing to
endanger her fragile peace.

Throwing off her pelisse as she entered the hall, Alicia

followed the scent of baking bread to the kitchen, where Becky idly punched down a bowl of rising dough while Bessie tested the doneness of the loaves in the oven. She smiled at Alicia's entrance and indicated she take a chair out of the way.

"Where is that hungry man of yours? I baked him something special."

Alicia was in no humor to be questioned more about Travis, and poured herself a cup of coffee from the pot bubbling on the wood stove.

"My father is after me to move again," she responded glumly.

Becky turned excitedly on the stool she used to reach the high table. "Ooo, you mean we get to live in that big house?"

Alicia glared at this defection "I'm not certain that pompous butler they have would allow you through the doors, Rebecca Whitehead, so don't go giving yourself airs."

"Oh, no, now! That's not fair!" Becky wailed before Mrs. Clayton overrode the uproar.

"Your father's quite right. You belong with him. It's not fitting for a young lady to be living on her own."

As Alicia opened her mouth to protest, a knock sounded at the kitchen door, and a second later Travis strode in, filling the heated room with the cold air from outside. Slapping his hands against the arms of his fringed coat with a shiver, he blew a foggy breath and grinned.

"Howdy, ladies! Mind some company?"

Irrationally irritated by his arrogant assumption that they wanted nothing better, Alicia sat in silence while the other two made a fuss over him. Mrs. Clayton bustled about, pushing him into the chair beside Alicia, producing the chess pie she had baked just for him, and clattering about searching for plates and forks.

Becky erupted into a tirade about those what didn't know what was good for them until Alicia gave her a stern look and asked her to pour Travis a cup of the coffee.

The small maid drew herself up to her most dignified stature, and gesturing toward her bandaged arm, demanded, "And how am I to do that with only one arm?"

"With the other!" Alicia snapped curtly. "If you had not been dancing on tables like an utter fool, you would not be in this sorry state."

"I was not dancing!" Becky replied indignantly. "I was scared of all them vicious, mean men a'rollin' all overs. I was just protecting myself."

"And what did you expect to find in a saloon? Pussy-cats?"

Before Becky could protest even more vehemently, Travis interrupted. "That's enough, Rebecca. Bring me my coffee and don't let me hear you speaking to Miss Alicia in that manner again, or I'll turn you over my knee and whip you until you're black and blue."

Startled and not just a little bit afraid that he might do as threatened, Becky leapt from the stool to the stove and awkwardly managed the process of pouring and serving coffee.

"Now, will someone tell me what the argument is about, or shall I guess? Would Lady Letitia have aught to do with it?" Travis threw Alicia's pale face and grimly set lips a shrewd look.

Alicia ignored his irony, but Mrs. Clayton and Becky erupted in rapid-fire explanations until Travis drew his own conclusions and held up his hands for peace.

"Alicia is a grown woman and entitled to live as she wishes. Besides, this is closer to the school than her father's. Perhaps if you just stayed with your father when school's not in session, he will be happy."

Alicia threw him a grateful look, and a wry smile turned up the corners of her mouth. "Now that you have solved that dilemma, Solomon, whose side will you take on the subject of marriage? They have quite decided on taking me to New Orleans in the spring, so I might find an eligible suitor. Shall you cut me in half and send part with them and keep the other here?"

An unholy gleam lit black eyes as Travis contemplated this proposition. "Which half would you leave here?" he inquired with a wicked leer.

Alicia threw her napkin in his face and rose from the table. "I should have known better than to expect sympathy from the likes of you. I think I shall go and run off with one of New Orleans's infamous pirates. I understand Lafitte is quite good-looking."

Travis hastily interfered before she could stalk from the room, catching her by the arm and forcing her to lift her chin to look up at him. "I'll be your pirate. Will the assembly Saturday night do in place of New Orleans for now?"

In her present mood she would have turned him down out of sheer spite, but the uncertainty and eagerness in his tone made Alicia hold her sharp tongue. Travis was always so abominably self-assured, but he had been listening to her after all. The mention of her father and marriage had given him cause for concern. As it ought, she thought rebelliously. If her father ever found out about them, he would most likely have them both hung.

Rebellion turning against her father and his irritating expectations, Alicia nodded agreement to Travis's plea. "I will be there."

"I will come for you," Travis amended.

That should upset a few applicants for her hand, Alicia decided grimly—arriving on the arm of the one man in town she had been denied. It should be amusing.

And even more so when they left together. She wondered how Travis meant to arrange that.

19

TRAVIS ASSISTED Alicia into the small two-seated carriage and adjusted the fur lap robe around her. Alicia buried her hands deep inside the ermine muff that matched the trim of her pelisse, and watched Travis as he checked the horses, rubbed their noses, and loped around the carriage to the other side.

Throwing a cautious glance to the house visible behind the crosshatching of bare tree branches, Travis bent a warm, quick kiss to Alicia's cold lips. "You make a beautiful snow maiden."

The snow had returned, leaving a thin covering over yards and rutted roads, turning them into white carpets for the ghostly coverings of evergreens and graceful tree limbs. Lights from the houses they passed only highlighted the pale grays and brown, and made shadows of solidity.

Alicia gazed out upon the scene and wondered why Philadelphia had never seemed so beautiful after a snow. Absorbing the warmth from the man beside her, she glanced to his angular profile. The break in his once perfect nose seemed more pronounced from this side, but the hard planes of his jaw sloping down from high cheekbones spoke of a strength and determination she might never match. He felt her gaze and glanced down at her.

"You are not having second thoughts, are you?"

"I gave up thinking for Lent," she replied airily.

Uncertain how to take that, Travis turned his attention back to the horses. "You are not worried about your father, then?"

"I have not heard from him all week. I do not know if that means Letitia has spoken to him or not. Perhaps he means to forget I exist."

Travis heard the hint of bitterness and shook his head. "I will assure you he has not forgotten. He may be peeved, but he knows what you're doing."

Alicia sent him a startled look. "How do you know?"

Travis set his lips in a thin line. "Because I told him. I will not let you bear the blame when it is reported we appeared publicly together. There is no point in hiding what the whole town will soon know."

"You told him! And he gave his permission?" Alicia's heart skipped a fast beat until she heard the irony in Travis's reply.

"He informed me his daughter did not belong at public assemblies and that he preferred she be escorted only by men who have met his approval and then only under proper chaperonage. He was not particularly pleased when I told him I did not seek his permission but only sought to inform him."

"That was foolish. He is not a man to offend, Travis."

"I did not offend him. He was not pleased, but he was understanding. He's a rational man and knows he cannot expect to take over your life after so many years. He thanked me for being honest and promised not to interfere in this evening's entertainment if this is what you wished. I suspect there may be opposition if you persist in your obviously mad infatuation with the likes of me, but you may rest assured that tonight is permissible."

A low gurgle of laughter sounded somewhere from deep inside the bundle of furs. "You are a conceited popinjay, Mr. Travis. I affect no infatuation for the likes of you, but merely desire to ruin myself forever by appearing in your company."

"Then I shall most certainly give you satisfaction, Miss Stanford." The suggestiveness of his tone gave the path of his thoughts, and Alicia blushed furiously as the carriage drew up before the assembly rooms.

Flinging a coin to a waiting boy to mind the horses, Travis strode rapidly around the carriage and lifted Alicia bodily from her seat. She gave a soft gasp of surprise as his hands encompassed her waist, and she found herself flying through the air before meeting the ground.

Travis held her there a minute, gazing into her eyes. "You are the only one who can prevent me from making you mine, and I intend to dispel any objections you may raise. Stand forewarned, Blue Eyes.''

Alicia had no doubt that Travis meant what he said. She could tell from the intensity of his black gaze and the strength of his hold on her that his desire was not likely to dissipate under any pressure her father might bring to bear. She wasn't even certain her own objections would stand in his way very long. For the first time she realized she had set out on a course from which there was no turning back. The man she had chosen for lover had all the instincts of a wild animal and the same fierce protectiveness of what was his. She could not escape him even had she wanted.

A band tightened around Alicia's chest, constricting her breathing as she read this knowledge in his gaze. As if to confirm his possession, Travis slid one hand caressingly to her breast, the gesture hidden beneath the folds of her pelisse. His knowing fingers found the hard crest beneath the thickness of velvet and played it persuasively until Alicia swayed helplessly into his hands.

Just that one touch excited rivers of fire that flamed through her midsection and left only molten lava in their place. Satisfied he had made his point, Travis trailed his hand upward to caress her cheek tenderly, then took her hand and escorted her toward the brilliantly lighted assembly room. Alicia clung to the muscled strength of his arm and wished they could be alone.

They doffed their outerwear in the lobby, and Travis's gaze swept approvingly over the wine-colored velvet of Alicia's gown. It was not one of her fashionable pieces of clothing, but a simple gown cinched in firmly at the waist, the neckline modestly filled by a gauze so fine he could see the valley between her breasts. It was a gown that warned to look but not touch—except he meant to divest her of it shortly.

As if reading his thought, Alicia blushed, but did not flinch from Travis's gaze. His black hair did not spill in fashionable curls across his forehead, but lay in a thick wave that threatened his eyesight, emphasizing the dark sideburns he had grown these past months. Someone had trimmed the soft curl along his high collar, and Alicia felt a moment's sorrow at losing this sight. Her fingers still itched to bury themselves in the thickness of that gleaming cap.

She did not dare look too closely at the rest of him as

Travis escorted her into the crowded ballroom. The soft
green wool of his coat fit him like a second skin and the
shoulders needed no padding. The long tail of the coat
outlined narrow hips and muscular thighs, and the waist-
length front emphasized the leanness of his flat stomach and
the tailored fit of his biscuit-colored buckskin trousers. Everything about him emphasized his virile masculinity, and
Alicia felt a sudden panic building inside of her at the vague
realization of what it might mean to be possessed by him.

Their arrival in the ballroom caused a stir. Heads came
together and whispers rippled around the room, while more
immediate acquaintances hurried forward to greet them.

Although all knew Alicia to be a schoolteacher, and she
had the opportunity to meet the parents of many of her
students, her quiet elegance still caused many of the women
to look at their old-fashioned dresses with dismay. Travis
too did not quite fit in, although the reason was not as
discernible. The overabundance of males in town produced
a wide assortment of well-dressed gentlemen at the assembly, but they appeared to pale in comparison to the tall
Indian keelboatman, who by all rights shouldn't even be in
polite society.

The fact that the new couple apparently walked in two
worlds created pockets of suspicion, but the ease with which
they mingled with the crowd soon erased whatever tension
had been aroused by their appearance. Society of any kind
was welcome here, and though gossips readily squirreled
away fascinating tidbits, the new arrivals soon made themselves at home.

Too at home, Travis grumbled to himself awhile later as
he watched the rich wine of Alicia's gown dance by in the
arms of one man after another in a reel. Sapphire eyes
laughed and sparkled as he had not seen them do before,
and he felt a twinge of jealousy. He quickly returned his
attention to his own partner. Although he fully intended to
make Alicia his wife, he did not intend for her to disturb his
life in any other way.

That thought lasted only long enough for Sam Howard to
discover Alicia's presence and dance her off in a spirited
quadrille that involved much laughing and swinging about.
They made an attractive couple, Sam with his polished,
blond good looks, and Alicia with her willowy, ladylike
grace. Telling himself he sought only to keep what he had

worked so hard to gain, Travis abandoned his conversation
with one of the local horse breeders and set out to retrieve
his partner at the dance's end.

Sam did not relinquish his prize willingly, but Alicia scarcely
seemed to notice as she literally danced from Sam into
Travis's waiting arms. Noting the less than laughing look in
Travis's eyes, she grinned wickedly.

"I am having a wo-o-onderful time." She drew the word
out with delight. "Sam says he might persuade the orchestra
to play a waltz."

Out here, under the eyes of an audience, Travis could not
draw her into his arms, and she knew it. She also knew he
wanted to and tormented him with it. It suddenly occurred
to Travis that by awakening Alicia's passions, he was un-
leashing an unknown quantity. The woman he had courted
and wooed had been beaten down by circumstances and
fate, and had turned to him in desperation. Now that she
was regaining her spirit and confidence, she could as easily
dance from his grasp as she had Howard's just a moment
before.

Travis did not linger long over that feeling of desolation.
In the past he had found flaws in every woman he had met.
This one had flaws he could gallop a horse through, but she
was perfect for him. He would not let her go so easily.

"The waltz is mine, Miss Stanford," Travis drawled casually, but Alicia did not mistake the steel in his eyes. Still,
she grinned impudently.

"So be it, then." She turned and gave Sam a sweet smile.
"You may tell the orchestra Mr. Travis would like a waltz. I
myself would prefer a lemonade." With that nonsensical
statement she swept off, leaving both men to stare at each
other ruefully.

Sam ran his hand through his smooth blond locks and
shrugged genially. "These Eastern women take some getting
used to."

Travis suppressed a sudden urge to laugh. There wasn't
another man in this room who could saddle Alicia once she
took a notion to take the bit in her teeth and run. Only her
father could claim any command over her, and that was an
illusory claim at best. The thrill of the chase sent excitement
racing through Travis's veins. She might elude him for a
while, but Travis relied on his experience to win her in the
end. He would gentle her and tame her to the bridle, and

see her well harnessed before summer arrived. And the lesson would begin tonight.

Alicia was well aware of his purposeful approach, and her heart skipped a little faster. Her boldness had shaken him, she could tell, but it hadn't discouraged him as it had Sam and dozens of her other suitors. She didn't think her tendency to say what she willed would discourage Travis in the least. She wasn't certain anything would discourage Travis. And that thought excited her more than any other.

He caught her elbow and peremptorily guided her toward the stairs leading to the ladies' powder room. "Go powder your nose or whatever ladies do up there," he commanded. "Just be prepared to fall into my arms when you come back down."

Alicia gazed at him in astonishment. "I could do no such thing."

Travis crooked one eyebrow. "You could if you tripped."

"Trip . . ." Her voice wandered off as she read the sheer devilment in his eyes. "I would look a graceless ninny."

"Which we both know you are not. Does it matter what others think if it gives me excuse to take you home early?"

The mellow murmur of this suggestion sent a shiver down her spine, but Alicia tried to ignore it. "Which home did you have in mind?"

"Mine, but let others think what they will. There are a few matters we have left undone, and I would see them completed to our mutual satisfaction."

Alicia gave him a speculative look, but obediently lifted her skirts and climbed the stairs. She could say no at any point; he would not force her. The knowledge that the choice was hers eliminated any irritation at his assumption that she would say yes. He couldn't be certain; he just made it uncannily easy to go along with him.

The sight of Travis's long, lean frame lounging against the newel post as she came down decided the matter for Alicia. She very much wanted to be caught up in those arms. She wanted to feel their strength around her. It seemed all her life she had been standing on her own. It would be very pleasant to let someone else take care of her for just a little while. With as much grace as she could muster, she tripped on the last few steps and gave a small cry as she fell directly into Travis's capable arms.

The women behind her clustered and clucked anxiously as

Travis lowered Alicia into one of the chairs along the wall. Alicia protested and tried to stand and sat abruptly down again. Someone cried they would fetch a physician, while others recommended hot packs and someone else began a long recital of what had worked for their grandmother when her leg had "swole up like a turnip." Alicia's grimace as she looked at Travis was not one of pain, and he held back a smile of sympathy.

Dr. Farrar hurried to the rescue and Alicia glanced at him dubiously. "It is just a small sprain, sir. It is really not worth your attention. Mr. Travis has been kind enough to offer me a ride home. I promise I shall be quite fit in the morning."

The young doctor smiled at the lady's reluctance to have her ankle examined. "A sprain can be very discomforting, Miss Stanford. Perhaps you would prefer it if I accompanied you home?"

That was more than Travis could tolerate. Even the damned physician was making eyes over her. Swiftly Travis knelt beside the chair and boldly took her slender ankle in his hand, expertly twisting it side to side. A few of the ladies gave shocked gasps, and Alicia barely maintained her dignity at this manhandling, but when Travis stood, everyone awaited his verdict.

"I don't believe it's serious, Bernard. I'll take her home and she can soak it, and if it's still sore in the morning, she can send for you."

The doctor nodded agreeably and bowed over Alicia's hand. Between them they assisted her to her feet. Someone went for their coats and the carriage. Within minutes they were settled behind the horses, cantering down the snow-filled street toward Travis's rooms.

Travis sent the proud tilt of Alicia's chin a worried look. "I went too far?"

"You went too far," she agreed. "I do not like making a public spectacle of myself."

"But you make such a pretty spectacle." Travis transferred both reins to his left hand and slid the right around her waist. "It gave everyone something exciting to talk about, so no one will even think twice about us leaving so early together. We have as long as we like."

She had consented to his madness and could not fault him, but she still had an uneasy feeling about this deception.

Perhaps Travis was accustomed to this kind of deviousness, but she was not. It worried her to be less than honest.

"What if we're caught? What if my father speaks to Mrs. Clayton and they both discover I was in neither place?"

"I think the likelihood is small, but I will take you to either of them at any time you wish. Just give me a little time, Alicia. Everything worth having is worth taking a risk for."

All her prior nervousness returned, but the strength of the arm around her gave her a courage Alicia did not think she possessed. She could not live in fear all her life. Already Travis had stripped away much of the horror until she could spend an evening like this one without recoiling from every man's touch. If he could take away the nightmare, replace it with the promises she felt in his words, in his touch, in his looks, it would be worth every risk taken. But one.

Worriedly she gave Travis a half-glance. Although he seemed to be concentrating on his horses, his grip on her tightened, and she knew he waited for her response.

"That is easy for you to say, but you are not a woman. What happens if I should bear your child?"

Reluctantly Travis withdrew his arm to steer the carriage into an alleyway behind Main Street where the horses would be stabled. His thoughts, however, had not veered from her question.

"Would you dislike that very much?" Travis asked quietly.

Alicia sent him a surprised glance, then considered the question. It was one she had carefully avoided until now, but logic demanded that she consider it before she set one foot out of this carriage.

She felt Travis's gaze turn questioningly to her, and she lifted her eyes to his. "I would like to have children, but I could not live through what happened to me before another time."

That did not entirely answer his question, but Travis understood this greater fear. "Don't let it worry you tonight. I will protect you."

The heat of his gaze sent a ripple of warmth through her, and suddenly everything was all right again. It was as if the snow stopped and the sun came out. Tentatively Alicia touched his gloved hand.

Travis seized her fingers and rewarded her with a grin of exuberant joy. In a leap he was on the ground and swinging her from the seat, leaving the horses to be tended by the stable lads.

Alicia squealed in surprise as Travis lifted her into his arms and set out with firm tread toward the back entrance of a large building looming ahead. She did not even inquire where he took her. Her hands slid behind his neck, and she buried her face against his broad shoulder.

Soon she would know what it meant to be loved by a man.

20

THE BACK ENTRANCE proved to be a stairway to an upstairs room Travis presently called home. The keelboat offered a retreat, but here was the hub of his many and varied interests. The constant murmur of voices from the rooms below was scarcely noticeable.

The large chamber reflected his Spartan lifestyle. A simple quilt covered a frame bed of a size necessary for a man of his height. A broad desk with numerous drawers and well appointed with the necessary instruments for writing dwarfed one corner. But these were not the objects to which Alicia's attention was drawn. On shelves lining the room sat an assortment of carved creatures, large and small, that had employed his talented fingers at one time or another.

Travis discarded his coats and watched as Alicia admired one after the other of these products of idle hours. He was half ashamed that these were all he had to show for these last few years he had spent escaping the two lives he could not live. But Alicia's awe as she lovingly ran her fingers over the detailed wingspan of a golden eagle restored some small part of his self-respect.

When she came upon the statue of the lady with the lovely hat, she studied it carefully, marveling over the detailing of her face and the miniature slipper peeking out from beneath long skirts. She glanced quizzically to Travis's impassive face.

"She is very beautiful. Is she someone you know?"

A woman's question, and Travis grinned at the hint of jealousy it invoked. "She is now. She's my good luck charm, but now that I have what I want, you may have her if you wish."

Alicia's startled look was quickly replaced with embarrassment as she read the meaning of his words in his dark gaze. Gently she sat the lovely carving on the bedside table and prepared to remove her pelisse. The room had grown suddenly very warm.

Travis quickly stepped to her aid, folding the heavy material over the desk chair. Although this room had higher ceilings and more space than the boat, Alicia still felt as if his masculine frame filled the room, making it impossible to avoid him. She was almost grateful for the noises below, reminding her civilization was still at hand.

"Alicia." Travis stood before her again, his hand reaching to touch gently at her cheek. The longing in those deep-set eyes sent a sea of churning waves crashing against weakened barriers. Alicia could not tear her eyes away.

"Are there more questions you would ask of me? Is there aught between us now that keeps you from me?"

Tall and lean, clothed in silk shirt and leather breeches, he appeared every inch the elegant gentleman, and Alicia could not ask for anything more. She did not want to know more. There were still episodes she would prefer not to remember, questions that could only have unsatisfactory answers. If she thought of nothing else but the warmth of his hand against her face and the desire in his eyes, she could forget his savagery and her fear. All her valiant vows faded beneath the look in his eyes. Travis was as inscrutable as any Indian. He could desire her wealth, her position, or just some idea he had formed in his mind, but she didn't think the longing in his gaze could be manufactured. He desired her, and for now that was enough.

"No more questions," she murmured, daringly meeting his eyes with all her own desires naked for him to see.

Instantly she was in his arms, hard muscles crushing her as Travis spun her around in an ecstatic dance. Alicia laughed, a full-throated golden tone that filled the room. Her arms slid around his neck, and very soon the exuberant dance slowed as Travis bent to taste the promise of full, rich lips.

Travis had lit only the one lamp and it sent shadows dancing crazily over the high-cheekboned planes of his bronzed face. Wonderingly Alicia smoothed her hand over these hard angles, finding them soft beneath her touch. No tension marred their strong lines as she lifted her lips to be kissed.

She found herself quickly caught in an undertow she

could not fight, drowning in a current so deep she could never escape. Travis's mouth came down hard and slanting across hers, drawing from her all the response she was prepared to give and more that she had not known she possessed. She knew his hands roamed over her body, but she could concentrate on nothing at all as the tumultuous current of his kiss drew her deeper into a world she had not known existed.

His mouth slid forcefully over hers, nipping, caressing, surveying the territory that was now his to explore. With devastating swiftness his tongue invaded the hidden recesses of her parted lips, and the probing heat proved Alicia's undoing.

Her gown and petticoats slid silently to the floor with the help of Travis's hands smoothing them past her hips. A draft blew around her stockinged ankles, but Alicia felt only the excitement of strong fingers at her breasts, loosening corset strings. This too soon fell away, and only her chemise and his shirt and trousers came between them.

His hands played skillfully along her sides, sliding along her hips and buttocks and drawing her closer while his tongue ravished the innocence of her lips. She responded with a need to match his own. The heated currents of his passion drew her closer, daring her to explore further. The clinging materials between them became a barrier to be breached, and her hands fumbled at the fastenings of his shirt. The hardness of the broad expanse of muscular chest beneath frightened her, but only enough to fuel her daring.

Impatiently, ignoring the sudden rise in noise level below, Travis stripped away his shirt and flung it aside, then reached eagerly for the prize he had sought so long. One by one he pulled the pins from Alicia's hair, scattering them far and wide, never to be seen again. With glorious abandon he buried his fingers deep in her thick chestnut curls, spreading them down and around her throat and shoulders, exulting in the rich lengths that entwined about them.

Travis stepped back to admire his handiwork, and Alicia stood proudly silent beneath his questing stare. The thick, curling cascade of chestnut fell across high, firm breasts scarcely concealed by the thin silk and lace of her chemise. Tendrils curled about a waist so small that Travis marveled over nature's miraculous impossibility. The full swell of her hips narrowed to slender, graceful thighs silhouetted by the clinging silk, and his heart thumped so loudly he could hear it. Soon, very soon, those thighs would part for him, and the lady would be his.

Alicia stifled a gasp as Travis lifted his gaze to hers, and she correctly interpreted the look in those deep, black eyes. The moment had come from which there was no turning back, and she could not speak. She could only stare into the depths of his eyes, fully conscious of the nakedness of his bronzed chest, not daring to glance lower to the tight breeches that concealed nothing of his narrow hips. She had felt the hard line of his masculinity when he had held her close. She dared not contemplate its purpose now.

Gently Travis circled her waist and pulled her close once more, giving her time to accept the intimacy of their bodies. His hand gently explored the fullness of her breasts, expertly teasing the hidden crests to aching points of readiness against the filmy material of her chemise.

Alicia shuddered as a slow heat took root somewhere in her midsection and began to spread with breath-taking ferocity throughout her body. She ached for his touch, wanted more than he was giving, and her arms went about his shoulders to persuade him to part with more.

With a groan of satisfaction Travis swept her up in his arms, molding his mouth to hers, taking possession, drinking deeply, and promising more. With effortless grace he laid her back against the bed covers and joined her before she could make her escape. One leg trapped hers while his hands and mouth explored and ravaged where they would. Once more she lay beneath a man's heavy weight, but this time Alicia welcomed it. Her hands roamed freely over the rippling musculature of his back, and her body strained against his, craving the union so long denied.

Wrapped in a world of their own, they refused to acknowledge the intrusion of loud shouts below. Travis had posted guards at either entrance to this room and knew none could invade their privacy this time. The brawl below would soon die down. The surging heat of many months' denial prevented any thought beyond the welcome haven lying compliant and eager beneath him. Just a few minutes more, just a little more patience, and she would open to him and sweet possession would be complete.

The heady perfume of chestnut tresses disguised the other fumes drifting beneath the rudely cut door. With Alicia's mouth pliant and vulnerable pressing into his, her breasts soft and yielding as Travis worked to uncover them, his senses could not absorb any more.

Not until a particularly ear-piercing shriek cut through their absorption did either wake to the danger.

Bracing his weight on his hands, Travis turned his head to listen. Alicia too tensed at the vaguely familiar sound. The scream repeated itself from a distance, and they glanced back to each other. Becky.

Only then did the fumes strike their senses. Taking a deep breath, Alicia began to cough, and Travis quickly leapt to his feet. Smoke poured in black clouds from beneath the door, stealing the air from the closed room, filling their nostrils with its suffocating stench.

Travis cursed and laid his hand against the door, tearing it away again as the heat scorched his skin. Weakly Alicia tried to rise and find her clothes, but the smoke filled her lungs, and she could only cough and stumble blindly in the growing darkness. Travis grabbed the quilt to wrap around her and swung her up in his arms. The rear entrance appeared untouched as yet.

"Wait!" Alicia cried, struggling to see out of the folds of heavy material wrapped around her. "Your carvings! You can't leave them behind."

"They're not alive," Travis muttered curtly, carrying her toward the door, "but you are."

Still, she couldn't let him lose them all. Extending her arm, she grabbed the lady from the bedside table as he passed by it, clutching it protectively in her hands even as another spasm of coughing overtook her.

Travis knew his way up and down the stairs in the dark, but the thick clouds of smoke slowed his progress. The roar of the fire came louder from out here, but no flames could be seen. Travis cursed all the way down the stairs. He had told Lacrosse after that last brawl that lamps would have to be nailed securely to the walls. To leave them where those fools could knock them over was the height of idiocy.

Frustration and anger and a niggling fear propelled Travis down the stairway. The slender burden in his arms coughed raggedly, adding to his distress. The sight of a bulky form clambering toward them eased several problems.

"Auguste! We're coming down," Travis warned, sending the big man running back down ahead of them.

"Becky?" Alicia coughed out, remembering those ear-piercing screams.

As they emerged into the shocking cold of night air, Travis repeated the question for her, sending an inquiring look to his right-hand man. Auguste nodded his shaggy head in the direction of a small figure scurrying toward them, one arm slung awkwardly across her chest.

"What in hell is she doing here?" Travis asked irritably, as if it mattered at all. The yard was filling with people come to fight the fire or just to watch the flames. Curious glances were already being directed down the alleyway.

"Get the carriage out," Travis ordered hastily as several of the crowd tentatively peeled from the rest and began to follow Becky down the alley. Auguste hastened to do as told.

"Miss Alicia?" Becky gulped frantically for air as her gaze jerked from Travis's set face to the bundle in his arms.

The fire would not be the only hell in this town tonight if Alicia were caught in her present state outside a tavern in his arms. Travis could feel her shudder against his chest and realized he was half naked, too. He would have to trust the brat to keep quiet.

"She's fine. We'll have to get her back to the house before—" Travis cursed silently as the shape of the young physician emerged from the alleyway.

"Is there anything I can do?"

That was twice this night the damned doctor had interfered. Already the conscientious concern in his eyes was being replaced as he recognized Travis and glanced suspiciously to the quilt-wrapped figure in his arms. At least Alicia had the sense to keep her tongue quiet, although her racking coughs worried him.

As another figure made the dash down the alley at the same time the carriage rattled into the yard, Travis had to make a sudden choice. Alicia might need a physician, but only after she was safely tucked into her own bed. And judging by the shape of the man running this way, that bed had better be at Mrs. Clayton's.

Shaking his head in reply to the doctor's inquiry, Travis began to lope toward the carriage turning around in the yard, Becky at his heels. Travis scarcely noticed the cold, but Alicia continued to cough and shiver against his chest. The whole damned town could go up in flames if it wanted, but he had to get her safely out of here.

The fates were against them, as they had been from the start. Even though Dr. Farrar gauged the reason for Travis's bolt for the carriage and attempted to delay the racing figure down the alleyway, Chester Stanford was a determined man. Spying the man who had sold him the saloon, he had sought to question him. Only after discovering the feminine bundle in Travis's arms did it also occur to him that Alicia was supposed to be attending the assembly with the treacherous half-breed this night. Stanford's shout echoed off the walls as he shoved the young physician aside.

Travis managed to get the carriage door open and Alicia settled inside before Chester Stanford reached him. Defying the older man's command to halt, he threw Becky in after her and shouted to Auguste, who whipped the horses to a jerking start. There wasn't time to tell Auguste where to go. By the look on Stanford's face, it didn't matter. Travis swung around to meet his furious foe.

"If that was my daughter, I'll have you whipped with chains!" Chester exploded. Although shorter than Travis by some inches, he was not a small man, and in his wrath he seemed physically capable of carrying out his threat.

Physical punishment was not Travis's concern, however. More people had followed Chester down the alley, seeking further excitement as the flames died down and word spread that the saloon had just recently changed hands and now belonged to the wealthy Stanfords. Grimly Travis attempted to keep the gossip to a minimum.

"This is not the place for a discussion, sir," he growled between clenched teeth. With a nod over Chester's shoulder, he indicated the men closing in nearby. "Name the place and I'll meet you there."

Dr. Farrar was moving among the crowd, dismissing them with calming words, but Chester understood the message. In a lower, if not calmer, tone, he said, "I ought to demand your seconds, but I have a family to consider. I want you in my study in ten minutes. Then I'll decide whether to shoot you or whip you."

Turning on his heel, he strode off.

21

By the time Travis appeared on the Stanford threshold, he had acquired a shirt and coat from the boat. He still smelled of smoke and his hair hung thickly across his brow rather than neatly off his face, but these things did not tarnish his gentlemanly image so much as the thunderous expression on his face. War paint was all that was needed, thought the terrified servant who ushered him into Chester Stanford's commodious and very civilized study.

Travis paid no heed to the leather-bound books lining the walls or the leather-upholstered Chippendale wing chairs at the hearth. He moved across the expensive Turkish carpet as one accustomed to such wealth. His black gaze met Stanford's wrath with an assurance that made the other man writhe with increasing fury. Standing, Stanford took the offensive.

"She is upstairs. Letitia is with her. I don't think there is an explanation you can give me that I will accept." Brandy and a glass sat on the desk in front of him, but Chester remained standing, his knuckles white as he leaned against the desk to face the unprecedented confidence of the dark man entering the room.

"I would not give you one, in any case," Travis replied coolly. "Alicia will tell you what she wishes you to know. How is she?"

The flush of rage deepened. "How is she! You want to tell me how she will be when word of this gets out? How many damned people know where she was?"

"That depends on how many of your servants saw her. Farrar will keep quiet. My man will say nothing. I'll not vouch for Alicia's maid, but I suspect she can be made to keep quiet. Rumors are bound to fly, but they will not be confirmed easily, if that is all that worries you."

Every word out of the man's mouth infuriated Chester to a greater degree. Travis behaved as if no harm had been done, as if a young lady of good reputation had not been ruined forever by a half-Indian keelboat captain. Chester wanted to smack the self-assured expression off that implacable face, but decades of gentlemanly training had taught him not to brawl with his inferiors. By all rights, he should have just ordered the man thrown in the river and not spoken to him at all. That Travis had been a guest in his home, a man with whom he had done business, presented a certain dilemma.

"Rumors will fly and Alicia will be ruined. Have you no remorse at all?" he exclaimed incredulously.

That touched a nerve, and a muscle ticked in Travis's jaw. "I regret any harm I may have done Alicia, but my intentions have always been honorable. If your only fear is for her reputation, then let me assure you that I am fully prepared to marry her. I am not certain that Alicia is of the same mind."

That outrageous blow was more than Chester could handle. Slowly he sunk into his seat and reached for the brandy, his horrified gaze fastening on Travis.

"Marry her?" He swallowed a gulp of brandy. "I am quite sure you are, as is every other fortune hunter in town. If that is your game, let me assure you, I will see you hung first."

Since the older man made no offer of the liquor, Travis poured himself a glass and settled into the comfortable chair across from the desk. His future lay in these next few minutes, and he had found boldness won more than timidity.

"I am no fortune hunter," he stated serenely. "I choose to live on what I earn, but there is a sizable fortune sitting in a bank in New York that would provide for Alicia for the rest of her life should anything happen to me. I will give you the name of the bankers if you care to verify it."

This audacious proclamation rattled Chester even more, but it was talk he understood. He sipped more calmly at his drink and examined the man his daughter had evidently chosen for a lover.

"Even if I could verify it, what makes you think I would find you a suitable husband for my daughter? Wealth can be had by many means, but good breeding is essential for a woman like Alicia. She has been brought up as a lady in polite society. Forgive my saying so, but your antecedents are not likely to meet those requirements."

A cynical smile turned a corner of Travis's lips. "I might argue several of those points, sir, but my father would quite definitely disagree with the latter. He himself cannot quibble if I choose a colonist for wife since he set the precedent with my mother, but he would find your quarrel with his ancestry laughable. We trace our title back to William the Conqueror."

Chester choked on his last swallow of brandy and came up sputtering. "Title? Colonist? What in hell do you take me for? Madman?"

Travis sipped slowly at the brandy, though his pulse raced. He had not dared consider so precipitous a move before, but he had no choice now. If he could not win Alicia's father, she would be lost to him. He did not fool himself by thinking she would take such a step as marriage without her father's consent. He would draw the whole damned family tree if necessary to convince this man.

"No, sir. I respect your concern for your daughter and give you information I have revealed to no one on this side of the world. Again, I will give you the address of my father's agents in New York, or if you prefer, my father's direction if you wish to address him directly. That will involve some months, I fear, but I am prepared to wait whatever time is necessary."

Fearing perhaps he had drunk too much brandy already, Chester shoved the glass aside and glared at this arrogant impostor. "That is very fine," he declared scathingly, "but what is to be done in the meantime if she shows signs of increasing? Or is that your next strategy?"

Anger twitched a corner of Travis's mouth. "Your daughter has suffered enough from neglect, Mr. Stanford. You must ask her at whose hands she has suffered, but I can assure you that they were not mine. My only interest is to keep her from harm. That I must go about it in a manner other than normal is through no fault of my own. My references are impeccable. It is only society's view of me that gives you reason to question my integrity. I resent your insinuations."

Stanford sighed and sank back in his chair. Damned if he

wasn't beginning to believe the bastard, though he only understood one word in two. It made no sense, but it certainly sounded sincere.

"Believe me, I would heartily like to accept your explanations, but you must admit, they are just a trifle farfetched. There are not too many titled Indians among our ranks."

Travis made a rueful grimace. "There would be none had my father's elder brother and his son not died in a smallpox epidemic two years after my birth. My father never thought to inherit the title. Admittedly, it is presumptuous to ask you to take my word, which is why I give you references I would give no other. However, I am perfectly willing to prove my integrity in any way that you require. I have been aboveboard in all my dealings with you and every other man in this town. Although I could not acquire a taste for the life my father's society requires of me, I have been to Oxford and have the education any husband of Alicia's would require. Perhaps I have lived too long outside the boundaries of civilization, but I am prepared to change my habits for Alicia's sake."

Chester swore under his breath as he considered the alternatives. He did not doubt that Travis could pass for a gentleman in any society when he turned his mind to it. He had heard nothing but praise and admiration for the young man from his associates since his arrival. If he were truly the legitimate son of a titled Englishman and wealthy enough to support his daughter, he could have no other grounds for objections. It was obvious Alicia favored him.

The alternative was to allow Alicia's reputation to be smeared by rumors and hope she might overcome them, or to give her up to the life of unmarried teacher as she had declared she would do. Chester rather suspected the latter would be most likely. Alicia could be as bull-headed as her mother. The fact that she had taken a lover relieved some of his fears of his former wife's influence, but it did not mean Alicia would agree to marry. An incident like this might be the impetus to persuade her.

Reluctantly Chester Stanford began to nod his agreement to the younger man's arguments. If Alicia did not bear his brat, there would be time enough to verify his story. A long betrothal would be a requisite.

Rising and coming around the desk, Chester offered his hand. "A formal betrothal should put an end to flapping tongues. You understand the marriage cannot be formalized until I have received answers to my letters?"

Travis rose to accept Stanford's hand. Neither man noticed the opening of the door or the robed figure hesitating in the doorway. Only when Travis spoke did any sound reveal her presence, and then it was too late.

"I thank you for your regard, sir. You will not regret your decision. I promise that as my wife, Alicia will receive all the respect she deserves."

Alicia's gasp of fury sent them swinging to face the doorway. Garbed only in a long, flowing robe of maroon velvet, her hair pulled back in a ribbon, she still bore herself regally. Only now her face was pale with emotion.

"Traitor!" she hissed as she met Travis's dark gaze. Then turning to her father, she spat, "I am not yours to give."

In a blink of an eye she was gone, but those brief moments had been sufficient to bring months of planning to the brink of disaster. Travis leapt to chase after her, crying her name with anguish, but he could hear the bedroom door slam before he made it halfway up the stairs.

Letitia appeared on the stairway, blocking his path. Gazing down into the torment of black eyes, she took sympathy on the handsome young man, and a smile formed on her lips.

"I do not know what you have said to upset her, but I beg you wait until the morrow to apologize. She is not in a state to be rational tonight, *n'est ce pas?*"

Travis would not let Alicia's stubbornness defeat him. It would have been better had he been given time to win her properly, but the man at the bottom of the stairway would not understand that if Alicia had not told him her history. Somehow he would have to persuade her, but he didn't think logic would work as well as it had with her father.

Travis turned to meet Stanford's angry gaze. "That wasn't the best way to tell her."

By Sunday afternoon Alicia had tired of hiding in her room, but she could not organize any other plan. Travis had blocked her at every turn.

Staring out the window at the muddy remains of last week's snow, she realized she should have presented herself at church this morning as if nothing had ever happened. If it had just been the stares and whispers of the congregation that she would have to defeat, she could have done it somehow. But she never could have done it and faced Travis at the same time. That was asking more than a saint could manage.

She could not believe Travis had manipulated her this way. Surely, he could not have planned the fire, but he must have had other plans that would have had the same result. How else could he have persuaded her father to this idiocy so easily? Marriage! Perhaps if she told her father the atrocities she had seen Travis commit . . .

But she had known of those before she had gone up to his room. Everything came back to that. Everything she knew about him should have told her he was not suitable, but she had ignored all the warnings. How could she possibly explain to her father why she had gone up those stairs with a man not even suitable to be her husband? She wasn't at all certain she could explain it to herself. Idly she stroked the smooth wood of the carved lady she had rescued from the flames, not attempting to bridge the incongruity between the sensitive carving and the violent man who had created it.

Alicia grimaced as Becky knocked and poked her head around the bedroom door, but she preferred any diversion to her thoughts.

"Mr. Travis is downstairs. He brought something for you." Becky entered the room and produced a small pot of gardenias. Their aroma immediately filled the room with summer, and the glossy leaves brightened the dreariness of winter outside.

Curtly Alicia pointed to the door. "Take it back. I do not take gifts from traitors."

Becky stared at her in astonishment. "He ain't no traitor. He saved your life for you, and he's plumb worried about you. You've got no call to treat him like that."

"He nearly cost me my life and more. Let him worry." Alicia turned to stare out the window again. If she let herself think of Travis as a gentleman whose feelings would be hurt, she would give in to these pleas. She must remember he was no gentleman and his pocketbook, not his feelings, were involved.

"Mr. Travis didn't go settin' that fire. 'Tweren't his fault. He lost everything. You should be commiseratin' him."

Dully Alicia spoke to the window. "What were you doing

there to know how the fire got started? Didn't you learn your lesson the first time?"

"You were there. Don't talk to me about learning lessons," Becky responded defensively. "I was just keeping Auguste company—in front of a whole room full of people, which is more than you can say!"

When even this did not draw a response from Alicia, Becky turned and left the room, slamming the door behind her.

Travis accepted Alicia's message with a grim nod and left the flowers for Becky to dispose of. She would have to come down out of her ivory tower sooner or later.

Returning to the boat that had become his only abode now, Travis discovered Auguste had taken up residence there. The big man gave his employer's black look a passing glance before settling down against the banquette cushions again.

"What are they saying in town?" Travis asked wearily, throwing himself down on the bed and jerking at his boots.

"Nothin' much, just speculatin'." Auguste shrugged laconically. "Dr. Farrar, he tell them it was just one of the bar girls, but not too many as believe him."

"The other story is just so much better," Travis reflected bitterly. He had promised to keep Alicia from harm, but he had certainly made a botch of it. Perhaps she was right. Civilized gentlemen wouldn't have found themselves in this situation. But civilized gentlemen wouldn't have won Alicia, either. There had to be a way.

Travis flung one boot to the floor and started on the other. "What was Becky doing there last night?"

Carefully nonchalant, Auguste shrugged again. "She like to have fun, too." He grinned in remembrance. " 'Bout screeched the house down when I wouldn't walk through fire for you."

Travis grunted his appreciation. "Her screams were sufficient." He stopped in the middle of pulling the last boot off. "Stanford had to leave town on business today. He won't be back for a week."

Not quite following this train of thought, Auguste simply waited for the remainder. Travis's dark face began to glow with devilish mischief. He had seen that look before and spent many a night in jail for it.

"Becky's on our side. Give me that writing desk . . . No, she probably can't read. You'll have to carry the message."

The message he dictated brought a wry lift to Auguste's eyebrow and a hint of a smile to his lips, but he left to carry it with a jaunty swing of his shoulders.

Travis wondered if the message or Becky had produced that unusual reaction from the taciturn boatman, but he did not consider it long. He had enough troubles of his own.

22

UNABLE TO SLEEP, Alicia kicked off the covers, rose from the bed, and donned her dressing robe. The cold air felt good against her heated body as she lit the lamp wick. Travis had taught her more than she wished to know and left her restless for more. He must have known what he was doing to her, and counted on her wanting more.

She only hoped he suffered as much as she. Flinging herself into the bedside chair, Alicia picked up the book she had tried to read earlier. The words blurred together and she pressed her eyes shut, leaning her head back against the chair. Just that small action reminded her of the way Travis's lips had burned against her throat, and she flung the book against the far wall.

Why had he asked to marry her? It ruined everything. She had always been told that if men got what they wanted before marriage, they would never make it to the altar. She had been willing to accept that. She only wanted to be rid of the fear so she could live a normal life again. What had made him think she wanted marriage?

What was wrong with her? Why couldn't she find some nice gentleman like Sam Howard and marry him and live happily ever after like other women did? Why did she find herself falling into the arms of a savage like Travis, a man whose proper name she did not even know? A man who had taken advantage of her loneliness and fear to seduce her and ruin her unless she married him?

If she thought about it carefully, rationally, she would realize Travis represented everything she was not and could never be. He had the savagery to turn on his attackers and tear them apart, the freedom to go where he willed and do what he wanted, while she had not the daring to break out of this shell of civilization that protected her. Without that protection, she would be nothing. She would be no better than that knife-wielding harlot in Pittsburgh. She could never be like Travis, and she could never marry a man who so threatened her precarious existence. But her thoughts did not flow in that direction.

They kept returning to that burning look in Travis's dark eyes when he looked at her, the hunger in his kiss when he held her. Why couldn't some other man make her body ache and yearn for something she had yet to discover and may never know now?

The cold air wasn't enough. Alicia strode to the window, flinging it wide and breathing deeply of the night. Even the weather betrayed her. The night was mild, carrying the first hints of an early spring, and she nearly wept with the frustration as the gentle wind lifted her hair in a soft caress.

A sound at her door caused no reason for alarm. Becky came and went as if the room were her own, somehow sensing when Alicia's spirits were at their lowest. She waited for the latest impudent excuse as the door swung open.

When it closed again without a word being said, Alicia swung around.

Travis turned the key in the lock, then removed it from the door and reached to deposit it on the top of the high door frame. Only then did he turn to confront his hostage.

He wore a black silk shirt and trousers, incongruously completing the outfit with moccasins and his fringed buckskin coat. A strand of black hair trailed across his high forehead, and he flicked it back in place, not tearing his gaze from Alicia's tense pose.

Loosely belted, the velvet robe did little to disguise the gosamer gown beneath. Full breasts thrust against the flimsy material, and Travis could almost imagine he saw the rose-tipped peaks in the flickering lamplight. The memory of how they had tautened eagerly against his palm brought a surge of heat to his loins, and he stepped boldly into the room.

"What are you doing here?" Aghast, Alicia stared at him as if he were a ghost conjured by her sinful longings. He could not be here. She had given in to her father's advice and stayed in his well-guarded house instead of returning to Mrs. Clayton's, and still Travis walked through it with impunity.

"We have unfinished business, Alicia." Travis discarded the heavy leather coat, throwing it across the blanket chest. He advanced closer.

Alicia began to edge around the wall toward the door. "I don't trust you anymore, Travis. It will have to stay unfinished."

Travis's lips curved cynically. "Other women would have cried foul if I had not offered marriage last night. You ever were a backward creature, Blue Eyes."

He had her backed into a corner now. His forward movement was so swift, Alicia stepped backward in surprise, only to find her path blocked by the bedroom chair. She braced her hands against the chair arms to keep upright, but her knees bent against the seat as he stopped in front of her.

"Get away from me, Travis," she hissed, but even as she said it, she knew she did not mean it. The heat of his body matched the fire in her own, and she wanted to grasp his shoulders for the support she needed. She wanted to feel his hard chest pressed against her, know the power of his heart pounding close to hers, and feel the bliss of his mouth on hers once again. Instead she sat abruptly in the chair.

Placing his hands on both arms of the chair, Travis leaned tauntingly over her. "Say it with more conviction, Alicia. Scream it out loud. Let's hear a little emotion from those cold lips of yours."

"I will scream. Go away before they come and haul you off to hang. You can't get away with this."

A grim smile flickered across Travis's dark face. "Alicia, I have exhausted all my patience. I will have you if I must hang for it, but don't think anyone will come running tonight."

Alarm leapt to Alicia's eyes as one hand lifted to stroke her cheek. "What do you mean? Why won't anyone come?"

"Your father is out of town. Letitia is staying with a sick friend. And Becky is entertaining those of the servants still in the house with a game of cards in the kitchen. We have tonight, Alicia. Let's make the best of it."

She didn't have time to contemplate Becky's treachery. The hard line of Travis's mouth closed over hers, pressing her backward until he was half on top of her, forcing her to recognize his desires. Futilely Alicia strained to turn away, but the brush of his tongue against her lips released the flood tide of passion she had kept pent up for as long as she could. Her lips parted eagerly, and she began to drown in the waves of emotion his deepening kiss aroused.

Instead of shoving him away, her hands slid along his chest, alternately caressing and beating him helplessly. Ignoring this useless effort, Travis circled her waist with his hands, holding her still while his kiss roamed freely across her lips. Resting his knee against the chair edge, he could plunder at will, and she could do naught but surrender. His mouth burned downward, tracing the slender line of her throat, drinking of the hollow at the base, journeying deeper to that tempting valley scarcely concealed by filmy lace.

Alicia gave a helpless cry as Travis lifted her upward and parted her robe with his eager caress. Her arms slid about his neck and she arched to meet his ardent kiss, moaning softly as his mouth found the tender peak of one breast and drew gently at it. His tongue swirled over the hardening crest, driving her wild as the waves crashed harder and harder against the crumbling barriers of her defenses.

The robe fell open and Travis pushed it aside with a single sweep, letting it fall as he gathered her into his arms and lifted her from the chair. Alicia made no attempt to elude his grasp, and he lingered in the lamplight to admire the prize he had won. The seductive femininity of the gown she wore surprised him, and he smiled as his gaze traced the silhouette of the full globes of her breasts to the narrow valley of her waist downward to the darker shadow at the junction of her thighs.

"I approve your choice of nightwear, my love. Your taste has improved considerably since last we met like this."

Alicia blushed as she realized how much the gown revealed, but Travis did not give her time to grow timid. His muscular arms tightened around her as he carried her toward the bed. As he lowered her to the mattress, he caught his hand in the hem of the gown and drew it upward. Alicia gasped as she felt the heat of his palms slide along her bare legs, and then the gown was gone, pulled over her head in a move so swift she could not have anticipated it.

Travis caught her before she could roll away and burrow into the covers. Lowering himself to the side of the bed, he held her firmly by the waist while his gaze reveled in the beauty of the woman he meant to claim as his own.

Alicia found herself wanting to give him pleasure. She wanted him to look at her with desire, and her skin burned

with the heat of his gaze wherever it rested. Boldly she met
his eyes, reading the hunger behind that dark, implacable
gaze, judging the tension in the angle of his jaw. Long
lashes half hid his eyes from her, but she knew he wanted
her. He was frighteningly male; just the musky smell of him
warned her of the dangerous virility harbored behind gentle
touches. She knew the power of those muscled arms and
wide chest, a strength built by years of fighting a river's
current. She should be terrified by his possessive hold, but
she was not.

As his hand began to travel over her hip, Alicia daringly
reached to touch the place where his shirt had not been
fastened, her finger tracing the soft curl on a bronzed chest
just beneath the *V* of his collar. Obligingly Travis released
her long enough to unfasten the rest of the shirt, dropping it
to join her gown upon the floor.

In the same swift move Travis lay down beside her, his
hard hip pressing against hers while his hand tangled in the
loosened braid of her hair. Through the thin material of his
tight trousers, Alicia could feel the swelling line of his
masculinity, and a war of conflicting emotions arose inside
her. Travis gave her no time to pull away. His mouth settled
firmly over hers, reawakening the hungers he had so painstakingly taught her.

Alicia grasped eagerly at the familiarity of these sensations. Her fingers traced his bulging upper arm, and she
cried joyously as Travis bent to suckle one breast, then
the other. His kisses traveled as swiftly as his hands, drawing her close, demanding response, until her mouth sought
eagerly for his and her hands clasped desperately to his arms,
his shoulders, anywhere that she might come closer to him.

Travis slid his hand beneath her hips, pulling her up
against him while his knee came between her thighs. Alicia
groaned and buried her face against his shoulder as she felt
the draft of cool air rush over the fire he had aroused in this
vulnerable spot. His fingers began to stroke her there, while
his kisses poured across her hair, her forehead, her cheeks,
anywhere they could reach until the flame of these multiple
fires caught and spread and consumed every inch of her skin.

Alicia trembled against him, not knowing what to do or
how to tell him what she wanted. Her kisses fell lightly
against his hard shoulder and angular jaw, and her fingers
explored tentatively the vast expanses of his chest and back.

Nothing could dissolve the growing ache where Travis held his hand, massaging her into readiness. She rose against his penetrating fingers, and the ache grew bolder, more demanding, until she groaned aloud with her need.

Instantly Travis brought his mouth back to hers, pressing deep, penetrating and invading much as his fingers had done, until finally Alicia's tongue responded to his call. He sighed deeply at the sensual sweetness of this kiss, offering him the warmth and softness he craved. Slender curves filled his hands and pressed along his body and his desire became a pounding need to possess.

Alicia's fingers fumbled at the front flap of his breeches, and Travis held his breath at the exquisite sensations her innocent touch aroused. Hastily he unfastened the cloth and whipped the remainder of his hampering clothing off. Before Alicia had time to be afraid of his nudity, he gathered her close, fitting himself to her slender curves.

Alicia gasped at the heated flesh pressing against hers, but Travis's kiss soon drew away the fear, spreading the wildfire through her veins. His hands and lips played games along her skin until every inch was sensitive to his touch, rising eagerly for more, seeking some satiation for the turbulent currents of fire raging through her.

The loose braid of hair came undone and spread across her shoulders and down her back, where Travis gathered it in thick handfuls as he pressed his kiss along her throat and the ripe temptation of her breast. As his mouth closed over the peak, Alicia arched instinctively upward, crying out as she felt the burning brand of his masculinity press between her thighs at the same time as his lips made their claim.

"Tell me you want me, Alicia," Travis muttered thickly against her hair. "Tell me now before I burst with the need of you."

She knew what he wanted. She was terrified of what it meant. But the hunger inside her ached for fulfillment, and the hard masculine body holding her so demandingly seemed ideal for the purpose. She wanted him. She would be less than honest to say no.

"Travis, please," she pleaded, frantically burying her fingers in his hair, kneading the rippling muscles of his back, straining to be close to him.

"Tell me, Alicia. I want to hear you say it. Tell me you want me as much as I want you. Tell me you're mine for the taking."

Travis turned her on her back and stared down into the smoky blue of Alicia's eyes. Her lips were bruised and swollen from his kisses, and passion burned deeply behind those thick, dark lashes. She was soft and vulnerable beneath him. He could take her with ease, and his entire body ached for the possession and the release he so desperately needed, but he would not take her in fear or against her will.

His heavy weight pressed her down into the mattress, and his masculinity branded her thighs and rubbed achingly for entrance, but Alicia felt none of the fear or humiliation she had that first time. Travis rose above her in proud nakedness, his bronzed skin gleaming in the lamplight, his shadowed eyes like blazing coals as he gazed down at her. He heaped no blame or guilt upon her shoulders, but admitted his desire freely, leaving her opportunity to do the same. They were equals in this, each needing the other, and the longing within her grew to insurmountable proportions.

"Now, Travis, please. I need you." Alicia lifted her hands to his chest and slid them around his neck as Travis lowered himself over her.

Breathing raggedly, Travis slid one hand beneath her, pulling her close as he sent fervent kisses down her cheek to the sweet moistness of her lips. At long last he had what he wanted, and he would not waste it with haste. He drank deeply of her kiss while his knee nudged her thighs to part.

Alicia tensed as his maleness pressed where his fingers had been earlier, but Travis had worked his magic too well. The warm languor his caresses had produced stole over her now as his hand stroked and played and opened her to him.

She was ready when Travis entered her. Alicia gave a small gasp of surprise as his length filled her, expanding narrow passages until she thought surely she would burst, but she did not, and the sensation of his complete possession made her weep for the joy of it.

Gently Travis began to move back and forth, renewing the intensity of her need. Alicia clung to his shoulders, following his lead, surrendering her body to his as Travis drove them higher and higher, to peaks beyond imagination. She had no body beyond his, and it did not surprise her that when the violent quakes erupted and shook her insides, his did the same, and they moved together.

23

At last they lay together, the sweat of their bodies mingling on the sheets. Travis rolled on to his side so as not to harm her, but he did not release her. His hand rode gently up and down Alicia's spine, calming the shudders that occasionally shook her shoulders.

"Are you regretting it now?" he asked in a rough whisper.

"No, never." Alicia licked a drop of sweat on his shoulder, savoring the taste of it as she radiated in the closeness of his body next to hers.

Travis relaxed and pulled the covers up to hold the warmth, using the sheet to dry the moistness between her thighs. Already he felt his need for her begin to grow, but he had promised to protect her, and that promise did not come easily.

"Then you will not scold poor Becky for abandoning you to my savage lust?" Travis pressed a kiss to the vulnerable skin beneath her ear, then nibbled gently at the tempting lobe.

Alicia shivered with pleasure and cuddled closer into his sheltering arms. "She's incorrigible. You should not encourage her. Oh, Travis, what are you doing?" she gasped as he gathered her hair in his hands and tilted her head back to smooth the path of his kisses. She knew his direction, and she drew her breath in sharply as his lips covered her still tender nipple.

Drinking his fill at this succulent fountain, Travis raised his head to smile down at her. "No more incorrigible than I." His smile faded and his eyes grew dark. "I am not willing to give you up so easily, Alicia. Will you give me time?"

She did not want to think of these things now. She wanted

to explore the masculine figure that had produced such pleasure, discover the source of the hardness pressing insistently against her abdomen. She did not want to think.

"What time would you like?" she murmured nonsensically, trailing her fingers over the light fur covering his chest.

"A lifetime, preferably," Travis grunted as her fingers discovered the small peak of his nipple. He smoothed her hair down her back again. "But at least give me time to persuade you to be my wife."

Alicia glanced up sharply to his angular profile. "I thought you and my father had settled that matter between you."

"You would give me no chance to explain," he admonished softly. "You must learn to trust, Alicia. I would not take that choice from you. I did not want to give you up without first having the chance to persuade you, but if you decide against me, I will not keep you bound."

Curious, more than willing to listen to the voice of reason if she could remain in this haven, Alicia relaxed and listened. "How will you do that?"

With a certain amount of sadness Travis hugged her close. He didn't want to lose her, not now, not after tonight had shown him how it could be between them. But he knew his own shortcomings better than any. If her father had not been here, if she had found herself all alone in an alien world, she might eventually have turned to a man who could offer her some of both worlds. But why should she settle for the likes of him when she could have all of her own world if she wanted?

"We will have to let your father think you have agreed to this marriage so I can continue to see you. But if you find you cannot go through with it, that you cannot be my wife, then I will just quietly disappear from your life."

Alicia heard the odd note of bitterness behind his simple phrases, and her heart ached. There was no talk of love between them. There never had been. He had said marriage could be based on friendship and respect, and she supposed that was true. But after what had gone between them, she had hoped for more. That was romantic foolishness, of course, but she would have liked to hear the words.

"How can you do that?" she asked softly, daring to touch the taut plane of his face beneath high cheekbones. "You have invested your time and money here. You said you wanted to buy land here and settle down. How could you just disappear from my life?"

Travis trailed a line of kisses along her cheek. "One day I would say I had a shipment to deliver, some land I would like to look at, and the next day I would be gone. It happens all the time out here. I'm accustomed to traveling from town to town, I have no roots as you do. I can settle anywhere. When people begin to ask questions, you could look worried and say you feared something had happened to me. Before long, everyone would believe I was dead. I won't come back to prove you false."

The flatness of his voice told of the finality of such a decision. He would disappear, just like that. Gone from her life forever. It seemed a harsh choice, and Alicia had no desire to make it.

Her fingers rubbed lightly over the rough stubble forming on his jaw. Her gaze followed the path of her fingers as they trailed down his jaw and into his hair. She knew he watched her, but she did not meet his eyes.

"My father has no right to ask that of you," she replied evasively.

Travis had not expected more. It would take time to pry a commitment from her, and she had not denied him that time. He wouldn't ask for more just yet. His hand slid down her back, claiming her for now.

"I take what I can get," Travis said roughly, then proceeded to show her just what he meant.

This time he had no need to seduce her. Alicia responded eagerly to his caresses, daringly exploring his body until Travis could scarcely control his reactions. When he could wait no longer, he took her quickly, possessing her with a firmness that she could not fight.

Alicia knew she had forfeited control of the situation, but as Travis's body conquered hers and carried her away, she did not care. Come daylight, she might have to return to the struggle for her freedom, but tonight she surrendered it willingly to his expertise. Imaginary it might be, but in his arms she felt wanted and loved and wholly a woman again.

This time when her body rocked with the power of his thrust and the waves of pleasure they produced, she felt Travis withdraw abruptly. She cried out in surprise and held him as he shuddered within her arms, gaining his own release only after leaving her.

They lay together quietly, his large body covering hers with its heavier weight as their breathing slowed and their hearts' pace matched each other's. Alicia slid her arms wonderingly over Travis's bronzed back, not understanding much of this complicated man who had claimed her, fearing to know more.

"Why did you stop?" she whispered as he began to stir in her arms once more.

Lifting himself on one elbow, Travis stroked her cheek. "I said I would protect you." He gave a wry grin at her vaguely puzzled expression. "I did not think I would be given chance to take you once. Twice I was not prepared for. I fear you will have to make some choices quickly, Blue Eyes. I have no wish to leave you in the family way if you choose against me."

Alicia's sudden gasp of understanding wiped some of the bitterness from his eyes. With all her book learning, she knew little of men. Travis rolled on his side, taking her with him. If he accomplished nothing else, he would educate her in that subject.

Alicia lay against his warmth, feeling the stickiness of his seed along her thighs. She had accepted his promises without thought, but she could not continue much longer in this mindless state. As she had reason to know, he could start a child within her womb so easily. How was it she had placed herself in such a position again?

Perhaps because the child she had lost had left an emptiness within her that needed filling. To her shock, Alicia realized she wanted children. Now that she had no fear of the act that created them, she could be honest with herself. She wanted to make love to a man and feel his child grow within her. The question remained, could Travis be the man to father her child?

Despite the sleepy languor produced by their lovemaking, a tension remained between them. Knowing he would have to leave shortly, Travis buried his face in Alicia's hair and held her close so that he could feel the tips of her breasts pressed against his chest and her hips rubbed close to his. He watched in surprise when Alicia lifted her head from his shoulder to stare at him in curiosity.

"I do not even know your name." Wide eyes stared up at him, ablaze with some inner discovery.

Travis's lips twisted tenderly at this innocent amazement. "Max," he answered lightly.

"Max?" The question lingered there as she tried the sound upon her tongue.

"Maximillian," he amended with a shrug.

A small grin flirted about Alicia's mouth. "Maximillian Travis? And the Lonetree?"

"A name given me by my mother's family. It is written on no paper anywhere."

"I like it better than Max," Alicia announced firmly, as if deciding the matter.

"So do I." Comfortably Travis adjusted her against his shoulder and placed a kiss against her brow.

When he felt her breathing evenly, he gently began to extricate himself. Alicia stirred and reached for him, but only encountered the empty bed. He was already up and donning his clothes.

"Travis?" she murmured sleepily.

He came to sit beside the bed, admiring the golden glow of the lamplight along ivory breasts. "I must go," he warned her gently.

"Not yet," she protested.

Travis smiled at this petulant reply. "As it is, I may meet Letitia on the stairs or find myself locked in. I think we may have a hard time explaining that to your father."

"Not to Letitia." Gradually growing aware she caressed his muscular thigh, Alicia lifted her head sleepily.

"No, perhaps not to Letitia. She is a very understanding lady, but I would not trespass too far on her good nature. Will I see you tomorrow?"

Tomorrow. Another day when she must think. Everything seemed so much easier when wrapped in the languid sensuality of his presence. If she could just let her body think for her. Alicia smiled as Travis pressed a kiss to her temple.

"Tomorrow," she answered, and she slid her hand lovingly along his thigh.

Travis left her room that night in the same state that he had entered it: wanting her desperately and hopelessly uncertain of the future.

The next day, to Alicia's dismay, she discovered the narrowness of the velvet walls of her father's protection. A

carriage carried her back and forth to school, so there was
no opportunity to linger on long walks after classes. Instead
of Bessie's cozy kitchen, she entertained Travis in the parlor
after dinner under Letitia's watchful eye, and even that time
was limited to a respectable half hour.

When Letitia made it clear that the evening had ended
but understandingly left the room to give them a moment
alone, Alicia lifted a rueful eyebrow to her suitor.

"I have done it now, haven't I?"

Gently Travis touched the upsweep of hair that had fallen
in such abandon through his hands just the night before. He
did not do more for fear he would not be able to let her go.

"It was necessary. If we are to be a respectable betrothed
couple, you must live under your father's supervision."

A rebellious look leapt to Alicia's eyes. "I am nearly
twenty-one. He cannot think to treat me as a child."

"No, he can only love and try to protect you from rogues
like me." Touching full, pouting lips with his fingers, Travis
produced a wry grin. "But being the bounder I am, I will
find some way to see you alone. Last night was not enough."

Excitement shivered through Alicia at this admission, and
their gazes locked in understanding. The tension lingered
there between them, so taut it could be plucked like a guitar
string as their bodies yearned to touch and fought to stay
away.

Valiantly Travis kissed her quickly, scooped up his hat,
and retreated to the outer hall where he bowed politely to
Letitia with impeccable timing.

By Friday night Alicia could have cried with frustration.
She had not given thought to anything at all but the opportunity to be alone with Travis again. On Friday her father
returned and the opportunity seemed lost forever.

Letitia had invited Travis to dinner, and the three of them
were sitting down to eat when Chester Stanford arrived.
Sending Travis an anxious glance, Alicia sent for another
place setting while her stepmother ran to give her husband
an ecstatic hug of greeting. His exuberance at being home
was apparent to all until he entered the dining room and
found Travis sitting at his table.

He stiffened immediately, his gaze traveling from Alicia's
frozen features to Travis's noncommittal expression. With
formality he escorted his wife to her place and took his seat
at the head of the table. Exchanging polite greetings until

the servants returned to the kitchen, Chester immediately launched his attack.

"I will assume matters are settled since I would not elsewise be entertaining the man who destroyed my daughter's reputation." With precision Chester slit the fish on his platter and began to remove the bones.

Anger momentarily stilled Alicia's tongue, and she sent Travis an anguished look. Before he could reply, Letitia gaily broke the silence.

"Don't be such a Yankee Puritan, Chester," she admonished laughingly. "Everybody understands that Alicia cannot even announce her betrothal until her year of mourning is over. To have her intended escort her all the way out here to obtain your permission was extravagantly romantic, if a trifle foolish. Young love can be terribly impetuous." Letitia sent her husband a roguish look that discomfited him slightly.

Travis bit back a grin as he recognized the source of the story that had been making the rounds this past week. "You are too kind, *madame*. I had wondered why I was being treated so understandingly by the ladies lately."

As Chester struggled with his bewilderment, Alicia began to follow the drift of this insensible conversation, and she couldn't help but smile at her stepmother's quick-wittedness.

"I suppose you have also explained how I could have met Travis in Philadelphia?" she inquired demurely.

Letitia beamed. "But, of course, *ma cherie*. Your father has said he is acquainted with Mr. Travis's father, and how could that be unless he is of an old family back East? I think New York was mentioned, was it not, *cher ami*?" Bright-eyed, she turned to her husband, who appeared to be strangling on a fishbone.

Alicia caught undercurrents here of more than Letitia's active imagination, and she lifted an inquiring eyebrow. "New York?"

Since her father did not answer immediately, Travis shrugged and carried the jest to its limit. "East, undoubtedly, although I daresay my ancestors lived there well before the good burghers of New York. Definitely an old family."

Alicia smothered a laugh, knowing full well he referred to his mother's ancestors and not his father's. Noting her father had recovered his equilibrium, she sought more sense than she would receive from Travis or Letitia.

"You know Travis's family, then?" Letitia had exaggerated the truth, but she had not lied. It had to be assumed she knew something of the conversation between Travis and Chester that had resulted in this surprising agreement on the subject of marriage.

Chester sent Travis a baleful look. "If he is who he says he is, yes, I know his father. It is only for that reason that I have not had him tarred and feathered and run out of town on a rail." He turned a warning glance to his smug wife before addressing Alicia directly. "You have honored your mother sufficiently. It is time that this specious betrothal is announced publicly. People will talk elsewhere."

Travis read the rebellion in sapphire eyes and hastened to smooth the direction of this conversation before words were said that could not be undone and his cause be lost forever.

"Mr. Stanford, I understand your concern, but I would prefer it if you give me time to make my own case with Alicia. She is accustomed to making her own decisions. To expect her to change after all these years is a trifle unreasonable."

Caught by surprise at this rejection of her father's authority, Alicia stared at Travis with something much akin to approval and disbelief. She had thought they worked together against her. From the look on her father's face, it seemed Travis was as caught in this trap as she. It gave her food for thought, and she digested it carefully.

Chester Stanford had the grace to swallow his rage as he noted the look of admiration in Alicia's eyes as she gazed upon the bronzed visage of the man across the table. The devil knew what he was doing, and the good Lord only knew, he didn't anymore. The twelve-year-old who had once idolized him had become an independent woman he despaired of knowing.

"I am glad you understand, Mr. Travis." Alicia carefully sipped her wine, grateful for this reprieve. "Then you should also understand that I enjoy teaching and am in no hurry to give it up."

This brought protests even to Letitia's lips, but only Travis's quiet words overcame the chaos to be heard clearly.

"I will not ask you to give it up. If your father will just give us some time alone to discuss these things, I am sure we can come to some agreement."

Still holding her wine glass, Alicia met his dark gaze and

felt the shock of it tremble down her spine and settle in her stomach. Travis did not mean to allow any argument to dissuade him from this marriage. She could see it in the way he looked at her, hear it in his voice. He meant to pound away at all the careful walls she had built until they became dust at her feet. It would just be a matter of time before she was his wife and sharing his bed every night—wherever that bed might be. That thought brought a flush to her cheeks and Alicia slowly lowered her eyes with her wine glass.

Sensing victory at hand, Chester genially agreed that the couple should have some time alone to talk things over, then changed the subject to the effects of the shipping embargo on Britain and France. The two men instantly fell into an animated discussion as to whether Congress ought to continue the embargo or declare war on Britain in retaliation for their insolent and proprietary treatment of American ships. Letitia and Alicia listened quietly, their own thoughts closer to home.

Immediately after dinner, Chester dismissed the young couple while he and Letitia caught up on a week's worth of news. Quietly Alicia led her would-be fiancé to her father's study, where Travis firmly closed the door behind him.

He watched as Alicia escaped to the far end of the room, ostensibly to stir the fire. She wore her thick chestnut curls stacked loosely, and a number escaped in fetching wisps about the nape of her neck as she bent over the hearth. The high-waisted, tawny gold velvet gown she wore emphasized her slender waist and hips and revealed more of the soft curve of her breasts than her usual attire. Travis could almost believe she had dressed purposely for him, except that she would not face him now.

"Alicia, don't hide from me." He strode into the center of the room, willing her to meet him halfway.

Alicia turned to find Travis's rather awesome masculine presence filling her field of vision, erasing the rest of the book-lined study. In a sober frock coat of brown wool, fawn trousers, and soft, polished boots, he appeared every inch the gentleman. But Alicia knew the breadth of his shoulders did not come from fashionable padding, that the weathered bronze of his face did not stop at his shirt collar, and that beneath the respectable silk waistcoat were the scars of untold battles. The clothing was only a disguise. She did not yet know the man beneath.

Still, she could find no cruelty in his hawklike features, and the depth of his black eyes hid no secrets. He had never failed to be honest with her, and the fact that she knew little about him had more to do with her lack of questioning than his reluctance to answer. She felt the heat of those eyes now and knew their magnetism. She stepped forward a few paces, leaving some distance between them.

"I am not hiding from anyone. I simply do not know what to say. My father has put you in an awkward position."

"No, I put myself there. I knew what I wanted and did not fear the consequences. You are the one who took the risks. I would make the consequences as agreeable as possible for you, if I could."

The light of the lamp on the desk threw shadows across the hollows of Alicia's cheek and gleamed softly in the folds of her dress. Travis longed to take her in his arms and force her to understand the foolishness of her reluctance, but the time had come for Alicia to make her own decisions. He wanted her, but he would not force her. That was not the way he wished to spend the rest of his life.

"There is no other way, then?" Alicia inquired almost wistfully. She harbored no romantic notions. She had never expected to be wooed and courted and swept off her feet, but there ought to be more to a marriage proposal than this.

Travis felt some small part of his heart twist within him as he saw the sadness behind the lovely blue of her eyes. Against his will he reached out to touch her hair and to run his fingers over the delicate rose of her cheek.

"Do you wish me to go down on bended knee and lavish you with words of love and praise? I can probably remember some very pretty poems if I turn my mind to it." His mouth quirked at one corner as he read the flicker of amusement in her eyes.

"I think my father would come to investigate should he hear me laughing hysterically. Please, do not pretend what isn't there. A friendship based on mutual respect is more than many couples have."

No, she wasn't quite ready to take the initiative yet, to admit to feelings that frightened her still. He had hoped . . . But that was his impatience showing. Travis closed the gap between them, gently enfolding her in his embrace.

"Perhaps you will admit to just a little bit more than

mutual respect?" Without waiting for an answer, he bent to taste her lips, to find her reply without need of words.

The warmth of his kiss swiftly melted her reserve, and Alicia stepped readily into Travis's hold. His strong arms tightened around her, and his kiss deepened until the dizzying wave of passion unleashed by his touch threatened to inundate her senses, and she pressed her palms against his chest to hold him off.

Travis obliged by turning his lips to sample her cheek, her hair, anywhere within his reach as he held her firmly to him. His craving for the slender woman in his arms might never be satiated, but he was willing to spend a lifetime in trying.

"I am not certain marriage can reliably be based on this," Alicia protested, hiding her face against his shoulder so he could not tempt her more. "Any woman could fill that need for you."

Travis caught her by the shoulders and set her back so he could see behind those distressingly uncertain eyes. Sometimes he could just shake her, she was so stubbornly blind.

"If any woman would do, I would not be considering marriage now. Are you telling me you could lie with any man? Bear any man's children?"

The intensity of his tone made Alicia stare at him in wonder. "It is different for a man—" she started to object, but Travis shook her to a halt.

"No! That is too easy, Alicia. I will admit that I have never pretended to be a monk. I have known more women than I will admit to myself, and actually enjoyed some of them. If it were not for the fear of pregnancy, you could do the same, and then you would understand the difference. A moment's pleasure is a fleeting thing. That's not what I want from you. I draw pleasure just from looking at you, touching you, knowing you are mine and that I share you with no one else. The way you look at me excites me. The sound of your voice, the way you smile, no other woman can duplicate. I wanted a lady to raise my children and grace my home, but it is the woman beneath that I want in my bed. In you I have everything."

Travis's impassioned words sent shivers of longing through Alicia, and her body reacted to the timbre of his voice as thoroughly as it did to his touch. Heaven forgive her, but she wanted him to make love to her. She wanted his touch, his kiss, the length of his body against hers, and her cheeks flamed with the knowledge.

Travis noted the rising color in her cheeks with satisfaction and brushed his thumb against the delicate skin. Alicia bit her lip, meeting his dark gaze uncertainly.

"I am not a very courageous person, Travis. Sometimes you frighten me. It is very hard for me to believe in happily ever after. I don't want to hurt you, but if we agree to this for my father's sake and I find I can't—if I can't go through with it, it will hurt you, and I will lose a friendship I have learned to cherish."

"Alicia, I have gambled for worse reasons. I am willing to take my chances on this. The prize is worth losing everything."

He almost made her feel as if it was. Staring into the shadows of the bronzed planes of his face, she felt the urge to gamble on the impossibility of such a marriage. To have a man like this at her side, a man who understood her fears, her need of independence, and still wanted to share his life with her—that would be worth the possibility of making a fool of herself. If only she knew more of him, or perhaps a good deal less. She had trusted wrongly once before, with a man she had known for a lifetime. She could never trust fully again.

"I want to teach, Travis. I like teaching, but I would lose my job if we married. There are so many uncertainties . . ."

Travis pressed a finger to her lips. "There are many things we need to discuss, yes. A long betrothal is fine if that is what you wish, but do not worry yourself over this one subject. If you want to teach, you shall. Perhaps not at a lady's academy, but there are plenty of others out here who would benefit from your education. I would like to own a farm. I have one in mind that would require a number of hands. They would live on the farm, have wives and children who would work and live there, too. Most of them, like Becky, will scarcely be able to write their names. They need teaching as much as your pampered little ladies."

Alicia's eyes widened at the prospects opened by this barrage of information. "I have not thought of teaching adults, but I could try. And the children? I could teach them during the days while their mothers worked." She frowned suddenly. "You are not talking of slaves, are you?"

Travis chuckled at the wide sweep of her concerns. "I said

a farm, not a plantation. If I breed horses, I will need good, willing men. I do not want the responsibility of owning other human beings. But we cannot cover all subjects to-night. As it is, your father will soon intrude to see what takes us so long."

He slid his hand in his coat pocket and brought out a small box wrapped in plain paper and string. "I found this down at M'Knight and Brady's. They claimed the monks from Cahokia traded it for blankets and food; they are known for their silver work, so perhaps it's true. It's not as elegant as what you are used to, perhaps, but I thought of you as soon as I saw it."

Alicia accepted the small box with trembling fingers, not daring to meet his gaze. He made it impossible for her to refuse. Just the mention of her father brought the impossibility of refusal home to her. She had shamed him with her behavior. By accepting this outrageous proposal, she would make Travis happy and return her father's pride in her. There could be no harm in doing something that made so many people happy.

Alicia opened the box and gazed in delight at the exquisitely wrought ring within. Delicate bands of silver supported an oval sapphire and two tiny diamonds. She could almost feel the love that had produced such workmanship, and she raised her eyes to Travis without a hint of doubt.

"It is the loveliest ring I have ever seen," she murmured softly, her eyes as bright as the stone in her hands. "Are you certain you want me to wear it?"

Travis lifted the ring from the box and, taking her hand, slid the band gently over her finger. The whiteness of Alicia's skin contrasted sharply with the brown of his as he held her hand, and his eyes turned to look into hers.

"I want the world to know you are mine, Alicia," he whispered huskily before drawing her into his arms and claiming the kiss that it was now his right to take.

Alicia's bare arms slid gladly around his neck, and her tongue tasted eagerly of the heady wine of his. The ring burned against her finger, but not more so than the heat of Travis's body where her breasts pressed against his hard chest and her hips molded to the growing fire in his loins. She ached for the touch of his hands along her skin, and as Travis brought his hand up between them to caress her breast, she groaned softly.

Neither heard the sharp rap against the door. Not until Chester Stanford abruptly threw open the study door did they remember an outside world existed. His loud "Harumph," brought a sudden distance between the lovers.

Sharp blue eyes gazed at them over wire-rimmed spectacles. "I take it this means the evening has come to a successful conclusion," he remarked with irony. The glow of happiness in his daughter's face softened his tone considerably.

Shyly Alicia circled Travis's arm with her hands, causing the lamplight to glitter against the ring on her finger. "Travis speaks faster than I can think. I believe we may be officially engaged."

Travis bent his smile on her dark head before boldly lifting his gaze to her father's. "With your permission, of course." His expression said that he had no doubt that he would receive it.

24

AT THE SAME time Chester Stanford's letter to New York launched the first leg of its journey, a stagecoach rumbled down the muddy streets of Pittsburgh and came to a halt in front of a local tavern. A well-dressed young man of average height and build swung down from the uncomfortable confines of the interior, and surveyed the hostelry with studied arrogance.

The coach driver and the other occupants hurriedly set about unloading, but the young man complacently threw a coin to the driver and waited for his trunks to be handed down. Pocketing the coin and delivering the trunk to the porch, the driver wiped his nose with the back of his hand and eyed his wealthy passenger warily.

"Be there anythin' else you need?"

"The boat maker you mentioned, he is close by?"

"Down to the river, bottom of the hill here. Don't know that she took my advice, though. 'Twas mighty late in the season."

"I thank you for your time." Another coin comfortably exchanged hands, the grizzled driver tipped his hat and returned to his tasks, while the young man entered the tavern.

A short while later, his luggage and his room comfortably arranged, the new arrival set out in the direction indicated. Dark blond hair growing slightly thin waved fashionably above a sloping forehead. Despite the exigencies of travel, his expensively tailored suit clung neatly to rounded shoulders and trim waist. The caped greatcoat thrown over his shoulders produced a dashing effect that did not quite suit his surroundings. Several of the town's occupants turned to stare as he strode rapidly toward the river.

As he walked, he mentally counted the coins remaining to him. His debts had been such that he had found it difficult to borrow cash, even from his father. The supply was dwindling rapidly. Information had a high price, but it would be worth it in the end. By now she should be more than grateful to be rescued from barbarian society.

The widow's weeds puzzled him, but they certainly made it easier to trace her. The boat maker remembered her instantly.

"Quiet lady, real respectable-like. Shouldn't 'a been traveling alone. Thought she was a widow, though." The old man looked at the younger with a hint of suspicion.

"She nearly was. I have only just regained my health and returned home to find myself declared dead. You can imagine how I felt when I learned my poor wife had fled in grief to her father. I must find her and bring her home."

The boat man accepted that story with a shrug. He had heard stranger. With his finger he indicated the direction of the keelboat captain who had agreed to take on a passenger for one final run downriver.

When located, the keelboat captain grinned and looked the fashionable young dandy up and down while he repeated his story of widowed wife. The man didn't doubt that the haughty miss belonged to this arrogant Easterner. His interest lay solely in how much he could make out of it.

"Sure, I remember the lady. Didn't take the ride well; sicker than a dog most days. I'll take you down to where I left her off for thirty dollars." He watched shrewdly as the young man eagerly grasped the bait. With any luck he could persuade Lonetree to kick back some of his take when he left the dude off in Cincinnati. That is, of course, if Lonetree had ever delivered the lady at her destination. Still, at thirty bucks, it was worth telling the sucker any tale.

Edward Beauchamp III accepted the captain's offer with satisfaction. Alicia had never been sick a day in her life. The widow's weeds began to make sense. A hasty calculation told him if his guess were correct, she ought to look like a pear by now. She would be more than eager to take his name before the child was born.

Eying the icy floodwater of the Ohio, he inquired, "How long does it take to where you left her?"

The keelboat captain looked out over the swollen river and spat. "A month maybe, if the river don't kill you."

*   *   *

Unaware of events taking place elsewhere, Alicia and Travis spurred their horses down a soggy road across the open plain beyond the city limit. The March wind whipping her hat and hair, Alicia raised sparkling eyes and rosy cheeks to the road ahead, daring her steed to fly faster than the stallion Travis had begged, borrowed, or stolen.

They had long ago lost sight of the wagon rattling slowly along behind them. As they approached a grove of oaks just around the bend, Travis gave his mount full rein, and the stallion thundered across the finish line with several lengths to spare.

He brought his horse to a rearing halt and waited with a grin for Alicia to catch up with him. Far from being irate at his ungentlemanly display, she laughed and eyed his horse with admiration.

"If that is the kind of horse you mean to breed, you should be eminently successful."

Swinging from the saddle, Travis caught her by the waist and hauled her down against him. His kisses tumbled what remained of her pins to the ground, and hat and hair fell in wondrous disarray about her shoulders. Alicia's protest did not last beyond the fervent press of his lips against hers. With joyous abandon she clung to his shoulders and returned his kiss with an excitement that increased each time he touched her.

Reminded by a horse's snort that they were not quite alone, Travis reluctantly returned his fiancée to the ground and gathered the reins of both horses in his hands, leading them off the road to the protection of the oak grove.

"I would like to know what story you have told my father that he so foolishly allows you to accompany me with Auguste and Becky as chaperones. He is not normally so gullible." Alicia fumbled fruitlessly with the tangle of her hair, searching for the few stray pins that remained.

"I thought offering to bring my groom along a rather gallant gesture," Travis disputed with a mocking air of ruffled dignity.

"A groom who is terrified of horses?" Alicia laughed at his aggrieved expression. The new leaves of the oaks did not yet shade the sun from this clearing amid the trees, and dappled sunlight danced along Travis's dark hair and skin. With a daring she had learned these past weeks, she lifted her fingers to the sharp cheekbone accenting his angular jaw.

With the horses tied and content, Travis was free to return to his earlier pursuit, and he shamelessly grasped this opportunity. Circling her waist with his arm, he buried his face in the thick mass of hair at her nape. His other hand slid provocatively down her back to the curve of her buttocks.

"A groom terrified of horses is as good as a maid who cannot tell the front from the back of a corset," he murmured wickedly against her ear.

"Who told you that?" Alicia gasped, as much from the sensation of his hand rubbing her tender seat as at this outrageous piece of information.

"A little bird told me. Is that why you wear none now?" he inquired daringly, his hand sliding beneath her heavy riding jacket to the linen shirt beneath.

"Travis!" Alicia struggled against his prying fingers, but the desire to feel his hands on her was stronger than her protest, and she leaned into his embrace. "Becky shouldn't tell such things."

"Becky didn't. Do you think I am quite blind?" Travis leered convincingly when she glanced up at him. Unerringly his fingers found the fastenings beneath the lacy jabot, and in seconds his hard hand had invaded her shirt. "It was an unfair advantage. I could have fallen from my horse just watching you bounce."

"Oh, you are a terrible, terrible person!" Alicia squirmed with embarrassmant and not a little pleasure as his hand took liberties that brought her breath to short gasps.

"That will teach you to hire useless maids," Travis whispered as he removed her coat and flung it aside. Before Alicia could escape to retrieve it, he divested her of her unfastened shirt, and the cool spring breeze blew over fair skin as fine and unblemished as precious porcelain.

Alicia did not feel the chill. The heat of Travis's eyes as his gaze slowly swept over her warmed her to the bone and set small fires in her belly. So seldom could they find these rare moments alone that she reveled in each one, savoring each brief second. Never before, though, had they enjoyed the light of day. It was wickedly naughty, daring discovery, but she could not have denied him had she wanted. And she had no desire at all to deny him.

The blanket from the horse found its way to the greening grass, and they fell upon it, discarding clothes that hampered eager caresses. The shoulders of Alicia's chemise fell away as Travis sought greedily for the rose-tinted peaks hardening achingly beneath his fingers. Her skirts quickly followed, riding up about her waist as his hand found the smoothness of her thighs and sampled their hidden warmth.

Alicia arched eagerly against him, wanting his desire, wanting the pleasure of his body. She could feel the surge of his sex against her, and her hand boldly strayed to explore along the taut line of his trousers. Travis groaned as she instinctively stroked there, and in an instant he was on his feet and jerking off the offending clothing.

Lying beneath him, Alicia gazed in awe at the masculine physique so arrogantly displayed. Dappled sunlight played along the bronzed skin over muscular thighs and back. The scars along his ribs gleamed palely. Not until Travis turned to kneel over her did she discover the full knowledge of his manhood, and the sight struck her with both fear and longing. He was as much one with this natural environment as the ram in the herd in the far field, and he possessed her with the same urgent needs.

Alicia clung desperately to the deep demands of Travis's kiss, wanting to know there was more to what they did than just this burning hunger of their bodies. She found reassurance in the gentle command of his hands, in the patience of his kisses as Travis sought those places that pleasured her most. And when their need was so strong that neither could fight it any longer, she gave a cry of pain and delight as he sheathed himself inside her, and her body opened slowly to his thrusts.

All doubt fled as Travis showed her once again how completely he could fill her. He took her, yes, and possessed her, but no more so than she possessed him. Alicia could feel him straining against her, wanting her as desperately as she did him, and the knowledge of this small power released the last of her inhibitions. He might take her body over and over again, possess her and claim her as his own, but he would never own her mind and soul, as she would never know his. With delighted abandon she rose to meet him equally, and together they found that sweet release they craved.

As Travis quickly withdrew, spilling his seed upon the grass, Alicia wrapped her arms around his shoulders and held him close, seeking to return to that fiery warmth he had so abruptly taken away. His kisses did not serve to fill the emptiness within her, and a small tear rolled from the corner of her eye.

Travis found its track and fingered it wonderingly, lifting himself on one elbow to gaze into her lovely face still flushed with lovemaking. When long-lashed eyes opened to reveal their wells of blue, he watched them with concern.

"Is it something I have done? Have I hurt you?" Travis questioned softly, pulling the blanket's edge around them to hold their warmth.

"I did not want you to stop," Alicia admitted mournfully, turning her face away from that penetrating stare, not wanting him to know the intensity of this need inside her. He was still a stranger to her, but more and more she found herself accepting the inevitability of his claim. That she found herself wanting him to complete his possession, to make it permanent, she hid from him as best she could.

She did not succeed very well. Travis had learned the responses of her body—not only the hardening tips of her breasts pressing into his chest and the eager arching of her belly to meet his hips, but the open welcome of her womanhood and her despairing struggle to hold him there. Just bringing her pleasure was not enough, and knowing Alicia, he understood why. Gently he pressed a kiss against her temple.

"When you are ready to be my wife, when you are certain that you will welcome my child, you need only tell me yes, and I will not stop, Alicia. I do not want to take your choice from you."

Alicia shivered as Travis lifted himself enough to brush her skirts back into place, and her gaze sought his face uncertainly. "What if I cannot have children, Travis? What if I lose them all like the last? Or if the fever has made me barren like my mother? What will happen then?"

Only this proud and haughty lady could smite him so thoroughly with just the tremble of a soft, vulnerable lip.

Never before had he found himself crying inside for the plight of another, and Travis gathered her reassuringly in his arms, pulling her on top of him and covering her hair and face with kisses.

"Do not bring troubles before their time, my darling. We have many years to make children, and if it is not to be, it could be as much my fault as yours. As far as I am aware, I have never fathered a child. Perhaps it would be better if we should not. The world is an unhappy place sometimes, and there are so many children out there who have no homes or families. Your little Penny was lucky to have grandparents. Many others do not. We can always have children if you want, Alicia."

Alicia relaxed in the reassurance of his strong hold. "You would not mind if you have no son to carry on your name?" she asked with curiosity.

Just a hint of bitterness touched his reply. "It may be better if I did not. My existence creates enough problems. I suspect both families would be relieved should the line end with me."

"Travis!" Shocked, Alicia stared down into his closed face, trying to understand what his life must have been like, but failing as usual. "You cannot believe that."

Naked, he needed only war paint to complete the image of a savage. The taut muscles of his jaw emphasized high cheekbones and black eyes, and there was nothing of gentleness in his expression.

"Believe it, Alicia. My father's family was more than relieved by my decision to return to my Indian life, and my mother's family did not mourn my loss when I left. You will have no interfering in-laws to contend with. Letitia's story to the contrary, you are not marrying into any family at all, just the lone black sheep."

There seemed something terribly sad about being an outcast for no reasons of his own, and Alicia curled against his shoulder, wishing she could offer him what his family did not.

"Red sheep," she corrected mockingly. "And even had you loving family all over New York or Boston or wherever, they would all be too far away for me to meet, so it matters not. Should we not dress before Becky and Auguste arrive?"

Travis grinned. He had feared her need of the security of family would lead her to reject him eventually, but she did not seem much concerned by the lack. They just might possibly make this work after all. His hand sought the soft weight of her breast beneath the blanket.

"By now they will have decided we are lost and will be consuming our lunch. We will have to go back and find them—when we are ready."

As he drew her across him and his lips began to consume hers, Alicia realized lunch would be long gone before they were ready to find it.

25

"I HAVE RECEIVED a reply from your bankers, but not from your father's agents." Chester Stanford struck a light with his flint and applied it to his pipe as he regarded his daughter's tall fiancé.

Garbed casually in buckskin and linen, Travis seemed to lounge unconcernedly in the room's center. In reality, he listened intently to every nuance of the other man's conversation.

"The blockade in New York harbor will prevent any quick correspondence with England. I daresay your letter has rattled my father's agents into a state of confusion, and they will not know how to respond without his consent. They have not heard from me in some considerable time." Travis wondered if his father too would be rattled at the news that his son and heir was well and alive in the wilderness, but he did not let it worry him. He intended to make no claim on the estate. His family could relax and pretend he did not exist after the effects of the news wore off.

From beneath heavy brows, Chester studied the younger man's easy nonchalance and gave a mental nod. He no longer doubted Travis's claim. He remembered Lord Royster well enough to see many of the same mannerisms in his son. The looks obviously favored the mother more, but he could see Royster about the nose and eyes. The arrogance, of course, was all Royster. Damned British aristocrats, always looking down their noses at the "colonists," even when one was his son.

"Don't see how Madison can tolerate any more British insolence. He'll be looking to reenact the embargo soon, I don't doubt. And if the war hawks have their way, we'll see war by year's end. Whose side will you be on then?" Chester drew deeply on his pipe, savoring the smoke before releasing it into the air. He left the young pup standing, knowing Alicia would arrive any minute.

"My own," Travis responded cynically. "I can't see that either government has done me any favors. British insolence may be intolerable, but American arrogance killed my mother and my friends. An army that assumes all Indians are killers and murderers accordingly is not organized to protect the citizenry, but to espouse racism. If anything, my sympathies lie with Tecumseh, but I will not go to war for him either. I will fight only to protect what is mine."

Alicia quietly drifted into the room, her first words indicating she had heard this last part of the argument, and her eyes shining with approval at Travis's philosophy. "The whole town is talking of Tecumseh's threats to raise an Indian nation. That thought is frightening enough, but his brother's predictions have made everyone uneasy. I cannot believe anyone can make the earth tremble or the sun go dark, but you must admit the portents are frightening. First, the terrible cold, then the floods. We have had no spring. Is this normal out here?"

Travis had not known she was there until she spoke, and he was not quite certain what had brought the warmth of admiration to her eyes, but he basked in the glow. Claiming her hand, he tucked it into the crook of his arm, bringing her close enough that he might enjoy the scent of her perfume. Gardenias, he suspected. The plant he had sent some months ago had been reinstated to a sunny window. It bloomed profusely, and somehow she arranged to carry their scent wherever she went.

"After a harsh winter it is normal for rivers to flood. That takes only common sense. Admittedly, the rains on top of the heavy snows make things uncomfortable this spring, but fluctuations in rainfall are common."

Alicia smiled up into his eyes, feeling the ripple of excitement his dark gaze always produced when Travis turned it upon her like this. She felt the muscles of his arm tighten beneath her hand, and her heart began a steady thundering.

Chester watched the two of them together and smiled inwardly. Perhaps he had been hasty in forcing this marriage on them, but from the looks of it, he had decided rightly. They made a striking pair, both tall and well favored, Alicia's fair complexion contrasting nicely with Travis's dark one. They would give him handsome grandchildren, and he swelled a little with pride.

"Are you still planning on going downriver? The weather does not look promising."

"The journey by boat will be a short one, and the cabin is secure should it rain. I have Chouteau's old carriage down at the farm to take us back. That will probably be as quick as poling upriver against a flood, if we don't get mired in the mud. The distance is not great."

As her father continued to look dubious, Alicia put the stamp of finality on it. "'I have to see the house so I know which furniture to ask Aunt Clara to send. And measurements will have to be made for draperies and things. Travis can't be expected to know what a house needs."

Both men exchanged rueful glances and Chester shrugged in surrender. "Heaven forbid that I should stand between a woman and nest feathering. Just have her back here by dark. You are taking that maid of yours, aren't you?"

"Of course, Papa." Alicia kissed her father's cheek and triumphantly allowed Travis to escort her from the house. These hours stolen from prying eyes were too precious to be postponed by acts of nature as insignificant as a little rain. She had a decision to make, and only these hours gave her time to learn more of this man who wished her to share his life. Gazing up at Travis's strong profile now, Alicia felt the quickening of her heartbeat again. The decision had already been made, it needed only to be told.

Becky had already appropriated the seat beside Auguste in the Stanford carriage that was to take them to the river. The late March weather was still cold, and heavy, metallic gray clouds boiled up from the horizon and across the sky, but the wind held a hint of spring and a few brave daffodils decorated the lawns they passed by. In the shelter of sunny walls, forsythia bloomed, and Alicia crowed ecstatically at these certain signs of spring.

Feeling her anticipation, Travis began to grow nervous. Alicia was a city child, accustomed to the comfortable mansions and amenities of civilization. How would she view the farmhouse and acres of empty land he had chosen for his home? In front of her father, she played the part of eager bride enthusiastically. Only he knew that she had not yet agreed to be wife in fact. They never discussed it. Once she saw the kind of life he meant to live, would she reject the

solitude of rural living? To keep her, could he give up his
dream and settle for the city?

Not daring to hope, not daring to think at all, Travis
escorted the small group onto the waiting keelboat and
directed the crew to make preparations for departure. Glancing at the lowering clouds, Travis led Alicia to the comfort
of the cabin.

"The river is rough. I will have to remain with the men,"
he explained shortly when she seemed prepared to protest.

The cabin had not changed since last she had been invited
here. The big, fur-covered bed looked inviting, and a small
brazier kept the space cozy. Turning dark-lashed, sapphire
eyes to the buckskin-clad man in the doorway, Alicia studied his face wistfully.

"You cannot join me a little later?"

A corner of Travis's mouth crooked upward and he touched
her cheek tenderly. "That was what I had planned, had the
weather cooperated. I would like to make love to you to the
rhythm of the river."

Alicia blushed, and black eyes watched her with fondness.
Passionate though her response was to his lovemaking, she
still remained shy of this most natural of functions. Someday
she would come to him boldly with her desire, but that time
had not yet arrived.

Travis brushed a kiss against her forehead. "Keep your
kisses warm for me. I will find a use for them later."

With that, he strode off, ordering the untying of ropes
and the manning of poles while Alicia lingered in the doorway watching the grace of his animal stride. He had taught
her to be nearly as shameless as he. Pleasure rippled through
her insides as she watched the flexing and unflexing of
broad shoulder muscles when Travis grabbed a pole and
shoved the keel out of the path of a floating log. Those
same muscles would embrace her hungrily before this day
was out, and her blood flowed heatedly at the thought. She
did not know what she had done by falling into this man's
bed. She only knew she could no longer live without it.

Quietly Alicia closed the cabin door and went to lie down
on the bed that Travis slept in alone. Her hands smoothed
the fur as she tried to imagine sharing these quarters with
him every night. Could she sacrifice her privacy and independence to this arrogant keelboatman, who made no claims
of love but promised only the pleasures of his bed? For one

who had spent her life in terms of practicality without pleasure, it bore the certain signs of madness to even contemplate such a decision. But to the lonely, frightened woman
inside, Travis offered strength and security and the chance
for happiness. She need only swallow her pride and a lifetime of pleasure would be hers.

Had he ever treated her less than gently, ignored her
wishes, or tried to force her decision in any way, Alicia
could have rejected him without a qualm. As it was, to
reject him would be to banish him from her life forever, and
she could not do that. Her father had made it impossible to
keep Travis just as friend.

Restlessness made it useless to lie still. The fresh scents of
spring filled the air, and Alicia returned to the cabin door to
watch the river glide by. Straight and proudly tall, Travis
expertly guided the frail craft through the flood's debris,
making the dangerous chore seem as effortless as rowing a
canoe in placid waters. Was it possible to love a man like
that? A man who had no need of anyone, who walked hand
in hand with nature, without the trappings of society?

As Travis turned and caught sight of her in the doorway,
he winked, and Alicia knew it didn't matter anymore. Her
heart soared, and a blinding smile turned her lips; the elec-
tricity crackling in the clouds overhead only reflected the
surge of power between these two. The magnetism that
drew them together was such that it could not be denied
with logic or intellect. Nature would have its way.

Thunder rolled ominously overhead as the boat landed at
a makeshift dock at the foot of a bank covered in blackberry
brambles and sassafras saplings. A narrow stairway had
been carved in the clay mud and lined with stones. Swoop-
ing Alicia up in his arms, Travis swiftly carried her up these
steps to the land beyond, leaving his crew to tie the boat
securely. Neither paid any attention as to whether Becky
and Auguste followed.

The land lay in gently rolling pastures as far as the eye
could see. Streambeds could be detected from the fringe of
willows and sycamores along their banks. To the right a
grove of hardwoods interspersed with loose-limbed evergreens disguised much of the hill and house that commanded
a view of all these acres. It was in this direction that Travis
carried her.

"Travis, for goodness sake, let me down," Alicia whis-

pered nervously. From the things Travis had said, she knew
there would be workers in the fields and the outbuildings
beyond the main house. It would not do to arrive in this
uncivilized fashion.

Grinning, Travis ignored her. Alicia was a good head
taller than most women, but she was slender as one of those
willows and just as light. He had wanted to do this since he
had first laid eyes on her. The opportunity might never
come again.

The path though the field and the drive up to the house
were muddy from the spring rains, but Travis didn't seem to
notice. The men gradually drifting up from the river grinned
and kept a respectful distance behind them. Many of them,
like Travis, had chosen to settle in St. Louis after that last
trip from Cincinnati. Newcomers to the crew had already
been apprised of the erratic romance their captain had waged
throughout the fall and winter. Now that spring had arrived,
it seemed the captain had won his prize.

As they came through the curtain of trees, Alicia surrendered her battle and turned to gaze upon the house that
could soon become her home. As Travis had warned her, it
was little more than a farmhouse, but the most elegant
farmhouse she had ever seen. The bricks must have been
painstakingly made and carried from some nearby clay pit.
They had mellowed to a deep rose almost completely hidden in places beneath some intertwining vine. Leafless now,
the vine revealed arched windows and deep green shutters
that could be closed against winter winds.

The previous owner had abandoned the building, unfinished, after his wife and children had died in a smallpox
epidemic some years before. Alicia immediately spotted
Travis's handiwork in the scrolled columns of the shaded
portico and the massive eagles spreading their wings on the
entrance gate. The birds seemed capable of taking flight to
protect the house's occupants, and Alicia fell in love with
them immediately.

"Oh, Travis, put me down. I want to touch them. They're
even better than the ones you lost."

With a pleased grin Travis halted long enough to allow
her to run her fingers over the wooden creatures, but he
refused to loosen his hold until they crossed the threshold.

As he climbed the steps to the front porch, Alicia admired the carved flowers hidden beneath the roof at the top

of each column and adorning the entrance. There wasn't a house in all of St. Louis that could boast such refinements, and she knew Travis had added these touches to please her. Her eyes glowed with delight before he even opened the door to carry her inside.

Travis halted just within the front door, gazing down at Alicia as her eyes swept the elegantly wide entrance hall. In summer, the doors at front and back could be left open to air the house with breezes from the river, and the heat would be banished to the high ceilings. But it wasn't just the high ceilings and beautifully polished oak floors that held her attention. The gracefully sweeping front stairs brought a gasp of awe to her lips.

"Travis, how can you call this a farmhouse? It is magnificent!"

Carefully Travis lowered Alicia to her feet, his eyes searching her face for any sign of disappointment. What he found there brought a rapid beat to his pulse, and his hand went out to stroke the lustrous thickness of loosely stacked curls.

"Would you care to tour the upstairs or down, first?" he muttered huskily, his gaze following the sudden flush of her cheeks and the quick intake of breath. With pleasure he noted the leap of excitement in sapphire eyes, and his hand traveled suggestively downward, caressing her cheek, brushing a straying curl, coming to rest on the rounded curve revealed by the tight fit of her woolen bodice.

Butterflies flocked nervously to Alicia's stomach, and began to leap and bound in an inexplicable manner as Travis's hand grew warm and inviting upon her breast. He had discarded his jacket on the boat, and she was all too aware of the virility of the masculine body beneath that loose linen shirt. She didn't dare look downward. The tailored construction of his leather breeches disclosed every secret they were meant to cover. She knew what she would find there.

Patiently Travis awaited her decision, dark eyes boring holes to her insides as he watched her face. Without another thought to what she did now or what she would do later, Alicia lifted her arms to his shoulders and daringly planted a kiss to the corner of his lips.

"Upstairs, first."

26

SCHOOLING HIMSELF to patience, Travis offered his arm and escorted Alicia up the elegant flight of stairs to the second floor. If any other occupied the house, they were unaware of it as they slowly traversed the polished stairs and upper hallway, coming to a halt at a door on the far end.

Travis didn't need to explain why he had bypassed the other doors in the hall. Alicia clutched his arm a little tighter as he threw open the door to the room she knew he meant for them to share.

As the door slowly swung open, Alicia emitted a small gasp of surprise. She had not expected the house to be furnished, and had seen no sign of so much as a rug in any other part of the place. But in the center of this one room stood a high four-poster bed adorned with a sapphire blue silk canopy and draped in graceful folds of netting. Behind the netting Alicia could see the glimmer of a blue coverlet, but the slender posters held her attention. Releasing Travis's arm, she drifted into the room, her gaze lovingly stroking the highly polished and intricate carving of the dark wood.

Sheaves of abundant wheat wrapped the delicate pole, interspersed with some flower Alicia could not identify. The heavens in the form of the sun and moon overlooked the harvest, and a river wound between them, nourishing the plants. She did not know the exact meaning of the symbols Travis had chosen to mark their marriage bed, but she could guess.

Her eyes filled with tears of happiness, Alicia turned her gaze up to meet Travis's anxious one. "I'm not certain I deserve such beauty," she whispered.

"To me you are worth the moon and the stars, Blue

Eyes." Travis touched a drop of moisture threatening to spill from one lovely lash. "I want this house and this bed to be yours as much as mine. I want you to be happy here. Do you think you could be?"

A slow smile formed on full, rose-tinted lips. "Yes, Travis." As she lifted her arms to encompass his shoulders and move closer against him, Alicia repeated huskily, "Yes, yes, yes."

Fireworks exploded in his brain as Travis heard more than he dared hope behind that single word. Thunder rolled in the distance as he wrapped his arms about her slender waist and searched her face carefully. He could not disguise his eagerness as she rested willingly in his embrace.

"Yes, Alicia? Do I dare hope that yes, you will be happy here means yes, you will be my wife? Do not answer if you still have doubts, for I could not ever let you go once I thought you mine."

Raked with emotion, his voice was almost harsh, but Alicia heard the loneliness and the hunger behind the words, because they rang these same chords in her. "I don't want to be alone anymore, Travis. Please, let me love you."

Choked with a wild surge of joy, Travis could only scoop Alicia up in his arms and rain kisses upon her face, nearly squeezing her to death in the process. Alicia's laughing protests were quickly silenced by hungry kisses as his mouth found hers and pressed demandingly for reassurance. She gave it without restraint.

Alicia buried her fingers in his thick hair and melted willingly into Travis's heated embrace as he nearly bent her backward in his eagerness to take possession. His tongue filled her senses with fire, and she responded with urgency, bending her hips to his, pressing her breasts against the strong shield of his chest until their bodies became a single plane upon which danced a sheet of flame.

With suddenness Travis set Alicia back upon the floor. His eyes burned like coals as they traveled the length of her. With a swift movement he returned to the open bedroom door and slammed it shut, throwing the wooden bolt across it.

As he returned, Alicia watched him with a question in her eyes, and Travis smiled. "I installed the bolt myself. I'll not have my nights with you disturbed for any reason."

Thinking of all the times they had been interrupted in their lovemaking, Alicia could appreciate his thought. Even

Becky would not have the nerve to protest that locked door. A shudder of desire swept through her as she read the import of Travis's heated gaze.

"I cannot wait until our wedding night, Alicia," he murmured thickly, reaching for the pins in her hair.

She ought to protest. This was barely the end of March, and June was a long way away. She knew from the purposefulness with which he undressed her that Travis had no intention of restraining himself this time. And she did not care.

With uninhibited delight Alicia pulled his shirt tails from his trousers and ran her hands over the warm, hard planes of his chest. Travis grunted in surprise as she found the hardening points of his nipples and stroked them eagerly, but nothing she did slowed his hands. Her bodice fell forward and he shoved the hampering gown to the floor with a swiftness that caught Alicia by surprise. Neither noticed the lack of heat in the room as thunder rumbled overhead and their hands tore determinedly at each other's clothing.

Flicking aside the netting, Travis whipped back the bed covers to reveal the sheets beneath. Alicia gave a quiet cry as he lifted her by the waist and flung her in among the pillows, but she quickly wriggled out of her chemise as he sat down to remove his boots.

The sheets were smooth and icy beneath her bare skin as Alicia slid to the luxurious center of the bed, but the fire inside her kept her warm. Brazenly sitting naked amid the pillows, her hair streaming in thick waves down her back, she watched hungrily as Travis stood to strip the remainder of his clothes off. The gray light through the bedroom windows shadowed the broad, bronzed muscles of his chest, but she already knew them by heart and could see them with crystal clarity.

When Travis came to her, erect and ready, Alicia was prepared for him. His kiss sealed her lips with desire as his hard, lean length pushed her down into the feather mattress. A stroke of lightning flashed outside the window and the crash of thunder struck immediately overhead, but these forces of nature provided only a background to the act performed here. Spread against the sheets, Alicia opened willingly to him, and embraced his broad shoulders as Travis pierced her to the quick.

Their cries mixed with the thunder as their bodies rose

and fell with an urgency that matched the sudden downpour of rain against the windows. As the rain pounded harder, so did they, until no part of them remained separate. No longer alone, they merged as one, their bodies quaking with the thunder of their passion until the flood tide of life erupted and flowed through fertile valleys, filling them with contentment.

Alicia sensed the heated liquid of Travis's seed spilling into her womb, and she cried with the joy of it. This was what lovemaking truly meant, and she rejoiced in finding a man with the patience to share it with her. Her mother had been wrong about so many things, it did not come as a surprise that she was wrong about this. There was pleasure in this act of becoming man and wife, and the pleasure was not all the man's.

Finding the tears, Travis kissed them away. His body worshiped at the altar of hers, not leaving the welcoming warmth she offered, but growing stronger within her. The storm pounded with abandon outside, but the satin haven he had discovered gave all the shelter he craved.

"Alicia, my love, I have not hurt you?" Anxiously aware that he could not withstand her nearness much longer, Travis searched her flushed features with concern.

"No, never. It is too beautiful." Meaning this love she felt growing inside, the ferocity of the storm outside, and the man sharing them with her. Such perfection had no place on this earth, and she basked in it.

Travis understood. With gentle kisses he explored her face, turning on his side to ease his weight from her. Those things that were supposed to be done could wait for another day. Today he would win the future.

Alicia abandoned herself to his demands. His kiss took away her breath while his hands coaxed and teased her breasts until a river of molten lava seemed to spill from some hidden source to overflow her senses. Her hips moved instinctively to search for his, and she gasped as she felt him surge along the walls of her womanhood. Catching her waist, Travis held her impaled, and she could only writhe with the exquisite ecstasy he extracted as he moved slowly back and forth within her.

The thunder rolled into the distance and the rain eased to a gentle patter as Travis tumbled Alicia once more against the satin sheets. The rhythm of the rain measured their tempo, and this time they enjoyed each other slowly, savoring each moment that carried them higher and higher until they reached a crescendo and exploded with the passionate storm of the finale.

Afterward, lying in Travis's strong arms, her legs entwined about his muscular thighs, Alicia sighed with contentment. Months of indecision had come to an end, and she could look forward to the future. With Travis's seed still warm inside her, her thoughts traveled back to the prior spring, when another man had planted his child within her. Would it happen again? Like the newly plowed fields outside the window, would she begin to burgeon with life in the months to come? The horror of that previous time still clung to her, and she burrowed her face deeper against Travis's large shoulder.

"Travis, I am scared." Overwhelmed, frightened, terrified of what she had done. This total loss of control he had taught her was not so terrifying as the violent anger that had once caused her to carry a gun, but it was still beyond her ability to handle. She craved the freedom she found in his arms, but she also feared what it could do to her.

Not understanding, Travis ran a broad, callused hand reassuringly down her side. "There's no need to be. The storm is almost past, and the sun will be out shortly."

It was too much to expect that he would know the fear of her woman's body, how easily it could be hurt, how vulnerable it made her. She had learned that lesson the hard way, but in his masculine strength Travis would never understand. She had to trust him, had to allow this small bud of love and hope to flourish in his protection, the alternative was too lonely and painful. But the fear and insecurity stayed with her.

Daringly Alicia leaned back to gaze upon the masculine physique that had so frightened her when first they met. Never had she seen a man like this, and her fingers trailed admiringly over the rounded bulge of Travis's shoulders and upper arms, falling to stroke lightly the muscled pads of his chest. Her hand looked pale and fragile against him.

Travis gave a gasp of pleasure as her palm moved lower. He nuzzled her ear, biting lightly at the lobe to catch her attention. "When will school let out?" he murmured as her fingers unerringly found the source of greatest pleasure.

"Commencement exercises are scheduled for the first day

of June." Understanding she gained some control over this alien male by doing what she was doing, Alicia continued to stroke and explore. He could not be strong in everything. Already she had learned this one weakness. His body responded to her every touch.

Clenching his teeth with the intensity of the pleasure Alicia's innocent explorations produced, Travis managed to growl, "Then we shall have to set the wedding for the second day."

Alicia glanced up in surprise, then laughed low and joyfully as Travis's eyes opened and she read the heat of his desire. Her hand returned to rest gently against his chest. "Perhaps you are right." The need between them was so strong, if they did not actually get caught before then, she would most likely be swelling with his child. That thought excited her and her cheeks flushed.

Travis kissed the growing pink in her cheeks and cupped her breast in his palm. "I am glad you are so agreeable. I look forward to having you in my bed every night, to waking up beside you in the mornings. I cannot think of a better way to start the day."

Since his eyes and the timbre of his voice spoke clearly what his words did not say, Alicia blushed even deeper. Her nipple tautened achingly beneath his caress, and she knew what little control she possessed over him was lost beneath his greater experience. She was his to do with as he wished. He would take her to his bed every night and claim her more certainly than a deed of sale. She had made the choice to give him that right, and although it frightened her, she felt confident what she received in return was well worth the risk.

Alicia stroked the sharp-bladed bone of Travis's cheek. The first tendrils of love began to unfurl like the fragile shoots of a flower as his expression softened beneath her touch and he kissed her palm. She wanted to make him happy, but knew too little of him to feel confident she could do it.

Her fingers came down to brush against the tattooed band of blue around his arm, a symbol of those things that separated them. "Did it hurt?" she inquired softly, inspecting the scar with her touch.

"Yes, but I was so caught up in becoming an adult and a part of the tribe, I did not notice the pain too greatly."

Sensing some of the bitterness behind his words, Alicia sought some way of relieving it. "Did you not say some of your tribe lives near here?"

Dark eyes watched her with a hint of wariness. "Yes, just south of here. They have been driven farther and farther west to avoid conflict with settlers, but once this land is made a territory, they will be driven on again."

"Have you been to see them?" Alicia ignored his political diatribe. She could not control the country, but people she understood.

"Yes, before I bought the land." Travis could not see the direction this conversation took, but he followed it cautiously. She had a right to know more about him than he had offered, but experience had taught him not to reveal more than was asked. "My cousins and their families live inside the southern boundaries of this property. The previous owner never cleared the land, but had the legal deed showing it was his. It was one of the reasons I bought it from him, so my people did not have to move on again. Someday they will have to learn the white man's laws so they will not be cheated out of their lands anymore."

That he had bought this land to protect the people who had rejected him told her much, and her reply was soft. "Someday, will you take me to meet your family?"

Travis jerked with surprise, but the blue eyes innocently meeting his did not waver. Cautiously he agreed. "If that is your wish, I will arrange it. Do not expect approval, however."

Alicia smiled faintly. "That is fair. I'm not certain you would have my family's wholehearted support, either."

Travis grinned and relaxed. It was going to be all right. She knew him for what he was, knew the obstacles they faced, and did not seem to care. He had known he had chosen rightly when he had picked this independent lady. Everything was going to work out fine.

"I will most certainly lose what support I have and probably half my hide if I do not get you back to town this day. Much as I hate to mention it, we had better consider getting dressed."

Closing her eyes, Alicia attempted to memorize the feel of Travis's long length and greater weight pressing against her, but she knew the memory would not serve so well as the fact. Sighing, she slid her leg along his. "We shall have to go to church in the morning and pray soundly for our sins."

With a kiss to her cheek Travis rose from the bed. "I shall pray soundly that they may be repeated soon."

Alicia flung a pillow at him, and grinning triumphantly, Travis leaned over the bed, capturing her between his arm and body before bending to drink slowly at the fountain of her breast. She squirmed gratifyingly beneath this torture, and he smacked her buttock lightly as he stood up again.

"Remember, I don't fight like a gentleman," he warned before drawing on his trousers.

Quite naked and utterly unashamed, Alicia slid from the bed and raised her arms to pull her waist-length hair into some semblance of order. Perhaps this ploy wasn't as bold as his, but it was equally effective. She could feel the heat of his fascination as his gaze rested on the upward thrust of her breasts.

"Then I shall just have to learn not to fight like a lady," she replied grandly.

"Then let us hope we shall not have to fight at all," Travis prayed fervently, reaching to grab her by the waist.

It might be a long time before he had this opportunity again. Her bare breasts crushed against his chest as his lips captured hers with grinding desire. He could not let her go just yet.

27

HE DID NOT let her go at all, Alicia thought dreamily as she stood in front of her mirror some weeks later. Early morning sunlight streamed in the bedroom window, caressing her fair skin as she gazed wonderingly at her reflection. Her fingers rose to the dark peak of one breast, where Travis had left his mark the night before. He took advantage of every stolen minute together, and even when they were apart—like now—he was with her.

Their wedding would be in less than a month, and excitement colored each passing day. She had not believed it could be like this. She had once dreaded surrendering her freedom to a man, but with Travis it seemed as if the narrow confines of her present life opened to whole new dimensions. He made everything seem possible. She had already sent for the furniture she wished to use in her new home, and he had turned over the decorating to her. She had never been allowed this pleasure before, and she delighted in it. But most of all, she delighted in the plans for the school his workers were renovating for her in one of the outbuildings.

Running her hand assessingly over the fullness of her breast to the flatness of her abdomen, Alicia sought for some sign that her wishes had come true. A school of her own she could teach in even if she married, but pregnancy might slow her down some. Still, she wished for a child of her own as much as she did for the school. And she had some reason to believe it just might be possible, that she might very well be carrying Travis's child already.

Excitement at the thought made logical reasoning difficult to maintain. That was the reason she stood here now, forcing herself to consider this logically. She had been pregnant before. She knew the signs. The most obvious, of course, was that she had not had her monthly flow since well before that day Travis had first taken her to the farm. It was possible for a month to go by without her regular cycle if she were not well or if their lovemaking had interrupted the way of things, but this was the beginning of the second month. Yet she had suffered none of the morning sickness, none of the weakness and pain that had accompanied her previous pregnancy. And there were no outward signs as yet, she finally decided with a small sigh of disappointment. She wanted this child so badly, she could imagine herself pregnant easily. But it would probably be best if the seams of her wedding gown did not have to be let out just before the wedding.

Turning away from the mirror, Alicia reached for her chemise. She didn't care what the mirror said. It might be early yet, but she knew Travis's child had already taken root within her womb and begun to grow. Logic had naught to do with it.

Becky met her in the foyer, and carrying baskets over their arms, they ventured out into the warm May sunshine. After the cold dampness of the previous months, it felt delightful to turn their faces to the sun and breathe in the fresh scents of lilacs and honeysuckle. Spring had arrived at last.

Perhaps spring had much to do with Alicia's secret conviction that life blossomed inside her. With the mock oranges bent under the weight of their heavy blooms, plump robins hopping about greening lawns to feather their nests, and new life springing everywhere from damp earth, she felt as new and alive as the season. A year ago her mother had died, and she had been lost and alone in an empty house with an empty future. Travis had changed all that. She wanted to do the same for him.

Singing softly to herself, Alicia perused the latest shipment of lace trimmings in the mercantile store, stopped to admire a lovely silk in the dress-goods window, and waited in the sunshine while Becky stopped in the greengrocer's for a few items the cook had requested for tonight's dinner. Alicia waved as the carriage carrying Dr. Farrar rolled by, chatted with the mothers of several of her students, and smiled to Sam Howard from across the street. Already she felt a part of this community, and she seldom gave Philadelphia's faraway streets a second thought.

The arrival of a keelboat at the landing below had produced the usual shouts and curses, but the din was settling now. Alicia contemplated taking a peek at the new arrival to see if any new house goods had arrived, but a sudden dizziness caught her by surprise. She swayed and grabbed for the wall behind her. Faint, feeling as if she might fall to the ground if she stood a moment longer, she sat abruptly on the flour barrel outside the store. Her head spun crazily, and she closed her eyes against the motion, holding her forehead with her hand.

This was foolish. She had never fainted in her life. She was not even wearing a corset. But she could not stand. She felt so light-headed that she would surely topple should she try to rise. What was happening to her?

And as Becky came out with her basket full to stare at her with concern, Alicia knew the answer. Gripping the flour barrel for balance, she sent a blinding smile of delight to her anxious maid. She had wanted a sign. Now she had one. The child within her had quickened. She was going to be a mother.

Not fooled by Alicia's smile, Becky continued to watch her with concern. Garbed in one of her elegant, lace-edged muslins, this one of white with blue Swiss dots, topped by a blue velvet spencer and matching hat, Alicia looked every inch the lady she was. That made her perch on the flour barrel all the more incongruous.

"You all right?" Becky asked suspiciously.

"Never better in my life," Alicia declared grandly. "That basket will make your arm ache if you carry it long. Why don't you take it back to the kitchen while I look around some more? I'll follow you shortly."

She wanted to find Travis and tell him the news. She could picture the delight on his face now. He wanted a family so badly, and she could provide one. The thought made her ecstatic. Perhaps then he would realize how much she loved him, could love him, if he would let her. She couldn't wait to let him know. She had to tell him now.

But not with Becky hanging around. Travis was in town today, she knew, because he had promised to stop by after lunch. He usually conducted business in the tavern that had been rebuilt since the fire. She couldn't let Becky know she went there.

With some misgiving Becky was persuaded to leave Alicia

behind. The dizziness was already fading, but not the euphoria. She would be able to make it to the tavern without difficulty. Just imagining Travis's reaction when she told him would carry her there.

Nursing a glass of cold cider while waiting for Auguste to return from the river, Travis idled away his time observing the other occupants of the new saloon. Stanford had built this place with an eye to the wealthier clientele. Polished mahogany and gleaming crystal adorned the walls and ceilings, and the men at the other tables spoke in low voices and wore snowy white cravats and top hats. The keelboat crews and trappers had been forced to find more suitable surroundings closer to the river. Travis rather regretted the loss of the informal bonhomie of the old bar, but this one was certainly a good deal easier on the nerves. These gentlemen were not inclined to fisticuffs at the drop of a coin. They fought in the time-honored, civilized tradition of dueling, with a minimum of yelling and a maximum of stoic blood. Bloody Island was the place for that, not taverns.

Travis watched with interest as the door swung open and a few more of the new arrivals from the keelboat drifted in. While Auguste was picking up news and information from members of the crew, Travis indulged himself in listening to the complaints of the passengers. It had obviously not been a happy journey, and so far he had learned nothing from their conversations other than that the British still had New York blockaded.

His eye followed the dignified progress of a young man turned out in high, starched cravat, wine-colored velvet, and shining new Hessians. The length of gold chain from his watch begged for removal, but it obviously had survived the perils of travel. He greeted several of the keelboat passengers with arrogant familiarity. They did not seem particularly pleased to see him, and Travis suppressed a grin over his estimate of the situation. The bantling obviously considered himself a cut above the rest.

So it was with great surprise that he heard the young rooster speak his name, followed by instant suspicion at the sound of Alicia's. Travis sank back in the shadows and listened covertly as the stranger badgered the bartender with questions.

"They told me down at the river that someone here could direct me to Stanford's house. If you cannot tell me anything of this Lonetree, surely you can give me the direction of Miss Stanford?"

Well aware of Travis's presence and his relation to the boss's daughter, the bartender warily avoided answering. "Perhaps you'd best ask around. I just work here."

Disgusted with this taciturn reply, Edward turned to contemplate the tavern's occupants. If it had not been for the card games aboard the boat, he would be penniless by now. As it was, he scarcely had two coins to clink together. He had to find Alicia here. He could go no farther.

Approaching a respectable looking elderly man at a table not far from Travis's, he inquired, "Could you direct me to Chester Stanford? I have been told he has recently built his home here."

The man lifted a steely gaze and asked coldly, "Who wants to know?"

"Edward Beauchamp III, sir." Sweeping off his hat, he made a graceful bow. When this did not seem to impress, he played his wild card. "His son-in-law."

A sudden hush seemed to fall over the room. Edward had not spoken softly from the first, and his dress had made him noticeable the moment he stepped through the door. His words now caught the attention of every man in the room. Chester Stanford was well known and well liked in this town. His daughter had danced on the arm of practically every man in here. And every man in here knew her fiancé sat at the corner table, listening to every word. They waited.

Not rising from his chair, Travis drawled casually, "You wouldn't be Teddy, by any chance, would you?" His expression remained as impassive as stone, but his fingers clutched his glass as if they would crush it.

Edward swung around, something in the tone of that voice warning him to be wary. The man who had spoken was dressed in shadow, but he could see enough to ascertain the speaker was no gentleman. Wearing what appeared to be a rawhide waistcoat over an open-necked linen shirt, the man still managed to seem comfortable in his elegant surroundings. His hawklike features and swarthy coloring produced a foreign effect, and Edward's eyes narrowed in suspicion.

"Who are you?" he demanded imperiously.

"'I'm not the one who's lost and asking directions." Travis made no attempt to keep the scorn from his voice as his gaze swept over the dandified traveler. Alicia had never

described her rapist, but he had known men of this ilk before.
There was little doubt in his mind that he had finally come face
to face with the bastard who had nearly destroyed his lady.

Shrugging when Edward made no reply, Travis declared,
"Suit yourself," and insolently lifted his glass to his lips.

"You're Lonetree," Edward suddenly accused him. "Where
is she? What have you done with Alicia?" His voice rose
with his fury, convinced this man held the secret that kept
him from his future.

"Are you Teddy?" Travis demanded again.

"She calls me Teddy, yes! Now what have you done with
her, you half-breed renegade?"

The few low murmurs around them quieted at this epithet. Travis was regarded warily by many of the established
members of society, but they had found him to be fair in
business and sound in his thinking. That Chester Stanford
had condoned Travis's betrothal to his only daughter sealed
their approval. The rumor that he was also of British nobility had been shrugged off as had his Indian ancestry. A man
was what he made of himself out here. And a man did not
accept an insult sitting down.

Travis calmly set aside his glass and rose to tower a full
head over his antagonist. "I take offense at the derogatory
tone of your voice, sir. And I also take offense at your
familiar use of my fiancée's name. I trust you have someone
you can call on to act as second?"

Mockingly Travis repeated the protocol of the duel, knowing full well the response he would receive. Never let it be
said that he had not at least attempted to settle this in a
gentlemanly fashion, when what he wanted to do was rip the
bastard's insides out and feed them down his throat.

The shock on Edward's face was quickly replaced with
wild laughter as he regarded this barbarian imitating his
betters. Alicia and a savage! That was rich! He howled his
amusement, expecting their audience to join in.

Instead men began to slowly rise from their seats and
edge their tables away, leaving a ring around the two men.
Travis's ancestry might be hazy, but his temper was legendary.

Travis's fingers rolled into fists of rage as he contemplated
this jackal's soft jaw, but he held his temper in check while
waiting for a reply. He would have no fault held against him
when this got back to Alicia.

Realizing he laughed alone, Edward assumed another

pose. "Your fiancée? You presume too much, Lonetree. I don't know what she's told you, but I'll not duel with a savage. You might consider another man's leavings fair game, but I've decided to forgive her and take her back. She won't have to—"

The rest of his sentence went unspoken. Travis's fist flew out and connected squarely with Edward's jaw. Edward staggered backward, blood streaming from the corner of his mouth. Travis hit him again, rage hammering through his blood and taking vengeance on the body of the man who had physically violated the woman he was about to marry. Whether the rage was for himself or for Alicia was a moot point. He fully intended to decimate the bastard.

Alicia wandered in off the street just as Travis sent Edward sprawling to the floor with a crushing blow to the abdomen. Edward folded up with a gagging gasp, and Travis was upon him in an instant, forcing him to fight back. Alicia's scream almost went unheard in the shouts and yells of the crowd.

Her first reaction was one of vengeful delight as Edward's hated figure crumpled to the floor. How she wished she could have done that herself! Her fists curled in anticipation with the sound of Travis's blows, until the memory of the knife Travis usually carried in his belt made her blanch with terror.

She had to stop him. She had to stop the violence that raged through her veins, rousing her to madness, destroying her life as it had before, as it would again if he continued. She screamed for Travis to halt, losing her self-possession as she fought for what had been stolen from her once before, what she could lose once again. Her fragile peace shattered further with every blow, returning her to the wounded, terrified creature she had once been. She screamed until tears formed in her eyes and shame filled every corner of her soul and she had nowhere to hide from herself.

When Auguste materialized at her side and tried to lead her away, Alicia jerked her arm away with a strength she did not know she possessed. The relentless smack, smack of fists against flesh tore at the lovely imaginary world she had created and ground it into ashes at her feet.

Desperately striving for sanity, Alicia broke through the circle of bystanders. Her hoarse cries went unheard as Travis vented a lifetime of fury on the bruised and swollen features of the man who had tried to steal his woman. Edward's tailored clothes lay in ribbons as he feebly attempted to protect himself from the rain of blows about his head. Terrified of the violence, Alicia screamed again for Travis to halt.

"You'll kill him!" she cried, trying to return rationality where there was none, but still Travis did not hear.

Panicking, Alicia rushed forward to where the two men fought, avoiding outstretched hands that tried to hold her back. Grabbing Travis's collar, she attempted to pull him away as the fools around them would not.

Strangled by the insistent grip on his shirt, Travis wheeled furiously to take on this next opponent. Eyes burning with lust for battle, fists raised in rage, he started to swing.

Alicia cried out in fear at the mindless violence in his eyes, the same violence that had been in Teddy's eyes when he had knocked her down and raped her. Even though Travis halted his swing before it could harm her, she reeled as if the blow had been a physical one. She felt sick to her stomach, and she closed her eyes in pain.

Auguste caught her elbow and tried to lead her away, but Alicia shook herself free of this interference. She knew what she had to do, what she should have done from the first. Stripping the sapphire ring from her finger, she dropped it at Travis's feet. Disdainfully meeting his dumbfounded gaze, she said, "A wolf in sheep's clothing still eats sheep."

She swung on her heel and stalked out, the pert tilt of her fashionable hat remaining elegantly in place as the door slammed behind her.

The crush of men and murmurs around Travis warned that unfinished business remained, but rage prevented clear thought. He barked a command to Auguste. "Heave him in the next boat out of here. Get him out of my sight before I do kill him."

With that, he bent to pick up the ring Alicia had so casually cast away.

28

THE RAGE roaring in Travis's blood boiled over at Alicia's regal rejection of everything he had worked to earn, for a reason beyond his comprehension. He had been protecting her name as well as his. Did she think he would let the filthy bastard go with no more than a pat on the back and a "So sorry, old chap, you lose"?

Without another look at the crumpled dandy on the floor, Travis stormed from the tavern, the sapphire engagement ring carefully resting in his pocket. He had no intention of letting her get away this time. They had made a commitment and he would see it honored, if he had to hold her at gunpoint to see it done.

Well aware of what Travis's reaction would be, Alicia practically ran back to her father's house, ordered the servants to refuse Travis entrance, then bolted up the stairs and locked herself in her room. Her father was gone on another one of his business trips, but Letitia should arrive soon. Surely another woman would understand her predicament.

Collapsing on her bed, Alicia began to shake all over. She pulled the covers around her, trying to halt the tremors while her mind sought out all the implications of what she had done. She had just thrown away her life, her hopes, and her child's father. Was she mad?

Her hand resting protectively over the place that held the future which had given her such happiness earlier, Alicia sobbed into the pillow. Travis would be back; she did not cry for that. He would be wild with rage, but he would be back. She meant too much to his plans to gain society's acceptance to allow her insults to hold him off now. But that was all he wanted from her. Why had she been so blind as not to see it until now?

He hadn't changed. He never pretended he had. She was the one who had imbued Travis with qualities he never possessed. He was a brutal barbarian who drank and fought and whored to excess. Why on earth had she imagined he would settle into a faithful, loving husband? Once he got her with child, he would be free to return to his other pursuits. Undoubtedly, the challenge of finding times and ways that they could make love had kept him from growing too bored these last months, but once they were married, that excitement would be gone. Would he then turn to violence to soothe his savage lusts? She could not risk it, not with a child involved.

Her revulsion to her own reaction at the naked rage in Travis's eyes blinded her to logic. She only knew she must flee from here, flee from the violence a man like Travis could do to her life, flee from the madness of hate within herself. She had thought Travis offered the peace and security she craved, but she had only been fooling herself. What could a savage like that do to her or to their child if his temper were roused? And what would she do if he turned that temper on her? She could take no chances. She would not lose this child as she had the other, and she would not allow him to reduce her to a knife-wielding harlot. Somehow she must have the strength to stay away from Travis as a drunk must stay away from drink. She willingly admitted her weakness. Now she must find the cure.

Only one cure came to mind. A drunk could throw out the bottle, and it would not get back up and come in the door. Throwing Travis out would have no such effect. Sooner or later he would find the way into her presence and sweet-talk her into doing what she knew now she must not. Instead of hiding the bottle, she would have to hide herself.

The only means of doing that would be to leave St. Louis. Gradually Alicia's tears began to fade as she put her mind to work instead of her torn emotions. She had been through this before. She knew what to do. It could work, if she planned it carefully. The first thing she must do was not confide in Becky. Her maid's loyalty was uncertain at best.

Travis glared at the message from Stanford House and, wadding it up, heaved it in the river. Letitia promised to talk sense to Alicia as soon as she calmed down, but he knew Alicia better than that. It had taken months to break down those stubborn barriers of hers. Anything could happen in those months if he had it to do all over again. There was no justification for it, none at all. He would have to force her to see reason.

When Becky slipped away from the house to inform him Alicia had locked herself in her room with a trunk, Travis felt his future slipping away through his fingers. He could not let her go. Would not. If she thought of him as the same spineless caliber as that fish bait she had left before, he would have to teach her differently. He might not have the piece of paper to prove it in a court of law, but she was his wife. He would fight until his dying breath to keep her.

With that thought in mind Travis made his plans discreetly. He knew Alicia's mind as well as his own. The river swarmed with boats this time of year. One had already obligingly carried Teddy away for a small fee. Alicia would most certainly be seeking another. It did not take a genius to verify this suspicion and set his plans in action.

The hired wagon appeared at the rear of Stanford House before dawn the next morning. Alicia quietly led the driver to her trunk and followed him out to the wagon as he loaded it. For a few coins he transported her to the river and none was the wiser.

She had no difficulty in locating the keelboat the kitchen boy had described to her. It was the only one tied to the bank at the foot of the hill. Already men were stirring aboard, preparing for departure, just as the note had promised. They would be gone before the town woke.

The kitchen boy might remember the exchange of notes later, after Alicia had gone, but it would be too late by then. This current would carry her straight downriver. Not even Travis could catch up with her. She would have to be careful to disguise herself and use another name so she was not so easily traced this time. She'd had no idea Teddy would come after her, but she could count on Travis's trying to follow. The brink of madness gave her a craftiness she had not possessed before.

She prayed she would not run into Teddy anywhere south of here, but she doubted he would be in any state to interfere if she did. It would just be a matter of looking over the cities that they stopped in and deciding which one would be her new home. New Orleans sounded pleasant. She wondered if it would be large enough to lose herself in.

Disguised behind a long gray traveling veil, Alicia followed the wagon driver aboard the keelboat. A flatboat full of settlers would have been preferable, but few traveled south from here. The captain had promised her a private berth among the cargo and a keelboat would be faster. She would have to take her chances.

As soon as the driver returned to shore, the crew cast off. Alicia vaguely recognized one or two of the men, but the boat's captain did not seem in the least familiar. She breathed a sigh of relief. She had done it.

The weather had never truly warmed as it should have by this late in spring. After an excessively icy winter and wet spring, it seemed as if the summer might never arrive. Alicia pulled her pelisse more securely around her and watched the few familiar landmarks pass by. She was really leaving. She could scarcely believe it herself. She hoped her father would forgive her.

Pacing restlessly up and down the planks, Alicia could not bring herself to retire to the stuffy interior. It was simpler and less painful to act than to think. If she kept moving, she would not have to think. Before long they would be passing the landing that led to what would have been her home. She wondered what would become of her furniture when it arrived, but she preferred not to think about it. Nervously she strolled to the other side of the stern to avoid watching the passing bank. The violence of yesterday's rage still lapped at the banks of her mind as the river did those far shores.

The sun did not reach the shaded expanse of the river until some hours after dawn. They had gone by Travis's landing, Alicia felt sure as she turned back to face the shore again. Pink redbud laced the barren forest, creating a haze of color through lifeless trees. Never had she seen anything lovelier, but her spirits did not lift as they ought. She might never see these shores again. She must set her sights on the cold, civilized future ahead.

She had almost resolved to go inside when the boat began to drift toward shore. It could not yet be time for lunch. There did not seem to be any landing out here in this wilderness. Why were they stopping?

Irrational instinct produced immediate panic. Frantically Alicia searched for some cause for this diversion, and her gaze swept the deck, finding her answer in the man emerging from the cabin. Travis!

Without sending a glance in her direction, he took over the lead pole and began to guide the keel toward a small outcropping of land. The air had warmed sufficiently so that he did not need coat or jacket, and the loose sleeves of his shirt whipped in the brisk breeze off the water. In the unforgiving sunlight his sharp visage looked more Indian than usual, and Alicia clenched her teeth in genuine fear. She knew without a shadow of doubt that she was being kidnapped just as surely as if he had held her at gunpoint. Where was he taking her?

She did not have long to find out. In moments her trunk was being thrown overboard and Travis was stalking the deck in pursuit of her. His black eyes glittered with a fury Alicia had never seen addressed to her, and she started to back away. She could jump overboard. The river's current was swift and would carry her out of reach, but that was suicide. She could not swim. She could jump for land and run, but the heavy thickets along the bank would slow her considerably. With a sinking feeling Alicia knew Travis could outrun her even were she not hampered by skirts. She was trapped.

Travis took one look at her set jaw and did not bother to argue. Grabbing Alicia by the waist, he threw her over his shoulder and lifted her bodily onto shore. With a grim wave of his hand he dismissed the boat. Not until the crew silently shoved off and the boat drifted into the current did Travis lower his kicking, squirming burden.

Alicia lifted her hand to smack the grim look of satisfaction from his face, but Travis caught her arm and rapidly twisted it behind her back, bringing her up against him.

"Don't start what you can't finish, Alicia. You're on my turf now. It will pay you to follow the fashion of whatever society you find yourself in. I am speaking from experience, so heed me well."

Without another word of explanation he turned his moccassined feet to a path winding up the bank, leaving Alicia to follow in his footsteps. For a wild moment she contemplated fleeing in another direction, but a glance up and down the bank taught her the foolishness of that notion. Her slippers would be torn apart upon the rocks and thorns, and her fragile gown would disintegrate should she try to beat her way through the underbrush. She should have remembered one of the first lessons he had taught her—dress sensibly.

It mattered little. She could not survive in the wilderness on her own even if Travis allowed her to run. And he wouldn't. Grudgingly she turned her feet to the one slender path through the bushes. The trunk stayed behind.

At the top of the bank they found themselves on the edge of a neatly furrowed cornfield. Because of the late spring, the green shoots were not tall yet, but they were readily recognizable. Alicia gazed past this sign of civilization in search of the farmhouse that must contain the inhabitants who had produced it. Perhaps she could attract someone's sympathy and free herself from the rigid anger of the man beside her.

What she saw made her insides quake and her small store of courage fail. On the far edge of the field and as far as the eye could see were the domed bark wigwams of Travis's tribe. Smoke curled from the holes in the center of each hut, and small figures roamed the streets of the village in the distance. Kidnapped and held prisoner by Indians. It seemed only fitting.

Fighting tears of terror, Alicia marched silently at Travis's heels. She ought to run. Perhaps they would bring her down in a hail of arrows. That outcome would be infinitely preferable to the more likely one. Travis would simply outdistance her, bring her down in the middle of this muddy field, and either beat her or rape her or both. He was angry enough to be capable of anything.

She felt certain his temper would assert itself sooner or later, but she preferred to put it off as long as possible. Time might soften his anger and give opportunity for logic to prevail. Travis was not a fool. Surely he knew he endangered himself and his people by bringing her here. Trading went on between the Indians and the town. Someone would surely learn a white woman was being held here against her will. But how long would it take?

Her father would think she had gone downriver. It could take weeks, months before he learned she had not. By that time the child would be obvious to all, and she would be trapped. Tears burned behind her eyes as Alicia lifted her chin and tried not to think of the future that loomed ahead. Somehow she would find her way out of this.

Travis led her silently through the village. Children ran

out to stop and stare, and their mothers scolded and dragged them back to their huts. No one greeted them. Only a few old women bothered to send them curious looks, though Alicia sensed their progress was followed by unseen eyes. No one tried to halt them, either, and Alicia understood that Travis was an accepted intruder in the village.

They halted before a hut slightly larger than the others, more oblong than circular. The door was pinned back to allow air to circulate, and Travis gestured to indicate that Alicia enter first. Her eyes hardened as her gaze met his, but she stooped to enter. Argument would be pointless.

She felt Travis enter behind her but she concentrated on examining her surroundings. A slight, half-naked Indian woman stirred at something in a pot over the open fire. She glanced up with surprise at their entrance, but her smile of greeting for Travis was warm. Avoiding gazing too closely at the woman's uncovered breasts, Alicia wondered if these Indians allowed two wives, as she had heard some tribes did. That would be all she needed, to become Travis's second wife.

But the conversation between Travis and the woman seemed perfunctory, and Alicia gave up trying to translate the rapid spate of words. The hut had a dirt floor, but the ceiling was high enough to allow her to stand comfortably. A few colorful blankets littered the floor. Baskets whose contents she could not identify sat in one corner. A stack of furs adorned another. Surely Travis couldn't mean her to live like this?

He did not tell her his intentions. Ordering Alicia to remain with what sounded like "Homasinee," he bent through the doorway and disappeared.

Left suddenly alone with this stranger who could not even speak her language, in a place that was totally alien to everything she had ever known, Alicia nearly panicked and ran after him. Only pride prevented her. Hiding her despair, she met the woman's dark gaze bravely. At least Travis had not taken his anger out on her physically. Yet.

The thought of what might happen when night came made her shiver, and Alicia wished desperately for the courage to run, but she did not have it. The fear of the unknown was greater than her fear of Travis. She had to stay, come what may.

The Indian woman—who appeared little older than

herself—gestured for Alicia to have a seat among the blankets. Feeling awkwardly tall beside this petite savage, Alicia accepted the seat, but that did not ease the awkwardness. She could not converse. She had nothing to do with her hands. She could scarcely look at the other woman without embarrassment. What on earth was she supposed to do with herself?

Almost shyly the young woman sat on a blanket nearby and picked up one of the baskets. Her deerskin skirt gave room for her to cross her legs and sit comfortably with the basket in her lap. Alicia would never have dreamed of sitting in such a position, even had the delicate length of her muslin allowed it. She watched as the woman swiftly shelled what appeared to be some kind of pea into another of the baskets.

It did not look too difficult. Tentatively she held out her hand, and the woman obliged by filling it with a number of the slender pods. It took some practice and concentration to keep the peas from spurting out and rolling about the floor, but Alicia finally succeeded in getting the knack of it. She did not work as swiftly as the other woman, but she had something to occupy her hands. Anything to make the time go by.

When the sun was directly overhead, the woman stopped work to dip two dried gourd bowls into the pot simmering over the fire. Alicia stared in dismay at the greasy stew presented to her without utensils. She was starving, but she could not imagine how to eat this. Cursing Travis with every epithet in her limited repertoire, Alicia again fought back tears of despair. She couldn't live like this. If Travis wanted to humiliate her, he had succeeded. So why wasn't he here enjoying his triumph?

The rumble in her stomach reminded her she had more than herself to think of. Biting back a grimace, Alicia lifted the bowl to her lips and sipped at the broth. She had tasted better, but at least it seemed edible. Covertly watching her companion, she tentatively stuck her fingers in the bowl and fished out one of the larger chunks of meat as the other woman did. The meat was tough and stringy and the gravy made her fingers sticky, but the nourishment settled some of her stomach's demands.

The day dragged on. Alicia followed Homasinee down to the river where they washed and took care of their bodily functions. Alicia became aware that the other woman was several months along in pregnancy, and jealously she again wondered if this was Travis's Indian wife. The humiliation would be even greater than she could bear once he learned that both of them carried his child. She would drown herself first.

By the end of the day Alicia was beginning to wonder why she had not gone ahead and sought the oblivion the river had to offer. All around her, she was aware of the men returning to their homes, the shouts of children at play, and the light scolding chatter of the other women as they prepared their evening meals. There was no sign of Travis, but Homasinee kept glancing eagerly to the doorway each time a footstep sounded outside or a shadow darkened the doorway.

Alicia felt slightly nauseous from the greasy meal earlier, and the smells rising from the various camp fires did nothing to improve her appetite. She wished for nothing better than to roll up in one of the blankets and close her eyes to the world around her, but she would not admit her weakness. Straightening her aching back, she slowly chopped the root vegetables that were her contribution to the evening meal.

She had discovered earlier that Homasinee knew several words of English, but she seemed shy of using them. Since Alicia had lost all interest in communicating as the day dragged by, she had not attempted to converse further. But now, in her irritation at being abandoned and left to fend for herself, she began to mutter dire imprecations under her breath.

Homasinee sent her a curious look, but continued beating the cornmeal batter. The day had faded to twilight outside, and the shadows inside concealed the details of their faces. Feeling safer in the darkness, Alicia contemplated what weapon she could use to break Travis's head when he came through the door. Something of her threat must have escaped out loud, for Homasinee gave a gasp of surprise and horror.

"Lonetree work hard," she protested, startling Alicia into looking up.

"I don't deny that," Alicia agreed grimly, not knowing whether the Indian understood a word she said.

Sensing Alicia did not understand, Homasinee tried again. "He build wigwam—home, for you."

That set Alicia back on her heels. She stared through the growing dusk to Homasinee's eager expression. She could find only one meaning for these words, but she was not ready to accept them. Travis had a home, had a house and lands and more. Why would he need a hut in an Indian village? Unless he meant to keep her there.

The utter horror of such a life added to the weariness and degradation she already felt, creating a burden too heavy to carry for long. The second Travis ducked to enter the doorway, Alicia lifted the basket of unshelled peas and flung it at his head.

29

HOMASINEE CRIED OUT in surprise, and then began to giggle softly as Travis straightened his half-naked frame and glared at his recalcitrant "wife." He had obviously bathed in the river before returning here. His hair lay plastered against his head and neck, and rivulets of water glistened down the bronzed width of his back and chest. His temper appeared none the cooler for the dunking, though.

Homasinee's giggles prevented him from venting his ire, however. That would come when he had the vixen to himself. Travis satisfied himself by barking curtly, "You had best pick up the mess before my cousin returns home. He is likely to blame Homasinee."

With that, he turned his back on Alicia to converse in a low voice with his hostess. Alicia wondered what would happen should she bury her nails deep in the bare flesh exposed to her. The knife in her hand would be more satisfying, but that would be a betrayal of all she hoped to conquer, and she had not the courage to do it. She stifled her rage.

Coldly she began to gather the scattered pods, eyeing the beckoning opening of the doorway. Now that Travis had returned, she could not bear to be in the same room with him. Escape seemed essential. Perhaps it would be easier to elude him in the dark.

As if her thoughts had triggered a silent alarm, a massive figure blocked the doorway, slipping through and closing the flap behind him. Alicia fell back as the tall savage stepped into the room, stinking of smoke and something rancid. She had thought Travis formidable, but this man was terrifying. He scarcely gave her a second glance as he stepped around her and greeted the other two occupants with a guttural growl.

272

The exchange of words in a language foreign to her irritated Alicia further, and she drew away into a dark corner by herself. The knowledge that she had only herself to blame did not ease the pain. There were reasons why she had been expected to choose among a select group of suitors, men of her own kind who shared a common background and breeding. Why had she thought she could throw aside centuries of cultural caution, and marry a man who came from a world as alien as this one?

She cringed as Travis sought her out and gestured for her to join them at the fire. She didn't want to sit near that beast that must be his cousin. She didn't want any of that ghastly gruel they called food. She wanted to go home to her own bed and wake up in the morning to find this was all just a horrid dream.

Instead she found a seat at the edge of the firelight some distance between Travis and Homasinee and far from the tall savage. The man stared at her across the flames, but when Homasinee handed him a bowl of food, he turned his attention to it.

Ignoring the others, Alicia stared at her hands until Travis's curt words made her jump and look up.

"It is the custom for the women to serve the men first. Homasinee cannot eat until you serve me."

Serve him! She would just as soon hit him over the head as to serve him. Something of that message must have conveyed itself through her glare, but Travis continued to stonily await her obedience. Feeling as if all eyes in the world were upon her, Alicia reached for one of the bowls.

Travis fully expected the hot stew to end up in his lap, but Alicia's training as a lady overcame her fury, and she served the stew as if it were a delicate bouillabaisse in a porcelain bowl. Only he could see the trembling of her hands and judged the extent of her controlled anger.

When Alicia took nothing for herself, Homasinee scooped out a bowl and pressed it upon her. Alicia could not refuse the food, but she made no pretense at eating. Her stomach was so tense it would have rejected anything put in it.

Lost in her own painful thoughts, Alicia ignored the low murmur of conversation around her until a small cry from Homasinee made her look up. The petite woman had grown pale beneath her dark coloring, and her hand leapt to cover the small mound that was her stomach. Without a word she leapt up from the fire and ran outside.

An anxious spate of words flew between the two men and
Alicia tried to follow them, her gaze occasionally drifting to
the doorway she had been denied. When the men grew
silent, Alicia spoke sharply.

"What is it? Why did she leave?"

Travis frowned, but his voice reflected his concern. "She
does not carry the child well. She has lost others, but there
is nothing they can do."

With a cry half of anger and half sympathy, Alicia leapt to
her feet and rushed toward the door. Travis rose to stop her, but
she brushed past him and disappeared into the darkness.

She returned in a few minutes with Homasinee clinging
to her arm. Ignoring the men at the fire, Alicia helped the
young woman to lie down on a bed of furs. Folding a stack
of blankets, she placed them under Homasinee's feet, ele-
vating them above her head. The two women exchanged a
few words in voices too low for the men to hear, then Alicia
coldly returned to her seat just outside the firelight.

"She ought to have a doctor." The tone of her voice indicated her lack of expectation that this advice would be heeded.

"There are no doctors out here," Travis pointed out,
though his gaze strayed anxiously to the prostrate figure in
the shadows.

"And, of course, the custom is for the women to work
until they drop," Alicia answered scornfully. "Tell your
cousin he may as well punch her in the stomach and have
done with it. It is his child, is it not?" The scorn hid her
anxiety over this point.

"Yes." Fighting back another wave of rage at the fates,
Travis turned away and spoke rapidly to his cousin. The
man glanced to his wife and nodded with a concerned frown.
Travis rose and crossed the room to Homasinee's pallet.

Watching him kneeling beside the Indian woman, speaking to her gently, Alicia felt the day's tears begin to spill
from her eyes. This laughing, loving, bright-eyed little creature who had treated her with such kindness throughout the
day was the woman Travis had loved and lost. She could tell
it in his gestures, the way he looked at her, the unspoken
exchanges that went between them. Homasinee was the
noble wife he had wanted and should have had, but for the
circumstances of his birth.

Without a word Alicia rose from her seat and went out
the flap. She didn't know where she was going or what she

would do, but she needed the sting of the cold night breeze against her skin, blowing away the stench of the close air of the hut.

As she walked toward the outskirts of the village, she wished she had brought her pelisse with her instead of leaving it lying somewhere in Homasinee's hut. The night would get colder before dawn, but she had no intention of turning back.

She felt no surprise when Travis's hard arm snapped around her waist, snatching her from the ground. She had no hope of escape as long as he wanted her. She made no effort to struggle as his other arm circled her knees and lifted her into the air. She just could not bear to look him in the eyes, but buried her face against his bare chest. The heat of his skin warmed her cheeks but not her insides.

Travis carried her to the hut of bent saplings thatched with strips of bark and insulated with river grass that he had spent the day constructing. The interior still smelled of green wood and the pine boughs he had used for their bed. Furs covered the soft bed of branches, and a variety of blankets lay scattered across the top. It was not as elegant as the home he had intended for her, but it would serve its purpose.

He set her down and watched with hands on hips as Alicia retreated to a far corner.

"You cannot run from me any longer, Alicia. You are my wife now."

Alicia jerked nervously at the word "wife." She could see his masculine silhouette against the open doorway, knew the strength of the muscles in the arms outlined against the night sky, and knew there was no escape. No escape but pride and he had left her precious little of that. Still, she shook her head blindly, fighting the inevitable.

"No, Travis. I was wrong. I cannot live my life with you."

She did not hear the painful intake of his breath beneath the blow of these words, but she saw with fear his steady advance into the room.

"It is too late for that. In the eyes of my people we are married. I have built my home for you to share. You will sleep in its shelter and everyone will know you as my woman. When you are ready to exchange our vows legally, I will take you back to your father and we can have the ceremony repeated officially in the church. But understand me, Alicia, we are husband and wife already."

"No! No, we are not." Alicia backed against the wall as far as she could go, protesting the fate he assigned to her. She would never submit to this coercion. But if she did not, she might never see her father and civilization again. She could not accept either alternative.

"Be reasonable, Alicia. It is late and we are both weary. Take off your clothes and let us sleep. Perhaps in the morning we can look at this rationally."

Never. She could never look at it rationally. He loved that woman back there in that hut, a woman who would never be his. He only wanted her as a salve to his pride, a showpiece to decorate his arm just as the elegant farmhouse paraded his good taste. He wanted the power and money she could give him and the children she might bear, but he wanted the woman back there. Not her. And she did not want him. Not ever again.

"I want my trunk," Alicia demanded irrationally. Where was her trunk? Where were her clothes? She wanted some semblance of civilization to fall back on.

"You won't be needing it." Travis dismissed the subject callously. "I want to go to bed, Alicia. I don't want to have to fight you. Turn around and I will help you with the buttons."

He stepped closer, the breadth of his bare shoulders closing in on her, blocking her breathing. Alicia tried to slide along the wall out of his reach, but Travis caught her shoulder and held her still.

"No, Travis, don't!" Alicia pressed back against the wall and crossed her arms over her breasts, terrified of his closeness. She didn't know this man. He was a stranger to her. And just his presence was a threat to her existence.

Impatiently Travis dropped his hand and stepped back. "Take it off yourself, then, but if you do not do it immediately, I will rip it from you. You're not likely to see another for a long while."

The import of his words sunk in with the weight of lead. She could undress for him now or go naked until he chose to return her to her father. Without clothes there was no possibility of ever leaving this room. With trembling fingers she began to unfasten the row of tiny buttons.

Satisfied, Travis moved about the room in darkness. They would be warm enough without a fire, and he did not bother to build one. By morning he hoped to have persuaded

Alicia from her foolishness. He heard the soft rustle of her gown falling to the floor and he began unfastening his breeches. This night he would not have to get up to dress and return her home. She was his.

Travis stripped off his clothing, and when Alicia did not come to him, he strode across the room to find her.

He found her still wearing her chemise and cowering against the back wall. With a curse, he ripped the frail silk away and threw it aside.

"Don't hide behind false modesty now, Alicia. It doesn't become you."

Alicia cringed as he pulled her against his nakedness. She could feel every sinew of the hard arm holding her, knew the steel-like trap of his chest, and unsuccessfully avoided the unyielding trunks of his thighs. Once she had come willingly into the suffocating walls of his embrace. Now she fought like a caged tiger.

Travis ignored the useless kicks of unshod toes and easily trapped Alicia's fists behind her back as he carried her to their bed. Lowering her to the pallet, he fell beside her, swiftly catching her legs beneath his to prevent further exertion.

"Alicia, stop it. You may be angry with me now, but you cannot deny everything that has gone between us before. You are my wife, you could be carrying my child, and I don't intend to let one argument destroy it all. Let's call a truce, Alicia, and enjoy what we have of this night together."

Never! She couldn't. He mustn't know of the child. She had to get away. Just the pressure of Travis's heavy weight lowering over her brought irrational panic, and she struck out at him again.

Travis didn't flinch but captured her hands, holding them over her head while he bent to sample the moist sweetness of her mouth. Alicia refused to yield, but undaunted, he continued to spread his kisses over her lips and cheek, locating a tender earlobe and nibbling there.

Alicia strained against him, trying to fight off the prison of his body, but Travis held her more effectively than steel bars. His knee and thigh kept her trapped against his loins, where any movement brought her into closer contact with that which she wished to avoid. The strength of his hold on her wrists prevented any movement there at all, leaving only her torso free to squirm from his wandering lips. And that only with disastrous consequences. As she raised herself upward, Travis bent to capture the peak of her breast with his mouth.

Alicia screamed in rage as Travis's lips fastened on this sensitive crest, tormenting her with his tongue. The nipple hardened to an aching point beneath his ministrations, and desire stole slowly through her body, giving her one more opponent to fight. It was an unequal battle at best, and when Travis's hand released hers to travel downward along her breasts and between her thighs, Alicia could only grasp the blankets on either side of her to prevent her hands from straying to hold him.

She was powerless to prevent his invasion, but she did not have to surrender. She clung to the blankets and forced her body into stillness as Travis spent his kisses and caresses on an unresponsive statue. When his fingers produced no reaction, Travis trailed his lips lower, yielding the peaks to conquer the valleys.

A path of fire burned across her abdomen, and Alicia gasped and tried to wriggle away as she realized his intent. Travis caught her hips with his hands and slid lower, using his tongue to produce the response he desired.

Alicia had never experienced this sensation, and she whimpered softly as the moist heat of Travis's mouth invaded and conquered the vulnerable cleft between her thighs. Beneath the pressure of his hands, she parted her legs, and her hips rose of their own accord to greet this subtle victor. Her body's needs betrayed her, and tears slid from the corner of her eyes as Travis plied his victory well.

Travis quickly took advantage of this submission to gain the ultimate success. Rising to lean over her, his entrance was swift and unmerciful. Alicia cried her defeat as his body moved within hers, warning her of the futility of this fight.

As he came to a shuddering explosion inside her, Alicia knew of a certainty that if she did not already bear his child, she soon would. He had filled her and claimed her and there would be no escape. Tomorrow he might return to his other lover, but for the rest of her life, she would be his.

And she wept.

30

WAKING IN THE middle of the night, Travis felt cold wash over him, and panic-stricken, he reached for the woman who belonged at his side. He found her on the far side of the pallet with her back turned toward him, as far from him as she could go without sleeping on the earth.

Angry that he could not win her as easily as he had before, Travis sought resolution for his resentment. As his arm slid around her waist, capturing her in this position, he sensed her wakefulness, but he made no attempt to woo her as he had earlier. He had found no satisfaction in forcing response from her then and made no effort to seek it now. She was his wife and he craved the release she had once given him willingly. He would take it as he could.

Alicia muffled her cries in the blanket as Travis's arm held her against him while his hand traveled to the soft purchase of her breast. When she felt the hard thrust of his arousal from behind her, she bit her finger with shame, but made no attempt to fight him. It would be quicker this way.

She'd had no idea how thoroughly he could possess her in this position, and a moan escaped from Alicia's throat as Travis found his goal and thrust deep inside her. Unprepared and defenseless, she quickly succumbed to his rhythm, opening to his powerful thrust until she thought she could take no more and crying her dismay at his retreat—until the thunder overwhelmed them, rolling over them, making them quake with the power of this explosion.

They slept then, curled against each other, exhausted by their struggles.

When Alicia awoke, it was to an empty bed. Blankets had been carefully arranged around her to keep her warm, but there was no sign of Travis. Or her clothes.

Her body ached from the battering it had received the night before, and the first mild stirrings of nausea prevented any sudden movement. She feared this symptom as much as she had wanted it earlier. Perhaps it was just the unaccustomed food she had eaten yesterday. Now that Travis held her prisoner, pregnancy would be a cage from which there would be no escape. Exploring her still flat abdomen with her hands, Alicia allowed her gaze to roam the room in search of her clothes.

The pretty muslin gown had disappeared. A neatly folded stack of deerskin lay beside the bed, and Alicia eyed it with loathing. She could guess what it represented, and her pride rebelled at donning this uniform of subservience. He meant to make her his squaw, but she would not do it.

The alternative, however, became painfully clear when Travis entered the hut a short time later. After stacking his load of kindling next to the fire he had prepared, he rose to his full height and stared down at the woman still wrapped in blankets in his bed. Alicia felt the heat of his black gaze stripping away the rough woolens, and she clutched them tighter to her breast.

Grabbing his shirttails, Travis reached to pull the soft linen over his head. "If you are inclined to spend the day there, I will be more than happy to join you."

Frantically Alicia wrapped a blanket around her and sat up. Chestnut curls that had escaped loosened pins fell in long swaths over her bare shoulders as she stared at him in dismay.

"No, Travis. Don't." She inched away from his towering figure in fear.

Travis noted her motion with disgust as much at himself as with her. Lowering his arms, he pointed at the stack of clothing. "Those will be more suitable while we are here. Put them on and start breakfast. I will be back shortly."

He strode out without another word, leaving Alicia cowering among the covers, glaring at the deerskin. If he thought she would parade about half dressed for his prurient enjoyment, he would be mightily disappointed.

Gingerly she lifted the top garment, finding it to be a long, fringed skirt similar to what Homasinee had worn. It tied with leather thongs, adjusting to any waistline; a convenience to a growing one, Alicia judged cynically. Slipping it on, she found the open flap made leg movement easy, though exposing an unseemly amount of calf and ankle.

Beneath the skirt lay a simple cotton tunic without sleeves or collar. She had not seen any of the women in camp wearing such a garment, but she felt relief at its inclusion. Heavy blankets would have made a poor substitute. Still, after she had pulled it over her head, Alicia wondered if she should not wrap the blanket around her anyway. The thin material did little to disguise her unfettered breasts, and her arms felt bare and vulnerable without even a shawl to cover them. Once she had wrapped the beaded belt about her waist to hold in the billowing material, she had accomplished no more than disguising her skin. The dark aureoles of her breasts pressed visibly against the cotton, and the cut of the tunic emphasized every curve.

Despairing of ever living in decency again, Alicia slipped on the leather moccasins left for her and gazed anxiously about the hut. There was no washstand, no discreetly hidden chamber pot, no basin of water available. Before she even contemplated fixing food, she had to wash and relieve herself. The urgency of her bladder outweighed the churning in her stomach, and she dearly wished to rid herself of the stench of last night's activities. She refused to call it lovemaking.

Lifting her chin and trying not to show her consciousness of her near nakedness, Alicia stooped to leave the wigwam and find the river. Travis could try his best to strip her of civilization and reduce her to the level of a heathen savage, but there were some things too deeply ingrained to remove. The need for cleanliness was one of them.

As Travis left his cousin's hut with a bowl of cornmeal, he watched Alicia's progress through the village with suspicion. Noting her direction, however, he guessed her intention. Leaving the bowl inside the hut, he followed at a discreet distance. The clothing he had provided for her hung well on her tall, slender frame, and he admired the graceful sway of her hips as she strode over the rough terrain. Judging from the lascivious smirks on the faces of the hunters emerging from their huts for the day, others appreciated the sight also. Cursing, Travis glared his warning at any appearing to look too closely. He had been too long from this world and had forgotten the easy acceptance of sexuality here. If he had not already claimed her, Alicia would be easy prey to every man here. His stride grew faster.

Travis did nothing more than stand guard as Alicia cautiously lifted her skirt and waded out into the river. The current was strong, but she had chosen a shallow eddy that would be safe enough. He tried not to watch as she threw the skirt to shore and waded out farther, but the urge to join her there was almost crippling. Never before had one woman driven him to such obsessive lengths, and he struggled to control the raging desire in his loins. He had meant to teach Alicia a lesson, but he was rapidly learning things about himself that he did not wish to know.

Just when he thought he could endure it no longer, Alicia waded back to shore and wrapped herself securely in her skirt once again. When he saw her safely on the road back to the village, Travis stripped off his own clothing and dived into the icy river. Short of raping her again, there was only one solution to his problem, but even the icy bath could not rid him of the burning desire flowing through his veins.

Alicia glanced up warily as Travis entered the hut the next time. His hair was plastered to his head from bathing, and she ducked her head to hide her blush in the heat of the fire as she imagined him swimming where she had just been. Surely she would have seen him if he had been there.

After her "bath" Alicia was starving, and she made no attempt to rebel over Travis's order to fix breakfast. The ingredients were far from promising, but she did what she could given the circumstances. She breaded the fish Travis had left with some of the cornmeal, and made a flat cake out of the rest. It would serve to fend off starvation at the least.

Travis ate her offering in silence. He could scarcely keep his gaze from straying to the hard points of Alicia's breasts pushing at the thin material of her blouse, and his hands ached to fill with the plump mounds thus hidden. He did himself no favor by forcing her into the trappings of his world. Why had he never discovered the temptations of this mode of dress before?

In his youth, he had found nothing to covet in the supple young bodies of the maidens of his tribe. When he felt the urge, he had lain with whichever one smiled upon him, and then had gone about his business without another thought. Why did Alicia have the power to drive him mad with

longing, even when he had possessed her as thoroughly as a
man could possess a woman? Why did her partially covered
breasts drive him insane when he scarcely noticed the nudity
of the other women outside the hut? Even Homasinee had
long since failed to arouse this kind of interest in him. If he
admitted it to himself, she had never aroused in him this
savage hunger and protectiveness. He must be losing his
mind.

She was just a woman like any other. He had best remember that lest he fall victim to irrational delusions. The argument here was merely over a point of law. She was his and
he could not let her throw away all his work over an emotional incident. He must prove to her the justness of his
claim. Emotions had no place in an argument of elemental
logic.

He had failed to make his case yesterday because he had
allowed his desires to rule his actions. He would not make
the same mistake twice. It might take time, but Alicia would
learn the folly of her rebellion. She had been brought up
having everything her own way. He would have to teach her
life wasn't like that. She couldn't make up her own rules.

"If we are to stay here, I will have to do my part in
bringing home food. While I am out, you may help the
other women in the field or stay with Homasinee and help
her. Which would you prefer?" He did not tell her Homasinee
had been assigned the chores given to old women or child-
bearing ones. He preferred she stay in the village.

Alicia stared up into Travis's hard, bronzed face. He had
wrapped a wide red cloth around his forehead to keep his
hair from his eyes, and he looked more than ever the part of
Indian. She had known him for what he was. Why had she
ignored this side of him? Love was truly blind, but now the
blinders had been removed. She could not stay here.

"I want to go home." She refused to accept his alternatives.

Travis raised one eyebrow in mild curiosity. "You are
prepared to go before a preacher and admit you are mine?"

"I will do no such thing!" Alicia rose from her seat at the
fire and stalked to the far corner of the room. "You cannot
hold me prisoner forever. Send me home before you bring
trouble on your friends."

Travis rose, too, but he made no attempt to follow her. "I
anticipate no trouble. Our pledge was binding, and your
father cannot object if I choose to take you to my family.

You are not mistreated, and you have your choice of homes.
We are wedded legally here, and so far, this is where you
have chosen to stay. Say the word, and I will return you to
the farm, where we may be legally wed under the white
man's laws."

"I will not marry a savage! I want to go home—to Philadelphia. I am not your wife and can never be your wife.
Why can you not understand that?"

"I defend what is mine, Alicia, and whether you will it or
no, you are mine. We will stay here until you accept that."

Travis walked out, leaving Alicia to decide for herself
how she would spend the day. She contemplated following
the river upstream until she reached help or St. Louis,
whichever came first, but she knew she could not do it. She
knew nothing of surviving in the wilderness, and the life
within her was too precious to risk. She had run that first
time and learned the consequences. She could not bear
another such loss. She wanted this child, even if she wished
its father in hell.

She chose to stay with Homasinee. The Indian woman
seemed surprised to see her, but readily acquiesced to Alicia's offer of help in exchange for learning something of the
Algonquin language. Alicia helped arrange the pallet so
Homasinee might recline comfortably with her feet raised
while directing Alicia in what needed to be done. The
mindless tasks gave plenty of opportunity for exchanging
tentative words into conversation.

Homasinee's understanding of English was greater than
her desire to speak it, but Alicia managed to interpret her
words and gestures with some measure of success. Like any
woman, Homasinee was curious about why Travis had brought
his white bride here, and why they spent so little time in
their marriage bed. When Alicia understood this last question, she blushed and looked away. It seemed even Indians
had the equivalent of a honeymoon.

Alicia did not try to explain that she was prisoner, not
wife. It was obvious to all that Travis took her as wife, and
the complexity of explaining the difference in a foreign
language was beyond her ability. Homasinee laughed at
Alicia's uninformative shrug, declaring that Travis was like
the moon and stars and wind in the trees. He did as he
pleased and no one could stop him.

That seemed an apt enough description of Travis's masculine arrogance, and his appearance later that afternoon confirmed it. Having caught more than his quota of game, he returned early, before his cousin. After exchanging a few words with Homasinee, he gestured for Alicia to follow him.

He led her back to the wigwam, where he had started a fire and heated a large pot of water. Alicia glanced at him questioningly, wondering if he meant her to cook something in that awkward pot.

Travis shrugged at her glance. "I would introduce you to the amenities of the bathhouse, but I do not think you would appreciate communal sweating. Nor do I think your constitution strong enough to risk a dive in the cold river afterward. This is the best I have to offer in exchange. Do not tarry long. I am starved and will make my own ablutions quickly."

Alicia stared after him as Travis disappeared out the door. She would never understand him, not if she lived for a thousand years.

Without further question she hurriedly disrobed and made the most of this impromptu bath. When she had sponged herself as clean as she could, she dipped her hair in the water and worked the harsh soap he had provided for her through it. Just having her hair clean provided refreshment.

Travis returned while she still bent over the pot, working the lather from thick lengths of chestnut. Gazing at the splendid sight of Alicia's slender nakedness kneeling upon his blankets, he praised the Lord and knelt beside her to help.

Trapped, Alicia could not refuse his offer, but as soon as the last drop of soap had been wrung from her hair, she reached for a blanket to wrap around her. Travis stayed her hand. His dark gaze told her all she needed to know, and she trembled as he reached to unfasten his buckskin trousers.

"No, Travis," she whispered, backing away from his half-dressed figure. He wore no shirt, and his broad shoulders still glistened with the moisture of his bath. The dark rings of the tattoo upon his arm flexed as he rose and removed the remainder of his clothing in one smooth motion.

Travis did not reply, but merely grasped her by the arm and lifted her to her feet. The heat of his bronzed skin seared hers as he drew her against him. With a groan she felt the hardness rising against her belly, but she had learned the folly of struggling the night before. When he lay her across his bed, she made no effort to flee. He could take her body, but she would never surrender her soul.

She was not so certain of that some hours later when she lay beside Travis's sleeping figure in the nighttime darkness. An owl hooted somewhere in the trees beyond the village, and a million chirping, whirring insects filled the air with music. She still felt the imprint of his body upon her flesh, knew the heat of his life's fluid within her. He had taken her not once, but several times. His lust had seemed insatiable, and she had consented to it.

The shame of her own responses was even worse than the shame of his rape, if rape it could be called. Sated, floating on a sea of languor, Alicia's body sought only repose. Travis's arm lay across her, trapping her at his side, one hand still circling her breast, and she did not move away. How long before her mind and heart succumbed to this addiction of her body? How long before he owned her soul?

Alicia blushed with shame as Travis stirred in his sleep and his hand unconsciously caressed her aroused nipple. Just that small gesture woke the ache between her legs, and she knew she had only to reach out and touch him, and he would be there to satisfy her. As long as he was within her reach, she could not escape. Her soul was lost, consumed by a desire worse than any addiction to opium or whiskey. No matter how wrong her mind told her this was, her body ached for the completeness Travis gave her. Hell could not be worse.

And as Travis discovered her wakefulness and bent to plunder her mouth, Alicia parted her lips in welcome. The silky fur slid along her skin as he pulled her to him, and in drunken abandon she wrapped her leg across his, offering what he sought without protest.

Somehow she had to escape, but not tonight.

31

TRAVIS'S COUSIN woke them at daybreak. He paid scant heed as Alicia scrambled to cover her nudity with blankets. His dark face pale and pinched about the mouth, he spoke a few sharp words to Travis. Still groggy from the night's exertions, Travis reacted slowly, forcing his cousin to repeat his words. Then nodding, he sent Bear Mountain away.

Clutching the blankets, Alicia watched Travis with uneasiness. She felt light-headed, and the churning in her stomach made her more certain than ever of the life growing there, but she kept this secret to herself.

"Homasinee is in pain. My cousin fears she will lose the child. He thinks you can help her." Sitting up, Travis groped for his pants. Just one look in Alicia's eyes told him he had not won, but there was no time for delay. It would be better if he could leave her here, but he could not trust his own people any more than he could trust her. She would have to go with him.

Alicia's gaze followed him with bewilderment. "How can I help? I know nothing of babies. She needs a doctor."

"I know." Curtly Travis jerked off her blankets and threw her her clothes. "We'll have to get her back to St. Louis."

That Alicia understood, and she grabbed eagerly for the buckskin skirt she had scorned the day before. "How will you get her there? I should think travel would be dangerous in her condition." She wrapped the skirt around her and reached for the tunic.

Travis scowled at the eager light in her eyes. He had not given her time to brush her hair last night, and it hung in wild profusion over her shoulders and down her back. Had it not been for her fair skin, she would look almost Indian in that outfit. Knowing she wore nothing beneath it satisfied

him momentarily. It would be the work of seconds to have
her under him again. He knew she still fought him, still
denied him the pleasure she had so sweetly given before,
but he could not complain. He had taken her against her
will and she had responded. With this woman that would
have to be enough.

"We will have to return by keelboat. A message will get
to Auguste by mid-morning. There's enough crew at the
farm to manage a short trip."

Alicia didn't dare ask if she would go, too. His black
scowl warned of interference, but raised her spirits. She did
not think he would leave her behind.

As she followed him to Bear Mountain's hut, she tried to
avoid thoughts of what would happen when they arrived in
St. Louis. If her father were there, she could hide behind his
protection and demand to be sent home. The scandal would
be enormous, but it had to die down sometime. Even if they
learned of it in Philadelphia, it would not matter. She had
no intention of marrying. If her father were not there . . .
That thought did not bear contemplation.

Homasinee smiled weakly as they entered. Alicia knelt
beside her to comfort her while the men spoke in low tones.
Seeing Homasinee's anxiety obliterated Alicia's small hopes
of freedom. It did not matter what St. Louis society thought.
Her first concern had to be saving this child.

Under Homasinee's direction she brewed a bark tea and
brought it to her patient. There seemed to be no bleeding as
yet, and Alicia brought blankets and furs to prop up
Homasinee's feet and head and make her comfortable. She
was aware that Travis had left, but she did not think about
it. He would be back.

He was in and out the rest of the morning, checking to
see if anything was needed, reassuring his cousin, joking
lightly with Homasinee. If anyone thought it strange that
he and Alicia exchanged only necessary words, no one
commented.

By noon word of the boat's arrival reached them. As
Travis arranged for furs and blankets to be taken to the
cabin to supplement the ones already there, Alicia tried to
reassure Homasinee's sudden fright.

When Travis appeared in the doorway, demanding to
know the reason for their delay, Alicia looked up at him
with anger and frustration.

"She is terrified. How do you expect me to explain to her where she will be going and what the doctor will do? You're her lover. She will listen to you."

Travis's black brows rose at this comment, but he entered the hut and began to cajole their terrified patient. Alicia retreated to the entrance and so heard the uproar outside before the room's other occupants. Lifting the door flap, she glanced out, and did not conceal her gasp in time.

Travis was on his feet in an instant, following her gaze and cursing. From the path through the woods rode Chester Stanford, Bernard Farrar, and the minister from Alicia's church, the first two bearing rifles.

In dismay Alicia glanced down at her state of undress and then up to Travis's set face. With terrible certainty she knew all decision had been stripped from her. There never had been a choice. A terrible fear for the future yawned within her, but quietly she slipped into the hut's interior and retrieved the pelisse she had left there two nights before. She would meet her fate respectably covered.

Travis stepped out into the daylight, silencing the angry shouts and commands being exchanged between the villagers and the intruders. An expression of relief momentarily swept across Stanford's face, to be quickly replaced by grim severity.

Trotting his horse down the dirt-packed street, he confronted Travis angrily. "Where is my daughter?"

Alicia appeared in the doorway, incongruously wrapped in a woolen pelisse on a brilliant day of sunshine. Her hair streamed in rich profusion about her back and shoulders, and the shadows of her eyes revealed her pain.

"I am here," she stated coldly. Had it not been for her father, she would never have encouraged Travis's intentions. He was as much to blame for this fiasco as Travis. She swung her gaze to the two white men hovering in the background. "Dr. Farrar, your services are needed inside."

Not understanding but preferring to be out of the line of fire, the young physician swung down from his horse and accompanied Alicia inside. The thin flap of animal hide over the doorway did not keep out the angry voices beyond.

"I am not going to ask what this is about." Stanford's first words carried with controlled fury. "I have a rifle and I know how to use it, but I trust you know your responsibility in this matter and will come quietly. I would prefer to see my daughter married in the church, but I will see it done right here and now if there are any objections. The choice is yours."

The heat of Travis's anger remained bottled up behind his stoic facade. "As I have told you before, the choice is your daughter's. As far as I am concerned, we are already wed."

Dr. Farrar glanced up at Alicia's pale face after these words, but when she remained silent, he returned to examining his patient.

"My daughter will do as I say. If she does not, I will see you hung. Rape is a hanging offense out here."

As she had known, there would be no choice. Men were violent and unreasonable by nature, her own father included, as she had so sadly come to learn. Much as he deserved it, the father of her child could not be hung. The future loomed dark and foreboding, but she could see no alternative.

The minister's placating words had no effect on the argument, and numbly Alicia acted as interpreter between doctor and patient. Not that Homasinee needed an interpreter, but her fear blocked her tongue, and Alicia explained the symptoms as best she could.

By the time Dr. Farrar had produced a bottle of strengthener and restorative and ordered complete bed rest, the argument outside had died to ominous silence. They awaited Alicia's appearance.

Dr. Farrar left first, giving Alicia time to reassure the patient and administer the medicine. When Alicia finally stepped into the street, it had been cleared of women and children. Men were beginning to drift silently from the woods as word of the intruders spread, but they maintained a respectful distance until they had some signal from Lonetree.

Chester frowned at his daughter's outlandish garb and disheveled appearance, but he spoke with authority. "Alicia, you are coming with me. Mr. Hale has agreed to perform the ceremony first thing on the morrow. Your fiancé will be kept under guard until then to assure his appearance."

Weary down to her very bones, Alicia answered without emotion. "You would do better to set the guard on me. Travis will be there."

She could almost feel the tension in the muscles of the man beside her, but Travis said not a word, merely sending her a scathing look.

"If you are not, he will hang." Chester gestured toward the woods and a group of riders trotted from the shadows carrying shotguns and leading Alicia's mare.

Bear Mountain instantly stepped forward, speaking sharply to Travis and issuing curt commands to the men around them. The confrontation could have been deadly, but Travis halted it with a few short words in his language and an abrupt agreement to Chester.

"My boat is at the river. Alicia will be more comfortable there. Make whatever other arrangements you prefer; I will follow."

Without expression Travis turned his gaze to Alicia. "Homasinee?"

"The doctor says it would be best if she did not travel. He has given her medicine and instructions. There is nothing more you can do."

By all rights she should hate him, but Alicia was too drained to feel anything. Even the embarrassment of all those men staring at her, knowing how she had spent these last nights, failed to reach that part of her that mattered. She felt like the condemned prisoner standing before the court. Tomorrow would be her day of execution. Or Travis's.

32

TRAVIS WAITED INSIDE the cool darkness of the church, surrounded by the bodyguards who had not left him since the village. These were men he had joked and laughed with on social occasions, but he could read the fear and anger in their eyes now. He was not one of them, would never be one of them, and he had proven it by his treatment of a white man's daughter. They would hang him without a qualm if Alicia did not appear.

That danger seemed eminently possible after giving careful thought to his actions these past days. Still, he did not see how he could have acted differently. He could never have let her walk out of his life as she had planned, but Travis began to develop some understanding of why Alicia feared him. He had reacted as a man who had lived the violent life of the river too long. A woman who had been raised out here might understand that, but not Alicia. He had been too long from civilization. She had some justification for her fears, and his hopes sank faster than stones in a pond as he contemplated her anger.

He could very well hang before this day ended if Alicia put her mind to it. Travis glanced out the church window, trying to judge the time by the angle of the sun. Approaching noon, he surmised. The few guests had begun to squirm restlessly in the pews.

A rustle of activity at the rear of the church made Travis's heart lurch violently. He could scarcely allow himself to believe she would give him a second chance. Perhaps Chester Stanford had arrived to order his execution. The men beside him had the same thought. They stiffened to attention, clutching their shotguns nervously. It would not be easy to outrun those guns, but Travis damned well planned

to give it a try. He would not let Alicia escape that easily.
He braced himself for a dash into the crowd, where they
would not dare fire.

To Travis's immense relief, Letitia appeared in the doorway garbed in brilliant blue and a collar of pearls, lending
every symbol of respectability to the occasion she could
summon. She clung to Chester's arm and proceeded up the
aisle gracefully, smiling as if it were the happiest day in her
life, occasionally stopping to whisper to one of the guests or
throw a laughing gesture to a friend in a far row. Travis
mentally applauded her performance while warily eyeing his
prospective father-in-law. Stanford never looked once in his
direction.

The church doors were thrown wide, allowing in a stream
of golden sunshine and the outpouring of a mockingbird in
the trees beyond. Heads turned and whispers of delight
billowed through the gloom. Travis fastened his gaze on the
doorway and prayed.

Alicia appeared in a satin sheath that trailed behind her in
a river of shimmering silver blue. A froth of intricate lace
descended to her shoulders, hiding the dark curls pinned
severely in a chignon. A trick of the light momentarily caught
the brilliance of sapphire eyes as she glanced toward Travis,
but she quickly turned her gaze back to the long aisle ahead
of her. She did not look at him again as a violin began to
play and she proceeded slowly to the altar.

Alicia started nervously when Travis stepped from the
shadows to join her. She knew he had dressed respectably
for the occasion in a formal suit and cravat, but she could
see no more than that from the corner of her eye, wanted to
see no more than that. It was easier pretending a nameless,
faceless man stood beside her than to admit she was actually
binding herself for life to a renegade keelboatman with the
morals of a savage. She had to be insane; this entire past
year had to be a nightmare from which she would soon
wake.

As the minister murmured the first part of the ceremony,
Alicia stood coldly, silently, as if listening to a sentence of
death. When it came time to repeat their vows, her voice
sounded hollow, even to herself. The minister referred to
Travis as Maximillian, making the ceremony even more
unreal. Only when Travis took her hand to place the sap-

phire ring upon her finger did the tolling bell of reality peal. Just as he took possession of her hand now, he would take possession of everything she owned or claimed later, including herself.

She tensed, and Travis had difficulty getting the ring over her finger. She jerked her hand away when it was done, and continued staring woodenly at a space somewhere over the minister's shoulder as the remainder of the ceremony was repeated in solemn, meaningless tones. Legally she had no rights, but if he thought it would be easy, he was mistaken. The battle had only just begun.

With the end of the ceremony Travis turned to kiss his bride and read well the rebellion in stormy eyes. He held her hand firmly but kept the kiss to a chaste peck. Now was not the time to create a scene. His collar still felt tight from the threat of the noose.

Before they could escape down the aisle, the minister muttered something about marriage papers that had not yet been signed. He led them hastily to the side of the church, where someone held out a pen and a writing desk and a piece of parchment.

Travis took the pen impatiently and scrawled his name on the line indicated. He handed the pen to Alicia, who gazed warily at the legal document. There seemed no point in refusing at this late hour, but she scrutinized the writing carefully, just to irritate the domineering men around her.

When she came to Travis's scrawl, her eyes widened, and she shot him a look of fury. In an undertone she asked scathingly, "Is this your idea of a joke? Or did you think you could nullify this whole miserable episode by forgery?"

Travis gave her a startled look, then glancing where she pointed, shrugged. "That's my name. Ask your father for the particulars if you do not believe me." He watched her reaction, wondering if the title that was part of his legal name would ease her anger any. It had not occurred to him that Chester Stanford had not immediately informed his daughter that she would be marrying into the British peerage.

Alicia stared in disbelief at the "VISCOUNT DELANEY" scribbled after a host of given names. She knew absolutely nothing about this man. She must be quite literally insane. It would be fitting if she spent the rest of her life behind locked doors.

Which gave her a perfectly workable idea of how she would even the score. Neatly penning her name across the document, she gave the minister a lovely smile and dutifully took Travis's arm to be escorted down the aisle. Her bridegroom would not be quite so confident of himself when she finished with him.

Travis was not fooled by the polite smile on Alicia's lovely lips. She was a lady first and last, and she would play the part of dutiful wife in public. What he could expect when he got her home was anyone's guess. He knew enough by now to realize the lady's mind was quick and unpredictable, and her temperament not the most stable. The knife in his back would be invisible but just as painful.

To his surprise Alicia demurred when her father offered his home for their wedding night. Chester appeared stunned at her refusal, but Letitia merely smiled knowingly and wished them well.

The usual merrymaking had been foregone, reportedly in deference to Alicia's mourning, and in no time at all a parade of horses, wagons, and carriages escorted the newlyweds to the river and Travis's waiting boat. Chester still seemed shaken by the suddenness of this departure, but he hugged his daughter and shook his son-in-law's hand with vigor.

"I'm trusting you with my most precious possession, damn you, Travis. If you hurt her, I'll have your hide."

Travis wished for the time to take him aside and ask why he had never told Alicia of his heritage, but it no longer seemed relevant or important. A title made no more difference to Alicia than his Indian ancestry. She hated him for himself alone. He wondered if that was an accomplishment to be proud of, but did not ponder the point. She was his, and there would be time enough in the future to correct any misunderstandings.

As the boat shoved off, Alicia waved smilingly to the gathering of friends and relatives on the shore, but as soon as they were out of sight, she strode silently to the cabin and closed the door. If Travis dared follow her, she would hit him over the head with the wine bottle left suggestively upon the bed, apparently a gift from the crew.

It had all happened too fast. She barely had time to comprehend it. She had lost her job. Her father had sold her to a British lordling. She didn't even know if arrangements had been made to send her clothes downriver. She had nothing but a few remnants of pride to cling to. And Travis was the reason. Or Lord Delaney, or whatever his name was. She wasn't even certain of her own name now. Lady Delaney? Mrs. Delaney? Mrs. Travis? Lord in heaven help her, how would she ever survive?

The crew had begun celebrating early, and their boisterous songs echoed off the riverbanks as they passed the jug around, casually guiding the boat downriver with little need of effort. Shadows had already grown long by the time they reached the landing Travis had constructed. Alicia felt the boat bump against the shore with dismay. Fight she would, but she felt little hope or joy in the outcome.

This time Travis did not carry her ashore, but politely lent his hand in assistance. Even this touch Alicia found repulsive, and she jerked away, sweeping up her skirts and maneuvering the tricky path on her own. Travis shrugged and followed. With his luck she would trip on a root in the semidarkness and break her leg. No one would believe it was not his fault.

The house loomed dark and empty when they reached it. There had been no time for preparations, no means of sending someone out here to prepare beds and meals and fires. Travis had no servants, and the lack stared him in the face as he gazed with Alicia's eyes on this unwelcome homecoming.

"Becky and Auguste will be out tomorrow," he muttered, opening the door so his bride might enter.

The coldness of the house seeped into Alicia's bones, and tears came unbidden to her eyes. The house had held so much hope and sunshine the last time they were here, the time their child could have been conceived. Now she saw only the bleak emptiness of marriage her mother had faced, and she could not meet Travis's eyes.

"I cannot fix dinner in this." She indicated the long train of her gown. "Have you something I can wear? An old shirt, some breeches?" She strode deeper into the gloom of the hall, away from the threatening presence of the man behind her.

"Upstairs in the wardrobe you will find one or two things that might suit." Travis breathed a sigh of relief at his forethought in acquiring these gifts he had meant to surprise her with. They might not be particularly suitable for cooking over a fire, but they would be better than the wedding gown. "I will get the fires started and see if they haven't got something cooking in the bunkhouse. You shouldn't have to cook your own wedding meal."

"It doesn't matter. I am quite capable of fixing my own." Proudly Alicia tilted her chin and proceeded up the elegant stairway, grateful for the shadows that protected her from Travis's view. Hot tears spilled down her cheeks.

In the wardrobe she found an assortment of dresses made up from materials she recognized as having admired in the dry-goods store at one time or another. Curse Becky's tattletale tongue. Without so much as a candlelight, she could only admire the workmanship in the gloom of dusk, but even in that, the colors shone like jewels. Travis preferred her in bright colors instead of the drab ones she had worn since her mother's death. Spite made her reach for the darkest one in there, a deep indigo with less neckline than she had ever worn, but she suspected they would all be of the same make. Travis meant to dress her to his taste, but after tonight he would be sorely disappointed. Becky would certainly bring her own clothes on the morrow.

The rich wool fit like a second skin and Alicia eyed the seams of the bodice with trepidation. She would not have to worry about wearing these gowns for very long, in any case. Shortly it would be obvious the gowns no longer fit.

The happiness Alicia had once found in this thought faded to an aching sorrow. Once Travis learned of her pregnancy, he would crow with pride and strut about like a rooster, knowing he had accomplished his goal. She was his, until death do they part. What little pride remained to her would be lost.

She would keep it from him as long as she could, however. She knew how to play the part of wife, how to run a household, how to cook. She was well trained for her place in things, as every lady should be. She would make a home of this place if it killed her, simply because her child must grow up here. Beyond that she would not go. She had given of herself once and been humiliated. Never again.

In giving Travis control over her physical self, she had forfeited all ability to maintain her own self-esteem. She would not give him such control again. He could only drag her down until she was dust beneath his feet. Her mother

had been right about men. They were not to be trusted.
Travis had humiliated her time and again. She had humiliated herself by turning to him. It would not be easy, but she
would not let it happen again, whatever the cost. She would
be her own woman, and no man would ever have the power
to destroy her.

Travis lifted his head from gazing at the fire as Alicia
entered the kitchen. He caught his breath at the beauty of
milk-white shoulders emerging from the satin sheen of blue.
No ornament adorned Alicia's graceful throat except the
tangle of a silken curl escaped from its pin, but that was
enough. He wanted to jerk the remaining pins from her hair
and bury his fingers deep in thick mahogany cascades, but
he could see by the iciness of her eyes that time had not
come. Might never come.

He gestured toward the tin plates set politely on the crude
table. "I have had no time to make this house a home. I
hope you will be able to do that."

Alicia cared not if they dined from tin or silver and gold.
What mattered was the company, and his made a hornet's
nest of her insides. She would not be able to eat whatever
revolting mess steamed in the kettle over the fire.

"My things should be arriving from Philadelphia any day
now. We can manage without for a while."

At least she was talking, and Travis allowed a breath of
hope to enter as he produced a bottle of wine and began
pouring it into two cups. Alicia spooned the thickened broth
and lumps of meat and beans onto the plates.

They ate in relative silence, Alicia barely picking at her
meal while Travis gulped his with all the gusto of a condemned man. He could not find the words to apologize for
his behavior, could not really find the need to apologize. He
had done what he had to. He was sorry he had embarrassed
her, but that would be easier to say in the aftermath of
lovemaking, when they both felt a little more relaxed with
each other. Gradually the anticipation of his wedding night
raised his spirits.

Water heated over the fire while they ate. As Alicia
began to rinse and scrape their plates afterward, Travis
carried buckets to the wash pitchers and tub upstairs. Someday he would have to build a bath house and teach Alicia to
enjoy it. For this night he would anticipate her wishes and
provide a hot bath.

When Travis returned downstairs, he generously offered Alicia what privacy he could, hoping to ease her tension. "I will check on the horses and leave some orders for the morning with the men. Don't worry about the fire, I will bank it when I come in."

Alicia dried her hands on a towel and nodded acknowledgment, but remained in the kitchen until Travis was safely out the door. Then she strode rapidly for the safety and protection of the bedroom upstairs.

Fire danced in the grate and a steaming bath awaited her. A gown of gossamer weave lay across the bed covers, another gift from her husband, she surmised. As usual, he had prepared all the trappings for seduction carefully. But this time he would not succeed.

Without a qualm she threw the bolt of the bedroom door.

Half an hour later, Travis returned to the house, hopeful hot water and wine had done their work and that Alicia had begun to thaw. They were married, for better or worse. They may as well become used to it. It was not as if they were strangers to each other's beds.

Repeating this litany of logic, Travis climbed the stairs with increasing anticipation. He could imagine the gown on her now, the soft folds of material clinging to Alicia's high, full breasts, silhouetting her supple waistline and slender hips, disguising the long limbs that drove him to distraction when they wrapped around him. He would have the whole night to make love to her, teach her the foolishness of denying what they both wanted, and with God's will, give her the child she craved. It would work, he would make it work.

When Travis encountered the barred door, he still did not grasp the future that lay in store for him. He rattled the wood lightly, calling out to wake Alicia from whatever reverie she sought in her bath. When he received no reply, he shook the door louder, setting up a thundering in his ears that seemed to come from his heart.

"Alicia, are you asleep? Unbar the door, please."

He heard a movement within and breathed a short-lived sigh of relief. The light under the door went dark and he could hear the creak of wood as the bed sagged beneath Alicia's weight. He continued to stare dumfoundedly at the barred door even as it became obvious that Alicia had no intention of unfastening it.

Once she had barred her door to him. Never had it occurred to him that she would try again. With disbelief Travis stared at the solid oak he had so carefully fitted with the precaution of an unbreakable bar to protect their privacy. Not even an ax would destroy that bolt without a night's chopping. And he would not lower himself to that level.

With a curse Travis swung on his heel and sought the cold comfort of the kitchen fire, the pleasures of his wedding night burned to unwelcoming ashes.

33

FROST ON THE ground would have been warmer than the reception Becky met when she arrived the next day. She found Alicia furiously sweeping months of dust from the front room while Travis merely grunted a greeting and hefted her trunk to his shoulder to carry it inside.

Even Becky's limited imagination did not require prompting to gather the cause for this iciness. The gossip of the kidnapping had spread like wildfire, and the speculation of what had happened in the Indian camp was on everyone's tongue. That was no way to treat a lady like Alicia, and for once she sided with her mistress. Travis had to face two cold demeanors each morning when he came down from the empty room he had chosen for his own.

Travis had no overt cause for complaint. Alicia bent over backward to be polite and efficient. The filth of a bachelor's establishment disappeared beneath the brooms and mops and scrub brushes of Alicia and Becky and the wife of one of his men. In the evenings a hot meal always awaited him. Once the supplies Alicia sent for arrived, the meals even included deliciously light loaves of bread and pies that made his mouth water just smelling them. All his creature comforts but one were satisfied. That one ate at his insides like an insidious disease.

Alicia consented to accompany Travis on his trips to the Indian village to see how Homasinee fared, and she sat at his side when they made the long trip into St. Louis for church on Sunday mornings. In front of others Alicia was unfailingly pleasant, deferred to his wishes, and behaved as any other new bride could be expected, making Travis grit his teeth in frustration.

Only at night, in the privacy of their home, did she openly

defy him. If Alicia retired first, Travis found her door barred to him. If he attempted to accompany her upstairs, she remembered some task to be done in the kitchen and refused to return to her room until she heard him settle down for the night. Once Travis tried waiting for her in the room he had meant for them to share, and she spent the night sitting in a rocking chair beside the kitchen fire. He never attempted that again. He would not force her, nor cause her further grief.

If Alicia had looked high and low for a method to drive him insane, she could not have found a better one, Travis swore as he swung his ax and splintered the firewood in the yard. This was far worse than her refusals on the trip downriver. Then he had known she had suffered at another man's hands. This time he knew it was himself who had driven her away.

That was not the least of it. As chips of wood flew in the air from his angry strokes, Travis cursed beneath his breath. At least on the boat, she had kept herself hidden from his eyes and not displayed all her charms to tempt him. But now, living together as they were, he could scarcely look around without finding her in her nightdress brewing tea in the kitchen, or with her scarf removed, revealing the round, firm globes of her breasts as she wiped sweat and dust from her face while cleaning. Even the sound of her splashing as she bathed behind locked doors drove him into a frenzy. He had taken to icy baths in the river for himself.

Stacking the wood by the kitchen door, Travis ducked his head beneath the pump to wipe off the sweat, then drying himself on an old towel, trudged into the house and up the stairs. Wryly reflecting on how the mighty had fallen, Travis contemplated the foolishness of his hope that a title might bring his lofty lady around. Instead, the Viscount Delaney, heir to an earldom, found himself performing the tasks of a common laborer and sleeping on the floor. He had more respect when he brawled in taverns and could outfight any man who challenged him.

Even with these satiric thoughts, his heart skipped a beat as he came upon Alicia standing on the landing, gazing out the window. Sunlight gleamed along her hair, throwing her slenderness into silhouette, and Travis's hands ached to encompass her apron-wrapped waist. She may have reduced him to a field hand, but the Philadelphia heiress performed all the tasks of the lowliest of maids. Even in this she left him no cause for complaint.

She turned at his approach, and Travis read her expression with curiosity. She showed no fear of him, no anger, not even coldness any longer. It was as if he merely existed, a fact of life to be dealt with appropriately, as the dirt she swept from the house. At the moment she chewed lightly at her lower lip, lost in thought, and he had the wild urge to taste that lip himself, but he coldly stifled that madness.

"Something worries you?" he inquired without emotion, watching the delicate features of her face as they turned up to him.

Under other conditions Travis's closeness might have made her nervous, but Alicia's mind was elsewhere, and she actually welcomed his timely arrival. She gestured toward the window where she had been standing.

"Look at Becky." Her tone held neither command nor question, only perplexity. She had been so concerned with her own problems these last weeks, she had given little thought to others. She had not even looked at her little maid closely for months. The shock when she finally opened her eyes unnerved her.

Travis came to stand beside her. Out in the yard below, Becky carried the hired hands' noon meal to the bunkhouse. Auguste evidently had come to help, and the two stood deep in conversation. Travis could see nothing unusual in this. He gave Alicia a quizzical glance.

"What is wrong? She seems perfectly normal to me. She has always preferred talking to working."

Alicia glanced out again and saw that Becky had turned her back to the house. She made an impatient gesture. "Wait until she turns around. There. They are going on. Look. Can't you see?"

With curiosity Travis followed the path of the couple. Auguste had taken away the heavy kettle and Becky carried only the tray of bread. The half-starved urchin they had rescued from the tavern had not grown much in height these past months, but she had certainly filled out. Mrs. Clayton's cooking had a lot to be said for that, and Becky had greedily learned everything she could. She would surpass boarding-

house standards if the prior night's meal was any evidence.
Travis could find nothing of concern in that observance.

He shook his head in ignorance. "She looks fine to me, a
little plumper maybe, but it looks good on her. She looks
less like a half-starved chicken."

He was surprised when his witticism was met with the
furious stomp of Alicia's foot and shake of her head.

"She is pregnant! Can't you see?" Alicia could have
screamed at his blindness. She need not worry about hiding
her own condition if he was too blind to see that Becky was
well advanced in motherhood. She overlooked the fact that
she herself had just noticed it.

Travis looked again and gave a low whistle. An apron and
full skirts disguised much of the fact, but now that he knew
what to look for, it was obvious. The tray Becky carried
rested on a distinct bulge beneath the discreet apron, and
she walked with an odd waddle that belied her usual jerky
gait.

"Auguste," he muttered, not in anger, but more in wonder. They made an unlikely pair, these two: the mountain-
ous keelboatman with his taciturn ways and the slight young
maid with her ever constant chatter. The ways of love and
nature were strange.

"Yes, Auguste," Alicia answered impatiently. "What are
we going to do about it?"

Travis almost laughed aloud at her prim righteousness,
but he managed to smother his grin. "Hold a shotgun to the
devil's head, I expect," he responded cheerfully. "It should
be amusing to be on the other end of the barrel for a
change."

Alicia would have gladly strangled him, but Travis had
already loped off without another word. In minutes she
could see him crossing the yard in the direction of the
bunkhouse. She should have looked after Becky more carefully, but how could a young girl know how to behave when
her mistress set a worse example? Upset with herself, Alicia
disappeared into the Spartan room she had made her own.
It was too late to prevent what had already happened. All
they could do now was make the best of it.

Becky came to her a half hour later, her brown face aglow
and tears in her eyes. "Travis says it's OK by you. Are you
certain, Miss Alicia? I mean, if you're going to go away and

leave him, I got to go with you. And you know Auguste, he'll stay with Travis. I been afraid to say anything, but if you really mean it . . ."

Alicia nearly cried at the ogre she must appear, and she shook her head blindly. "Of course, it's all right, silly goose. You should have said something earlier. You shouldn't be carrying those heavy kettles about and scrubbing floors and—"

Becky grinned cheerfully. "Don't make me no matter. If you can do it, I can do it. But it would be kind of nice to have a wedding and all. When I get so big Auguste can't bed me, I'll at least have his name to keep me company."

Slightly stunned by this attitude and Becky's indication that she knew of Alicia's pregnancy, Alicia searched for a way to divert the topic. "When is the baby due?"

Becky shrugged unconcernedly. "Three, four months, I expect. There's lots of time."

"Three or four months?" Shocked, Alicia mentally counted backward. This was only the beginning of June. The little devil had been carrying on since the first of the year or earlier. For all she knew, the wise little brat may have singled out Auguste back on the boat. Would she ever learn to know people? Even this child was beyond her comprehension.

Briskly Alicia chased away such thoughts and set about making plans. That was something she knew how to do.

The day of the wedding dawned bright and clear. Word had traveled to St. Louis and uninvited guests began to arrive the night before. Every keelboat crew on the river seemed to be in St. Louis this week, Alicia speculated as she gazed out upon her lawn. And they had all showed up for Auguste's wedding. She gave a prayer of thanks that her own wedding was so hasty they had not time to congregate. Obviously they intended to make up for the lack today.

By the time the circuit preacher arrived and the vows were said, their guests were already well on their way to a happy state of oblivion. Travis had thoughtfully provided kegs of ale and a collection of musicians to smooth the road to that state, and the front lawn thundered with shouts and song by mid-afternoon.

Much to Alicia's chagrin, wherever the boatmen went, women followed, and the reception quickly threatened to become an orgy if it did not rain soon. Glancing at the cloudless sky, she saw little chance of that. With dismay she watched as Becky and Auguste began the dancing with a rocking, bumping display that made a mockery of the art form. Physical contact seemed to be the main object of the dance, and the audience whistled in appreciation as Auguste swung his pregnant wife into the air.

Travis startled her by coming up silently from behind and sliding his arm around her waist. Alicia could smell the liquor on his breath, and her heart quailed, but he seemed quite sober as he watched the dancing.

"If we don't join in soon, they will begin calling for us," he warned, staring out at the crowd and not at the woman moving uneasily in his embrace.

"Travis, I cannot go out there," Alicia protested, terrified at even the thought of it.

"They'll be insulted if we do not. I don't think you want to insult the guests at Becky's wedding, do you?"

Alicia swallowed her distaste. These were his friends. Come hell or high water, she would see them entertained as they expected.

The touch of Travis's hand and arm about her waist sent nervous shocks through Alicia's system, and she did not meet his eyes for fear he would see the effect he had on her. If she could only hate him, it would be so much easier, but even the knowledge that he did not love her—scarcely seemed to respect her—could not abate her feelings for this man. He stood tall and straight beside her, his strength a bulwark she could rely on, but his gentleness a facade he used to deceive. She had seen his savagery with knife and fists, knew the lengths his fury would carry him. She must shut him out, preserve herself and her control at all cost, or he would destroy her as Teddy had tried to do, as her father had destroyed her mother. There could be no compromise, she saw that now as she had not earlier. She would not submit to this man or any other. That way lay madness and degradation, not the peace and safety she had thought. He had taken away her freedom and humiliated her beyond endurance. She would never forgive him.

Travis felt Alicia's shoulders stiffen, but her crisp nod of agreement brought a smile to his lips. She loved to dance. Music affected her as much as strong wine, he had already observed. This night he would melt her icy reserve and find surcease for the raging fire in his loins. To look but not touch was a torture he could scarcely endure any longer. Already the flames were licking along his veins as he guided her toward the open field where the musicians played. His hand clutched possessively about her waist as the crowd noted their appearance and cheered.

In the light of the setting sun, Travis's dark countenance gleamed in shades of red and gold as he turned to face her. The burning stare of midnight eyes swept Alicia's breath away, but obediently she fell into the pattern of his steps. The fiddle's tune was for a country dance, but Travis made no effort to release his hold on her waist. They swept briskly down the lawn, his strong arm providing all the guidance she needed.

Holding her gown up from the grass as elegantly as if this were a ballroom, Alicia slid easily into Travis's embrace as he whirled her around in an impromptu choreography of his own. The crowd whistled and cheered, but Alicia had already forgotten their existence. Dark eyes cast a spell on her, holding her fascinated as they moved to the steady rhythm of the rowdy music. His hands burned paths of fire down her spine as they guided her through the steps.

Aroused by the sensuous display of the couple dancing only for each other, others began to join in. As dusk arrived, a fire was lit, sending a golden glow over the assemblage of whirling figures. And still Alicia and Travis danced, their bodies speaking what their words could not.

Sweat broke out on Travis's brow as Alicia's hips moved close to his, and he had to stifle his sudden surge of lust. His body had been denied too long to respond any less than violently to the rapture of her sinuous movement in his arms, the heavenly scent of violets from her hair, or the sight of white flesh pushing temptingly above her bodice. If he did not have her soon, he would rape her right here on the lawn.

But he would not have to resort to violence, Travis surmised as he stared down into depths of azure. Desire was written on moist, upturned lips, parted softly as she met his gaze and did not look away. His grip tightened, and Alicia swayed against him, their thighs brushing and his readiness apparent. She did not flinch, and Travis muffled a groan against her hair. Tonight. It would have to be tonight.

The general rowdiness eventually broke out into the inevitable fight, and Travis hastily pulled Alicia from the firelight. His quick glance told him Auguste and Becky had safely retired, and he turned Alicia in the direction of the house.

"Go on. I will have to settle this before they set fire to each other and everything else. I will join you shortly."

A gust of cool night air blew between them, coloring Alicia's cheeks and forcing them apart. She dropped her eyes and nodded, then scurried toward the house, her heart beating an uneven patter as she reached the porch.

The heat of Travis's hands still burned where he had touched her. Moistness rolled between her breasts and thighs, reminding her all too vividly of what they had done together, what they would do together. She knew what he wanted, what he expected after this night's exhibition. She had been wanton in her behavior. The price would be extremely high indeed.

With trepidation Alicia fled to the safety of the bedroom, closing the door softly behind her. As she stared at the elegant poster bed, its symbolic carving flickering into life in the lamplight, she knew this would be a haven no longer if Travis were allowed to enter. Her body wanted him, ached for his possession, but her mind reeled from the shock of the sensations he forced on her.

He had raped her, humiliated her, and bought her with his noble name. How could she even allow herself to consider what she so obviously had let him believe? Once she let him in here, there would be no removing him short of physical force. Ever. Travis had a way of converting everything and everyone to his own use. She would be just another one of his possessions, a woman he had carved from stone and brought to life.

Taking up the wooden statue she had saved from the fire, Alicia wandered to the window and stared out into the starlit night. The flames from the bonfire threw dancing shadows across the lawn, illuminating grotesque figures as they parted from the company or sauntered back. Girlish laughter drifted through the open casement, accompanied by the shouts and merriment of drunken men. An occasional scream or curse warned all fighting had not ceased, and she sought for Travis's familiar masculine physique among the combatants.

Among all the burly, muscular shapes, his was not difficult to find. Silhouetted against the fire, Travis hovered half a head taller than most. Broad shoulders tapering to narrow hips distinguished him from those few who nearly matched his height. Alicia watched as he flung aside his lace-cuffed linen shirt to join the coat and cravat he had worn in honor of the occasion. Half-naked, he raised his fists to meet his opponents—Travis's way of establishing peace.

Even now, knowing how violence could so easily destroy a life, Alicia thrilled at the sight of Travis's powerful torso moving with such grace and precision. Perhaps men dealt differently with death and destruction, but she could not. She had lingered too long on the brink of madness to feel safe with these savage instincts lurking somewhere still inside her. Travis aroused things in her that were better left dead. If even Travis could turn on her as he had, she had no one to rely on but herself.

She wanted to believe he loved her, that his concern would protect her from the violence of this savage life out here, but she knew now it was not so. If he had loved her, he would never have kidnapped her, raped her, humiliated her as he had done, knowing what had been done to her before. No, he was as uncivilized as all the rest, and she must protect herself from him as well as her surroundings. He only saw her as a means to an end; she had allowed physical pleasure to blind her to her mother's warning that a man's concern was only for himself. She had been a fool to think Travis any different.

Even knowing that, she would allow him to take her to his bed again, just to experience the piercing pleasure of being wanted, if only just in this way. She craved the strength of his arms, the heat of his kisses, the joining that brought them so close she could almost believe his words. She would give him everything just for the sheer physical beauty of their lovemaking, if she could ever trust him again.

Looking out at the violence of the man who pommeled his opponent to the ground and swung around looking for any other challengers, Alicia knew her trust had fled. A man like that was alien to her. She would never be able to understand the reasons behind his inscrutable actions, and not understanding, she could never trust. She had already felt the brunt of his savage ways once. What would he do once he thought he owned her?

She had too much fear to find out. Men had made a ruin of her life. Why should she believe this one to be any different?

As Travis moved triumphantly and unscathed from the firelight, advancing toward the house to the cheers of his audience, Alicia quietly turned from the window.

It took only a few steps and a single motion to slide the bolt that separated the past from the future.

He could take his lust elsewhere.

34

TRAVIS TOOK THE back porch stairs two at a time, stopped at the washbasin to fling cold water over his perspiring back and shoulders, and carrying his discarded shirt and coat, strode whistling into the kitchen.

The fire had already been banked for the night, and he continued through the house, his heart pounding wildly as he contemplated the prize awaiting him. He had worked long and hard to gain the comforts of soft arms and willing body. Not just any soft arms, but the sweet-scented arms of a lady. For one who had been cursed at and spat on as a heathen savage for too many years of his life, this was a reward made in heaven. He had proved himself not only as a man, but as a gentleman. He need prove nothing else.

That Alicia was not just any lady, but a woman with needs and desires to match his own, propelled Travis up the stairs with an eager gait. All trace of liquor had evaporated with the anticipation of this moment. The nuisance of establishing his control of the party outside had irked him where once it would have given him pleasure. He had disposed of his boisterous challengers more quickly than was his wont so as not to keep Alicia waiting. He wanted nothing to cool the flames of desire that had circled them earlier. He would not give her time for second thoughts.

Travis hesitated at the door to the room he had occupied these last weeks. Should he wash a little more thoroughly than that hasty splash? Should he shave and put on something more suitable? Rubbing his stubbly jaw, he contemplated these niceties only briefly. Eagerness won out over gentility.

A few long strides carried him to the closed door that had barred his happiness since their wedding night. He would burn the damn bar in the morning. Tonight he would win his bride.

Travis softly turned the wooden knob and pushed the door to enter. Wood came in contact with wood with a loud thump that echoed in rage through the corridors of Travis's mind. His fist closed in helpless anguish around the knob, the knuckles turning white with the tension of controlling his fury.

Without giving another try, Travis spun on his heel and stalked back to his own room and the comforts of the whiskey bottle he had left there. Not even the companionship of his friends or the violence of a good brawl would relieve the pain and anger surging through his veins this night. He needed numbness in which to think.

Millie, the farmhand's wife who occasionally came in to help with the housework, passed on the message Travis had left for Alicia the next morning.

With none of Becky's sharp curiosity, she glanced up as Alicia entered the kitchen. "Travis done tole me to tell you he had business in St. Louis. He'll be back with the next boat downriver."

Alicia accepted the cup of coffee Millie poured for her and walked to the door to stare out at the brilliant June day. She had heard Travis at her door last night, listened as he retreated to the other bedroom, and lay awake the rest of the night waiting for his revenge. She had been surprised when it had not come. No axes at the door, no ladders at her window, no silent figure dropping through the ceiling. Perhaps he really did not care.

His leaving for St. Louis without speaking made Alicia a little uneasy. If Travis went back to her father and demanded an annulment, she would have to reveal her pregnancy. The idea of that kind of emotional scene made her nervous. She didn't want any more scenes. She only wanted to be left alone to make the best of what was left of her shattered life.

With that thought in mind, Alicia set aside her cup and went in search of Becky. There were few children on the farm as yet, just Millie's two boys and the son of one of the men whose wife had died. But few of the hands could read or write. Becky would encourage them to learn. It was time she offered to help.

When Travis returned home late one evening, he found the kitchen lighted and an odd assortment of men and women bent over slates at the kitchen table. The class was by no means a large one, but a studious one. Not one man looked up as he stopped in the doorway. Becky immediately glanced his way and winked, and Alicia looked up with a frown, but rather than disturb the lesson, Travis turned around and walked out again.

Alicia did not see him again until the next morning, when Travis strode in from the yard as she prepared breakfast. She had not heard him come to bed the night before nor heard him rise that morning. He walked on cat feet, coming and going as silently as a mountain lion in the hills. And just as lethal.

Other than a word of greeting, he said nothing now. Alicia waited tensely for the blow to fall, the announcement that he would send her back to her father, annul the marriage, whatever plan he had made to even the score. He ate his meal, made a polite show of kissing her cheek for Becky's benefit, and walked out again.

He drove her insane. No recriminations, no reproaches, no angry words. He simply went about his business, appeared in time for meals, and disappeared afterward. They exchanged nothing more than informal greetings or casual comments on the weather, like total strangers. Alicia calmly considered swinging the frying pan at his head to catch his attention.

But it had taken many months of weary practice to regain her restraint against any such excessive emotion, and her training stood her in good stead now. She would not let him know how she felt, would not let him see the pain. As the days passed, a pattern evolved, and Alicia began to understand that Travis had other plans.

He took her to visit Homasinee to see how she fared and to make arrangements for signals should help be needed. He hired new men with experience handling horses to take charge of the new mares and their foals he had purchased that spring. He showed Alicia where he kept the farm books and the money needed to manage day-to-day expenses and a copy of the letter he had given his bankers to assure her access to his accounts. Alicia stared at them with growing comprehension but no comment.

Not until Saturday, when it came time to prepare for their

weekly trip into the city, did Travis say one word of his
plans. As Alicia packed a change of clothing for Sunday
morning, he came in to eye her progress and offer advice.

"You may want to take in enough to stay a few days this
time."

Alicia's fingers tightened around the petticoat in her hand
as she glanced up at Travis's dark, noncommittal expression. "We will not be coming home Sunday night?"

Travis coldly stifled the wrenching of his heart as he
stared into the brilliant azure of her dark-lashed eyes. Shadows circled them, but he ignored that fact too. "I will be
leaving after services on some business for your father. I
thought you might prefer to stay in town for a while rather
than be out here alone."

There should be nothing frightening in those words. Her
father left on business trips all the time. It took time to
travel in the west. The space around them was vast, the
population limited. Doing business required going where
the business was. Alicia understood that. If Travis wished to
participate in her father's various business dealings, it would
help them both. She could have no objections. But a niggling fear took root in her heart and did not die.

"I like it out here. Millie has agreed to bring her boys to
class with her Monday night. They will be expecting me.
Will it be too much trouble to return me here before you
leave?"

Whatever expression flickered briefly behind black eyes
did not reveal itself in Travis's reply. "No. No trouble at all.
I simply thought you might prefer the company."

They left it at that, neither of them with experience enough
to speak their feelings. Travis kept his private hell behind
the walls he had long ago constructed to face the world.
Alicia held her tongue as she had been taught. They rode
into town discussing nothing more demanding than the unusual coolness of the season. They rode home the next day
with an aching chasm of loneliness between them and no
words with which to bridge it.

As Travis watched Alicia sway wearily up the long staircase to bed, he yearned for just one backward look, one
sign of encouragement to give him hope. He received nothing. In actuality, he probably deserved nothing. He had
gambled, and he had lost. Perhaps one of her civilized
Philadelphia gentlemen would have known how to win and

keep her, but he had been too long from civilization to react any other way than he had. He had tried to force her into the image he had in his mind, but Alicia insisted on being herself. It was obvious she would never forgive him, and he only made them both miserable by remaining. With that bitter thought in mind, he swung away and walked out the door.

When Alicia rose the next morning, he was gone. No tender parting, no words of reassurance, not even a simple farewell. The churning in her stomach became bile in her throat, and she could not even drink her coffee. How had what once looked so bright and promising become this dismal grayness so rapidly? Where was the joy and excitement that had once bubbled over with her eagerness to share it with the man who had fathered this child growing within her?

Perhaps if she told him of the babe when he returned, it would be better. Perhaps she had been wrong in keeping the news from him. Travis used to laugh and sing and smile hugely for no reason at all. Maybe the news of the child would return the arrogant pride, but it would also return the laughter. The grim, taciturn man who had left here was not the bold keelboat captain she remembered. Alicia tried to put a finger on the moment he had changed, but it eluded her. She only knew he had once looked upon her with pride and admiration—never love, she was certain there had never been love—but he no longer looked at her at all anymore. Perhaps by denying the only thing they had between them, this physical attraction, she had denied him the only happiness he found in this marriage. That sounded foolish even to her, but to admit there could be anything else between them would be to admit she had been wrong. She had only herself to rely on, and she could not admit to failure. She would make this marriage work somehow.

With the stubborn determination that had brought her this far, Alicia set about working away the days of Travis's absence. The men had their orders and followed them well, but she learned to deal with the day-to-day mishaps that no man could foretell. She taught her classes in the evening, rejoicing when a new member joined them, seeking out reasons when one dropped out. And at the end of each day, she left a lamp lit in the hall and went upstairs to kneel beside her empty bed and pray for her husband's safe return.

The days grew into a week without any word from Travis. He had not said how long he would be gone. She had just assumed it would be the few days he meant to leave her in St. Louis. It had been foolish not to ask. Perhaps her father would know.

She traveled into St. Louis with Becky and Auguste that week. Chester and Letitia welcomed her with open arms, urged her to stay awhile with them, and offered no information. Alicia could not bring herself to beg the answer to her questions. She would not have them think there was anything wrong between her and Travis. She would wait.

The next week crawled by without significant occurrence. July came in as cool as spring. The crops did not flourish. Travis did not write. Alicia's life had become a string of non-events, measured by what did not happen. Even the child did not seem to exist, for there was no one there to share it with. Becky was too enraptured with her newfound status to notice Alicia's growing waistline, and anyone else who might have noticed did not feel obliged to mention it. She quietly let out the seams of her bodice by herself.

Her furniture arrived in mid-July, delivered by keelboat, and her father and Letitia rode out to celebrate the occasion. By the time they arrived, Alicia was dusty and disheveled from running back and forth between house and river, guarding each of her precious possessions every step of the way, preventing their being carried upside-down or dropped in mud or worse when the men tired of toting their burdens. Letitia took one look at her stepdaughter's shadowed eyes, gazed quickly at her still slender figure draped only in thin muslin, her apron scarcely disguising the bulge where the child grew, and ordered Alicia back to the house.

Her sharp command was so surprising, both Alicia and Chester turned to stare at the normally undemanding Frenchwoman.

"This is madness! You are not to stir from the house, *ma petite*. Up the stairs. I will find that lazy, no-account maid of yours and she will bring you warm water and tea and you will rest. At once."

"But, Letitia, I cannot—"

"You want to lose the little one?" Letitia demanded.

Alicia's cheeks colored at her father's amazed look, and she shook her head. "But someone must direct the men—"

"I can do that." Firmly Letitia turned her toward the house. "To bed. Now."

Chester gaped after the retreating figure of his daughter. "She's pregnant? The bastard rode off and left her pregnant?"

Letitia granted him a scathing look. "And who sent him? Tell me, who? Men!" She flung her small hands upward in an expressive gesture and bustled off to find the lazy maid.

Her father and stepmother remained several days, returning order to chaos, ensuring that Becky and Millie knew of Alicia's condition and looked after her accordingly. They tried to persuade Alicia to return with them, but she adamantly refused.

"Alicia, this is foolish. There is no reason for you to stay out here in the middle of nowhere in your condition. You should be with family," Chester protested as they prepared to leave.

"Someone must look after the place while Travis is gone," Alicia repeated her argument patiently. In truth, she did not want to return to St. Louis. The town held no entertainment for her any longer. Her life was here, waiting for Travis to return, keeping his house for him, nurturing his child. She never admitted these thoughts to herself either, but her belief in them was firm.

Chester looked skeptical, then noting the stubbornness burning behind his daughter's eyes, he relented. Sorrowfully he wondered how long her mother had sat waiting in that big, empty house in Philadelphia for his return. He prayed Alicia would never have to suffer that fate, but Travis had been gone far longer than necessary to complete the business he had sent him on. The countryside seethed with unrest. Anything could have happened.

Not mentioning his fears to Alicia, Chester kissed his daughter good-bye and joined his waiting wife. Tecumseh had gone south not far from here, seeking recruits for the war he had declared on the Americans. The British had increased their virulent mischief upon land and sea, and the talk of war was on everyone's lips. Travis, with his torn loyalties, could be anywhere. It would not do to speculate.

Knowing little of current events and caring less, Alicia spun a cocoon of security about the nest she made. She continued to leave a lamp burning in the downstairs hall in case Travis arrived late. Each day she worked to arrange the house. A piano now graced a large corner of the front

room. Delicate china adorned the shelves of a graceful
Queen Anne breakfront in the dining room. A silver tea
service was unpacked, polished, and displayed on the
mahogany sideboard. Flowers filled cut-glass vases and
sunshine streamed through velvet draperies pulled back from
casement windows. She would give him a home to be proud
of, one that would welcome him when he returned.

What she was doing made no sense. In some dark corner
of her mind Alicia realized this way led to madness, but she
did not pursue the point. The man who returned would be
the same man who had left and nothing would have changed
between them, but Alicia preferred not to think about that.
She preferred to think of Travis walking through that front
door and gasping with astonishment at the changes she had
wrought. She imagined his black brows rising with pride and
excitement as he sought her out, his dark eyes dancing as he
discovered the burden she carried. He would know the child
was his, and he would sweep her into his arms, and everything would somehow be all right again. It had to be.

The cold summer continued into August, and Alicia shivered as she rose from her lonely bed and looked for her
slippers. The morning nausea had passed and she did not
yet move awkwardly, but the heaviness weighed upon her
heart. Travis had been gone well over two months now
without a word. She could see confusion and sympathy in
the eyes of their workers when she gave them orders Travis
should have been there to do. Even Becky, totally useless
now that pregnancy kept her pinned to her chair with her
feet up, spoke with extra caution when Alicia was about. It
was annoying to be treated like a particularly incompetent
child, but that would end when Travis returned.

If he returned. Staring out over the verdant fields with
unshed tears burning her eyes, Alicia finally considered the
thought. Her father had often taken months to transact
business. New Orleans was a long distance away, the far-
thest place she could think of that Travis might go. It was
quite possible he was on his way home now. But that did
not explain why he had not written, why he had not told her
his business would take the entire summer. He loved this
farm, had large plans for it, and he left it at the most
important time of the year. No, that did not make logical
sense.

The only thing that did make sense was that he was gone.

Forever. Perhaps an accident. Perhaps at the hands of the thieves and rogues that swarmed the countryside. A bear. A snake. Anything. Or perhaps he had just gone as he said he would. The Indian version of divorce, walking out and not coming back. In a few months, a year, people would call her widow, and Travis would be forgotten. As he had told her.

The tears began to trickle down Alicia's cheeks at last. Had she done this to him then? Driven him from his home, from his dreams? Was that sun outside shining on him now, poling a keelboat down some distant river, riding his horse across a grassy plain, escaping the horror of his life? She choked and turned away from that picture. It could not be that. He would not leave her like this. She had been left before and knew the pain, the anguish that did not ever leave. He would not do that to her. He had to return. Had to. She could not live with it if he did not.

35

On the only warm day that summer, the Indians arrived. Out in the chicken pen scattering feed, Becky saw them first, and screamed so loud doors flung open everywhere. Eight months gone with child, she could only waddle back toward the house. By that time Auguste had appeared from nowhere to grab her by the waist and propel her toward the kitchen.

Alicia stood at an upstairs window as she often did these days, polishing idly at the glass and dusting away the cobwebs, gazing out over the vast spaces to the horizon. Becky's scream alerted her and she focused her gaze on the reality of the view and not her daydreams.

From the woods along the riverbank advanced a party of feathered and tattooed warriors. She could not tell if the colors they wore were war paint or the fierce scars that designated their achievements and positions in the tribe. She had never seen them in war paint, didn't know if they actually wore it. She simply recognized the tattoos from her visits with Travis's tribe.

Noting the men drifting from the barn, rifles in hand, Alicia shook herself into action. She would have no bloodshed if it could be prevented. These Indians were friends of Travis, and though they dressed as if for war, they appeared openly and without weapons drawn. She could not fear them.

The band of warriors and the ranch hands had come to a confrontation in the field in front of the house by the time Alicia arrived, breathless. Auguste stepped backward as if to prevent her from coming any farther, but she pushed past him, breaking through the wall of men to meet the savagely garbed strangers.

Her gaze swiftly swept the band of Indians until it came to rest on a visage she recognized with confidence. Bear Mountain. At her look of recognition he stepped forward.

"Lonetree?" With more demand than question, he met Alicia's gaze with approval.

Auguste hastily stepped to her side, barring the way with his rifle. "What do you want with him?"

Impatiently Alicia shoved the rifle aside, but she waited for some reply before speaking. It would not do to reveal Travis was not here and was not expected if this were an unfriendly visit.

Ignoring Auguste, Bear Mountain spoke directly to Alicia. "Homasinee sends her gratitude. The child is strong and healthy and bears the mark of a man. She wishes to share her joy with the woman my cousin has chosen. Shall I take her word that Lonetree has planted a son of his own and that is why he does not come?"

The strangely formal, stilted speech came out much as the notes of a little-used piano, but Alicia caught the pride and happiness that his stoic training prevented expressing.

"Lonetree has gone downriver and has not returned yet, but he will be most pleased to hear of his cousin's son." She swung around and gestured toward one of the men behind her.

"Tell Becky to give you the shawl I have just finished knitting. Quickly."

Alicia turned back to meet the grave stares of her visitors. "Would you come in and refresh yourselves? You may tell Homasinee that I carry Lonetree's child and cannot come to her, but I would like her to have this gift for your child. Come, tell me how she fares."

A wry gleam very similar to one she had seen in Travis's eyes lit Bear Mountain's face as his gaze drifted over the armed and hostile farmhands. With wicked decision he nodded silent agreement to the solitary woman's hospitality. Lonetree had chosen a pale face, but one with the spirit and courage of a Delaware. He spoke curtly to his followers, and to the dismay of the others, deliberately followed Alicia through the gate.

Alicia ignored the hawking and spitting and muttering around her. Travis had friends in many worlds, and he

would want them treated equally. She saw no difference in
entertaining keelboat crews or Indians. It was time the rest
of them accepted that fact.

The Indians had brought gifts of their own, soft beaver
furs and baskets of gourds and corn in recognition of their
belief that Travis and Alicia had saved the life of Bear
Mountain's child. Alicia exclaimed enthusiastically over each
presentation, though she could scarcely conceive what could
be done with such largess. A gourd or two might be conve-
nient for dippers. A basket of corn would make a meal for
the evening. But what in heaven's name would she do with
all the rest?

The men obviously knew, however, and they crowed with
delight as they carried off the bounty. The quick about-face
confused Alicia, but she graciously covered her distraction
as Becky warily appeared on the porch with the shawl.

The delicately woven wool did not seem quite enough
after the goods the Indians carried up from the river, and
Alicia racked her brains for something of equal worth.
Auguste's whispered suggestion horrified her, but the enthusiasm with which the whiskey jugs were greeted proved
him correct. A niggling suspicion of the trade-off between
corn and whiskey entered her mind, but she ignored it. She
could not comprehend the male affinity for liquor and would
not try.

Wanting something of more value than spirits, Alicia remembered the carving Travis had been working on before
he left. She sent one of the men after it and presented it to
Bear Mountain along with the pale green shawl.

"For Homasinee and for the child. May he grow up to be
as free and independent as the eagle that soars overhead."

The wide span of the eagle's wings gleamed golden in the
sunlight and Bear Mountain stroked them affectionately,
gazing up to where the matching pair sat guarding the gates
to this house. Travis had possessed an aptitude for producing powerful totems since he was a little boy. He had no
doubt these eagles would carry the magic of the man. The
gift healed any breach there might have been between the
cousins. He accepted the offering with solemnity.

"Your son and mine will be brothers. The ill wind that
comes will not touch them. They will grow together as the
hawk and the lion and stand against their enemies." Then

incongruously meshing the Christian religion of his Moravian teachers with the beliefs of his ancestry, he added, "Blessings be to God."

That night, staring at the canopy of her bed, Alicia contemplated his words and wished desperately for Travis's insight. Damn the man to a hell of no return, but she missed him. If he did not return soon, his son would in all likelihood grow up as wild as the weeds in the field. His son! Listen to her. Even she began to think like these impossible men around her. She had no doubt she carried a son. Travis's firstborn would be no other. And she had no doubt he would grow up as Bear Mountain predicted, hand in hand with his Indian cousin, at one with the beasts and river. She would have no control over him, as she had no control over Travis.

That thought brought tears to her eyes and she forced it away. What had Bear Mountain meant by an ill wind? Did he know something that she did not? She had heard murmurings of Indian uprisings ever since she had come here, but other than stories of what had happened elsewhere, she had experienced none of it. Perhaps he referred to the unusual weather. Maybe winter would come early this year. Could Indians predict that?

Damn, but why wasn't Travis here to explain these things to her? How could he bring her out here like this, fill her with his child, and disappear? She could kill him for that, take one of those bloody knives of his and carve his hard heart out. She should take the damned lamp burning below and fling it to the ground and stomp on it. Let him find his way in darkness. But then, so must she.

As his child kicked restlessly somewhere below her heart, tears streamed down Alicia's cheeks, and she prayed silently, desperately, that he was somewhere safe and well.

With the heaviness of gold weighting his pocket and a mug of cold beer slaking his thirst, Travis stretched his long legs out in the Mexican bar and admired the scenery. The lovely senorita with the castanets made no secret of her admiration for the tall newcomer, and Travis returned her regard, lifting his mug in acknowledgment. Hell, he had money in his pocket, time on his hands, and the rest of his life to live. This Mexican beauty would be as good a place as

any to start. He could wile away the night in her arms
without difficulty. And maybe the next night and the next.
Scornful blue eyes faded in a haze of alcohol, so he could
almost imagine replacing them with these ebony fires.

Travis's body relaxed in anticipation of the relief to come
as the dancer swayed into his lap. Her lips were warm and
willing, her body, lithe and strong. Travis's hand curled
around her small breast and he tried to imagine it as full as
Alicia's. His mouth traveled over thick lips and longed for
the taste of Alicia's finely chiseled ones. The stench of
perspiration, however, could in no stretch of the imagination replace gardenias.

With a groan Travis tucked a coin in the dancer's
décolletage and departed. It was going to be another long
night. He might as well spend it in the saddle.

The advent of the Indians marked the end of a lifeless
summer. Hearing of the visit, Chester Stanford arrived several days later, demanding his daughter return to St. Louis
with him. Alicia's refusal resulted in a prolonged and noisy
argument from which there was no pacifying Letitia to rescue them. Chester left in a fury and Alicia spent the next
several days working off her anger in the kitchen, preserving
the foods needed to carry them through the winter.

Rumors that Tecumseh had succeeded in gathering a large
force of Indians to the south were verified by the keelboat
crews returning upriver and stopping at the farm to exchange news and goods. Other crews having made the de-
tour from the Ohio upriver to St. Louis brought news of the
bloody massacres to the north, instigated by the bounties
offered by the British in their few occupied forts near the
Canadian border. Civilization as they knew it seemed on the
brink of violent upheavals, and nature played its role in
confirming their fears.

Alicia overheard Millie and Becky whispering one day
and demanded to know the topic. Millie looked uneasy, but
Becky lifted her chin defiantly.

"Them Indians ain't no fools. They've been sayin' that
Prophet told them the earth was gonna open up and swallow
them and fire goin' to come out of the sky if they don't drive
us back into the sea. And you seen what's already happened. We ain't had no summer to speak of, the crops ain't

growin', and now look at them fool squirrels runnin' to drown themselves in the river. Appears mighty strange to me."

The behavior of hordes of squirrels as they had flocked in droves to meet their deaths had been extremely unsettling, but this was a foreign land to Alicia. The first time she had heard an owl hoot had sent her flying into Travis's arms. The cry of the occasional bobcat sent shivers down her spine still. She found nothing particularly ominous in nature's behavior, and despite her words earlier that summer, she was no believer in portents or omens. Leave superstition to the savage Indians.

"Tecumseh's brother made those predictions just to frighten silly fools like you. When you start blaming that child on the moon, I'll have Auguste teach you the facts of life."

Laughing, Alicia left the two women whispering and headed toward the stables. She could no longer ride, but she loved to admire the new foals. Travis had been excited by the little filly, and now that it had better control of its long legs, Alicia could see its promise. The child within her stirred in approval, too, and she smiled for the first time in weeks.

If Alicia had been a believer in portents, the one that next frosty September night would have left her shaken. As it was, Becky's screams alerted her as usual, but the screams and the sight that met her eyes had no relation to each other.

Pulling on her velvet robe, Alicia ran to the window expecting to see the farm surrounded or the barn in flames. The screams had died away, but the whole sky seemed lit in a mysterious haze. Mystified, Alicia searched for the source of the illumination. A fog rose off the river, floating out over the lower-lying land, carrying with it moonbeams when there was no moon.

Men came running out of the bunkhouse, staring up into the sky at an angle that Alicia could not see from this corner of the house. And then it was there, crossing the sky in a streak of flame, throwing the foggy landscape into shadow and light. Alicia gasped at the beauty of it, then shivered in fear as Becky's scream rang out again.

The comet ignited a cloud, disappearing behind the thunderheads, but the men stayed out in the open, gaping in wonder at the sky. One of the men glanced up to Alicia's window and seeing her, loped toward the house. She hurried downstairs to meet him.

"What was that? Why is Becky screaming still?" Holding her side as she leaned against the door frame, Alicia cursed her unwieldy size. Never would she ever dance again.

"Don't know what it was, ma'am, but Millie says the baby's coming. I'll send one of the boys over in the morning to light the fires for you. Reckon the womenfolk will be busy."

The man's down-to-earth practicality took some of the magic from the night. Alicia gestured for him to wait.

"Let me get you some linens and blankets to take to them. I'll get dressed and follow you shortly."

Millie's husband did as instructed and soon Alicia was following him across the yard to the cabin Travis had given the couple. The men did not seem eager to return to their beds and they stood about discussing the odd sight in the sky and ribbing Auguste, who nervously paced the lawn, accepting swigs of whatever was handed him.

He seemed relieved to see Alicia, and she spoke a few reassuring words before hurrying to Becky's side. She was as nervous as Auguste, but she strived not to show it. She had never assisted in the birth of a child and the prospect terrified her, but she could not desert Becky at a time like this. Her own was due in less than three months. It would be best to gain what knowledge she could.

The babe was born before dawn, a tiny, squalling girl that had the towering keelboat man wrapped around her finger at first sight. Exhausted by the night's emotions, Alicia nearly cried as she watched the proud father lift his child into his arms. Would Travis ever look at his child like that? Would he ever learn he had even fathered a child?

Wiping away the tears, Alicia slowly dragged herself from the cabin back to the lonely house. It was a good thing she didn't believe in portents because her mood was such that the night's happenings would be translated into evil tidings. She could imagine herself alone forever, living in this empty house with only the carvings on the bed to remind her of a time when she had been fool enough to believe in love. Even the child growing within her would soon desert her for the exotic life of his cousins. The blood in him would assure that. No son of Travis's would ever grow up tied to a woman's apron strings. Wandering would be in his soul.

Dousing the lamp at the bottom of the stairs, she slowly climbed to the bedroom to collapse in exhaustion on the warm feather ticking. The child kicked in protest but soon quieted.

October brought a killing cold from the north, and Alicia worked from dawn to dusk to store and preserve the last of the summer's harvest. With more than a dozen people dependent upon her for food and housing, the prospect of a long, cold winter loomed frighteningly. She could not retreat to the comforts of St. Louis now. Someone had to oversee their livelihood.

Becky was worse than useless now, confined to her bed for weeks and burdened by the demands of the child. Millie had two sons who were in perennial scrapes, and she bore all the signs of growing big with a third. As Millie complained of nausea and ran for the privy, Alicia slammed her dough against the board and practiced her ever growing vocabulary of curses. Surrounded by men as they were, it seemed inevitable that every woman in sight would be continually pregnant. There ought to be laws.

Her own back ached perpetually from the heavy weight she carried. She carried her burden low, confirming everyone's opinion that it would be a boy. Whenever Dr. Farrar repeated this homily, Alicia threw it back at him in rage.

"That's just what the world needs! Another male to go to war, to subject the innocent to his violence, to create more babies and leave them to raise themselves. If I've suffered through all this for a miniature Travis, I'll put him in a boat and float him downriver to find his father."

She began to rise from the bed where he had examined her, but the young doctor caught her shoulder and pushed her back again.

"If you do not get more rest, you will lose the child and not need to worry about its sex. Follow your father's advice, Alicia. Come back to town and let his house full of servants wait on you until the babe is born. Winter is coming. There is nothing more you can do out here. You deserve some pampering for a while. If Travis were here, he would insist on it, I am certain."

He spoke as if Travis were dead, and Alicia shook her head furiously. "Then let Travis come and tell me himself. He's not dead, Benjamin. I'd know it if he were dead. He's alive and I will be here when he returns. I will go nowhere until he does."

She knew the physician believed her half mad, but she would lose her mind entirely if she thought Travis gone forever. Everyone thought he had to be dead to not return to the riches he had won, but Alicia knew him better. He had left just as he said he would, escaping to a new life, leaving her to lead her own, just as he had promised. He just didn't know that she had changed her mind. Maybe she couldn't live with him, but she knew she could not live without him. He had to come home just so she could tell him so.

36

AZURE EYES BURNED warmly as soft arms welcomed him, caressing his shoulders, holding him tight as he bent to taste pliant lips. Travis's need stole away reason, and he grasped her harder, finding her bodice and stripping it away, pushing her beneath him so he could feel all of her supple softness against him. His loins ached for the sweet release she offered, and he groped desperately for the hem of her billowing skirt.

A noise jerked him to instant wakefulness, and Travis grabbed for his gun before he realized the sound was only his horse whickering. Cursing the horse, cursing the dream that left him overheated and unsatiated, he stared up into the starlit heavens, trying to will his unruly body to peace.

The comet shooting overhead captured his fancy. If he followed its trail, would he see Alicia gazing up at him in wonder? What was she doing now? Consoling herself with another lover?

Somehow Travis doubted that. He had taught her the pleasures of her body, but he had also taught her the pain. He did not think she would rush to put herself in another man's power too soon, not his sensible Alicia. He took comfort in that thought, selfishly ignoring the loneliness it condemned her to.

What would she be doing now? Setting Natchez or New Orleans on their ears? Would she return to Philadelphia? Or had she just returned to her father's house and the safety of teaching wealthy little girls?

The desire to know ate at Travis almost as much as his desire to have her in his bed again. He had promised to get out of her life if he did not make her happy, leave her to a life of her own, but it was the hardest promise he had ever had to keep in his life. She was his, a part of him, and he could not bear the thought of another man touching her.

If he could just know she was safe and happy . . . Travis's thoughts drifted back to those times when they had been together before their marriage, the laughter in sapphire eyes, the eager willingness of Alicia's body when he took her in his arms. That was the way she was meant to be, not cold and hard as he had left her. He had been so certain he had won that night of Auguste's wedding. What had happened to change her mind?

That seemed two eternities ago, but it had only been June. They had three good months together before that bastard had arrived from Philadelphia, three months in which the world had been his and he had been fool enough to believe in happiness. He could still remember the shock on Alicia's face when she walked in that tavern that day—the shock, and something else. He had always been able to read her eyes, but he had never been able to interpret that brief expression flickering over her face when he rose to meet her gaze that day. It was as if something that had been brilliant and new had suddenly died.

Uneasiness nagged at his thoughts as Travis played and replayed that scene in his mind. By all rights, she should never have been near that tavern. Alicia never did anything so publicly improper in her life. Why had he been cursed with the ill luck of losing his temper at the same time Alicia chose to step out of character? It had to be something mighty important to bring her there all decked out in her bright spring colors and looking as if she had just been given the world on a string . . .

The sudden realization of her purpose there hit Travis with a physical pain equivalent to a blow to the stomach. Could he have been such a fool as not to have seen it? Rapidly he tried to make mental calculations, but his mind would not function. It was possible. He knew it was possible. He just could not believe he had been so blind.

Why else would Alicia have shed all sign of mourning and traveled uptown to that tavern that day? What else would have brought such an expression of joy to her face, such excitement that she could not wait for him to come to her but she must seek him out? He knew of only one thing that Alicia wanted so badly that she had actually consented to breaking all the rules to get. A child.

Travis was on his feet in an instant, scuffing out the fire,
buckling up the saddle. No matter that he might have dreamed
this up out of simple desire to return. He had to know. He
had to see Alicia one more time. It was excuse enough to
retrace his steps over the thousand miles between here and
there.

Alicia slid on the patch of ice at the water pump, caught
herself on the bare branch of a nearby dogwood, and slumped
wearily against its smooth bark. It was time she gave up her
wishful thinking and return to the real world. Travis wasn't
coming and she couldn't continue any longer as she was.
The babe was due in less than a month. All her energy had
drained away, and she could not even face the thought of
teaching her few remaining students any longer.

Millie's boys had developed a fever a week ago, and she
had taken them into town, where Dr. Farrar could watch
over them. With the baby to take care of, Becky had long
since lost interest in her studies. Without either of the
women there, the men felt too uncomfortable to hang around
long. She would have to give up the school until spring.

Which gave her no further excuse to linger. Lifting the
heavy pail of water, Alicia once again attempted the icy
path back to the house. Her back ached from bending over
the stove all morning, trying to put together a decent meal
for the men to warm their stomachs after the morning's
work. Not that there was much to be done this time of year,
but they needed something. Becky had promised to be back
to help, but Alicia hadn't seen a sign of her since breakfast.

It was just as she approached the porch that the shriek
rang out. So sudden and unexpected did the sound echo
across the silent valley that Alicia dropped the pail to swing
around in horror.

Men came running from the barn, but there was naught to
be seen. The heavy frost of earlier had melted with the
noonday sun, and the landscape shimmered serene in the icy
air. Treacherous patches of ice lingered in the shadows,
remnants of yesterday's storm, but the sun lit all else in
stark relief. The shriek did not repeat itself, but a low wail
soon gave direction to the cause.

Alicia hurried after the running figures of the men in the
direction of the cry. Becky. It had to be Becky. Nobody else
could harness the squawk of chalk on slate and couple it

with the wail of a banshee to produce cries that could be
heard from here to St. Louis. Whatever the occasion, it
meant trouble, and Alicia's heart pounded fearfully as she
rounded the corner of the cabin to the chicken yard.

Becky lay sprawled in a crumpled heap of woolen skirts
and pails of feed in the frozen mud of the cart track. Her
wails reduced to whimpers as the first of the men reached
her, but she screamed in agony as he attempted to help her
up. Even from this distance Alicia could see the awkward
angle of Becky's arm, and she shouted for the men to wait.

Some people were accident prone, but Becky lent new
meaning to the words, Alicia muttered to herself as she
waddled hurriedly to where the circle of men waited for her
orders. Auguste had taken Millie and the boys in the keelboat to St. Louis, so she could not rely on his strength and
sensibility this time. Becky would be inconsolable without
him.

Crooning soft words to the sobbing girl, Alicia knelt carefully on the ground and examined the bent arm. There was
no doubt that it was broken, probably in the same place as
last time. Trying to keep calm, she ordered one of the men
to part with his large handkerchief and struggled to support
Becky's arm with it.

"At least dancing on tables must have been more fun than
feeding chickens," Alicia commented dryly as she tied the
kerchief behind Becky's neck.

"Don't be funny. It hurts like hell," Becky muttered
ungratefully.

Alicia sent one of the men back to the bunkhouse for
whiskey and another to check on the sleeping babe. With
the boat gone, she had no way of getting Becky to a doctor
beyond the wagon. It would be a nightmare journey, but
she could see no other course. The arm had to be set.

As she ordered the wagon brought out and piled with
blankets, the foreman acting in Auguste's place began to
watch her nervously.

"Look, ma'am, maybe you ought to wait 'til Auguste gets
back. The whiskey will ease the pain and then we can take
her nice and easy up the river with the babe and all."

Alicia looked up at him as if he were crazed. "Auguste
intended to bring back supplies and wait to see how the
boys fared before returning. It could be days before he
comes. The arm has to be set now. Can you do it?"

Becky gave a shriek of rage at the thought, but her audience ignored the protest.

"No, ma'am, I surely can't, but that old wagon ain't got any springs and it's going to be a rough trip. You'll have to stay here without any womenfolk around you. It ain't right."

"Nonsense. I'd planned on returning to St. Louis anyway. I can't let Becky go alone. Who would look after her baby?"

The shock kept most of the pain at bay as Becky listened worriedly to this argument. At Alicia's pronouncement she protested vehemently. "You ain't going in that wagon! That babe will be born bouncin' in a rut and then where will you be? We'll send Auguste back for you. I'll be OK."

The whiskey bottle was produced and Becky sipped gratefully at the heated liquor while the horses were hitched and blankets piled in. Torn by indecision, Alicia watched a hint of color return to Becky's cheeks, but noted the whiteness of strain around her lips. There was nothing else she could do to relieve the pain, but it felt like desertion to let Becky travel alone.

The decision was effectively taken from her hands when the men swaddled Becky and her daughter in blankets, surrounded them with bags of grain to prevent jostling, and announced there was no more room for Alicia. She could have protested, but she didn't. The pain in her back reminded her that she had other responsibilities and that Becky was a woman grown. The babe she carried would have to come first.

Dinner was a dismal affair, the meat burnt during the interruption and the bread unmade. The men ate as if starved, however, and the tin plates when returned to the house were already cleaned.

Alicia silently blessed their thoughtfulness and dragged herself up the stairs for a well-earned rest. The men could fend for themselves for the rest of the day. With half the crew gone with Auguste, there were few enough to do the chores. They would keep occupied. As an afterthought she returned downstairs and lit the lamp at the foot. It grew dark early these days.

Returning to bed, she could find no comfortable position but tossed restlessly until the sun went down and the room fell into darkness. Gradually, exhaustion took its toll, and she slept.

When she woke, it was to moisture running down her

thighs and a pain so excruciating it was all Alicia could do to keep from crying out. She bit her tongue and clenched her fingers in the covers and let the searing pain roll over her until sweat popped from her forehead and she thought she would die. When it finally let loose its grip on her belly, she was too exhausted to do more than lay there panting until the next one hit her a few minutes later.

Her mind screamed in anger as she realized what was happening again. She was losing the babe! She couldn't let it happen. She had to hang on, to pray, to plead with God not to let her lose this one too. It was all she had. Travis would never come back if she lost his child. Please, God, no!

Alicia writhed with the agony of her thoughts as much as the pain ripping through her insides. She couldn't control it, couldn't stop the unbearable pressure pushing at her middle, forcing the child from her. Desperately she stuck a corner of the quilted comforter between her teeth to keep from biting her tongue with the pain. Travis! Where was Travis when she needed him? He had to come, had to save his child.

Tears poured down her cheeks as her body convulsed once more with the searing brand of agony.

Travis walked his exhausted horse over the last ridge overlooking the farm. It was nearing midnight. He should have made camp hours ago, but he was too close to wait any longer. He didn't expect her to be there, could barely hope that she might be in St. Louis, but he had to see for himself.

As Travis entered the deserted farmyard, a loneliness so piercing that he nearly wailed his anguish swept over him at the sight before him. No one stood guard over the corral. No cigarette glowed in the darkness outside the bunkhouse. No light shone in the small cottage that was Auguste's. They were gone. The home he had harbored longingly in a corner of his mind all these months no longer existed.

He could scarcely bring himself to walk the last few steps around to the front gates, where he might see the house. It would echo empty and lonely if he set foot in it. It would be even worse than those few weeks before their marriage when he worked alone on fixing it for his bride. At least then there had been hope. Now hope was gone, replaced by ashes so bitter he could taste them on his tongue.

As Travis passed beneath the soaring eagles, a light flickered somewhere in the depths of the house, and his heart leapt to his throat. A lamp! Someone had to be there, then. Not daring to hope, not even daring to think, Travis tied his horse to the post and silently strode up the porch stairs.

The door gave at his touch, not even fastened. Travis frowned at that, but the lamp burning welcomingly on the newel post beckoned him onward. He had not meant to come this far. He had only meant to watch and wait and see if he could find the answers before turning around and leaving again, but the lamp drew him forward.

He picked it up and the light gleamed on a polished mahogany bookcase in the hallway. Marveling at this wealth of books that had not been there when he had left, Travis swung the lantern in the direction of the front parlor. Elegant damask covered sofas and chairs leapt into view, drawn together cozily by a soft Aubusson carpet over the paneled flooring. Had he wandered into a stranger's house, then?

Fearing that might be the case since otherwise he would have to admit to hope, Travis stepped toward the parlor rather than the staircase. If he could just find some sign of Alicia, some evidence that she remained . . .

A muffled moan decimated all thought of caution. The whimper came from overhead, and in two strides Travis was on the staircase, the lantern flinging crazy shadows up the hall as he raced toward the sound.

He found her in the back bedroom, the blood-soaked linens sending him reeling back to another place, another time. He roared his rage at finding her thus alone, unaware he made any sound at all as he set the lamp aside and bent to take Alicia's limp form in his arms.

She acknowledged his presence by merely grabbing his arms, digging her fingers into their strength while rising pain washed over her. Her hair was soaked from her efforts, and Travis brushed the damp strands back from her face while the contraction passed over. When it stopped, he silently began to remove her soaked and ruined gown.

This wasn't the first time he had done this, but that first time it had not been his own child coming into this bloody world. Travis's hands shook as he stripped away the hampering lengths of material and threw them in a corner near the dead fire. The room was icy, but sweat poured down his back as he worked to make Alicia comfortable.

The pain came again, and Travis leapt to hold her in his

arms while she struggled through it. There wasn't even time
to curse the women who had left her alone or rail at his own
ignorance. Alicia's whimpering cries flailed at his insides,
torturing him with anguish.

"Scream, Alicia! For God's sake, scream!" Travis commanded, unable to control his emotion as well as she. He
wanted to shake her until the screams shattered the walls
and brought help running, until some miracle came to save
them both. He could feel them slipping away beyond his
grasp forever, and a fever of panic brought beads of sweat
to his brow. He had been a damned fool for too long, but
this was too high a price to pay for stupidity. He clutched
Alicia closer against his chest, as if to prevent her escape.

"Oh, God, help me, Travis! Help me!" The words were
torn from Alicia's lips as the pain went on and on and she
knew it would never stop until the burden was torn from her
belly.

The plea shook Travis to his senses. If force of will could
save them, Alicia had enough for both of them. His would
have to be a more practical role. "Hold on to the bed,
Alicia. Hold that post." Carefully Travis wrapped Alicia's
hand around the carved cherry as he lay her back against
the pillows. He knew nothing of babies other than that this
one was coming and might need help. He knew he would
need both hands for that.

Alicia clung to the post, the screams welling up in her
throat as the pain pushed down into her very soul. She knew
Travis was there but held her eyes shut against the pain,
unable to concentrate on anything other than pushing out
the heavy weight tearing her apart.

Then the pain moved and the scream ripped from her
throat, filling the walls of the room and ringing out into the
night until it grew deathly silent again. Hands shaking,
Travis gripped the slippery shoulders emerging from the
womb, delivering his firstborn into the world with a sense of
awe. The babe screamed its outrage as he wiped it roughly
and wrapped it in linen, but even as he lay the squalling
bundle beside his wife, the silence from the bed was deafening.

Into this void the wails of a newborn babe coupled with
the sobs of the broad-shouldered man kneeling helplessly
beside the lifeless form on the bed.

37

A FAINT SOUND from the bed brought Travis to his feet, and his heart lodged in his throat as he watched Alicia move her head restlessly on the pillow. She was alive! Hope once again came flooding back, and as he sat beside her, massaging her fingers, Travis sent anxious prayers to a God he had nearly abandoned.

Let her live and he would do anything she wanted, be anything she wanted. If nothing else, this last half hour had taught him his own selfishness and the stupidity of pride. He had made a dream out of wood, but he should have known Alicia wasn't a carving to be manipulated at will. She was a woman, the woman he had always wanted and more, but he had refused to realize that until too late. If only he could have this one more chance, he would not make that mistake again.

It might be a long time before she ever trusted him again. The punishment of seeing her day in and day out and not touching would be physical torture, but he could endure it. He could endure anything if he were only allowed to see her smile and laugh again, hear the intelligence of her words, dwell in the comfort of her companionship for the rest of his life. That would be enough.

Red-rimmed eyes watched in desperation as Alicia's breathing grew slowly stronger. Sometimes miracles happened.

The foreman took one look at Travis's unshaven face and swollen eyes, and made no attempt to push aside the arm barring his way. He nodded at his employer's curt orders and sent the others back down the stairs, barking commands for fires and hot water. It didn't sound as if murder had been committed, and relief that he hadn't been left to tend to it alone kept him from questioning.

Once again wearing the mask with which he faced the world, Travis turned back into the room. Using the cold water in the washbasin, he scrubbed the wailing infant as best as he could, wrapping it in one of Alicia's shawls when he was satisfied.

The cries stirred Alicia, and weakly she turned to find their source. Not knowing what else to do, Travis lay the child beside her, where she could see him.

"What will you name him?" he asked gruffly, unable to conceal the catch in his voice as the lamplight flickered over the pale shadows of Alicia's face.

"A boy?" Alicia carefully lifted a hand to touch the squalling bundle, afraid she dreamed and any moment she would wake. Could she wish something into happening? Did the child really live? Was Travis truly here? She was afraid to pinch herself to find out.

"A son." Now that he had time to think, Travis felt the first stirring of anger at all he had been denied, but his fear for Alicia kept it hidden. Those damned fools downstairs had better be riding like the wind to St. Louis by now.

"Then he should be named after you," Alicia murmured wearily, her eyes closing. She had given little thought to names. She had done her part. This was something Travis could do.

"Maximillian? Not over my dead body." Travis stared in disbelief at the tiny creature he had created. The infant had already found his fist and quieted. No son of his would carry the trail of names that had been his inheritance from his father.

Alicia smiled faintly at the annoyance in his tone. Travis was back. She need not worry any longer.

The messenger arrived at the Stanford house before dawn, arousing the household with his shouts and knocks at the front rather than sensibly locating the kitchen door. The maid who finally came to answer his call stared at the disheveled ranch hand with dismay, but his words gave him instant admittance.

"Miss Alicia's having the baby! She needs help, fast!"

A cry of dismay came from the stairway, and the man glanced up to the petite lady wrapped in a dressing gown standing on the landing. Behind her Chester Stanford stumbled sleepily down the stairs. A step behind that came a gentleman the ranch hand did not recognize, except to dislike his mincing air and haughty appearance. The messenger spoke directly to Alicia's father.

"The baby's coming early and there ain't no one out there but Mr. Travis to see to her. He says send the doc quick. Auguste has the boat down at the river. I'll go wake him if someone else will find Doc Farrar."

Letitia murmured, "*Mon Dieu!*" and dashed back up the stairs. Chester instantly pelted a dozen commands at the poor maid's head, sending her spinning for the kitchen. The eyes of the stranger behind him widened, and he too hastily returned upstairs. Ignoring the chaos he had created the messenger took to his heels in search of Auguste. He took orders only from Travis.

When the small party arrived at the river landing an hour or so after dawn, Travis had fallen into an exhausted sleep on the floor beside Alicia's bed. He had done all he could to make her comfortable, but she was unconscious of his efforts. Still, he would not leave her alone.

The knock on the bedroom door woke him, and he cautiously checked his patients before answering it. They seemed to be sleeping quietly, and Travis slipped out into the hallway to greet Dr. Farrar.

The young doctor took in Travis's travel-stained and rumpled attire, his collar-length, dust-coated hair and unshaven beard, and shook his head. "I see you arrived in time. How is she?"

Travis shoved a dark strand of hair back from his face and rubbed a weary hand over his eyes. "They're both alive. That's all I can say. And when I find out why she was here alone, I'm going to cut some throats."

"You may as well start with your own," the doctor informed him curtly. "If you don't, the ones below probably will. I recommend you wash before you greet them. Let me by. I want to see Alicia." Not offering further explanation, he pushed past Travis and closed the door firmly behind him.

Not caring who or what waited below, Travis staggered down the stairs in search of warm water and a cup of coffee. It already felt like a long day. He didn't dare allow the joy of his son to overwhelm him. Too much could happen to rob

him of that joy. He had learned long ago to take things one
step at a time.

At the bottom of the stairs he was greeted by Chester
Stanford and a stranger flanked by two uniformed British
soldiers. With a groan Travis ran his hand through his hair
and cursed his birth, the fates, and English perseverance.
Under the circumstances there was little else he could do.
His past had finally caught up with him, and there was no
escaping this time.

The stranger, garbed in high white cravat and an immaculate buff coat trimmed in gold braid, stared at the grimy
apparition on the stairs with varying emotions ranging from
hope to disbelief. "Lord Delaney?" he finally ventured.

Travis turned a bleary eye beneath a skeptically lifted
brow. "Who asks?"

Relief swept over the man's face at this arrogant tone. A
small man, he stepped forward bravely, offering his hand in
salutation. "Jeffrey Scott, my lord, Lord Royster's agent
here in the states."

Travis gazed coldly at the two red-coated soldiers. "Did
you come to arrest me and haul me back to London just for
my father's amusement?"

Chester Stanford looked slightly startled at that, and he
moved almost as if he meant to interfere with any such
action, but the agent shook his head cheerfully.

'No, no, nothing like that. These men merely helped me
to arrive here safely. The route is rather dangerous and
Lord Royster insisted I have accompaniment. We need to
talk when you have a minute. I have come a long way to see
you, but I understand you have just become a father. I can
wait awhile longer."

Travis grunted agreement, nodded in the direction of the
parlor indicating that they wait there, and headed for the
kitchen. To hell with his father and the British army, he
needed coffee and a shave.

The dapper gentleman stared after Travis's retreating back
with amazement, finally turning to look at his host for these
past days. "My word! He is just like his father! I would have
known him anywhere."

Chester Stanford choked on this outlandish comparison to
the dapper earl but without comment he ushered his guests
into the parlor. With a worried look over his shoulder, he
sent a prayer winging up the stairs to Alicia.

By the time he returned, Travis had scrubbed and shaved and changed into a clean linen shirt from his saddlebag. Carrying a cup of the bitter brew his men had cooking over the stove, he strode into the front parlor with an air of angry defiance.

His first question, however, was to Alicia's father. "Has the doctor come down?"

Chester Stanford shook his head. "Not yet. Sit down. You look like hell."

Jeffrey Scott throttled a gasp at this disrespect, but the viscount seemed to accept it without rancor. The agent continued watching the young lord warily.

Travis sank gratefully into a high-backed chair beside the fire, and gazed with interest at the changes Alicia had wrought in this room. Although he could not begin to name the style in which it was furnished, he felt instantly at home among the lovely woods and warm blues and golds. He propped his boots up on a needlepoint stool at his feet and set his cup on the Sheraton table beside him. Alicia had thought of everything.

"All right, Mr. Scott, I assume you did not come all this way to verify my identity. What does my father want?"

"He is a very ill man, my lord. He has been searching for you these past three years. When I wrote him that we had word of you, he booked passage at once. Since I left New York to come in search of you, he has arrived in New Orleans and even now awaits news. That is how anxious he is to see you, my lord."

Travis gritted his teeth at the man's unctuous tones and tried to curb his temper. "If you want anything from me at all, you had best stop calling me 'my lord.' I am not your lord or anyone else's. I am a citizen of the United States, a resident of St. Louis, and a farmer. You will find no nobility here."

The agent boldly objected. "You are heir to an earldom and entitled a viscount by birth. That cannot change. I will honor your request and address you as you choose, but you cannot deny your inheritance."

Travis rose and paced restlessly to the window. "Oh, but I can, and I do. This is my home. My father has a son who will be more than happy with the title I deny."

"But there you are, my—" Scott stopped and rearranged his wording. "Sir. Your brother died three years ago. A pestilent fever. It almost took the life of one of your sisters, but she recovered, the Lord be praised. There have been no other children. You are all he has, my—sir."

Travis swung around in irritation, his eyes blinded by the light outside, dimming the interior to shadows. "He has two fine, lovely daughters, a young wife, and the rest of his life to breed sons. He does not need me."

Nervous, aware he had started out on the wrong foot, the agent attempted to change tactics. "He is your father. He is ill, maybe dying. He simply wants to see you. Can you not give him that much?"

Travis walked to the doorway and stood listening for sounds from above. He wanted to see Alicia, talk to her, find out where he stood. That was what he wanted. His father had ceased to be a part of his life a long time ago.

"I cannot give you anything. My wife is seriously ill. I have a newborn son and no idea how he fares. I cannot and will not leave them alone. You have come at the wrong time, Mr. Scott. You should have been here six months earlier."

Not giving Scott time to question that enigmatic remark, Chester rose from his seat and confronted his son-in-law. "Don't turn your back on the man, Travis. I don't know what has gone between you and Alicia, but I believe you owe her the opportunity to speak her opinion. It might be she would like to meet her father-in-law when she has recovered. Don't close your mind to the possibilities."

That idea struck Travis like a slap on the face. Of course, she would want to meet his father. What woman could resist meeting British nobility? The world his father offered was more her world than his. Perhaps if he could offer it to her, it would right his earlier wrongs, and they could find some semblance of happiness together again. He was no fool. He knew what his father wanted. Once the noble Lord Royster had a second son to carry on the line, he had not shed a tear when his ill-mannered, half-breed first-born had walked out of his life. Only now, that first son was the only male heir he had.

Having just learned the pain and joy of bringing a child into this world, Travis could understand some of his father's grief at losing the son of his old age. Leaning his broad shoulders against the door frame, Travis accepted his father-in-law's wisdom.

"When Alicia is well, I will talk to her. I make no more promise than that."

Chester Stanford sent a warning glance as Scott appeared ready to protest. Throwing a look at the stern, hawklike profile of the man in the doorway, he knew argument would be futile right now. Black eyes had fastened on a door opening above them.

Travis was halfway up the stairs before the doctor could traverse the hallway.

"How is she? May I see her?"

Dr. Farrar gave the taller man a shrewd look and nodded his head. "She is asking for you. You did a good job last night. Both mother and child are exhausted, but otherwise fine."

He had scarcely time to get the words out before Travis was on his way down the corridor to the back bedroom.

Alicia glanced up from where she was uncertainly trying to guide her starving son to her bared breast. She blushed at Travis's hasty entrance and reached for the shawl on the bedside stand, but he was quicker than she. He placed the soft wool around her shoulders and brought it down around the bundle she held in her arms. His gaze could not leave the sight of his son's tiny fist kneading at Alicia's breast as his eager mouth finally located the tender nipple.

Alicia gave a cry of surprise at the eagerness of his tug, and Travis chuckled. She sent him a baleful glance, but allowed him to arrange the pillows more comfortably behind her back.

"We could call him Hercules," he suggested laconically, settling on the edge of the bed beside her.

"You wouldn't dare!" Feathers already ruffled by his possessive air, Alicia reacted defensively. She had forgotten his arrogant assurance, but despite her momentary irritation she was grateful for Travis's reassuring presence. Never would she admit it out loud, but she needed him right there beside her, where she could watch the laughter play across his dark eyes or his cheek muscles tighten with anger. It didn't matter which, just so she could touch him when she needed.

Travis shrugged, amused. "It is better than Maximillian or 'Hey, you.' We have to call him something."

"One of your names is Delaney. Wouldn't that do? It has a nice sound to it."

"Delaney Travis, Lord Delaney? They'd laugh him out of school. Besides, it would get shortened to Dell."

"Dale," Alicia corrected. At his quizzical look she explained, "Around here they can't even pronounce Dell. It would sound like Dale."

Travis grinned, and an enormous flood of relief swept away all the doubts and fears he had harbored these last hours. His lady hadn't changed. She would never dispute his right to be here, never scream and curse and throw things at him, but she would argue until she dropped to get the last word.

"Dale, then," he agreed.

"Delaney," she amended firmly.

His laughter caught her by surprise and startled the infant lordling into a wail, but one look at Travis's face and Alicia relaxed, soothing the babe with a crooning voice. He might not love her, but he came when she needed him. That ought to count for something.

With a house full of guests and no servants, Letitia took charge.

The two British soldiers were persuaded to part with their uniforms lest the farmhands take umbrage, and then they were billeted in Auguste and Becky's cottage. She and Chester took over the room Travis had once used—now neatly furnished with a stately Queen Anne bed and highboy—and Jeffrey Scott was given the guest room. Travis had a choice of the nursery or Alicia's chamber, and quickly rigged a pallet in a corner of the larger room. Alicia made no protest.

Visitors flowed through the front doors like a river. All the farmhands had to stomp across the polished floors to shake the proud father's hand and admire the squalling progeny. Dr. Farrar notified St. Louis society, and the unusually warm November weather allowed most to travel southward to offer congratulations and eye the father with curiosity. Mrs. Lalende and Bessie Clayton traveled together bearing gifts from the girls and teachers at the school and Bessie's famous pies. All stopped to admire the gracious home that had appeared in the midst of wilderness and to press invitations on the young couple and their guests. The arrival of Travis at the same time as the British soldiers had impressed society at large with the truth of his title.

The appearance of Bear Mountain and Homasinee with their son almost overwhelmed even Letitia's gracious hospitality, however. As the maid who answered the door shrieked and ran for the kitchen, Letitia appeared in the hall and stared in confusion at the buckskin and feather-clad visitors standing in the doorway. They stared back at her with equal confusion, giving Letitia time to spy the retinue of half-naked savages reclining in the yard behind them. Mercifully Travis came down the stairs at that moment, for she was at a total loss.

As it was, Travis came bounding down the stairs to hug his friends and draw them in, and Letitia had time to recover her poise. Before the visit ended, she was holding the dark-skinned, black-haired baby and meeting its blank stare with a grin of delight. She declared later she could almost see a family resemblance, throwing Alicia into a fit of jealousy and crippling Travis with laughter.

The debonair Mr. Scott absorbed all of this with interest, taking mental notes for further communication with his employer. Travis had yet to commit himself to anything, successfully evading the topic with references to Alicia's health. It became obvious to the agent that the momentum of his journey would need a helping hand if he were ever to deliver his prize to New Orleans.

The agent caught Travis coming out of the kitchen one day and gestured for him to halt a moment. Travis eyed him impatiently, eager to see how Alicia was faring, but politely waiting for the man to speak.

"Have you had time to discuss your trip to New Orleans with your wife yet? I must write your father and tell him something."

"She cannot even be allowed downstairs yet. I see no reason to trouble her with any decision. Traveling in midwinter is not a wise idea in any case."

"The weather has been mild and will be milder yet south of here. It would be healthier for your wife and child," Scott reminded him.

"The decision as to whether or not to go is Alicia's, but I will decide when and how." Curtly Travis put an end to the conversation, and returned upstairs to Alicia.

Scott stared after the viscount and pondered the consequences of these words.

Travis found Alicia sitting in a rocking chair beside the fire, the maroon velvet robe wrapped warmly around her as she admired the sleeping infant in the cradle by her side.

She glanced up as Travis entered and met his troubled frown with instant concern.

"What is it, Travis? Have they let one of the horses loose again? I've told them—"

Travis grinned and pressed a husbandly peck against her cheek, then scooped the infant from his bed to cradle him in his arms. "Auguste has told me how you have nearly nagged him to his grave. You'll have to confine your complaints to me from now on, I guess."

Alicia sent him a quick look, but Travis's gaze had turned tenderly to his son's sleeping features. "You mean to stay this time?" she asked cautiously.

"I mean to stay," Travis agreed firmly, touching a gentle finger to his son's soft cheek. "All bets are off, all promises ended."

Alicia glanced away from the tender scene, brushing a tear from her eye. He meant to stay, perhaps, but because of the child and nothing else. Somehow she would have to learn to accept that, for Delaney's sake. He needed a father, as she knew only too well. What it would mean to herself she feared to contemplate. It would have to be enough to know he stayed. She had married Travis for better or worse. Somehow she would have to come to terms with that fact.

She turned back to watch him, feeling her heart twitch achingly at the love in Travis's eyes as he admired his child.

"Then I gladly return the reins to you," she answered softly. "I know nothing of managing men or a farm. If it isn't the horses, what has made you frown?"

Travis glanced down into the pale oval of Alicia's face, and silently thanked the heavens for preserving her life. A lucky star had looked over them. Now he must do what he could to protect her from all other harm. He returned the child to his cradle and settled into a chair across from her.

"You have met Mr. Scott?" He knew she had. His father's agent had been eager to see the child and meet the mother. Travis suspected everything went into letters to his father.

"Yes. Fancy your father sending someone all the way out here to meet me. Does he approve?" Alicia's lips turned up with a wry twist.

"That wasn't his only reason, my dear. My father is even now in New Orleans, waiting impatiently for us to join him." At Alicia's quizzical glance Travis explained the reason for his father's arrival.

When he was done, Alicia watched him quietly. "You will have to see him."

Travis set his jaw and met blue eyes defiantly. "I go nowhere without you."

Startled and vaguely pleased by the intensity of his stare, Alicia made no comment. It would be December before she was well enough to travel. Whether it would be safe for Dale to travel with them was another consideration. If Travis had made up his mind, she would not argue. All she wanted was to stay by his side, if he would let her.

Jeffrey Scott shrewdly timed a visit to Alicia when Travis was not there. He admired the dark-haired, long-limbed babe as proudly as if he were a godparent, then worked the conversation around to New Orleans.

"Lord Delaney tells me he will not travel without you, and I must agree. His father is quite anxious to meet you, but I fear his lordship doubts your desire to go with him. Have you some objection to meeting your father-in-law?"

Alicia looked at him with astonishment. "Of course not. I will do whatever Travis wishes. He has made no mention of his plans to me, and I have expressed no opinion on the matter. The choice of whether to go to see his father or not belongs entirely to Travis."

Jeffrey Scott nodded approvingly. "I knew you were a sensible woman. His lordship fears you do not wish to leave your home and family, but the opportunities for him are enormous if a reconciliation could be made between him and his father. I know you would not want to stand in his way."

Alicia ignored the sinking feeling these words produced. If Travis wished to return to his home and family, she would not stand in his way.

That night, as Travis arranged his blankets in the corner of their room, Alicia took a deep breath and inquired bravely, "When do you intend to visit your father?"

Travis slowly finished folding his blanket and moved to poke the fire before answering. He should rejoice that she again showed some interest in him, but it saddened him that it had to be on this topic. He should have known that a woman raised as Alicia had been could not resist the temptation his father's society offered. He would just have to be grateful he had been given this second chance, if only for their son's sake.

"As soon as you are well enough to travel, I suppose," he admitted grudgingly. There seemed no purpose in putting off the inevitable.

Alicia checked the leap of her heart as Travis turned his dark eyes to her. Then he had meant what he said. He would not leave her alone again. It was for Delaney's sake, she knew, but it fed her hopes.

Offering a tremulous smile, she surrendered all other dreams in pursuit of this one. "I will ask Dr. Farrar in the morning."

38

BY THE FIRST week of December Travis had the keelboat
scrubbed and sealed and prepared for the long journey to
New Orleans. Doctor Farrar had announced his patients
were improving rapidly, and if they could be kept warm and
dry and rested, he would not object to their traveling.

Travis watched cautiously over every detail of the planning for this trip, and when the time came, he insisted on
carrying Alicia to the boat himself. Snuggled warmly inside
her fur-lined pelisse, she objected mildly to this patroniza-
tion, but the sensation of Travis's strong arms around her
once again silenced further argument. Clinging to his broad
shoulders, she allowed herself to be carried aboard but
insisted on remaining on deck to wave farewell.

The crowded boat offered limited accommodations for a
winter trip, and both Chester and Letitia and Auguste and
Becky chose to stay behind. They watched worriedly as the
little party gathered on deck and the boat prepared to
launch, but Travis's efficient commands reassured their
doubts. He had done this many times before. There was no
reason to question their safety now. As the boat drifted into
the current, tears fell and farewells were exchanged. Then
the river carried them around a bend and out of sight.

As Alicia turned away from the last sight of the home she
had called hers for so brief a time, Travis came up beside
her and wrapped a comforting arm around her waist. The
wind off the river blew her hood from her hair, and the pale
winter sun gleamed on rich chestnut tresses and frail features colored pink by the brisk breeze. There had been little
chance of intimacy between them these past weeks with a
house overflowing with guests, and there would be even less
chance now on the narrow boat. Perhaps it was better this

way. They would have time to start all over again. Only this time, they would be sharing the same cabin.

"I don't want you getting cold, my love. Come inside, out of the wind." Travis steered her in the direction of the door.

Alicia glanced up to Travis's dark, angular face with curiosity. Since his return he had showered her with endearments and concern, but there had been nothing more physical between them than a peck on the cheek. She knew the doctor had warned him she was not ready to share his bed yet, but Travis gave no indication that he even wanted to do so. Admittedly, he came to her room every night, but it was only to sleep on a pallet on the floor. She still slept in the grandeur of their marriage bed, alone.

Perhaps in these last months he had found another woman and no longer wanted her. Knowing Travis, there had been more than one woman. She could not blame him for that. It was her own fault, but the idea of facing a lifetime of marriage with a man who no longer desired her was a somewhat daunting one. The idea of sharing such a life in another country among strangers was even more terrifying, but Alicia admitted none of her fears aloud. She could learn to cope with anything as long as Travis stayed by her side.

"How long will it take to get to New Orleans?" she asked as they entered the cabin. Dale slept peacefully in his cradle beside the bed.

"A month, maybe more, depending on the weather and the current. I fear it is a poor way for you to spend Christmas." Travis watched her steadily as she bent to check on the sleeping babe.

A month. She would be well then. There would be no other women on board to pleasure him. Would she be able to seduce him to her bed when they arrived in New Orleans? The thought sent shivers of excitement and fear down Alicia's spine, and she did not even consider the wisdom of such a move.

"I have never seen New Orleans. I should think meeting your father and seeing the city will be a lovely Christmas present."

She smiled up at him and the radiance of it nearly staggered Travis. He still could not believe she had allowed him to walk back into her life without a word of recrimination or complaint. That she actually seemed to welcome his company kept him walking on clouds. After all she had suffered at his hands, he was willing to give her anything in reparation. If that meant returning to England, so be it. He could learn to live with anything, but he could not live without Alicia.

Travis grinned ruefully. "I will have to do better than that. As Lady Delaney you will need to be decked in gold and jewels, and I have given you nothing. You will pardon the lateness of the gift if I wait until New Orleans to find the proper ornaments?"

Alicia glanced up at him, half smiling; then seeing he was serious, she shook her head. "I have a trunk full of jewels if they are needed. Give me time to adjust to the fact that you are not only half horse and half alligator, but half aristocrat too, and I will garb myself accordingly."

Travis's appreciative grin warmed Alicia's insides, and his parting remark left her shaken.

"Whatever else I may be, I'm a man, and you're my woman. Don't ever let all the other nonsense get in the way."

He walked out, leaving Alicia speechless. "His woman"! The man had his nerve! But even as she thought it, her cheeks glowed with the pleasure of his possessiveness. It was good to know the Indian still ruled the viscount.

The journey downriver was swift and oppressively warm for December. The comet's light had diminished in the night sky, but the crew kept suspicious eyes on its direction. Wild predictions that the fiery light would scorch the earth or crash into the mountains had flown up and down the river; coupled with nature's unusual behavior, anything could be expected, and the superstitious crew watched the skies warily.

As his men rolled up in blankets around the fire on deck at night, Travis contemplated sharing the warmth of Alicia's bed. He came in from the fire to find her curled between the feather ticking and the quilts, and he could imagine himself beside her, holding her within the curve of his body. The temptation was too great, however, and he settled into the unsatisfactory blanket roll beside the brazier. His body had been too long denied the release it needed to settle for sleeping in Alicia's arms. He would have to wait for the day when she was ready.

Lying with arms behind his head, staring at the ceiling,

Travis wondered if that day would ever come. She seemed quite content with this arrangement, accepting his presence but giving no evidence of desiring more than that. Could her passion be destroyed so easily? If so, he had condemned himself to a life of misery, for his desire was so great it was like a physical aching in his bones. He would never find surcease until she was in his arms again.

Travis revealed none of these thoughts in Alicia's presence, however. Not wishing to scare her any more than he had, he remained stoically impassive when Alicia bared her breast to feed their hungry son. If he walked in to find her undressing or washing, he found some excuse to go back out rather than torture himself with the silky whiteness of skin he could not touch, soft curves he could not caress. When they were in New Orleans, maybe. . . He did not dare think beyond that.

Alicia watched him with a confusion of hope and fear and bit her lip each time he walked away without touching her. She knew nothing of flirting or seduction. Travis had pursued her so relentlessly before, there had never been a need to learn. She didn't know where to begin now, but she wished desperately to be held, to be reassured she had not become ugly in his eyes. Perhaps after the birth of his son he did not need her anymore and his fine words of before were just lies to obtain what he wanted. If so, she would have to kill him, because she could not bear to watch him the rest of her life and never be allowed to touch again.

Word of the battle at Tippecanoe between Governor Harrison and the Indians in the Ohio Territory had been received several weeks earlier, and the crew kept a constant watch for signs of further trouble. Familiar with the various northern tribes, Travis detected signs of movement among the Shawnees, but it was winter and the farther south they went, the less noticeable became the traces. He had the uneasy feeling that trouble would reach them by spring, but he would in all likelihood be far away by then, playing the role of English lord. He might never know the outcome of the tensions building along the upper river.

He might also be on the wrong side of war if and when it came. The cries for action against Britain had become more vehement these last months, though the Americans had no navy and few troops. How would he be able to take his place in a society determined to wipe out the way of life he had known the better part of his years? The thought chilled him, but Travis was determined to do what was best for his small family. Alicia deserved the privileges of rank and society, and his son should be made aware of them. He was the only one who would not fit in.

The weather continued oddly humid as the swift current carried them past the mouth of the Ohio and the spit of land that marked the edge of Kentucky. Flocks of trumpeter swans erupted from the forest for no apparent reason, beating the air with the sound of thunder and providing amusement for the crew's rifles, until Alicia cried for them to leave the beautiful beasts alone. They desisted, but began to grumble uneasily as other flocks of ducks and geese took to the air, unprovoked by gunshot or human presence, squawking and flying aimlessly.

The hackles on the back of Travis's neck began to rise when they stopped to make camp that night, and a herd of deer stood boldly and waited for his approach rather than running. He had lived off this land for many years, and never had such a thing happened before. Instinct told him to get the hell out of there, but darkness had arrived, and he had a boat load of hungry people waiting to be fed. A deer would be too large to prepare. From the shelter of the trees he felled two ducks in quick succession, and wondered at the ease of his kill.

Glancing at the darkening sky, Travis calculated the distance to New Orleans. This was mid-December. They had passed the small town of New Madrid about noon that day. There would be no other sources of supply until they reached Natchez, hundreds of miles away. They were making good time and should be at New Orleans by the beginning of January if things continued as they were. Their supplies would last that long easily. He would prefer to avoid the notorious docks under the cliffs at Natchez if at all possible.

He had ordered the boat anchored on the Tennessee side of the river, beneath bluffs that provided some protection from the dangers that abounded on land. As the crew cooked the day's catch, Travis checked the hawser, circled the deck to make certain their cargo was secured, and continued to eye the threatening sky. No sign of the comet tonight. The thick air obliterated all sight of the stars. The weather was ripe for a vicious thunderstorm if he read the warnings rightly. They should be safe enough here beneath the overhang.

Satisfied that they were as secure as he could make them, Travis went to join Alicia in the cabin. His days of taking his leisure with the crew had come to an end. He had other pursuits on his mind now.

The company of his father's agent and the two British soldiers put a certain damper on his progress. Travis picked at his food and ate silently while the men entertained Alicia with the tales of their journey to St. Louis. Alicia's apparent interest heightened their oratory skills, Travis noted with ill humor. She still had little idea of the effect she had on men, and he'd be damned if he'd let her know the power she possessed in this wilderness.

When the infant began to cry, however, the guests quickly excused themselves and retreated to the shelter Travis had built for them on deck. Relieved of their intruding presence, Travis relaxed and stretched his moccassined feet across the cabin floor while Alicia retreated among the quilts to feed their son. For the first time in a long while, he felt at home, and the tensions he had carried with him most of his life began to slip away.

When Alicia looked up again, Travis had fallen asleep among the cushions from the banquette, and she smiled softly. In sleep his harsh features relaxed, and he was even more handsome than when awake. A dark lock of hair fell over his high, bronzed forehead, and his black brows slashed across his angular face, emphasizing the sharp cheekbones in their shadow. His mouth rested in a firm, narrow line above a square chin, reflecting the strong character behind it. All in all, though, she preferred it when his eyes were open and alive with interest and his mouth curved upward in that intimate smile he sometimes bestowed upon her. Perhaps he was not conventionally handsome, but she loved him just the same. Fool that she was.

She wasn't even certain that she completely trusted him, and she certainly had reason to doubt his stability as a husband, but there was no logic to her feelings. Ever since Travis had walked through that bedroom door the night of Dale's birth, she had known she would not part with him again. Moments like this almost made it a sensible decision.

After placing the infant in his cradle, she covered Travis with the blankets from his bedroll, and climbed back in among the covers. Soon she would have to find some way to entice him to share this lonely bed.

A wild jerk of the boat and a violent crash like thunder tossed them from their contented slumbers. The roar that followed shivered the wooden timbers as effectively as the crash of water against the keel. Alicia rolled over and grabbed the cradle while Travis leapt to his feet with a curse.

A scream splintered the air, but the violent rocking of the boat prevented swift response. From above them the horrifying crashing of trees on the bluff warned of immediate danger, and Travis ordered Alicia to remain inside. No patter of rain or flash of lightning explained the ominous thunder that shook the air and raised the boat as if it were a splinter on a river current. Travis stumbled across the heaving floor to the deck.

The air stunk of sulphur, and flashes of blue flame illuminated the far shore, but these were minor evidence of hell compared to the violent eruptions of land and water around them. The river seemed to be rising from its bed on a tidal wave that rightly belonged only on a sea, and the land trembled and shook and heaved upward as if some tremendous sleeping giant had awakened and chose to rise from the depths. The upheaval sent trees crashing to the ground and tumbling to the water, and the rock bluffs above began to crumble, cracking with ominous popping sounds, fissures appearing as if drawn by unseen hands. With a scream of command Travis ordered the hawser cut and the boat released from shore. He preferred death by drowning to being crushed beneath a mountain.

Even so, two men fell victim to falling debris and rising currents before the boat could be shoved from shore. There was no time to mourn their loss or even try to recover their bodies. As they poled the boat out into the rampaging water, the bluff tumbled and crashed into the river, flinging the keelboat like an old log into the air and out into the current.

Through a miracle the hull held, and Travis had to live the nightmare of wondering how his wife and son fared while caught up in the desperation of trying to pole around and through the turmoil of a world gone mad. Frantically the crew grabbed what poles could be found and leapt to obey his shouts. They had no time for thought, only action, as fallen trees shot past them like bullets and the river leapt and swirled and crashed against a disappearing shore.

It was the terrified New York dandy who managed to cling to the deck and crawl to the cabin to check on Alicia and the babe. He found them wrapped in quilts, trembling, but otherwise unharmed as Alicia braced herself in the far corner. The constant jarring motion had bruised every bone in her body, but she clung determinedly to the crying child. At the sight of Scott she nearly screamed her frantic inquiries of Travis, but she did not attempt to make herself heard over the chaos any further than that.

Unable to walk the deck with the same assurance as the experienced keelboatmen, Scott propped himself in the doorway of the cabin and shouted the news of Alicia's safety to the young lord in the prow. Silhouetted against a night sky of blue flame and crashing waters, Travis had the appearance of a demon from hell as he fought to keep the boat afloat, but his relief at word of Alicia was all too human.

All through the night they battled a river that had no shore, no landmarks, no resemblance to anything they had ever known. Water spread out across what once had been acres of forest; bluffs and islands crumbled and heaved and disappeared forevermore. Travis kept his keel aimed at the swiftest current, praying this marked the deeper river channel, but even this method wasn't foolproof. The swifter current carried with it all the debris of the devastation farther upstream, and often swept under precariously overhanging cliffs. The stench of sulphur permeated their lungs as they fought to keep the boat from the deadly reach of fallen trees and jagged trunks.

All through the night and the next day the earth continued to tremble and shudder, creating new crevasses for the river to pour into, toppling towns and forests, opening up geysers of gas and coal and sand. By dawn a sulphurous haze hung over the water. Tangled trees leaning madly backward against the current cluttered the landscape. Terrified birds flew aimlessly over their heads, occasionally landing on the deck, totally disoriented by a world they no longer recognized.

With morbid interest the crew watched the cargo of untold boats bob on the current, barrels of flour, tobacco, and corn provisions for flatboats that had disappeared during the night. Bodies too, caught in the debris or borne dancing and bobbing on the water, floated past. Gathering courage to face the dawn's light, Alicia stepped from the cabin in time to catch sight of a child's golden hair disappearing into an eddy between a tangle of trees. Turning pale, she returned inside, reassuring herself with the sight of her son's healthy breathing.

Shortly after dawn the earth shook with renewed vehemence, and they could see in the daylight what they had endured throughout the night. The earth had literally opened up, swallowing trees and abandoned cabins and anything else in the way. The gas spewing from fissures carried with it hailstorms of debris and water that hissed and steamed with unholy implications. The superstitious crew crossed themselves and muttered uneasily.

As the rushing waters carried them southward, Travis dared not land in the treacherous eddies that marked what remained of both shores, and he could not rest for dodging the debris that jammed the river. Worn to a state of collapse, he ordered his men to take turns resting and reviving themselves. With each shudder of the unstable river, he murmured a pleading prayer. He had come too far to lose to vengeful gods of nature.

If Auguste had been there, Travis would have dared surrender his pole long enough to grab a bite to eat, but the majority of his crew was too new to be trusted. Battling exhaustion and nature, he sought some escape from the hell that followed them well past islands he recognized as being far downstream from the prior night's resting place. He had to get them out of there, but he couldn't even be certain whether they were heading away from or into the center of the devastation.

By nightfall they had either become accustomed to the shudders racking the earth, or the shudders had begun to lessen. Darkness made it nearly impossible to successfully navigate the logjams and sawyers and other snags that could rip the bottom from the boat if not seen in time. Knowing to continue would be more deadly than to stop, Travis chose to anchor on the slope of the protected side of one of the remaining islands. Helping himself to the stale bread and cheese and apples that Alicia had dug out from among the stores to feed the crew, he ate without tasting, and collapsed immediately into the sleep of exhaustion afterward.

In the middle of the night another shock struck, and again they jumped from their beds to pole the boat to safety if necessary. This time they watched in disbelief as the island just downriver from them disappeared from sight, but their own remained steady.

In this way they fought the river for what seemed like eternity, growing gradually more weary and filthy and hungry with each day, but still alive, which was more than could be said for the bodies they passed along the way. To restock for supplies was impossible. No towns remained along the shores. The few people they passed appeared dazed and homeless and offered no solution. No boats traveled upstream to give them news of what lay ahead, and they knew there was no sense in turning back to the devastation behind them.

They lost count of the days, each passing much the same as the rest. Tempers flared, but exhaustion prevailed. With aching backs and empty stomachs, fighting each other had little appeal. The raging river took the fight out of them.

One morning a roar and rumble and hiss not dissimilar to those they had learned to fear broke what had been a momentarily quiet dawn. This sound had a more mechanical note to it, and the rhythmic thumping that accompanied it was nearly as frightening. Finding Travis gone from his pallet beside her bed, Alicia stumbled to the doorway to stare in amazement at the creature risen from the water.

A boat of unheard-of size and length bore down on them with a speed greater than the current, although no sail or polemen could be seen. Smoke belched from a tall stack, and water flew from a churning wheel along its side. She could see men gathering idly on the deck, occasionally looking over their shoulders to shout to some invisible guide inside the monster but otherwise making no concerted effort to steer the boat through murky waters. If a monster had risen from its grave during the earthquake, this must surely be it.

More aware of the rumors that traveled the river than Alicia, Travis recognized the steamboat *New Orleans* for what it was—the invention of a genius and the accomplishment of a persistent man. Like others, Travis had doubted that the craft would ever float, but that it had traveled this distance was a wonder to behold. Built in Pittsburgh, it must have traversed even the treacherous shoals at Louisville to come this far. Better yet, it must have survived the violent upheavals of the earthquake unscarred, and in much greater safety than his own frail craft. It provided the first glimmer of hope Travis had seen in days, and he instantly took advantage of it.

The gray clouds overhead threatened turbulent weather to multiply the dangers of the already flooded, debris-choked river. The keelboat had survived this far only through prayer and luck and what skill he possessed. Their chances of making it to New Orleans safely were running out. He could not risk the lives of Alicia and the babe while another alternative existed.

Leaping to the roof of the cabin, Travis signaled the oncoming boat. A whistle indicated the other captain had seen him, but the chances of communicating over the noise of the boilers was small. He would have to take his chances they would understand.

Quickly Travis dashed into the cabin and, lifting his son from the cradle, shoved him into Alicia's arms. Glancing around, he grabbed one of her smaller trunks and, ignoring her questions, pushed her out the door.

More passengers had appeared on the deck of the steamboat, including a woman and a huge black dog. As they spied Alicia with babe in arms on the foundering keelboat, a general shout went up, and the larger craft seemed to slow. Maneuvering through the jam of logs and debris was tricky, the engines were not thoroughly reliable, and stopping in mid-river was out of the question. Still, the passengers bent eagerly to the task at hand.

As the steamboat passed closer, Travis heaved the small chest aboard. Men reached out to assure its passage and, certain now that the breach was passable, leaned over for the real reason for this encounter.

Frozen into immobility, Alicia clutched the bundle in her arms and stared at Travis's implacable face with terror. She tried to twist free as he lifted her from the deck, but he gave her no opportunity. Like so much baggage she was shoved from his arms into that of strangers and hauled onto the decks of the smoking monster.

Even as Alicia's feet landed safely on the sturdy deck, the churning paddle wheel carried them away from the keel-

boat, creating a wave that tilted the smaller craft dangerously. As Alicia screamed in horror, Travis was tossed from
his precarious perch into the frothing current. The wails of
the infant in her arms made no impression as Travis's dark
head disappeared beneath the muddy waters. Alicia's screams
vibrated over the river, but grew faint in her own ears as the
shock took hold.

Gentle hands reached out and caught her before she
crumpled to the deck.

39

ALICIA WOKE to the stench of smelling salts and the screams of two irate infants. She scarcely had time to take in the comforts of her surroundings before her memory returned and she sat up, screaming for Travis.

The woman hovering over her pushed her gently back against the pillows. "Nicholas brought him aboard. Rest now. You are safe."

That wasn't enough. She had to see for herself, hold his hand and touch his face. How could anyone survive the icy waters of the treacherous river? It was impossible. Travis might have the lives of a cat, but even a cat could not survive that devastation. Alicia rose from the bed and looked frantically around.

"Where is he?"

Lydia Roosevelt led her to the makeshift bed that held the two infants, and Alicia gave her son a perfunctory glance. She recognized his cry as one of temper and knew him to be safe. Larger, although apparently much the same age as the other infant, Dale flailed his legs and arms and proved his health. That was not her concern. She wanted to see Travis.

"My husband? Where is my husband?" Finding the opening of the curtain that must lead to another cabin, Alicia hurried toward it, determined to find out for herself what had happened.

Noting the tired shadows of her guest's face and guessing her to be near hysteria, Lydia relented. This cabin led to the larger men's cabin, badly damaged by a recent fire. Beyond that a small hall led to the cubicles the engineers and pilot used. She directed Alicia across the damaged room to the pilot's door.

Frightened now, Alicia turned the knob gingerly. She did not know what she would do if Travis were not alive and well beyond this door. After the death-defying ride they had just endured, her state of mind was in chaos, her emotions too near the breaking point to act rationally. If he were not there . . . the point did not bear considering. She shoved the door open gently.

Drenched and shivering, Travis was shaking off the helping hands of the men who had dragged him aboard. His only thought was to get to Alicia and to hell with the blood streaming down his face from the blow with driftwood. When she opened the door, he glanced up, and relief flooded his frozen expression.

Without words Travis opened his arms and Alicia ran into them. Tears streamed down her face, indistinguishable from the rivulets of water that fell upon her from his dripping hair. She felt the deep shivers running through him and pressed closer for a moment, giving him her warmth. Then she pushed away and began working at the sodden ties of his shirt.

"You must get out of these clothes before you catch your death of cold," she admonished shakily.

Now that the responsibility for her safety was momentarily in other hands, weariness overcame him, and Travis clasped her hands to keep from collapsing in front of her. "Go back to Dale. I can take care of myself," he ordered curtly, through lips blue with cold.

She wanted to slap him. She had almost died watching him disappear beneath those waters; he had almost died in going under. She wanted him to know her fear, her love, but all he could do was send her away. Aware they were being watched, Alicia lifted her chin grandly, and eyes flashing, picked up her skirts and left without a word.

One of the men behind Travis chuckled as the door slammed behind the two women. "The last time Lydia looked at me that way, I slept with the damned dog for a week. I hope you're better at mending fences than I am."

A small quirk of his lips recorded Travis's acknowledgment of the remark's aptness, but he said nothing. Even his bones trembled as he worked to remove his sodden clothing. He wasn't about to let Alicia see his weakness.

Before the day was out, fever raged through Travis's exhausted body, and he had no awareness of who saw him.

At first the two maids and the cabin boy took turns looking in on him, occasionally accompanied by one of the Roosevelts or their companions. When Alicia awoke from an exhausted sleep that afternoon and was apprised of the situation, she immediately moved herself and Dale into the sickroom.

For the most part Travis lay quietly, his body too drained from the exertions of these past days to stir needlessly. Alicia kept the bandage on his forehead clean, pressed cold compresses to his fevered brow, tried to keep him covered, and sponged his lips with water. Beneath the sheets and blankets he wore nothing, but Alicia tried not to concentrate on this detail. The muscular breadth of bronzed shoulders moving restlessly against the pillows created havoc enough with her insides.

The wife of the man who had dreamed this trip into existence stopped in occasionally to see how the patient fared. Not long out of childbed herself, Lydia could offer little help beyond company, and the room was too narrow for much of that. It was from this indomitable woman that Alicia heard the tale of the steamboat's miraculous journey.

Alicia found it difficult to believe Lydia's assurances that this odd contraption could travel upriver as well as down without the need for men or oars or sails, but she did not spend much time wondering over it. That Lydia had chosen to undertake the dangerous journey even though eight months pregnant by the time all the mechanical and technical difficulties had been overcome gave Alicia cause to wonder if her hostess should be admired or judged insane. The difficulties of travel and giving birth under such conditions, however, Alicia could understand better than the workings of the ship.

The fire that had destroyed most of the elegance of the forward cabin just days before they had joined it did not damage the ladies' aft cabin or the small cabins of the officers and engineers. While one of the maids took a turn beside Travis, Alicia was persuaded to explore the lovely living quarters Lydia had designed herself, and she marvelled at the conveniences that could be had on such a boat as this. The ladies' cabin had four comfortable berths, damask hangings, gilded looking glasses, carpets, and high windows to fill the space with light. The gentlemen's cabin was much larger, but badly damaged by the fire. This longer

room contained the dining table and stove and a galley in
the forward section, but no carpet. The habit of tobacco
chewing rendered carpets unsuitable. Appropriately placed
spittoons marked the wisdom of this decision.

The thought of traveling in such comfort amazed Alicia,
but she did not ponder the delights for long while Travis lay
burning with fever. If he were awake, Alicia knew he would
enjoy probing the inner workings of this new kind of shipping, questioning the intrepid Nicholas Roosevelt and his
engineers, and exploring the possibilities such a marvel offered. That he could lie here still and unwaking while this
opportunity passed conveyed the seriousness of his illness
more thoroughly than anything else.

Alicia possessed only the few clothes the small trunk had
held, while Travis owned only the clothes on his back when
he fell in the river. These had been carefully laundered and
ironed and laid upon a chair, but Travis had no need of
them while he lay motionless upon the bed. Each night
Alicia carefully smoothed her gown on top of the stack of
his clothing and crawled in between the covers beside Travis's overheated body. In this way she knew when he woke or
grew restless and could offer him liquids or cooling compresses
without disturbing others. Through her thin nightgown she
could feel his excessive warmth, and hot tears rolled down
her cheeks as he lay unmoving beside her.

On Christmas Eve, Travis's temperature soared, and he
thrashed restlessly in the bed, throwing off the covers as
quickly as Alicia put them on him. Worn to a nervous
frazzle, she cursed and threatened him with ropes, and
finally weighed down one side of the blanket with the trunk
while she sat on the other to nurse Dale.

When the babe fell asleep, she moved to return him to his
pallet. It was then that Travis cried her name, and she
nearly dropped the child before she recovered herself. Restlessly Travis repeated her name while she lay Dale upon the
quilt, and again as she stepped back to sit beside him.

He still did not wake, but his brow was drenched in
sweat, and gently Alicia rubbed a cool cloth across his face.

"Alicia!"

She jumped, startled, even though she sat beside him.
She watched him warily, but he remained unconscious.

Travis called her name again, then began to mutter. Irritably, he threw aside the cover and tried to rise. Alicia

hurriedly covered him again, her forehead creased with
worry.

His mutterings grew increasingly louder, though Alicia
could distinguish little more than an occasional curse. He
thrashed about, calling for her, until she ached with the
need to offer him solace. When she bent to hold him,
however, he shouted "Leave me alone!" and threw her
from him.

Flinging the sponge at his aggravating frame, Alicia rose
to escape. Even in illness, the man was a pestilence upon
the earth. He shouted her name again, and she ignored him.
Muttering, he seemed to shove someone or something aside
and tried to rise, still calling her name.

"I'm right here, you fool!" Alicia pushed him back against
the pillows again and jerked the blanket back over his bare
legs.

"Alicia!" A grin spread across Travis's face, though Alicia could swear he was still not conscious. The fever raged
beneath her hand and his brow was still damp to the touch.

He jerked from her gentle touch, yelled, "Go away!" and
returned to his muttering. Giving in to curiosity, Alicia tried
to interpret his ravings, catching the word "lady" once or
twice. Then suddenly, Travis sat up, tried to shove her
away, said distinctly, "Go away. You're not Alicia," and
rose from the bed stating, "I'm going home."

Alicia didn't know whether to laugh or cry as Travis's
boldly masculine physique strode naked across the tiny cabin.
She could see what he wanted from her, even in his illness,
and she wondered hysterically what poor woman's favors he
had rejected. Before the chill of the room could kill him,
she went after him.

"You're a fool, my worthless viscount," she berated him,
wrapping her arm around his waist and steering him in the
direction of the bed. "Any woman could give you what you
want. You don't need me."

Travis followed the sound of her voice willingly, but she
could not pry loose his grip on her shoulder when she tried
to return him to bed. Not until she climbed upon the bed
first and pulled him down would he follow. Suspiciously
Alicia touched his forehead when she had him between the
covers, but he was drenched in sweat and unaware of her
concern.

As she tried to pull away to find the sponge, Travis

caught her in his still powerful grip and pulled her against him. Through the thin linen of her gown Alicia could feel the pulsating heat of his flesh, and she shivered involuntarily. Not since that night in the Indian camp had he held her like this. He had taken her against her will then. This would be little better now. Her body was not fully healed, and he knew nothing of what he did. She didn't want it like this, though the heat of his touch sent rivers of excitement flooding her veins, and the place between her legs ached for his filling.

Travis muttered incoherently, repeating her name as his hand rode down her back, pressing her closer to his heat. Alicia cried out as her gown rode upward and he grasped her buttocks, surging forward until his maleness slid between her thighs. Without thought she slid away and captured his swollen member with her hand. Travis cried out in relief and began to move urgently. Within seconds his seed spilled across her hand and thigh, and he fell back against the pillow, sound asleep.

Wonderingly Alicia touched a hand to his forehead and found it cooler. She curled up beside him, resting her hand against his lightly furred chest so she could feel him breathe. Then rejoicing in the musky scent of life he brought to their bed, she slept.

In the morning Travis was awake, and Alicia blushed crimson as she noted his gaze had fallen on the valley between her milk-filled breasts. Hastily she rose to answer her son's cries, self-consciously aware that Travis's gaze followed her scantily-clad figure across the floor and back. She ought to find her gown, but there seemed no purpose in it. She had not even had time to wash.

Travis stacked the pillows behind her so she could sit comfortably, and he lay with his hands behind his head as she fed his son. The bed was narrow and Alicia could feel his heat next to her, but it did not feel so much like a furnace as it had the day before. In her joy and relief she did not resent his stare, but basked shyly in his admiration.

When Dale had drunk his fill and seemed prepared to play, Alicia tied her nightgown ribbons and lay him beside his father before rising from the bed. Strangely content, Travis watched as his son chased dust motes in the air and made gurgling noises that pleased them both, while Alicia washed and dressed.

The scratchiness of his bearded jaw and the weakness of his muscles reminded Travis that all was not well, but it did not seem to matter. He stretched to test his strength and lifted his son atop his chest while his gaze roved in fascination to his wife's slim curves in petticoats. He did not attempt to examine the vague visions that returned to nag his memory. He only knew that he had woke to find Alicia in his bed. After all these many months of loneliness, that was accomplishment enough.

Starvation he did not take lightly, though, and Travis grunted in appreciation at the smells coming from the breakfast tray carried into the room. The little maid carrying it looked flustered when dark eyes fastened hungrily on her, and she quickly handed the tray to Alicia and scurried out.

Startled by this abrupt departure, Alicia swung around to regard her husband, and began to grin as she realized the appearance he made.

"It is a good thing you don't have a tomahawk in your hand." Setting the tray down on the table beside the bed, Alicia smiled at the craggy visage of her husband. With black hair tumbling across his brow and down to his shoulders, and his dark eyes gazing wickedly from behind high cheekbones, he appeared more savage than any Indian she had ever seen. "Mayhap I have a bandanna and earring in my trunk that you could wear to complete the image."

Suspiciously Travis's gaze swept over his wife's slender, primly garbed figure, then back to her laughing sapphire eyes. Vague memories of the prior night came clearer, and his mocking grin spread slowly.

"I think the lady's been left alone too long and needs to be taken in hand," Travis informed his gurgling son, setting him to one side, though his gaze never left Alicia.

Before she could guess his intentions, Travis's hand shot out and tugged her down beside him, tumbling her across his chest in one swift movement. Before she could cry out, Travis pressed his beard-stubbled mouth against hers, drawing her breath away, while his hand explored the full curves he had captured. Exulting in her apparent willingness, he drank hungrily of lips he had long been denied.

Alicia did not protest as the welcome strength of Travis's arms wrapped around her. Her senses reeled at the swift invasion he mounted, capturing her breath with the depth of his kiss. Not until she realized he was still quite naked and that anyone could walk in on them did she recover enough sense to squirm from his hold.

"You're out of your mind," she retorted, brushing down the wrinkles of her gown and attempting to retrieve some respectability from the disheveled remains of her coiffure.

Travis shrugged unconcernedly, his grin still glinting behind ebony eyes. "Just making certain you hadn't grown too cold. Do you intend to join me at breakfast or just glare at me?"

"I think I'll just give you back to the Indians." Still flustered, Alicia strode out, leaving Travis to tend the babe. She needed her privacy for a little while, and, she suspected, so did he.

There was little enough privacy to be had, though certainly more than the keelboat offered. Besides the Roosevelts, the crew boasted a pilot and engineer, six hands, a cook, a cabin boy, and two maids. The main cabins gave no hiding place; there would be no avoiding Travis for very long.

However, once Travis's recovery was discovered, they were left little opportunity to be alone, and Alicia's only concern was that he would make himself ill again. Her concerns were needless. Shedding his illness like an old skin, Travis rebounded with more energy and interest than before. As Alicia had predicted, he was all over the boat within days, and the incorrigible Nicholas was right beside him.

Only at night, when there was time for quiet conversation behind closed doors did they have opportunity to meet without the buffers of strangers around them. It was awkward at first. They had never really shared a bed together, but it was not to be avoided now. Alicia could not ask Travis to return to sleeping on the floor, and she did not feel inclined to join the crew or Lydia and Nicholas in the main cabins. That first night Travis waited patiently while Alicia turned her back to him and drew on her nightgown over her chemise. Thereafter he waited out on deck until he was certain she had retired beneath the covers.

As Travis blew out the lamp and undressed in darkness, Alicia lay quietly waiting for his weight to sag the narrow bed as he climbed in. She had grown accustomed to his company, and now that she understood Travis did not intend to ask for more, she enjoyed these moments before they slept. As long as he did not touch her, she could drive away the images that haunted her mind's eye, and pretend he was bodiless there in the darkness. That worked best, for to be reminded that he was flesh and blood stirred cravings she had no desire or ability to succumb to yet.

She sensed that Travis lay on his side, those eyes that seemed to penetrate darkness fastened on her, but curled securely around her pillow, Alicia did not mind. Gazing at his shadow beside her, she asked, "Are we far from New Orleans?"

"Not far. The river is clearing, so it won't be quite so dangerous."

"The others? Is there any way we can find out what happened to them?" The keelboat that had carried them so far, so long, had become a part of her life. Surely the crew would have made it to safety by now, but whether the boat had survived was questionable. The city man and his soldiers must be feeling out of place in the middle of the wilderness they had left them in.

"The crew will be fine if they did not let Scott bully them into carrying on. I imagine they'll lay over in Natchez until the river clears. I'll leave word where I can, though, in case they decide to finish the run. Do not worry over things you cannot control, Alicia."

"It was horrible," she stated decisively, the memory of those frightening days not dying easily. "I don't know that I'll ever dare make that journey again."

"Perhaps you will not have to, my love," Travis whispered soothingly. The journey to England held worse dangers, but he did not tell her that. He would prefer to stay here, explore the possibilities of steamboat travel, raise his horses, and put an end to his wandering life, but the nightmare of his past had come back to haunt him. He would not be like poor Robert, carrying his childhood bride to the wilderness only to watch her die of the loneliness and the dangers. He wanted this woman by his side, and he would do everything necessary to keep her there.

Sleepy, Alicia did not question his words. He had every right to return to his father's home and claim his heritage. She only prayed that he meant to take her with him.

"Will your father mind terribly that you did not marry a Lady Somebody-or-Another?"

Her whisper scarcely reached his ears, but Travis heard

her fears. He grinned in the darkness and touched her cheek. "He will be so thrilled with you that he will most likely leave me behind. Don't fret, Alicia. It will be all right."

It would have to be, for just that touch of his finger told her nothing had changed. Her strange addiction to this overbearing man had not faded with time. It had grown more demanding.

40

THE ARRIVAL in New Orleans of the first steamboat to traverse the Mississippi River caused great excitement and celebration, and Travis's small family managed to slip away without notice. The Roosevelts deserved to have this day to themselves, and farewells had been exchanged the night before. The friendship that had formed would be left to flourish at another place and time, particularly since Travis had agreed to purchase a share of the steamboat company Nicholas planned.

Nervously Alicia clung to her son and stared out at the exotic sights of New Orleans as the hired carriage carried them away from the docks. Her best gowns had been left behind on the keelboat, and the lovely French designs she saw around her put even them to shame. The dowdy muslin she wore now would never be presentable in fashionable society. How could she face Travis's aristocratic father wearing muslin?

Leaving behind the chaos of the dock, the carriage carried them past the street vendors and the crowds of the levee up the wide expanse of Canal Street. Alicia stared in wonderment at the delicate filigree of the wrought iron railings and the crowded narrow streets of shops in the Vieux Carre as they passed, glimpsing only a small portion of the walled side yards and lovely old homes of this French quarter of the city. On the other side sprawled the bare expanses and more American construction of the city's growing suburbs, but the carriage did not stop here either.

Under Travis's instructions the carriage turned down a narrow side street in one of the older sections, past the more pretentious homes but in an area of respectable modest two-story residences. In the French style, many of the homes had shops on the street level, but the one Travis pointed out was wedged in between two others that had obviously been converted to simple residences. The graceful iron balconies provided the only accent to the townhouse walls, although the others around it displayed magnificent pots of geraniums and the green traceries of ivy. The one the carriage stopped before was blatantly abandoned.

As if he had only just returned from a brief trip, Travis leapt from the carriage and unlocked the front door. With a gesture to the driver he indicated their one trunk should be unloaded. Then with a gallant bow he assisted Alicia from the carriage and led her into the house.

"It is small and neglected but private. You will not mind too much? Just for a few days?" Anxiously Travis watched her face.

Alicia glanced at the cloaked furniture and high ceilings with amazement and shook her head, unable to voice her surprise. It was small, but lovely, and they would have to share it with no one. Or would they?

Hesitantly she turned her gaze up to Travis's dark face. "Who does it belong to?"

For an instant Travis debated the wisdom of telling her, wishing to avoid the questions that were sure to follow. But he had betrayed her trust once too often. Gazing down into beguiling eyes, he knew it was time to begin sharing his life. "It is ours, Blue Eyes." He watched as her eyes widened. When her cheeks began to color and she turned her gaze away to examine the furniture, Travis knew she had guessed he had once kept another woman here, but to his surprise, her sharp tongue remained silent. He did not know whether that augured well or ill, but he did not dwell on it.

He had not called her Blue Eyes since he had returned home. Alicia contemplated the meaning of his choosing to do so now as she carefully removed the dusty sheets from the parlor furniture. He had used all the meaningless endearments men tended to use when they wanted something, but this term of twin affection and aggravation that he had given her had eluded him recently. Had he called the woman who had chosen this furniture by a pet name? She wanted to fling it all out the door, but ladies did not indulge in fits of jealousy. For that was what it was.

She was jealous. She was jealous of all the other women he had known, even that flamboyant Molly in Cincinnati.

How long had Travis kept the mistress he had installed here? Longer than the few months it had taken him to bed her and get her with child and disappear? Was she so unsatisfactory that he no longer desired her but merely kept her because he had decided it was time to marry and settle down? Could he not be interested in any woman for more than a few months?

Blithely unaware of the hornet's nest he had stirred up, Travis explored the house for leaks or damage, noting the work that needed to be done, and making mental lists. Coming back to the bedroom, he found Alicia at the dressing table attempting to return order to her rebellious curls and his son lying contentedly amongst the bed covers. Resting his hand on the flawless skin of Alicia's shoulders, Travis met her gaze in the mirror.

"I thought we might relax and mend our wardrobes before calling on my father, if you do not mind. Or would you prefer to go directly to his hotel this evening?"

His hand burned against her flesh, and the look in his eyes sent shivers down Alicia's spine and into the pit of her stomach. Why did he have to look so damnably masculine with his wide shoulders straining at the seams of his old shirt and his buckskin trousers stretched tight across narrow loins? And why did she have to notice? She ought to punch holes in his male arrogance, but she no longer could find the fury to run from him. Too much had gone between them to fire the flames of anger. Anger no longer suited her needs. What she wanted now she saw reflected in the mirror, and her hand came up to rest on his.

"I am in no hurry, though your father may be sick with worry by now. Perhaps you should go to him and leave me here."

"I go nowhere without you." Travis repeated the words that had begun this journey. "I will send a message to my father that we are well and arriving shortly. Will that suit?"

Alicia did not comprehend the vehemence of his words, but they sent a warm current of hope rushing through her. Surely he would not be so adamant about her company if he did not feel anything for her? She nodded imperceptibly in agreement.

Travis felt the movement, but did not let relief take command. He wanted to be certain of her feelings this time, and the only way he knew to do that was persuade her to his

bed. The tension of not knowing if she would accept him or
if he had permanently damaged their relationship warred
with his concerns for her health. Perhaps she was not well
enough yet, or perhaps he should not risk the chance of
another child so soon. With any other woman he would
have swept her from her feet and thrown her in his bed and
had his way. With this woman he never knew where he
stood, and he cared more than he dared admit, even to
himself. He had discovered that too late last time. This
time, he wanted to make no mistakes.

Reluctantly he let his hand fall and, bending a kiss to her
cheek, said, "I'll go find a messenger. Then I will take you
somewhere to eat."

On silent feet he disappeared through the doorway, and
Alicia cursed the image in her mirror. Why hadn't she given
him some sign, made some movement, done something to
let him know how she felt? Would she ever be able to
unbend her stubborn pride to let him see that she loved
him, that she wanted to be his wife again, that she had been
wrong to deny him before? Or was she still avoiding the
violence in him that had separated them the first time?

Certain of nothing, Alicia went to bed that night in a
room with a high, carved poster bed similar to the one they
had left behind. With daring, she had donned a pale, batiste
nightgown heavily embroidered along the deep décolletage
and at the long slits in the seams from her ankles to her
knees. Every movement revealed an unseemly amount of
flesh and the nearly transparent material left little to the
imagination. She almost lost her courage and sought another, but the sound of Travis's feet outside the door warned
her it was too late.

Travis caught only a glimpse of a slim ankle as she ducked
beneath the covers. Slowly he closed the bedroom door
behind him, his glance taking in the sight of Alicia's un-
bound hair cascading in rich abundance over a creamy gown
that appeared to cling to rounded curves like another skin.
His gaze traveled from the ripeness of firm curves to the
heightened pink of Alicia's cheeks as she avoided his gaze.
Cautiously, he advanced further into the room.

"I don't think I can share the bed you slept in with your
mistress," Alicia announced firmly and clearly, the words
coming out without thought.

A corner of Travis's lips quirked upward as he sat down

to pull off his shoes. "That is my bed. I shared it occasionally with a bottle of whiskey, but nothing else."

His coolness irritated her. Determined to provoke him, she refused to let the subject go. "Where is she now? Did you find her when you went out walking after dinner?"

Calmly Travis drew off his shirt and dropped it over the bench. Lamplight flickered over the lean lines of his torso, throwing shadows across the bronzed expanse of his chest.

"We parted ways years ago. I don't even remember her name. What's the matter, Alicia? Do I detect just a small glimmer of jealousy?"

She sent him a scathing glance. "I would wear myself out if that were the case, wouldn't I? With your whores telling me how good you are, your Indian lover living on our land, the untold women you've been with these last months, and now this. . ." She threw her hand out to indicate the bed and all its trappings. "Did you carve this for her, too?"

An unholy light sprang up behind his dark eyes as Travis rose from the bench and stalked across the room to the maligned bed. Alicia jerked the covers up to her chin and glared at him defiantly, but he scarcely seemed to notice the obstruction. In a single sweep of his hand, the blankets slithered to the floor, revealing the enticing confection beneath. Travis had to catch his breath to keep from gasping at the splendor thus uncovered, and the light in his eyes flared brighter. She had donned that gown for his pleasure, not her own.

Long legs flew over the side of the bed, but Travis caught her by the waist before she could escape and they both tumbled into the center of the mattress. Travis held Alicia pinned beneath his greater weight, his hands grasping her shoulders as he stared down into unfathomable depths of blue.

"I have not had a woman besides you since we met. You are the only woman in my life, Alicia, and you're making me crazy. I admit, I deserve everything you toss my way. I've embarrassed and humiliated you and frightened you beyond the bounds of necessity. But somewhere it has to stop, Alicia. You've tormented me more than enough to make up for everything I may have done. When can we call a truce?"

His hands burned against her skin, and his buckskin-clad leg rode uncomfortably close to the source of her desire, stirring a turmoil of emotion not easily controlled. When Alicia gazed up into that rigid face, she wanted to touch and stroke and return the laughter. Instead she froze.

"When you treat me as something more than a horse to be rode and put out to pasture at your convenience," she whispered hoarsely, heart pounding with fear at this reckless challenge. She wanted him any way she could have him, but she wanted his love even more. Did she dare hold out for more?

Travis stared at her pale face in its circlet of dark curls with incredulity. His body ached for the possession he had thought surely won, but she wasn't going to let it be that easy. She had taken him back without a word, registered no complaint at being hauled from child bed to the treacheries of the river, nursed his son, his wounds, and his temper, but she would not submit to his bed without a fight. Why?

Slowly Travis released his grip on her shoulders and rolled over to stare at the ceiling. The vague scent of gardenias drifted to him as he lay there, and he knew it came from the soft curves of the woman at his side. He had only to reach out and pull her to him, stroke the firm lines of her body until she responded, and she would be his. He knew that. The current of desire between them was too strong to be ignored. His loins ached for the freedom she would grant him. He could almost taste the sweet honey of her lips. And he knew the urge was reciprocated, that if he just caressed the soft juncture of her thighs . . .

He sighed. That was what he had done the first time, seduced her into surrender. And then he had tried rape. Both times she had given her body but nothing more. That had been enough then, but was it still enough now?

"Alicia, I do not know how to give you what you want." With a violent motion Travis flipped on his side to stare down into her face, their bodies touching. "I thought by giving you marriage and a child, I was giving you what you wanted. You once said you would laugh in my face if I quoted poetry to you. I have no experience in whispering pretty words in your ear and wooing you with my wit. What would you have me do?"

Alicia had to smile at the look of pained puzzlement on his face. If she accomplished nothing else, she had forced him to admit there was something he could not do. Unfortunately, they had reached an impasse, for she had no talent for such things either. How then could she make him love her?

"We're a sorry pair, aren't we?" she murmured. "I do not have the words to tell you what I seek, and you do not have the knowledge to provide it. Perhaps we should have stuck to being friends."

Frustrated, Travis got up to blow out the lamp and finish undressing.

"To hell with friends. Right now I'd settle for lovers," he muttered.

The faint trill of laughter from the bed did nothing to alleviate his mood.

41

GARBED IN AN expensively tailored suit that had been poorly
mended and not recently cleaned, the fair-haired gentleman
slouched in his chair at the café, and stared blankly at the
passing crowds of elegantly dressed strangers. The little he
had won at the game the night before he had spent on
whiskey, and his stomach rumbled a complaint at the lack of
solid fare. Wondering where his next meal would come from
had taken precedence over his pride in his good looks. As
he drank his coffee, he scarcely noticed the parade of fashion before him.

Until the sight of a tall, well-dressed couple caught his
eye—and alarm bells clamored somewhere deep in his be-
fuddled mind. His eyes narrowed as he followed the progress of the black-haired, bronzed gentleman and his graceful,
blue-eyed companion. Neither wore the finery of the New
Orleans society surging around them, but no one would
doubt their wealth or status. They carried themselves as if
the world belonged to them, and they entered the doorway
of one of the most exclusive clothier establishments on the
street. Edward Beauchamp III ground his teeth together
with rage and focused his eyes on the dressmaker's, waiting
for these apparitions to reappear.

Inside the shop, an elegantly dressed young lady hurried
forward to greet them, her eyes darting speculatively from
Alicia's simple but exquisite muslin to Travis's arrogantly
informal attire. Generally, the people wealthy enough to
shop here she knew by name, but these two she could not
recognize even by face.

"May we be of assistance, madame, monsieur?" she murmured softly, noting the babe wrapped in the softest of
shawls in the lady's arms.

"Is Madame Helena not in?" Dark eyes searching the interior, Travis scarcely heeded the clerk. He had brought Alicia to the best seamstress in town, and he had little patience for those in between.

"Madame is very busy. Perhaps if I could . . ." Tactfully the clerk attempted to divert his attention. Madame had time only for her most important clients, and this couple did not appear to meet the standards.

Travis finally focused his hawk-like stare on the impertinent young assistant, recognizing her ploy and losing his patience. "Tell Madame that Lonetree is here and insists that his wife have the very best. If she no longer qualifies, I will be happy to take her next door."

"Travis!" Horrified at this impoliteness, Alicia took him to task in muted tones. "I'm certain this lady can help me find what I need . . ."

But the assistant had already hurried away, terrified she had made some faux pas of which she was not yet aware, but of which Madame would most likely inform her in no uncertain terms.

Within minutes a short, stout, black-haired Frenchwoman with wings of gray above her temples hurried out to greet the newcomers. "Monsieur Lonetree, you are a sight for these old eyes! *Bienvenu!* And, madame, it is a pleasure."

Effusively she made over Alicia, the babe, and Travis, dragging them back into her office, ordering refreshments, assigning one of the young girls from the shop to watch over Dale while others were sent scurrying for materials and designs. Alicia lifted a faintly mocking eyebrow to Travis over this confusion, but he merely grinned and lifted a shoulder nonchalantly.

If Alicia had any illusion that she could merely choose a few gowns and materials and be done, Travis effectively shattered it within the first few minutes. Pointing to a design of a simple Empire gown with a high-necked frill modestly covering the bosom that she wished done in a dark blue muslin for a morning gown, Alicia found Travis standing beside her, shaking his head.

"You may want one of those later for teaching school, but you don't need one now." Travis pierced Madame Helena with his dark gaze. "Our luggage was lost on our journey downriver. We need whatever the lady chooses as soon as possible. She will need at least one day gown and a dinner dress for tomorrow, and as many more as possible by the day after, including an evening gown. Bring out what you are working on that might be suitable, and then we shall decide on those to be made up."

Over the protest of the women, Travis had his way, and Alicia found herself trying on a yellow silk that even with the matching chemise showed a scandalous amount of bosom. As the seamstresses pinned and basted, she chose from the designs that Travis had the frantic modiste carrying back and forth. Alicia had to admit that his choices were admirably suited to her taste with a minimum of frills and furbelows, but his eye tended toward the more sensual patterns that she had always avoided. When he appeared in the fitting room to demand why she had rejected the silver-blue silk for the low-cut evening gown he had chosen, Alicia nearly flung the cushion full of pins at him while the seamstresses went into a twitter at his masculine presence.

"I cannot wear a gown that conceals nothing but my shoes, Travis! I will not be gawked at by every man, woman, and rake in the city! That silk leaves nothing to the imagination. I would have to hide behind potted plants all evening."

Since the silk in question was the most expensive in stock, Madame hastened to intervene. "*Non*, madame! It is of the very most elegant quality. With a figure such as yours—" she gestured toward the stars—"you will be the envy of every woman, and monsieur will be the envy of every man. It is not every woman who is so lucky to have a man who appreciates her loveliness. You will see, the choice is perfect."

Alicia scowled at being thus outvoted, but the silk was admittedly of exquisite quality. She just could not imagine herself wearing it. For too long she had worn the dark, modest clothes her mother had chosen for her. She might be daring and try the prettier, livelier colors, but this. . . !

Travis won nearly every battle, though Alicia managed to neutralize most of his victories by ordering shawls and spencers and high-necked chemises to match his more extravagant choices. Perhaps in England and France they wore these fashions, but they were still in the United States, and she could not help but imagine the eyebrows of St. Louis society should she wear these styles in public.

As they prepared to leave, Travis with a bundle of packages Alicia could not bear to part with under his arm, the young girl tending Dale reluctantly returned him to Alicia's arms.

"*Le petit est tres bon*," she murmured wistfully.

Struck with a sudden thought, Alicia tugged at Travis's sleeve until he looked down at her. "A maid, Travis. We will need someone to look after Dale and help me with my hair if we are to do much visiting. Would Madame Helena know of anyone?"

The young girl overheard and bobbed a hurried curtsy before Travis could speak. "I am very good with the little ones, monsieur. And I have the practice at coiffures. Madame says I am a very poor seamstress, for I have no experience in needlework, but I have been maid to Mademoiselle Dubonnier for these three years."

Travis glanced over the girl's head to Madame Helena, who had hurried over to issue last minute promises. He raised an eyebrow in inquiry, and Madame understood at once.

"She is very trying with the needles, but indeed, she does have the experience she speaks of. She is my niece. Foolish thing that she is, she did not wish to return with the Dubonniers to France, so I have kept her with me. She is a good girl. She would work hard."

Pleased with the girl's manner and fondness for Dale, Alicia eagerly awaited Travis's decision. Accustomed as she was to making her own decisions, it did not come easily to defer to someone else, but this morning's battle had taught her Travis had his own very certain opinions on many matters. If she were to make this marriage work, it would be best to at least enlist his thoughts on the matter.

After a rapid spate of French, negotiations were concluded and Anne-Marie was sent to pack her bags. Madame Helena promised to see her delivered with the first finished gowns in the evening.

As they left the dressmakers and roamed on to the haberdashers to replenish Travis's wardrobe, neither were aware of a sullen gaze marking their progress. Too caught up in the novelty of acting as man and wife, Alicia and Travis had eyes for no one but each other.

Garbed in new finery for the first time in weeks, free from the burden of child care for an hour or two with Anne-Marie's arrival, Alicia and Travis slowly walked the streets of New Orleans after dinner that night, simply enjoying the time together.

"Is there any city you do not know?" Alicia asked jealously as he pointed out the sprawling hotel where his father was staying.

"Philadelphia," he answered promptly. "Someday, you will have to show it to me."

Somewhat mollified by this prospect, Alicia wrapped both gloved hands around Travis's arm and strolled delightedly through the mild January night. Her pelisse kept out any chill the night air might hold, and Travis's proximity warmed her blood. The heated glance he bent to her now sent her temperature soaring even higher.

"How much longer must I wait before you admit that you are my wife?" Travis murmured huskily, his gaze roaming hungrily over her eyes and mouth, not daring to drop lower.

Heart pounding rapidly, Alicia struggled for some reply. She knew what he asked, and it was past time that she gave her consent. Perhaps he would learn to love her with time. Surely he did not find her totally lacking when he looked at her like that.

Slowly, softly, she offered what reply she could. "I am your wife, Travis, for better or worse. I do not want you to go away again."

The first part of her reply sent his hopes soaring, the latter brought them to an abrupt halt. Turning her gently toward home, Travis contemplated her meaning, knowing her past only too well.

"I am not your father, Alicia. I left because you did not want me, and I could not stay without hurting you. I thought that was what you wanted. I think I know better now, but I would hear it from you. I want to stay as your husband, not as a replacement for your father."

No one could guess the wicked mischief in blue eyes from the stately grace of Alicia's carriage as they moved down the street toward home. Eyes hooded, she murmured, "I am quite glad to hear that. My father sends me off to bed with a kiss on the cheek, and I was beginning to think you had decided to do the same."

Travis stopped in his tracks, forcing the people behind to eddy around them as he stared down into Alicia's composed features. Only her eyes gave her away, and the laughter and the love he found there demolished all restraint. Catching her up in his arms, Travis hugged her, his lips searching out the wicked mouth he had hungered for these past months.

His kiss sent Alicia's senses swirling, giving her no time to protest this public exhibition. Her hands flew around Travis's neck and wrapped themselves in his thick hair, while her heart pounded a wild tattoo against his chest. Her lips clung to his, drinking thirstily of his warm breath and intoxicating her with his masculine scent, while her body rejoiced in the strength and power of his embrace. She was back in his arms again, and nothing could part them now. The addiction was too strong to resist any longer.

Stunned by the ease of this surrender, Travis feared to let her go, but they were still some blocks from the house and he could not make love to her here in the middle of the street. Reluctantly he returned Alicia to the ground, ignoring the knowing grins around them.

Anxiously he searched her face. "You will not change your mind and attack me for my past transgressions before we reach the house? I can find us a room for the night right here if you think your resolve will waver before then."

Alicia laughed and lovingly stroked the high cheekbone of Travis's dark face. "You will have to take your chances. We cannot leave Anne-Marie alone with Dale all night, even if he is well behaved and consents to sleep the remainder of the evening."

"Who mentioned all night? I would settle for an hour. Just an hour. I can whisk you right up those stairs over there and—"

Giggling at his eagerness, Alicia caught his hand and turned toward home. "You can tell me what you mean to do on the way home. That should keep me from straying."

'No more complaints about the bed or my checkered past or my unromantic behavior?" Still astounded by his good fortune, Travis tested his limits.

"Oh, no, you go too far. I must have something to complain of. Your high-handed arrogance and bullying behavior is not enough. I prefer specifics."

Travis roared his laughter and hand to the small of her back, hurried her down the street. "Fine. Then you may complain of the way I unbutton your gown or my slowness in removing your garters or the number of times I intend to ravish you before dawn. That should be specific enough."

A shiver of pleasure coursed down Alicia's spine at the

combination of his touch and his words. Tonight would be
the wedding night they never had. Whatever doubts she
might still possess she intended to ignore. She loved Travis.
That should be enough for now.

A lamp shone in the parlor window as they hurried down
the narrow street toward the little house they had claimed.
Upstairs, a candle flickered in the nursery where Anne-
Marie and the babe slept. All appeared serene, and Alicia's
heart pounded faster as they approached the door.

The scream that split the night came so suddenly it nearly
rocked her backward. Travis reacted with the swiftness of
a man whose life depended on quickness of thought. Not
daring to leave Alicia alone, he half carried, half pushed her
into the house with him. Then leaving her with the lamp and
an iron poker from the fireplace, he dashed up the stairs in
the direction of the scream.

Hearing Anne-Marie's excited chatter, Alicia followed,
clutching the poker nervously. Dale's surprised cries urged
her on. Before she reached the landing, she could hear
Travis dashing down the backstairs to the kitchen and the
small garden leading into the alleyway. Fear began to take
the place of shock. Travis carried no weapon. If he chased
an intruder, he could be killed.

The little maid grasped her cotton robe and tried to
soothe the babe's cries at the same time. Relief flooded
Anne-Marie's face as Alicia scooped her son into her arms
and spoke to him softly, reducing the cries to sobbing hic-
cups. Responding to Alicia's questioning look, the maid
broke into hasty French, repeating what she had told Travis.
She had woke to find a man smelling of whiskey and holding
a candle in her bedroom. He had run out the back when she
screamed.

Wondering if the drunks of New Orleans were prone to
wandering in and out of houses, as the Indians were in St.
Louis, Alicia attempted to calm the frightened girl. Not
feeling secure until Travis returned, she made a pallet for
Anne-Marie next to the big bed in her chamber, and settled
Dale among the pillows in the bed with her. When Travis
returned, he could move them back to the nursery.

Travis did not return for some time. Finally losing the
intruder in shadowy, unfamiliar streets, he returned home
to find the lamp beside the bed guttering low, and his wife
sound asleep beside his son. The sight of the young maid

sleeping on the floor next to them smashed what few hopes he might have held of waking Alicia to announce his return and claim his reward. He discarded his coat and cravat and found a narrow spot among the covers in which to lie.

Lying beside her while she slept, feeling her soft breath against his neck, Travis felt the emptiness and the tension gradually slipping away, banished by the woman in his bed. Wanting more of this comfort, he gently pulled her into his arms, cradling her softness against his chest. The peace he found in just this action made him realize what he had missed—and what he had found. All his hopes suddenly coalesced into a single flame, a flame that would never die, no matter what the future held.

He had always fought for what he wanted, stalked his prey and conquered his foes and claimed his rewards as rights he had earned. He had learned to protect himself against rejection that way, but he had never learned to accept what was given willingly. Why couldn't he see that Alicia was a prize he could not win, a foe he could not, did not want to conquer? His mistake had been in thinking he had stalked and won Alicia, when in truth she had captured him. He didn't want her as a prize; he wanted her as a woman who gave of herself willingly, offered her love without fear or strings attached, offered as Alicia had tried, had he ever understood.

Gently, so as not to wake her, Travis kissed her brow and vowed to give her what he had not known existed until now. Perhaps he no longer deserved to be loved, but that would not prevent him from loving. He would give her England and pray that his chance would come again.

42

"IF MADAME HELENA has finished your gown, I mean to take you to a dance this evening," Travis stated calmly, throwing down his gloves and an assortment of cards on the foyer table as he returned home from his walk.

Alicia glanced up from her mending to stare at him in surprise. "A dance? But we don't know anyone here. And after last night, I could not think of leaving Dale and Anne-Marie alone."

"The invitations are right here." Travis dropped them in her lap. "And I have thought of that. It is a charity ball being held at the hotel. I have already taken two rooms. We will be able to go up and check on them as often as we like and they should be perfectly safe."

At the hotel, Alicia searched Travis's noncommittal expression with nervousness. His father stayed at a hotel. "We will have to send Anne-Marie around to tell her aunt to hurry. It will add to the cost of the gown." She made no mention of her fears. She had vowed to stay by his side. She would have to learn to deal with the British aristocracy when he returned to his proper home. She might as well begin now.

Travis smiled. "The cost is the least of my worries. My most pressing concern is how to keep you out of the potted plants long enough to meet my father."

"I'm sure you'll manage," Alicia responded wryly, hurriedly setting aside her mending. There were at least nine dozen things that must be done between now and then before she could be presented to anybody. Leave it to Travis to spring these things on her at the last possible moment. It would take every ounce of organization she possessed to prepare for the evening. She would worry about the night to come once it got here.

The moment arrived sooner than anticipated. A carriage carried them to the hotel, where Anne-Marie stared around her at the elegantly dressed assembly gathering in the lobby as Travis hustled them upstairs to their connecting rooms. Once the maid and her charge were settled, Travis relieved Alicia of her pelisse, throwing it across the bed he meant for them to share this night.

His hand came out to caress a perfectly placed curl shimmering in the candlelight along a creamy cheek. Her sapphire eyes rose to meet his, and the silver-blue silk dimmed in comparison. His hand traveled to the diamond earrings dangling from delicate lobes, and he smiled.

"I should have worn mine. Would you have disowned me?"

The jest eased her tension, and Alicia smiled involuntarily. In his properly wrapped cravat, white embroidered waistcoat, and elegantly blue coat and trousers, Travis looked the part of wealthy viscount without fault. His abandoned gold earring would have portrayed his true nature more effectively.

"I will give you one of mine," she offered, reaching laughingly for the bauble.

Relieved that she was not fooled by the disguise he donned, Travis caught her hand and kissed the palm. "For once, for the sake of peace, I will try not to shock. Are you ready?"

"If you stay close." Alicia wrapped her fingers around Travis's strong arm and felt prepared to meet the world. Whatever his faults might be, he always gave her confidence. Although the skirt of her gown clung sinfully to every line and curve as she moved, and the bodice came so low she feared to breathe deeply, just a look from Travis made her feel as beautiful as the Empress Josephine.

She could feel his pride in her as Travis escorted her down the curving stairway, his tall frame hovering protectively close as gazes below turned up to stare. The blatant admiration in the eyes of the men brought a slight flush to Alicia's cheeks, but it only enhanced her appearance as Travis led her through the crowd of strangers. Black eyes flashed with wicked delight as the well-bred gentlemen of New Orleans were forced to turn away in disappointment, for Alicia made it plain her interest lay only in her husband.

Intent in avoiding the stares of the men around her,

Alicia did not notice the company Travis led her toward
until they were almost upon them. Feeling the muscles of
his arm tense, she glanced up, and had to gulp back a cry of
astonishment.

Standing with what appeared to be the remains of a
reception line was an awkwardly tall, dark-haired gentleman
of craggy visage but urbane air whom Alicia recognized at
once. Startled, her gaze swept from this polished gentleman
to Travis's handsome, hawklike features, and back again.
Why had she never seen the resemblance? Travis might
have much of his mother's coloring, but he had no choice.
His father was as dark and fiercely featured as he.

Lord Royster looked up to discover their approach at this
same instant. His recognition of his son came immediately,
but the slow realization of the identity of the ravishing lady
on his son's arm caused his mouth to fall open. The woman
at his side noted this sudden gap in polite manners, and she
too turned to stare at the approaching young couple.

Not understanding the excitement rippling through his
bride as they stopped before his father and stepmother,
Travis made a polite bow. Before he could offer greetings
and introductions, however, Lord Royster pounded him
heartily on the back.

"My word, Max, I should never have doubted that you
would pluck from any less than the top of the trees. Alicia
Stanford! Why in the name of all that is righteous did that
rascal Scott not tell me you had filched Philadelphia's most
precious jewel? Don't ever tell me you found the likes of
this one out in the wilderness?"

With that astounding greeting Lord Royster claimed Alicia's hand, bowed politely over it, then offering a laughing
curse, he hugged her heartily, much to the enjoyment of the
crowd in their vicinity.

Alicia returned the hug, then embarrassed at her forward-
ness, stepped back to cling to Travis's arm. At his sardonically lifted black brow, she hastened to explain. "Lord Royster
has always been a guest of Aunt Clara's when he is in
Philadelphia. I have known him since I was a very little girl.
He used to bring me the most outrageous gifts . . ." She
threw the offender a belligerent look. "Oyster eggs you
called them! I could never have accepted pearls, but you
told me they were oyster eggs and I could hatch them if I
wore them! You are worse than Travis!"

At this irate proclamation, even Travis and Lady Royster had to laugh, and the tension of this meeting began to dissipate.

"So that is how you spend your time when you come here?" Pleasantly well rounded but shorter than Alicia, Lady Royster had lovely golden eyes to match her locks. Obviously much younger than her husband, she appeared devoted to him, and once advised of Alicia's background, she opened up warmly. "Flirting with little girls is a dangerous pastime."

Grinning widely, Travis murmured a wicked "Amen" in agreement, while his father beamed with pride. "Not so little now, is she? Splendid woman you've turned out to be. Where's your father? I suppose he wants the credit for this match, does he?"

Before Alicia's honest tongue could trip them up, Travis interceded smoothly. "He too is only recently wed, and thought to get us out from under foot by seeing us married and out of his house. He sends his greetings and apologizes for not making the journey. There is some possibility that he might have a son, at last."

Travis turned his grin to Alicia at her gasp. "Did you think Letitia would allow you to be sole heir to the Stanford fortune?"

"You wretch! Why didn't you tell me? Why does nobody tell me these things?"

Laughter smothered awkward explanations and eased the path between father and son. Lord Royster gazed with pride and affection upon the man his eldest son had become. The boy had become a man any father would be proud of, and he had chosen a wife who would make people sit up and take notice. Gazing fondly on the handsome young couple, he changed the topic to one uppermost in his mind.

"I've only had one letter from Scott since he found you. Said you could not travel immediately due to the birth of your son. Is he here? Did you bring him with you?"

With a straight face Travis assured his father, "Unfortunately, we had to leave Scott somewhere north of Natchez. I'm certain he will follow any day now."

Alicia had to bite her tongue, and meeting Lady Royster's eyes, they both rolled their gazes heavenward. It was no wonder father and son never got along. They were too damned much alike.

"Dale is asleep in one of the guest rooms upstairs. Our maid is with him now, but I will be happy to show him off anytime you ask." Since Travis seemed determined not to utter a sensible word, Alicia answered for him.

"Dale?" Lord Royster lifted his eyebrows in inquiry, directing the question to his son.

Maintaining an impassive demeanor, Travis explained, "Delaney Rochester Travis. We call him Dale."

"Delaney?" Lord Royster looked pained. "Is this another jest?"

Travis shrugged merrily. "No, just the American way of recognizing a title for what it is worth. Alicia is not fully convinced I am who I claim to be."

That puzzled the earl even further, but quite satisfied by the evening's events, he did not try to pry the entire tale from them on the spot. With the courtliness of another era, he bowed gallantly over Alicia's hand and asked for a dance. Not to be outdone, Travis offered for his stepmother's hand, and the two couples swept out onto the floor.

Relieved by the happy outcome of events, enchanted by the music and the company, Alicia danced in an euphoric haze. Knowing Travis's dark gaze followed jealously wherever she went, she smiled blindingly, happiness rising in her like the bubbles in champagne. Perhaps Travis didn't love her, but he never looked at another woman, and her confidence rose another notch. If everything would work out as well as this meeting, she would teach him to love her by the time they sailed for England.

Each time a dance ended, Alicia was surrounded by eager young men begging introductions from Lord and Lady Royster and the other sponsors of the ball. To reach his wife, Travis had to shove through the throng, but the blaze of happiness in Alicia's eyes as she lifted them to him eased his temper. Cries of "Foul!" followed their progress as Travis snatched her out from under the noses of her suitors and carried her to the dance floor. He'd been more than patient long enough. Tonight was his.

As the orchestra struck up a waltz, Alicia melted into Travis's arms without reserve, moving with the music and his motion as if they were all of one piece. She could feel the muscles of his arm tighten around her waist as the tempo increased, and the animal grace of his long legs guided her with superb instinct. Aware of the pounding of his heart close to hers, she dared look upwards and found herself captured by the heat of his stare.

"Do you have any idea how much I love you?" Travis demanded fiercely, his hand tightening its grip on Alicia's silken waist as he felt her start of surprise.

Incredulous, not believing she had heard him rightly, Alicia blinked and grasped for words. "I don't believe I have heard the subject mentioned," she admitted haltingly. "When should I have taken notice?"

A wolfish grin crossed Travis's face as he watched his elegant wife's discomposure. "I daresay the very first time I saw the delicate lady dressed in black dismissing an entire keelboat crew for bad behavior, but you will have to forgive my ignorance of the exact moment. I have never been in love before."

Feeling her breath catch in her throat and her heart playing skip rope, Alicia could scarcely tear her fascinated gaze from his. "What makes you think you love me now? Perhaps it is just a bad case of indigestion. Or too much champagne."

"I have had indigestion and champagne before," Travis intoned solemnly. "They did not make me feel as if I own the world or spin me in such a turmoil that I don't know if my feet are touching the ground. It has taken me a long time to admit it to myself, so I don't expect you to accept it all at once. Just keep it in mind when I behave too outrageously; it's all for the love of you."

Spirits soaring, Alicia slid her hand to the place where Travis's hair fell down over his immaculate cravat, rubbing her finger against the exposed flesh of his neck. The immediate effect was to find herself so closely entrapped in his embrace that she could scarcely move and embarrassingly aware of the sway of his narrow hips against hers.

"I think I fell in love with your gold earring first," Alicia replied inanely, but Travis's response was instantaneous.

With a crow of delight he stopped in the middle of the dance floor to crush her against him. Then, to the delight and shock of everyone within sight, he bent his head so that his mouth could claim hers with all the passion and happiness he had long suppressed.

The sight of the tall, handsome couple locked in tight embrace upon the dance floor sent heads turning throughout the ballroom. But when the orchestra struck the final

notes and the young lord danced his lady out of the crowd
and toward the stairs, a ragged male cheer shook the chandelier. Time was too short for young lovers to waste on
holding hands in public when there was a bed to be shared
elsewhere. More than one couple disappeared in a similar
manner that night.

Lifting her narrow skirt, Alicia started up the stairway,
Travis's possessive hand burning a hole in the small of her
back as he half pushed, half guided her upwards. Watching
the sway of slender hips beneath the slippery silk, Travis
groaned his impatience, and with decisiveness, caught her
by the waist and swung her into his arms.

"Travis! Everyone is watching!" Alicia buried her burning
cheeks against his shoulder as she caught sight of the laughing looks below.

"Let them. There will be no doubt in their minds whose
woman you are. And by dawn there should be no doubt in
yours."

The throaty rumble of this promise sent shivers through
Alicia's middle, and she clung desperately to Travis's shoulders as he opened the door of their room and carried her in.
Without putting her down, he kicked the door closed, and
his mouth swooped down to fasten upon hers once more.

Sucked in and spun around by the whirlwind of his passion, Alicia found herself nearly drowning. Her lips parted
beneath Travis's hungry demands, and the onslaught of his
invasion swept her along.

Travis tumbled her on the bed. Stripping off his coat and
flinging it aside, he quickly joined her. His hand slid from
the slender curve of her hip to the fullness of her breast
while his mouth returned to plunder hers.

As his hand and mouth worked their magic, Alicia's palms
roamed the breadth of Travis's shoulders, then traveled
downward to explore the supple movement of his chest.
Sliding her fingers beneath the opening of his shirt, she
succeeded in unfastening it enough to feel the rough fur of
his chest against her hand.

The fragile silk of Alicia's gown slid from her shoulders
beneath Travis's questing fingers, and she gasped as his
hand came in contact with her bare breast. Not satisfied
with this small touch, Travis quickly located the bodice
fastenings and released them, pushing silk and chemise together to Alicia's waist.

The chill of the room did not reach her as Travis lowered his head to kiss the soft curves thus exposed. His weight pressed her down into the mattress and she circled his neck and arched upward, excitement shooting through her at this touch.

Desire burned too heatedly to linger long. Raising her hips, Travis drew off her remaining clothes. Alicia cried out as his lips followed the path of her clothes, and she struggled to remove the last barriers between them.

With a laugh of triumph at this show of her eagerness, Travis sat up and tugged off his shoes, though Alicia hampered his efforts by running her fingers under his shirt and tickling his ribs. He caught her and pulled her over his lap, finding her kiss-swollen lips and tumbling backward until she lay over him, her breasts pressing against his half-fastened shirt. Alicia quickly undid the rest of it and ran her hands over the hard musculature of his chest, eliciting a gasp of shock from him as she kissed a hardened nipple.

Travis dug his hands into her upswept hair and sent all the pins flying with a tug that brought her lips back to his. "Now tell me it is my earring that you love, vixen," he muttered against her mouth as his lips laid claim to hers once more.

"Your earring and your mouth and your son and your boneheadedness," Alicia agreed as his kiss whispered across her lips and up into her hair while his hands played erotic games against her skin.

"Fie on you, woman, for not telling me sooner. I'll make you pay for this, you know." With those words Travis flipped her back to the mattress and stood to remove the remainder of his clothing.

Wearing only garters and stockings, Alicia watched him boldly. Free of the confinement of tight trousers, Travis did not even bother to remove his shirt before falling back into the open arms waiting for him. It had been too long to delay with the niceties.

Alicia cried out in joy and surprise as he entered her without further ado. Within seconds she was riding high on the swiftness of his thrusts, and the world outside this searing sea of heat no longer existed. When he reached the apex of her being, Travis struck his claim, and Alicia exploded with the intensity of his possession, her body quaking and quivering as he dipped again and again into the depths of her soul.

Travis covered her cries with his kiss, his hands searching out the soft purchases they had ached so long to claim. Once would never be enough, and as he grew hard and strong within her again, he moved gently against her hips, teasing her with his need.

"Travis, you cannot!" Shocked as much by her response as his recovery, Alicia tried to wriggle free.

"Oh, but I can, all night and all day." With that warning Travis rolled on his back and carried her with him, holding her firmly in place so she could not escape his impalement. "Just think of all the time we have lost, Blue Eyes, and resign yourself to a lifetime of catching up."

As he caught her hips and pressed them downward, Alicia learned the folly of thinking she could rid herself of this addiction. Her need for him came flooding back stronger than before, and she surrendered wantonly to the pleasure he forced upon her.

The need for him surpassed any reservations that remained.

43

LYING BESIDE Travis in the soft glow of dawn, Alicia curled closer to his warmth, despairing the time lost for listening to her head instead of her heart. Travis might possess the nature of an untamed beast, but she understood now that he did not intentionally hurt her. She might never understand the violence with which he protected what was his, but she would have to learn to accept it. To live without him had become unthinkable.

"Do that again and I assure you, you will be ravished before you have time to protest," Travis muttered thickly as Alicia daringly explored the length of his body with her fingertips.

Propping herself up on one elbow, Alicia gazed down at his closed eyelids and the relaxed line of his mouth and could not resist a good-morning kiss atop his nose. "Protest? Not I. But your son will wake the dead should I linger longer."

Travis slowly lifted one eyelid to peer at the disheveled temptress leaning over him. Noting the liquid warmth of azure eyes, he sighed with satisfaction and closed his eye again. "I thought, p'raps, I'd died and gone to heaven last night, but I can see you're not an angel after all. Angels wear more clothes than that."

Giving a gasp of outrage, Alicia swatted him with her pillow. Travis instantly pinned her to the bed and began to tickle her, until they were rolling among the bed covers, ruining what remained of the bed's original tidiness.

A knock on the connecting door returned them to propriety, and Alicia slid hastily from Travis's eager grasp. Grabbing a robe, she made some attempt to straighten her tangled tresses while Travis groped for sheets with which to cover himself.

The day slipped away without control after that. A message arrived from Lord Royster commanding their presence—and Dale's—at once. Suitable clothes had to be sent for. Alicia nervously had Anne-Marie rearrange her hair half a dozen times before declaring herself satisfied. Dale had to be properly adorned in his best gown. And Travis simply watched the confusion with a jaded eye. He knew the import of the summons and was in no way eager to meet it.

The interview went more smoothly than expected. Dale became the focus of attention. The mention of the loss of the Roysters' son brought instant sympathy from Alicia. The assumption that Travis would now return to England to take his rightful place went unspoken but undenied by anyone. In the event of Lord Royster's illness or death, someone had to take the responsibility for the large estates, a young wife, and two little girls. Better Travis than an indigent second cousin with the brains of a turkey, as the earl quite succinctly put it over lunch.

Watching Alicia as his father spoke, Travis contested none of his father's assumptions. For the first time since spring Alicia appeared happy and content. She laughed and talked with Lady Royster with more animation than he had ever seen in her. This was her natural element: surrounded by the warmth and comforts of a gracious home and well educated, well mannered people of her own kind. He owed her the right to live as she had been accustomed. In time he would grow used to it, too.

They returned to the townhouse that afternoon, preferring the privacy to the public attention of Lord Royster's suite. Alicia sighed with relief as she sought the solitude of the bedroom while Anne-Marie tucked the fretful babe to bed in the other chamber. It had been a long day, and although delighted with her new in-laws, she had much to come to terms with before accepting the new role Travis's past demanded of her. She needed time to think.

Travis found her standing in the center of the room, staring blankly out the window, her coat and hat discarded upon the bed, but no other semblance of unpacking in evidence.

He came up from behind her and circled her waist with

his hands, pressing a kiss to her temple. "Do your thoughts rate a penny?"

Alicia smiled and leaned gratefully into his embrace. "I believe I am too tired for thought. Perhaps, like Dale, I need a nap."

Concerned, Travis turned her so he could see her face. Shadows underlay her eyes and she seemed paler than she should be. He stroked her forehead and finding no fever, he concurred with her assessment. "You have done too much, too soon. Dr. Farrar will be furious with me. Lie down while the little monster sleeps and get some rest."

When he would help her with the buttons of her gown, Alicia sent him a mischievous look. "You had best go on about whatever business you are itching to get to or I will get no rest and you will accomplish nothing. Anne-Marie can help me."

Travis caught her look, and with a wry grin lifted his hands from her shoulders. "I agreed too eagerly, didn't I? Very well, I will be off, but make certain you rest. I cannot promise I will be so easily rid of tonight."

He kissed her lips lightly, just enough to warm them and leave them yearning for more, before striding rapidly from the room. Alicia watched him go with swelling love and pride. It seemed impossible to conceive that a man like Travis would even look at her, no less harbor any strong affection for her. She had thought him invulnerable to such weak emotions, but she had been wrong about many things. There was nothing weak about the love she felt for him. It burned bright and hard, and flamed higher with each passing day. Could she possibly believe that he felt the same for her?

After she woke from her nap, Alicia felt more confident than ever about the path she had chosen. She loved St. Louis and her father and Becky and Auguste and their lovely home, but she loved Travis more. It would be hard to slip into the role of useless socialite once again, but for Travis, she could do it. She would be the grandest Lady Delaney London had ever seen. Let the arrogant British see what an American can do.

Pleased with these thoughts, Alicia sent the little maid out to the market for some fresh vegetables for dinner while she searched the kitchen for ingredients for a pie. She would have Travis come home to a meal he could enjoy in the privacy of their home, where they could adjourn shortly after to the big bed upstairs.

Dale lay in his cradle in the sunshine from the window, cooing contentedly in accompaniment to his mother's singing. Rolling her sleeves up and covering her gown with an overlarge apron she had found in the cupboard, Alicia began to work the butter into the flour. She had seldom been allowed in a kitchen long enough to enjoy the pleasure of creating something on her own, but she had learned the knack these last months and used it willingly now. In due time she would be banished from the kitchen again. It was best to make the most of what freedom she had now.

Engrossed in her work, the song on her lips concealing all else, Alicia did not hear the sound of the front latch opening. Not until Edward leaned against the kitchen door frame was she even aware of another presence.

Her heart stumbled to a halt, and her fingers knotted in the ball of dough as she recognized the sardonic smile on the intruder's face. It had been a long time. Except for that brief glimpse of him on the tavern floor, Alicia had not seen Edward since that day he had torn away her pride and self-respect and reduced her to a quivering madwoman. She would not have recognized him but for that cruel smile. She would remember that to her dying day.

"Get out," she ordered firmly, without a qualm. They had nothing to discuss, and she had no sympathy for his unhealthy pallor and disreputable clothes. He deserved whatever had happened to him since she had seen him last. As he had grown weaker, she had grown stronger. Travis had taught her courage.

Edward just laughed. "Is that any way to treat an old friend? Living with savages has seriously rusted your manners, Alicia, my love."

"Out, Edward, before I scream bloody blue hell and bring my savage husband running. You wouldn't like that, would you, Edward? You can't bully Travis as easily as you did me."

Edward made a clucking noise with his tongue and folded his arms complacently across his chest. "Such language! Your mother must be turning in her grave. There's no need to scream, Alicia. I watched while everyone left. Your husband, if that's what he is, is nowhere within hearing. I owe him one, but I'm not here to even scores. Is that my son?" He nodded toward the swinging cradle. Contented coos had turned to fretful whines when Alicia stopped singing.

"Your son?" Alicia stared at him with incredulity. She scarcely knew the man who stood there now. Eyes that had once watched her with admiration now appeared hard and cold. The elegance with which he had once carried himself had dissipated into a casual slump, and his sardonic smile held a hint of petulance. She loathed the very sight of him, and fear crawled along her skin.

"Don't play the innocent with me. Beauchamps have a long history of getting their wives with child on their wedding nights. If you hadn't been so damned mule-headed, we could have been married before anyone guessed we had jumped the gun a little. You didn't have to go looking for savages to give the child a name. I was ready and willing."

"We have no child, Edward." Alicia said the words slowly and clearly, but she could tell by the gleam in his eye that he did not believe her. As he straightened himself and stepped closer, she caught the smell of cheap liquor, and her fear multiplied. If he could rape her when completely sober, she did not wish to consider what he could do while drunk.

"I'll take you back to Philadelphia where you belong, Alicia." His hand reached out to touch the gold locket about her throat. "This little bauble will pay our passage. Do you have others, Alicia? I would prefer to travel in style."

Hurriedly, she wiped her hands on a towel and unfastened the necklace. Holding it out to him, she said, "Here, take it. You can travel comfortably on its worth. Now go, before Travis comes."

He slid the chain into his pocket, but his hand did not release her shoulder. "We will be gone before he returns. Get the child, Alicia. My father will be quite pleased when I return with both you and a child."

His whiskey-laden breath seared her cheek and Alicia turned her head away from the icy look in his eyes. His fingers bit painfully into her shoulder, and she felt her courage fading. She had no strength against him, but she would rather die than submit to that fate again. If only there were some way . . .

She caught a glimpse of the knife she had been using to chop apples and she backed away from Edward, closer to the one weapon she possessed. "The child is Travis's. He would hunt you into hell before he allowed you to take him."

A feral gleam flickered behind cold eyes. "Don't lie to me, Alicia. You were carrying my child when you left Philadelphia. If that one isn't mine, where is it?"

She couldn't reach the knife. Edward's other hand caught her hair, twisting her head painfully as he forced her to look at him. She saw the danger in his eyes but did not understand the implications. She wished only to hurt him, as he had hurt her.

"It's dead, Edward. I'll bear no bastard of yours, ever," she spat in his face.

The blow came so swiftly, Alicia had no time to prepare for it. Pain shot through her jaw, and she stumbled backward against the table. Blood trickled into her mouth, and she stared in dazed surprise as Edward advanced upon the cradle.

"Then we'll even the score, Alicia. A babe for a babe. Why should his brat live if mine does not?"

Alicia screamed as her hand reached desperately for the knife.

Lord Royster glanced up with mixed annoyance and affection as his son's long strides grew more rapid the closer they came to the townhouse. Maximillian had never been an easy person to know. His mother's serenity had seemed sullenness in the boy. His volatile likes and dislikes had disrupted many a conversation. His opinions had been contrary to all of polite society's on almost every subject. He had terrified houseguests by his ability to appear and disappear without a sound, and he had been the terror of the younger set with his swift temper and faster fists. All this and more had built a barrier between them until the birth of a second son had come as a relief to both. A particularly violent quarrel soon sent the lad furiously back to his American home. The young viscount had never relented, never apologized, never offered one word of his health or well-being in all these years. It had taken a woman to make a man out of him. Lord Royster had a lot to thank Alicia for, but his son's eagerness to return to her was about to wear him down.

"Have pity on an old man, Max, and slow down. We should have hired a carriage."

Travis glanced at his father with surprise, then slowed his steps. "I'm sorry. My mind was elsewhere. Alicia will be delighted to hear Scott has arrived safely, but I'm not certain the rest of your surprise will be greeted with the same enthusiasm. For a woman with her upbringing, she seems supremely oblivious to class distinctions."

Royster grunted in disbelief. "I know her mother's family too well. Snobs to a first degree. When we let it be known she is descendant to both the Neville and Clarendon lines, she will be accepted by royalty. American, indeed! It is all folly. Her parents were British citizens when they were born and so is she. It is time somebody informed her of it. I don't give a groat for most of the hobble-de-hoy who call themselves Americans, but I daresay nearly every last one of them have British blood in them. This talk of war is ridiculous. We can't have it. Like brother fighting brother. Family squabble, that."

Travis let his father ramble on and listened with amusement. Perhaps the earl had enough power to put an end to British blockades and navy impressments, but he knew nothing of the American mind. They wanted revenge, and they would have it. Right or wrong, war was nearly inevitable.

When his father rambled to a halt, Travis merely shrugged his shoulders. "Nevertheless, Father, Alicia married an Indian keelboat captain, not a viscount. The fact that she is a scion of two noble houses will not impress her, as Scott seems to believe it ought."

The earl stared at his handsome son with disbelief. "Keelboat captain! You had the audacity to pass yourself off as a keelboat captain and still court a lady like Alicia Stanford? Are you out of your mind?"

"That's what I was—a keelboat captain. A damned good one, I might add. This title you would force on me means so little here that Chester Stanford didn't see fit to inform Alicia of it. Probably for very good reason. When she saw it on the marriage documents, she very near murdered me. The British don't have a savory reputation in these parts." Travis stopped a strolling flower vendor and bought a bouquet of early daffodils. Alicia had been thrilled at the March ones in St. Louis. Wait until she saw these. They would excite her more than news of her trunks or her ancestry.

"Title I *force* on you?" Royster wasn't certain which of his son's outrageous statements he wished to protest first, but this one stuck in his craw the longest. "That title has a long and venerable heritage. Your ancestors fought hard to give you the freedoms you shrug off so lightly. That title gives you honor and wealth and a position in society because of what they did for you. Have you no respect?"

They turned the corner and the townhouse came in sight. Travis's strides became noticeably longer. "You forget my other ancestors, sir," he answered calmly, his gaze focusing eagerly on the house ahead. "They fought nobly and with honor, too, but I am scorned for that heritage. I prefer to earn my own wealth and honor, but I will be satisfied to have won Alicia. Just do not press me too hard on the subject of respect—"

A scream rose and fell and echoed through the street. Travis's long stride instantly broke into a run for the few remaining lengths to his home. He should have seen that the door was ajar. He was getting soft already.

Alicia's hands had found the knife and her fingers wrapped vengefully around the wooden hilt as Edward tried to get past her to the wailing infant in the cradle on the floor. Terrified and furious, she had no concern for anything other than protecting her son. She held the knife clasped protectively in front of her, holding Edward in abeyance.

Edward heard the slam of furious boots across the uncarpeted floor and knew it was now or never. He dived for the knife at the same time as the kitchen door flew open.

The swinging door threw Edward off balance, and Travis's abrupt entrance diverted Alicia's shocked attention at the same time. Still clinging to the upturned knife, she stepped backward but not soon enough. Unbalanced, grabbing for the weapon, Edward tripped and fell forward. The knife swiftly glanced off his collarbone and into his throat.

Death was instantaneous, but Alicia's screams did not die so rapidly. As blood spurted from the man crumpling at her feet to splatter across the floor and over her apron, she clung to the knife and continued to scream, until Travis stepped over the body and slapped the weapon from her hand.

She collapsed into his arms then and sobbing, allowed him to half carry her from the room, not even noticing the scandalized expression on Lord Royster's face as they passed, scarcely aware that he existed. She shivered and could not stop, the tremors shaking her so violently that Travis wrapped his coat around her as he led her toward the stairs. She felt as if screams were tearing her throat apart, but Travis murmured soothing words in her ears and drowned the silent cries. He held her tight, kept her safe, and guided her into a room full of sunlight. Absurdly, he still held a hand full of brilliant yellow flowers, and Alicia's gaze fastened on them, blocking out all else.

"They're beautiful," she said wonderingly, touching her finger to the velvety texture of one petal.

Worriedly, Travis handed her the bouquet and began to strip his coat and the bloodied apron from her shoulders. "Daffodils. For you," he replied, humoring her.

"I killed him, didn't I?"

Azure eyes turned upward, piercing Travis with the depth of their pain and anguish. He had to take that pain away, drive it off now before it destroyed her and everything they had, but hearing the sound of the door and other feet below, Travis had to take a chance on leaving her alone. The wail of an infant drifted hauntingly from the kitchen.

"Let me get Dale for you," he murmured hastily, avoiding the question.

When he returned with the child a short time later, Alicia was arranging the flowers in a vase on the vanity. Her gown lay in a heap upon the floor, but she maintained the decency of keeping her chemise. She swung around at Travis's entrance, the panic still in her eyes, but she reached normally for the crying child.

"He is hungry. I must feed him." She held out her arms.

"Fine. Get into bed where you will be warm and I will give him to you."

Travis watched warily as she obeyed him. Once he saw her safely tucked beneath the covers, he handed her the soggy infant. Alicia gazed at him reproachfully and pointed to the diapers on the dresser.

Once the infant was dry and nursing contentedly, Travis sat on the bed and began to remove his boots. Alicia watched him with curiosity.

"What are you doing?"

"Joining you." Not bothering to remove his clothes, Travis climbed into bed beside her, enclosing her in his arms while the babe suckled, undisturbed, at her breast.

He could feel her tension, feel the shivers involuntarily rocking through her, and forced himself to remember the first time he had killed a man. He had been younger than she, but he had also been drunk. He had vomited all over the floor immediately afterward. Alicia did not have that advantage. She said nothing as he pulled her head down on his shoulder and made a cushion of his chest.

"It was an accident," he stated calmly.

"I killed him." The words came out cold and unemotional. "He was going to hurt Dale and I killed him."

That sent a ripple of shock through Travis and he clenched her tighter. The bruise on her face had spoken of self-defense. It had never occurred to him that the bastard would threaten a child.

He sighed and stroked her hair. He had no gift for explaining. What could he say to take away the pain? "You were defending the one you loved. You could not have done less."

"I killed him," she insisted.

"He is dead, yes," Travis partially agreed, "but you did not kill him. It was an accident. But if he had not died, I would have killed him. Can you understand that, Alicia?"

Alicia shook her head, not negatively, but trying to comprehend. "I am trying, Travis, but it's too horrible." She glanced down at the warm, fat, healthy babe in her arms. Edward would have killed him without even thinking about it. Instead, the knife had gone into Edward. There was no logic in it. "I couldn't let him kill Dale."

"No. Nor could I let him harm you. It is not something you think about, Alicia. It is something you do. It happens without thought. The instinct is there. Stronger in some than others, perhaps, but there. If you love someone, they are a part of you, and you will fight to protect them."

A wary light rose to Alicia's eyes as she turned them to meet Travis's troubled gaze. "The time in the tavern with Edward, you were protecting me?"

Travis sighed and kissed her eyelids, closing her accusing eyes. "Yes, I was protecting you, just as I tried to protect you from those rogues on the river. Although if you had questioned me then, I would have been too blind and hard-headed to admit I did it out of love. If Edward had been in that cabin with us when you lost the child, I would have killed him then. As it was, he made the mistake of coming after you. I knew what it would do to you, and I tried to stop him. I had not realized then that love is not ruled by reason. If I had known this would happen, I would have killed him then."

"Do not try to pacify me with lies, Travis. Edward is dead because I killed him. He would have been just as dead if you killed him, but it would not have been out of love. If you had loved me, you never would have left me."

Travis heard the sob in her voice and clenched her tighter. She had not cried since he had come home. Everything was kept bundled up tight and hard somewhere in the cellars of her soul, and she would not let loose of it for a minute. It was not natural, but he had not known how to touch her, how to free her from the heavy weight she insisted on carrying. This one more burden would crush her if he would let it. He could not. She had to let go sometime.

"I left you because I loved you and could not bear to harm you. I thought you would be happier without me. I thought it would be easy. I thought I could just walk away and never return and everyone would be the better for it. My God, Alicia, you don't know what a fool I am. Even when I could not touch another woman for wanting you, I would not admit your hold on me. I've walked away from family and home before, but I could not stay away from you. I heard of gold in Mexico and thought I would try that for a while, but I didn't want gold. I wanted you. I had to trick myself into returning, tell myself it was the possibility of a child that made me go back, not my need for you. But when I found you and thought I had lost you forever . . ."

Travis's voice broke, unable to find the words to describe his despair that horrifying night. His arms reached out to circle both mother and child, clasping them as if he would never let go. A tear slid down a bronzed cheek, coming to rest on Alicia's hair. She had to understand.

It was then he noticed the sobs shaking her shoulders, the

desperate struggle to hold back tears that kept her silent. Gently removing the sleeping infant from her arms and placing him safely in the bed's center, Travis cradled Alicia against his chest.

"Cry, Alicia. It is nothing to be ashamed of. Cry and let the grief out. Hit me, if you like. Curse me, for I deserve it. But then, let me kiss you and let us start anew."

She cried. She cried until her voice shook and her breath came in short bursts and she could cry no longer. She cried until all the tragedy, all the misery, all the festering madness that had been stored inside her since that long ago day in Philadelphia escaped, and the wound began to heal. And then she lay against Travis's strong chest and slept.

44

SHE HEARD the angry voices below, and sleepily she sat up in bed. The last rays of daylight still played along the walls and she frowned, not understanding why she was in bed.

Sharp words caught her attention again and she reached for a robe. The absence of the infant in the bed returned memory with a jolt, and Alicia's stomach lurched violently. The urge to give in to the nausea was overcome by her panic for Dale. What was happening below?

Jerking on the robe, she ran in stockinged feet to the door. The voices rose clearer in the hall: Travis and Lord Royster. Glancing in the nursery, she spied Anne-Marie rocking the babe, and she gave a sigh of relief. Her footsteps continued to carry her down the hall.

"The scandal will be impossible to control!" Royster raged. "I have done all I can, but too many people know of it. I can keep her from being arrested, but I can't keep people from talking. It won't do, I tell you!"

"Don't you understand anything? She's my wife, damn it, and I don't care if she murders a dozen bastards like that one! I would have done it myself if I had arrived sooner."

"That would have been easier to deal with. A man is expected to defend his family, but ladies do not wield knives with deadly intent. No one will understand."

"You expected her to faint, perhaps?" The sarcasm traveled clearly up the stairs. "This isn't London, Father. Women who faint don't last long out here."

"I'm just asking you to let the scandal die down some. Come back with me and leave Alicia here for a while. Once society grows accustomed—"

Alicia's appearance on the stairway halted the conversation. With the pins loosened, her hair hung in disheveled strands about her face. Her fingers clasped the velvet robe at the neck, but it was obvious she wore very little beneath it. It was her eyes, however, that caught the earl's attention and held it. They flamed furiously, like blue lightning.

She spoke calmly, with an authority that brooked no argument. "I killed a man to save your grandson, sir. If that makes me a murderer, then I am a murderer, and I will have to live with it for the rest of my life. But I don't have to live with the whispers and the lies and the innuendos of an arrogant, antiquated society. I want to teach. I want to feel like I create my own destiny. I'm tired of fulfilling the destiny society assigns to me. I'm returning to St. Louis and my home, where I belong. I'll sign any documents you wish granting Travis an annulment."

Without even looking back to see how Travis accepted this decision, Alicia raised her chin and swung around to go back up the stairs. Travis had told her some people acted on instinct more than others. She might as well finish the day as it had begun, without thought.

Below, a wicked grin began to play upon the corners of Travis's mouth as he watched his father's reaction. Alicia's words had filled him with relief and a great sense of freedom. His father registered only shock. There was no time like the present to clear the air.

"I have no intention of annulling my marriage for you or for anyone else, you realize," Travis stated calmly.

Lord Royster's shocked gaze swung back to his son. Before he could reply, Travis handed him the final blow.

"The only reason I consented to return to England was because I thought that was what Alicia wanted. You will have other sons. This one belongs here."

Travis started for the stairs, but his father grabbed his shoulder, forcing him to meet his panicked stare. "You can't do this! You can't be so cruel as to allow your sisters to go homeless should I die. They need you, if you will not consider my needs."

"That time could be many years from now. Name me your heir in the event no other son is born if you wish. I'll not neglect my duties, but I'll not neglect my wife or son either. My address will be St. Louis should you need me."

Without another word Travis ran up the stairs in pursuit of Alicia.

He found her in the nursery, holding their son. When he

burst through the door, she raised startled eyes to meet his, and a slow smile formed on her lips as he spoke.

"We're going home, Alicia. That south field still needs clearing, and I know where I can get one hell of a stallion for stud duty this spring. You reckon Becky's forgotten how to make those jam cakes yet?"

"No, I reckon she hasn't." Mocking his slang and ignoring the ten thousand questions and objections she should raise, Alicia read the happiness in Travis's eyes and stepped into his welcoming embrace.

They were going home, at last.

Epilogue

September 1812

HOMASINEE SMILED HAPPILY as her eldest toddled after his father into the woods. Her gaze lifted to meet that of the tall man beside her.

Travis glanced down into her serene brown face and asked, "Are you happy?"

She knew what he asked, and she smiled away his anxiety. "There is war all around us, but there is peace in my heart. And you?"

Travis stared after his cousin, not really seeing him as he put together the words. "I cannot fight my brothers or my countrymen, but I cannot join them, either. The war is over different ways of living, and I am content with mine as it is. I will defend my right to live as I am, if I must, but I will not attack others for theirs. Someday men must learn to stop fighting to settle quarrels."

A sly smile crept around Homasinee's lips. "Lonetree speaks with tongue of happy man. Only the discontented fight."

Travis laughed at this homily, and with the mail crackling in his jacket pocket, loped back toward home.

Roses still bloomed along the trellis Alicia had planted in the spring. Where the chickens had once hunted and pecked in the yard, a neat kitchen garden grew. Inside, he was greeted with the smell of a fresh apple pie, but he avoided the temptation of sneaking a bite. He could hear Becky scolding her rambunctious young one as the little demon decimated the kitchen. The pie would wait.

The letter in his pocket would not. He took the steps two at a time, following the sounds of Alicia's happy humming.

He found her grading papers from her first class of students. They had progressed from alphabets to essays, and

410

Travis still felt a shock when he discovered some of his men arguing over an article in the newspaper. True, they read it more often to discover who had stabbed whom in the latest tavern brawl, but that was progress of a sort. Once it would have been their names on the list of brawlers.

She looked up at his unexpectedly early arrival, and quickly set the papers aside to run into his arms and welcome him with a kiss. Travis closed his eyes and drank in the heavenly scent of gardenias and the sweet taste of her lips as he crushed her closer. Never would he get enough of the weight of her supple curves in his arms, the press of full breasts against his chest, and the joy that spread through him each time she offered herself in this way. It had been a long battle to reach this point, he would not yield it easily.

His hand sought her breast, his thumb searching for the hardening crest surging against the thin cotton. Alicia gasped as he found his goal and played it cleverly. She melted against him as he stroked the firm curve of her breast, then rode his hand downward, over the narrow line of her waist to the slight bulge of her abdomen beneath the high-waisted bodice.

"I'll not miss a day of this one's growth," Travis murmured against her hair as he covered the small mound of her belly with his broad palm. "I want to feel him when he starts to move."

Alicia laughed low in her throat, her eyes turning lovingly to her husband's hawklike profile. "I will gladly give him to you when that time comes if he is anything like your first-born. I thought I was possessed by a devil."

"And so you were," Travis agreed, glancing over her shoulder to where his son casually demolished the wooden wagon he had made for him. "Do all children destroy everything they own?"

Turning her gaze to find what Travis spoke of, Alicia smiled. "Only those who want to know what makes things go. I think he has just discovered the purpose of a wheel."

Travis grunted at this heresy and returned his attention to the partially unbuttoned opening of Alicia's bodice. "Why isn't he with Anne-Marie? I have some time before lunch, and I have in mind a way to put it to good use."

"Travis!" Alicia scolded, blushing, but fastening one of her lower buttons, she went to the door to call for the nurse-maid.

Not daring to look Anne-Marie in the eyes as Travis firmly led her from the nursery down the hall, Alicia finally gave into her natural desires as soon as he closed the bedroom door behind them. She slid her arms around his neck and pulled his head down where she could reach him.

Travis bent eagerly to her demands and entirely forgetting the letter in his pocket, plied her lips with heated kisses. The buttons of Alicia's bodice pressed into his chest, plaguing him with their intrusion, and he swiftly set to work on their demise.

Within minutes he had disposed of the simple gown and was triumphantly carrying his prize to the sprawling four-poster where both his children had been conceived, and where they all would be born. Alicia reached to pull off his shirt as he dropped her to the mattress, and only then did the crackle of paper remind him of his news.

With a grin Travis dropped the letter on Alicia's stomach, then sat at the bed's edge to remove his boots while she read. He did not even need to look to see her in his mind's eye. He could feel her sitting up against the pillows, propping them behind her, unaware of how that pushed her chemise low over her full breasts so he could almost see the rosy peaks pushing from the lace. The frail material would ride high over rounded thighs, revealing garters and stockings and the pale flesh above them he intended to kiss in another moment. That was how he wanted her right now, and his loins leapt in excitement at the thought.

"Travis!" Alicia cried excitedly as she scanned the elegant penmanship on the expensive vellum. "This means your father has another son to carry the title. Lady Royster must have been pregnant when she was last here!"

"That's what these American winters will do for you," Travis agreed smugly, throwing aside his shirt and leaning backward to caress her thigh. The letter had lost its importance with the sight of silky skin hidden in the shadows of her lacy chemise. His hand slid to capture her stockinged knee and move upward.

Alicia could scarcely finish reading as her husband's hand made a stealthy invasion beneath her chemise. Heat spread through her veins, finding its center where Travis's hand roamed. She moaned and threw the letter aside as his lips followed the path his hand had stroked.

Burying her hands in his dark hair, she tried to halt his

advances. "Travis! You are mad. He says you are still his heir and he wishes us to at least come visit for a while. What are we going to do?"

"I don't know about you, but I know what I intend to do."

As he found his goal, Alicia emitted a cry of delight and protest, and the letter fell forgotten to the floor.

There would be time next week to discuss trips to England. For now, they had each other.